A THRILL in the Air

A Mosaic Christmas Anthology V

MILLA HOLT * LORNA SEILSTAD * ELEANOR BERTIN
SARA DAVISON * BRENDA S. ANDERSON
DEB ELKINK * CANDACE WEST * JOHNNIE ALEXANDER

THE MOSAIC COLLECTION

Minneapolis, Minnesota

Published by The Mosaic Collection

Minneapolis, Minnesota

mosaiccollectionbooks.com

Cover design by Roseanna White Designs

A Christmas anthology from The Mosaic Collection

Our mission is to change hearts with the gospel through fiction.

WELCOME

TO THE MOSAIC COLLECTION

We are sisters, a beautiful mosaic united by the love of God through the blood of Christ.

Several times a year The Mosaic Collection releases one or more faith-based novels or anthologies exploring our theme, Family by His Design, and sharing stories that feature diverse, God-designed families. Stories range from mystery and women's fiction to comedic and literary fiction. We hope you'll join our Mosaic family as we explore together what truly defines a family.

If you're like us, loneliness and suffering have touched your life in ways you never imagined; but Dear One, while you may feel alone in your suffering—whatever it is—you are never alone!

Learn more about The Mosaic Collection at
www.mosaiccollectionbooks.com

Join our Reader Community, too!
www.facebook.com/groups/TheMosaicCollection

BOOKS

IN THE MOSAIC COLLECTION

Learn more at
www.mosaiccollectionbooks.com/mosaic-books

PRAISE FOR AUTHORS

IN THE MOSAIC COLLECTION

Praise for Milla Holt

Milla Holt writes interesting, multi-layered characters and rich settings. I always enjoy her stories.
— Dalyn Weller, author of the Apple Valley Ranchers contemporary Christian romance series

Praise for Lorna Seilstad

Seilstad writes an engaging story with characters you fall in love with, plot twists that keep you reading, and an ending that makes you smile.
— Stacy M.

Praise for Eleanor Bertin

I felt such a connection with this story! The entire time I was reading I was very reflective. Jacqui, the main character, had quite a bit of inner dialogue that I would read, and then stop and ponder similar thoughts and situations pertaining to my own life. Jacqui has her own flaws, but you can't help but root for her. Leaving a toxic relationship and completely starting your life all over is exactly where I found myself ten years ago and, just like in Jacqui's story, I can see God's grace through it all.

What was really intriguing about *Tethered* was the parallel of Jacqui's repairing her father's childhood home . . . while at the same time searching for the truth about her family, repairing family relationships, and mending her own broken heart.

— Christy F., Amazon review

Praise for Sara Davison

To say *Every Flower of the Field* is filled with suspense would be an understatement. Sara had me on the edge of my seat for most of the read, as in the previous book! If you are interested in reading romantic suspense from a Christian perspective covering complex topics that are relevant and timely today, this book is a good choice. Sara does not skirt the issues and isn't afraid to share God moments in a meaningful, non-preachy way.

— Jeannine B. Bennett

Praise for Brenda S. Anderson

Wow does not begin to describe Jennifer and Chad's story! All the emotion, all the feels, all wrapped up so beautifully in *Broken Together*. It is a story I will never forget.

— Sharon Dean

Praise for Deb Elkink

Deb Elkink is a wonderful author whose writing engages you from the beginning, drawing you into the stories she spins and keeping you there to ponder life's circumstances.

— Judith Crewdson

Praise for Candace West

I didn't think it was possible but Ms. West did it. She made a vile character redeemable. I admit I didn't want to see him find redemption. He's a rogue. But Candace did it with grace. Awesome story. Get caught up in Valley Creek.

— L. Austin

Praise for Johnnie Alexander

Johnnie Alexander is an amazing writer, who has some wonderful original works. This is an interesting and well written novel tackling a WWII mystery and a friendship turned love story. The characters are likable and engaging. I enjoyed finding out that it is based on true events.

— An Amazon review

SING, MERRILY SING

BY LILLIAN GRAY

There's a thrill in the air, there's a joy in the heart;
There is generous stir in the home and the mart;
For the Yuletide is with us, make ready to greet
The Child in the manger; lay gifts at His feet.

Sing, merrily sing,
Yes sing, merrily sing,
All hail him that cometh with peace,
Merrily sing.

Let the glad carolers ring, put all strivings away,
Deck the chapel and church in His honor today;
Let the great organs swell with their symphonies grand;
And send for their tidings all over the land.

Little children rejoice! join the song young and old,
Tho' the joys of the Christmas can never be told,
But rejoice and be glad, with your banners unfurled,
For the Christ that has come is the hope of the world.

CONTENTS

THE PRODIGAL'S FEAST

Milla Holt

* * *

Every family has a screw-up, but Linnea is done with that label. To show her loved ones how far she's come, she volunteers to host this year's Christmas dinner. But when things don't go as planned, will her family ever see beyond her past mistakes?

GLOSSARY

Mormor - Grandmother (literally "mother's mother")
Morfar - Grandfather (literally "mother's father")
Takk for mat - Thanks for the food (a polite acknowledgement to the cook after a meal)
Vær så god - You're welcome
Lille venn - A term of endearment toward a child
Bestemor - Grandmother
Medisterkaker - Pork patties
Fårikål - A dish of mutton boiled with chunks of cabbage
Lefse - A Norwegian pastry
Rømmegrøt - Sour cream porridge served as a festive dessert

And the son said unto him, "Father, I have sinned against heaven, and in thy sight, and am no more worthy to be called thy son." But the father said to his servants, "Bring forth the best robe, and put it on him; and put a ring on his hand, and shoes on his feet: And bring hither the fatted calf, and kill it; and let us eat, and be merry."

Luke 15:21-23, KJV

CHAPTER ONE

"Mamma, I'm hungry."

"Already?" Linnea Moen pivoted to face her four-year-old daughter. "Didn't you just—oh."

Her question trailed off as she caught sight of the kitchen clock. It was after 2:00 PM and Trondheim's meager allowance of December daylight was already fading.

Somehow, as Linnea had dashed around her small apartment getting things ready for her guests, lunch had fallen by the wayside. Poor little Hanna had eaten nothing since breakfast.

What kind of mother forgot to feed her child lunch? Guilt gnawing at her gut, Linnea grabbed a plate. "I'm sorry, darling. I'll fix you some peanut butter and crackers. Our guests will be here soon, and then we'll have our Christmas dinner."

"Yay!" Hanna clapped her hands. "Will Mormor think my dress is pretty?"

The girl spun in a circle, the pink ruffles of her outfit fluttering around her like falling cherry blossoms.

"Of course she will," Linnea said automatically. But did she really know what her mother would think? Mamma hadn't seen Hanna since the child was an infant.

Back then, Linnea and her newborn were living in a mother and child emergency shelter. It was a season Linnea preferred to forget. But everything was different now. *She* was different, and her family would see it.

Today, she was having them over for Christmas Eve dinner in her own place.

She pushed the plate of crackers, apple slices, and peanut butter toward her daughter.

Hanna climbed onto the stool of the breakfast bar and set her stuffed toy next to the plate. She crammed an entire cracker into her mouth. "Can I have some juice, please?"

"Don't talk with your mouth full, sweetheart." Linnea brushed a lock of dark hair off Hanna's forehead and kissed her smooth, olive skin.

Hanna replied around a mouthful of crackers and peanut butter. "Sorry."

Linnea turned to hide her smile and filled a plastic cup with cranberry juice, then set it next to Hanna's plate.

Her daughter taken care of, Linnea turned back to her preparations. She picked up a tray full of decorative candles. These would be the final touch on her festive dinner table.

The table was one of those extendable ones. Normally, it was round with room for four. With the extra leaf added, it stretched into an oval that could comfortably seat six, although it nearly touched two walls in her compact apartment. Linnea had set seven places, so it would be an even tighter squeeze.

She put the largest candle in the middle of the centerpiece. She'd made the wreath herself, using red baubles and spray-painted gold pinecones. Did it look too tacky?

She stepped back to inspect her handiwork. Each place was set with a rolled-up red napkin tied with gold ribbon, and a name card in her best calligraphy. The forgiving candlelight would hide the fact that the plates didn't match. And although three of the seats were metal folding chairs, she'd dressed them up with festive cushions.

Perhaps it was a little overdone, but Hanna loved all the Christmas decorations. This might be the first Christmas her little girl remembered for the rest of her life, and Linnea wanted it to feel magical.

"Mamma!"

Linnea spun around at Hanna's shout. The little girl's plastic cup lay on its side, and a spreading stain of deep red cranberry juice drenched the front of her dress.

Linnea dashed toward Hanna, grabbing a kitchen cloth from the counter. She dabbed at the large wet patch. "Oh, Hanna! You need to take that dress off. If I don't deal with this now, the stain won't come out."

"But this is my favorite one. I wanted Mormor to see it."

"I know." Linnea helped Hanna out of the dress. "Your purple one is really pretty, though, and purple is Mormor's favorite color."

"It is?" Hanna's face brightened. "Okay, I'll put it on."

"Wash your hands and face first."

Hanna picked up her teddy and trailed toward the bathroom.

Linnea blotted the stain with a mixture of rubbing alcohol and laundry detergent. What had she been thinking? She should have known better than to give Hanna cranberry juice. She put the damp dress into the washing machine. Might as well run a load of laundry now.

Turning the knob, she glanced at the relentless hands of the clock. Mamma and the others were due here in under an hour, and she still had so much left to do.

Five guests were coming—her parents, her twin sister Signy, Signy's fiancé, Roger, and Andreas.

Andreas. Just thinking of him eased the knot in her gut. He was one of the best things that had happened to her, next to her faith and her little girl.

Her cell phone rang, and she hurried to answer the call, smiling as she read the caller ID. "I was just thinking about you. Are you on your way?"

"That's why I'm calling," Andreas said. "I'm going to be held up, but I'll get there as quickly as I can."

Linnea's heart plummeted. She'd been counting on having his moral support when her family came. He knew how much today meant to her. But his on-call schedule was fixed months ago. If Andreas was going to be in her life, this kind of thing came with the package. "Well, I guess being on call means there's a chance you might actually get called in to work."

"Thanks for understanding," he said. "I'm praying it'll all go smoothly, and I'll be there on time to open the presents, at least. I really want to meet your family."

She hugged the phone against her cheek. "I'll save you a plate. I'm praying, too."

"Gotta go. Bye."

She ended the call and looked up. Surprisingly, Hanna hadn't come demanding to say hello to Andreas. She was probably busy changing into her purple princess outfit.

That was just as well. There was so much to do to get ready. She glanced at the clock. It was half past two now, and she still hadn't put dinner into the oven.

Linnea was making the traditional Christmas Eve meal her family had loved since she was a child: roast pork ribs served with potatoes, sausage, pork patties, red sauerkraut, and brown sauce.

She was using an online recipe because she'd never learned how Mamma used to cook the ribs. Come to think of it, she could only remember a handful of childhood Christmases that weren't spent with her sister, Signy, in the hospital.

Even when Signy went into remission and Linnea moved out of home, there hadn't been many family Christmases. The holidays she hadn't spent in a drunken haze she'd avoided going home because she didn't want to hear the nagging and be compared to her perfect sister.

That was all part of the past, though. This dinner would show everyone that.

Linnea pulled the ribs out of the fridge, where they'd been marinating for two days in a salt-and-pepper rub.

She transferred the slab of meat into a baking tray and poured a cupful of water over it, then covered the pan with foil, making sure it was tightly wrapped. The ribs would cook in the hot steam, and she'd take the foil off later to crisp up the fat.

When the pan was in the hot oven, she set a timer for forty-five minutes.

The biggest challenge with this meal was getting the timing right, since she had to cook the sausages at the same time as the *medisterkaker*. She'd thought about making the traditional Norwegian pork patties from scratch but decided to buy them ready-made and precooked. All she needed to do was heat them up just before serving.

It would be a good idea to peel the potatoes now, though. She picked up her vegetable peeler and scraped the first potato.

Then the silence hit her. Hanna was being very quiet. Too quiet.

Linnea's mom senses pinged an alert. It wasn't completely silent. She could hear something. It sounded like . . . water?

She threw down the vegetable peeler and ran over to the bathroom.

Water seeped under the door and onto the hallway floor.

"Hanna!" Linnea burst into the small bathroom.

Her daughter stood on a little plastic step that boosted her up so she could reach the sink. A flood of foamy water, replenished by a still-running faucet, overflowed from the bowl and spilled onto the floor.

"Hanna Kristin Moen, what are you doing?"

Linnea bounded toward the faucet, grabbing for the edge of the sink as she lost her footing on the slippery floor.

She landed on her bottom, the water instantly soaking her new woolen skirt.

Hanna looked down at her with wide brown eyes. "Buttons had cranberry juice on him, so I was giving him a bath so he could be clean when Mormor and Morfar and Aunt Signy come."

Buttons? Her stuffed teddy bear? "But if you've got Buttons completely wet, he won't be dry in time to meet them."

Hanna's pink lips rounded. "Oh."

"And now you've made a huge mess. You know you're not supposed to play with water."

"I'm sorry. And I wasn't playing—I was working. I was trying to help you."

Linnea hauled herself onto her knees and turned off the faucet. "Come on. We both need to change our clothes."

She took a firm hold of the doorframe to avoid another tumble and got to her feet.

The doorbell buzzed and her heart lurched. No! No, no, no, no, no! It couldn't be them already.

A loud knock followed. Her guests were here.

CHAPTER TWO

Linnea pulled open the front door, the blast of freezing winter air doing nothing to cool her flaming cheeks.

Her parents, a little grayer than the last time she'd seen them, stood side by side.

Mamma's eyebrows flew upward. "Oh, my. Are we early?"

Linnea stepped forward for a hug, then stopped herself as the cold weight of her sopping wet skirt pulled her back to her senses. "No, you're on time. Sorry, we just had a situation in the bathroom. Please come in."

Hanna peeked around from behind Linnea's leg, clutching her sodden teddy.

Mamma walked in, side-stepping the pool of water in the hallway. "What on earth happened here?"

"Hanna gave one of her teddies a bath and forgot to turn the water off," Linnea said.

"And this little imp must be Hanna." Pappa bent his tall, bony frame, so he was almost eye level with his granddaughter. "I hope your teddy got nice and clean after all that. Do you know who I am?"

Hanna nodded, pressing her small body against Linnea's

leg. "You're Morfar and this is Mormor. Where's Auntie Signy?"

"She's on her way," Mamma said. "She visited Roger's family in Oppdal yesterday and they'll be coming down together."

"I'm looking forward to meeting him," Linnea said.

Mamma beamed. "He's a wonderful young man, and so devoted to Signy. You may have seen him on TV—he's a news anchor."

Linnea shook her head. "I don't watch much TV. But that's impressive. I hear it's a very competitive industry."

"It is. He's a brilliant young man."

"The living room is over that way." Linnea stretched out a hand to Mamma. "Let me hold your bags while you take your coat off."

"No, no, I'm fine." Mamma whipped her purse under her arm as she shrugged herself out of her coat.

Linnea's face burned. Did Mamma still think Linnea would skim money out of her wallet? She wasn't that person anymore. But Mamma didn't know that.

Pappa held out a plastic carrier bag. "These are for you and Hanna."

Linnea took the bag, peeking in to glimpse a stack of wrapped packages. "Thank you. I'll put these under the tree. Look, Hanna. Morfar got you a present."

Turning to her daughter, she realized Hanna was still wearing only panties and an undershirt, both soaking wet.

"I'm sorry, but I need to sort out myself and Hanna and clean up this mess. Please make yourselves at home."

"I can help with Hanna if you'll show me where her clothes are," Mamma said.

Linnea's insides recoiled at the offer. The apartment's only bedroom, which she shared with Hanna, was a disaster zone. She hadn't thought anyone would be going in there. It was already untidy this morning, and heaven knew what it looked like now after Hanna had been ransacking her wardrobe on the hunt for the perfect outfit.

Was there any way to avoid Mamma seeing that room? Linnea chewed her lip. She couldn't clean the bathroom, sort Hanna out, and change her own clothes at the same time. Not to mention the Christmas dinner she was trying to cook. She'd just have to accept Mamma's help.

"Thank you. The bedroom is this way. Come on, Hanna."

She pushed the door open and stepped into the bedroom. The mess was even worse than she'd feared. Was there anything left in the dresser drawers and the closet? Every item of clothing Hanna owned must be on the floor, intermingled with stuffed animals, dolls, and—ouch!—Legos.

Stifling a yell, Linnea massaged her foot in its wet sock. "Sorry about the mess."

Mamma followed her inside, pursing her lips as her gaze roved about the room. "You use a bunkbed?"

"Yes, to save on space." Two singles side by side would have left the room with almost no floor space.

What must Mamma be thinking? She'd always been house proud, staying up long into the night to keep their family home spotless, only to get up just an hour later to deal with Signy's medical needs.

Linnea looked around. At least the room wasn't dirty. The scattered clothes were clean, and she vacuumed and dusted every week. The mess might look bad, but it was surface clutter.

She grabbed the first clothing items that came to hand, which were a pair of pink tracksuit pants and a green T-shirt. "Hanna can put these on."

"But I wanted to wear my purple dress," Hanna protested.

That mulish look on Hanna's face never boded well. The last thing Linnea needed was a tantrum. "Fine," she said. "If you can find it, you can wear it, but I don't have time to help you look. Mormor will help you dry off and get changed. Thanks, Mamma. I'll deal with the bathroom now."

She left the bedroom, her feet squelching in her socks. Her own wet clothes would have to wait until she'd mopped the flooded floor.

Pappa stood at the sliding doors, looking out into the dark evening. It wasn't even three o'clock yet, but night fell very early in Trondheim in December.

He faced Linnea. "That's a balcony, I suppose?"

"Yes. It gives us a little outdoor space, but not much of a view. It looks over the parking lot."

He rubbed his chin. "I guess that's typical of city apartments. Signy just closed on a lovely three-bedroom home over in Stjørdal."

"Did she? That's nice."

"Yes, she's done very well. It's very spacious and sits on a huge lot."

Linnea looked around at her living room. Compared to the sketchy places she'd crashed in over the years, this poky little apartment was like a palace. More importantly, it was a haven of peace for herself and Hanna. It represented her new life, and that was plenty to be thankful for.

"I hope I can see Signy's place soon. I'll just clean up in the bathroom now."

There was no quick way to dry the flooded bathroom floor. Linnea soaked up the water in a mop, then squeezed it into a bucket, repeating the action over and over. It could have been worse. At least Hanna hadn't clogged the toilet like she'd done a couple of years ago by dumping half a pack of diapers into it and then trying to flush them down. Linnea smiled. She could laugh about it now, but it hadn't seemed funny at the time.

She put away her cleaning equipment. Time to change her own clothes.

Mamma and Hanna came out of the bedroom as Linnea approached the door. Hanna wore the purple princess dress.

"Thanks for helping her get changed," Linnea said.

Mamma waved a hand as she sat next to Pappa on the sofa. "No problem at all. Hanna knew where to find the outfit she wanted. I don't know how she did it. It would have taken me an hour. You know, Linnea, keeping a tidy home really is a big time-saver."

Linnea accepted the implied rebuke. Mamma was right. She always was.

Mamma adjusted a cushion and leaned back. "How long have you been living here, again?"

"About six months. We used to live out in Klæbu, but this is much more convenient for Hanna's daycare and when I'm going to school and work. Lots of bus routes go by, so we're never waiting long for a ride."

"How are your studies going?" Pappa asked.

"Quite good. I hope to graduate this summer."

"A bachelor's degree in nursing, you said?" Mamma asked. "It should be easy to find work. When Signy was getting her master's, everyone was saying the economy was terrible and nobody was hiring, but she was offered a job before graduation."

"I hope I'm that lucky."

"It takes more than luck. You need determination and hard work. That's what got Signy noticed. Oh, have you brought a book? Do you want me to read that for you?"

Hanna walked toward her grandmother, holding a battered copy of *The Very Hungry Caterpillar*.

Linnea looked down at her wet clothes. "I'd better go get changed now."

"Yes, please do that before Signy and Roger get here,"

Mamma said. "Come here, Hanna. Your Aunt Signy loved this book, too."

Linnea went into the bedroom, closing the door behind her. What should she wear? This now-wet woolen skirt and matching cardigan was her best outfit. She didn't have anything else nearly so nice.

She found a pair of black slacks and an only slightly wrinkled yellow blouse. These would have to do.

Going back into the living room, her heart gave a squeeze as she saw Mamma and Hanna sitting side by side while Mamma read aloud.

This is exactly what she'd been praying for: for Hanna to get to know her grandparents and for them to be involved in her life. Thank God for new beginnings. He was a God not just of second chances but of third, fifth, twenty-fifth chances. She wouldn't be here today without his grace.

The doorbell buzzed and Mamma stopped her reading mid-sentence, her gaze snapping up. "Is it Signy and Roger?"

"It must be," Linnea said. Andreas had said he'd text her when he was on his way, and there were no messages from him.

Mamma closed the board book and set it on the coffee table. She sat up straight, a smile spreading over her face. Hanna retrieved the book and tugged at her grandmother's sleeve, but Mamma wasn't looking at her.

The doorbell buzzed again.

"Go on, Linnea," Mamma said. "Answer the door. Signy shouldn't wait out in the cold for too long."

Linnea went to the door.

CHAPTER THREE

Signy stood alone on the welcome mat huddled in a heavy coat, a bone-chilling wind whipping around her.

"It's so good to see you." Signy gave Linnea a side hug. "You look great."

"Thanks. So do you. Come in. It's freezing out there." Linnea stepped aside to let her sister past.

Linnea towered over her. She'd always been the bigger twin, as though she'd hogged the nourishment while they shared their mother's womb. Even before the cancer hit, Signy had been the dainty, waif-like princess, bringing out everyone's protective instincts while Linnea lumbered around, all elbows, knees, and feet.

Signy pulled off her beanie and ran a hand through her short, stylish blond hair, which was the same color as Linnea's. Both of them used to have long, thick waves before Signy got unwell. Signy's had never gained back its thickness and luster after repeated rounds of chemo.

"Darling, you're here!" Mamma walked quickly toward Signy, arms outstretched. "But where's Roger? I thought you were bringing him."

Signy's chin trembled. "He's not coming. We decided to end things."

Mamma's jaw went slack. "What? No! Oh, darling, come here."

Linnea stood by as Mamma enveloped Signy in an all-encompassing hug.

Signy's shoulders shook with silent sobs and Mamma stroked her back.

Linnea felt like an intruder in her own home. Should she walk away and let Mamma comfort Signy? She wanted to let her sister know that she cared, too. But perhaps Signy wouldn't welcome any words of consolation from the sister she hadn't spoken to in so long.

Mamma drew Signy along with her toward the living room, arm still wrapped around her shoulders. "Come, let's sit down. Linnea, a glass of water, please."

Water. At least that was something she could do. Linnea hurried into the kitchen and filled a glass from the faucet.

When she got to the living room, Signy was sitting in the middle of the sofa, her eyes red rimmed, a parent on either side of her.

Hanna hung back near the Christmas tree in the corner, forgotten.

Linnea handed Signy the glass, and Signy sipped from it in big gulps.

Linnea walked over to Hanna and brushed her fingers through the child's dark, silky hair.

Hanna leaned against her. "Why is Auntie Signy sad?"

Linnea cringed at the bell-like volume of her daughter's voice. She answered in a whisper. "She's not getting along with her friend. Let's be very quiet and gentle so she can feel better soon. Do you understand?"

Hanna nodded.

"Maybe you could play quietly in your room. How about that?"

"Okay."

Hanna went to the bedroom and Linnea stayed next to the tree, trying her best to be invisible.

Mamma clutched Signy's hand in both of hers. "What happened? I thought things were going so well."

"He's seeing someone else." Signy dabbed at her eyes. "He denied it at first but finally admitted it. I always had a feeling his ex wasn't completely out of the picture. I should have trusted my gut."

Mamma swelled like a furious hen. "So, he's been two-timing you? He doesn't deserve you, sweetheart. I know you're feeling bad now, but you'll soon see you dodged a bullet."

"Definitely dodged a bullet," Pappa echoed, patting Signy's shoulder. "I would never have expected that of him. If he's going to behave like that, it's so much better that we find out now rather than later."

Linnea's phone alarm pinged. She silenced it and stared at her handset, blank for a second. Of course, the ribs! It was time to turn the oven down.

Relieved to have something to do instead of stand on the sidelines, Linnea pulled the baking pan out of the oven and removed the foil. The ribs were nicely steamed, and now they needed to roast and crisp up.

Linnea adjusted the oven temperature and put the pan back in, resetting her timer for one hour.

She still had an entire Christmas dinner to cook, and she'd better get on with it.

Signy was in expert hands. Her parents had a lifetime of practice in caring for their older twin's needs. Linnea glanced at them as they sat on the sofa, the perfect nuclear circle of nurturing. Mamma and Pappa had supported Signy throughout her hellish illness and treatment, the rhythm of the Moen family life following the ups and downs of their daughter's cancer journey. And that was as it should be. Parents had to support their neediest child. And, growing up, Signy had needed every ounce of energy her parents could spare.

As always, Linnea would just be in the way if she tried to add her clumsy and ignorant words of comfort.

She focused instead on preparing the meal. She wasn't a wayward teen anymore, looking for love and attention in all the wrong places, adding to her parents' burden by acting out. By God's incredible grace, Linnea had come through her own dark period, scarred and bruised but whole.

She glanced at her sister. Signy seemed to be over the worst of her initial grief. At least she wasn't crying anymore.

Linnea moved quickly through the kitchen, peeling potatoes and putting them to cook. It would probably be a good idea to do the sausages and pork patties now as well and then leave them on the warming shelf until it was time to serve dinner.

"Oh, who is this? You must be Hanna, right?"

Linnea's gaze shot upward at the sound of Signy's words.

Signy was looking at Hanna, who stood in the bedroom door.

"Come over here and let me say hello," Signy said.

Hanna walked forward shyly and stood in front of her aunt.

Signy stroked the child's hair. "You have such pretty brown eyes and brown hair. Everyone else in our family has blue eyes. I guess that comes from your pappa."

Linnea's heart froze in the silence that followed Signy's words. She never talked about her daughter's father. During the alcohol-soaked period of her life when Hanna had been conceived, Linnea and her boyfriend at the time had what he called an open relationship. When they went out partying with their friends, it was anyone's guess who'd end up in whose bed. It was supposed to add spice and excitement to their relationship, but it left Linnea feeling dirty and used.

The sordid truth was Hanna's father could be any one of a handful of Linnea's barely recalled hookup partners.

The whole question made Linnea sick with shame. She still wasn't sure what she'd tell Hanna when her daughter was old enough to ask.

The only person who knew the degrading truth was Andreas. When they'd started dating two years back, Linnea had told him. To her shock, the strait-laced pastor's son hadn't dumped her immediately.

But Linnea had never brought herself to tell her own family.

The aggressive chemo and bone marrow transplant that had saved Signy's life had cost her the ability to have children, meaning Hanna was her parents' only grandchild.

Was it fair that Signy, always the good girl, the brave soldier who'd never put a foot wrong, would never bear a child? Yet Linnea, the screwup, fell pregnant after a drunken hookup.

The doorbell buzzed and Linnea hurried to answer it, praying that the new arrival would put a stop to any more awkward comments about Hanna's paternity.

CHAPTER FOUR

Andreas stood at Linnea's front door, tall and solid as an oak.

"You made it!" She leaned into him as he hugged her, his body shielding her from the blast of icy wind.

He stepped inside, shedding his coat as Linnea closed the door. "The baby was in a hurry to make his appearance, and everything was over quicker than we expected. Are all your guests here?"

"Yes. Are you ready to meet everyone?"

He squeezed her hand, then followed her into the living room.

"Andreas!" Hanna leaped to her feet and ran toward him.

He scooped her up. "Hello, *lille venn*. Merry Christmas."

"Guess what?" she said. "Mormor, Morfar, and Aunt Signy are here."

"You didn't tell us you were expecting another guest, Linnea." Mamma stood and extended a hand to Andreas. "Are you going to introduce us?"

"This is Andreas Nygaard. He's my . . . my boyfriend." The word felt frivolous, weak, and silly. She'd used the same title for men with whom she'd had the most depraved and seedy encounters. She hated using it to describe her relationship with Andreas.

She turned toward him, heat radiating from her face. "These are my parents, Kjersti and Per-Einar Moen, and my sister, Signy."

Andreas set Hanna down and shook Mamma's hand. "Delighted to meet you, Mrs. Moen. Linnea has told me so much about you."

"Really?" Mamma threw a sidelong glance at Linnea. "She hasn't told us much about you. Call me Kjersti."

Linnea squirmed. She hadn't been sure how much to tell her parents. In the end, she thought it best for them to meet Andreas with no expectations and just get to know him. Perhaps that had been a mistake.

He shook hands with everyone and sat in the armchair across from the sofa.

Linnea sneaked a peek at her sister. Springing her relationship with Andreas on her family was doubly awkward following Signy's bad news.

Signy sat with her arms crossed and her expression unreadable.

Hanna climbed into his lap and poked in his jacket pocket. "Where's your stettiscope?"

"I left it in the car."

"Stethoscope?" Signy leveled her gaze at him. "Are you in the medical field?"

"I'm an obstetrician. That's why I'm late. I'm on call tonight and a patient needed me."

"An obstetrician?" Mamma looked at Linnea, surprise written all over her face, then back at Andreas. "I see. And how did you and Linnea meet?"

"I used to see her at church, but we never really spoke. And then she came to St. Olavs on one of her practice rotations and we got to know each other better." He winked at Linnea. "I had to work really hard to convince her to go out with me."

"Is that so? And how long have you been seeing each other?"

"It was two years in October. Right, Linnea?"

She nodded. "Yes, that's right."

"By the way, Linnea, my parents said hello, and they're looking forward to tomorrow."

"Do your parents live nearby?" Mamma asked.

"In Melhus, so not too far."

"And you're having Christmas Eve dinner here instead of with them?"

"Linnea told me you were coming, and I was very keen to meet you. Plus, since I'm on call, the twenty minutes from Melhus is farther away from the hospital than I want to be."

Pappa leaned forward. "You're very different from any of Linnea's previous friends that we've met."

"How so?" Andreas glanced at Linnea, with a half chuckle.

She clenched a fist, bracing herself for Pappa's remark.

Mamma burst in as Pappa opened his mouth. "She's never gone for the professional type, is what I think Per-Einar means."

Linnea stood. This was a good time to make her getaway. "Since Andreas is here, I'll get a move on with dinner before he's called in for another emergency."

"Do you need any help?" Andreas asked.

"No, I've got everything under control."

Hanna twisted her body and looked up at Andreas's face. "Could you read a book for me?"

"Let me guess. *The Very Hungry Caterpillar?*"

"Yes! How did you know that?"

"Because I know you very well."

Linnea went into the kitchen, welcoming the bustle of

dinner preparations and the temporary escape from further questioning. Why had she thought it would be a good idea to just introduce Andreas without preparing her family? It would have been far better to tell them earlier.

But she'd thought Signy's fiancé was going to be here, to take some of the spotlight off her own relationship.

Andreas was handling himself well, though, with his usual unflappable grace. She'd have to apologize to him later for the awkwardness she'd caused.

The first of the pork patties went into her largest pan, sizzling as it hit the hot oil. She added the rest of the patties and put the Christmas sausage into another pan.

When everything was coming along, she sneaked a glance into the living room.

Done with *The Very Hungry Caterpillar*, Andreas was on the floor with Hanna, laying out the cards for one of the child's memory games.

Mamma and Signy chatted to each other, and Pappa sat staring at Andreas. Were they all just going to ignore him?

Linnea prayed under her breath as she put the rest of the meal together. The ribs needed to rest, so she got them out of the oven, then heated the sour cabbage. The brown sauce was coming from a package mix, so that needed to go into a pot now, too.

Finally, everything was ready. All that remained was to bring the food to the table.

Andreas sat up as Linnea brought out the dish of steamed potatoes. "Do you need help carrying anything?"

"Yes, I'd appreciate that."

He ruffled Hanna's hair and stood. "What should I do?"

"Take the red cabbage, sausage and *medisterkaker* to the table, and I'll bring the ribs and sauce. Hanna, would you wash up, please? We're about to have dinner."

"Yay! I'm really hungry." Hanna scrambled to her feet.

Andreas laid out the dishes, then grabbed a couple of bottles of sparkling grape juice from the fridge.

Finally, the table was set. "Dinner's ready," Linnea said, just as her gaze landed on the now-extra place setting that was supposed to be Roger's, Signy's ex-fiancé. She'd forgotten to clear it away.

Would it be more awkward to remove it now or just leave it where it was? Indecision froze her brain as everyone approached the table.

"Oh, what lovely place cards," Mamma said, picking hers up. "You always were very clever with your hands."

Signy reddened as her gaze homed in on Roger's name card on the place next to hers.

Biting her lip, Linnea shambled forward and grabbed the card, putting it face down on the plate. She piled the cutlery on top and picked everything up. "I'll just clear these away."

Lips pressed tightly together, Signy sat down without a word.

Linnea caught Andreas's quizzical look. She shook her head and put the plate on the counter.

When everyone was seated, she said, "Could you give thanks, please, Andreas?"

"Of course. Shall we all join hands?"

And now she realized she'd seated Andreas at the head of the table, yet another decision she was second-guessing. Was it presumptuous?

Linnea took hold of Hanna's hand to the right and Mamma's to the left. Nothing but a miracle would make this awkward meal turn out well. She just wanted it to be over.

Andreas waited for a moment, then prayed. "Jesus, thank you so much for this time of the year, as we come together to celebrate how you came to live among us and show us your love. Bless this wonderful meal and the strong, skillful, and gentle hands that made it. Amen."

"Amen," everyone mumbled.

Andreas smiled into Linnea's eyes, and she could feel the comfort of his encouragement from across the table.

She let out a slow breath. "Please help yourselves."

CHAPTER FIVE

The food was perfect. The pork ribs were tender and falling off the bone, and the crackling beautifully crisp. Mamma hated soggy potatoes, so Linnea exhaled a sigh of relief since these ones turned out fluffy, with not a single water-logged or undercooked bite.

But as Linnea looked around the table, only Andreas and Hanna ate with any enthusiasm.

Signy pushed the food around her plate, and Mamma picked at hers. Pappa plowed through his meal with slow deliberation.

Mealtimes were never chatty occasions in the Moen household, but the silence around this table weighed heavy, like brooding storm clouds. Was this what the Bible meant about a dry morsel being better than a feast with strife? No one was fighting or arguing, but Linnea struggled to swallow each bite. She couldn't shake the feeling that something was about to explode.

Hanna held out her plate. "Could I have another *medisterkake*, please?"

"Mm, I'd like some as well," Andreas said. He put another pork patty on the child's plate and helped himself to more of everything.

"Do you live on your own, Andreas?" Mamma asked, just as he put a forkful of sauerkraut and potato into his mouth.

Andreas held up his hand, chewing quickly. He swallowed his food and sipped some water. "Sorry, you caught me just as I was stuffing my face. Yes, I live on my own."

"Renting, or do you own your home?"

Linnea cringed. Why was Mamma asking such a personal question?

"I own it. Or, rather, the bank does," Andreas replied with a smile. "But I'm very grateful not to be renting in this economy."

"Where is your house?"

"It's in Lade."

"Lade," Pappa echoed, staring at Andreas with raised eyebrows. "You must be doing very well to own a home there at your age."

Andreas's face reddened. "God has been very gracious." He looked at Linnea and smiled. "He's blessed me in very many ways."

"God is gracious to everyone, but we don't all own a home in Lade."

Linnea's grip around her fork tightened in the hush that followed Pappa's remark. She didn't understand the weird vibe in the room. It almost felt as though her family were going out of their way to be cold toward Andreas.

She trawled her brain for a question to ask Signy, but every topic that came to mind related in some way to her sister's now-broken engagement. She finally landed on something that seemed safe to ask. "Pappa says you've recently got a new place."

Signy poked at a piece of sausage. "That's right."

She didn't follow up her response, and Linnea's mind went blank.

Mamma broke in. "She got Flora Ekeberg to do her interior design. *Adressavisen* featured it in their lifestyle spread last month, didn't they, Signy?"

"Yes." The shadow of a smile touched Signy's lips.

"That's very impressive," Andreas said. "No newspaper is coming to photograph my interiors."

Silence fell again until Andreas sighed, placing his cutlery next to his plate. "That was absolutely delicious, Linnea. *Takk for mat.*"

His compliment radiated warmth into her chilled heart. "*Vær så god.*"

Mamma's lips stretched in a thin smile. "That was a great effort. I don't believe I've eaten your cooking before."

"She's an amazing cook." Andreas beamed across the table. "She's the first person to make me actually enjoy *fårikål*. I didn't think that was possible until she made it for my parents and me this autumn."

Signy looked at Linnea. "That's quite a feat. I'll never understand how boiled mutton and cabbage can be made appetizing. Our grandmother made that whenever we visited, and we always hated it. Remember how we used to slip bits to the dog under the table?"

Linnea remembered coming up with creative ways to hide her mutton and cabbage. But she mostly recalled the kind woman who loved to fuss over her and show her love through food, with plate after plate of *lefse*, waffles, and bowls of creamy *rømmegrøt* smothered with butter and cinnamon.

Bestemor's death was the first big blow in her life, sending her into a tailspin of depression and poor choices. Her grandmother was the only person in her family who didn't shove her aside in a rush to cater to Signy's huge needs.

The much-maligned *fårikål* sparked memories of her beloved grandmother. After Linnea started getting her life back on track, she'd been almost fixated with recreating and perfecting Bestemor's signature dish.

"*Fårikål* isn't that bad," Pappa said to Signy. "Remember, you were probably struggling with the effects of your chemo. That made everything taste horrible."

"Maybe. But please don't make me ever eat it again, Linnea. *Takk for mat.*"

"*Vær så god.*" Linnea stood. "I was thinking we'll have dessert and coffee after we've exchanged our gifts, unless everyone would rather eat dessert first."

"When do we get our presents?" Hanna asked.

Mamma leaned forward. "You'll get your gifts after everything is cleared away. Little children must learn patience."

Hanna pushed her lower lip out. "But I've been waiting so long!" She gazed at the tree that glowed in the corner, the colored lights reflected in the shiny paper of the gifts that sat piled underneath.

"I have an idea, if it's okay with your mother," Andreas said to Hanna. "Shall we take a little walk around the block? We'll get our tummies ready for dessert, and by the time we get back, it'll almost be time to open your presents."

"Aw, would you mind? I'd really appreciate that," Linnea said.

He smiled back at her. "No problem at all. I'll feel less guilty about the massive helpings I'm going to have if I take a bit of a walk first."

"Okay. Come on, Hanna. Let's get your coat and gloves."

Hanna jumped off her chair and skipped toward the front door.

Linnea helped her slip on her boots, coat, scarf, mittens, and hat, bundling the little girl up against the cold.

His own coat and scarf on, Andreas bent forward and brushed his lips against Linnea's cheek. "See you soon. Let's go, Hanna."

Hanna slid her mittened hand into Andreas's as they left the apartment.

Linnea closed the door behind them, a warm glow washing over her heart until her gaze met Mamma's.

Mamma folded her arms. "Is it safe for Hanna to go for a walk now? It's dark outside."

"It's only half past five. Of course it's safe for her to go on a short walk. It's not like she's gone on her own. She's with Andreas."

Signy glanced at her mother, then faced Linnea. "Does he often spend time alone with her?"

"Every so often. He's taken her to the park before and watched her while I do errands." Linnea walked to the dining table and began to stack the dinner plates.

"And you don't see anything wrong with that? You know, in this day and age."

A tight, icy ball formed in the pit of Linnea's stomach. "What do you mean?"

Signy shrugged. "I'm just saying you can't be too careful."

Mamma chimed in. "He does seem like a very pleasant and successful young man. He's got a good job, and he's very attractive. I would imagine he doesn't struggle to get female attention. In fact, I would think he needs to beat them off with a stick. So, no offense, of course, but I've just got to wonder, what's his interest in being with a single mother?"

Linnea's gut clenched like a fist. "What are you trying to say?"

"You're a lovely person, don't get me wrong. You have some really good qualities, and I can see how hard you've worked on yourself since . . . Since you were younger. But I'm going to be frank with you. If a man could have his pick of any woman he wanted, he's going to consider what benefits him most. Why choose a person with a young child? Unless the child is his." She raised her eyebrow. "Is she?"

Reeling under the onslaught of guided verbal missiles, Linnea grasped at the one question she could answer. "No, Hanna isn't his."

"Does he know everything about the circumstances of her birth?"

"Of course he does. I told him as soon as he expressed an interest in being more than friends."

"Well, then, either he's very forgiving, or he has reasons of his own for wanting to be with someone more vulnerable or dependent on him. And since Prince Charming only exists in fairy tales, I think you need to be careful."

"I don't believe in fairy tales." Linnea hated the way her voice wobbled. "But Andreas is a decent, God-fearing Christian man."

Mamma glanced at her husband. "Per-Einar?"

Pappa took his turn in the tag team attack. "I think your mother is trying to say you need to approach this without rose-tinted glasses on. It doesn't matter how Christian he says he is. What's in this for him? He's an obstetrician who owns his own place, which makes him a catch, as you young people would say. We live in a really depraved world, which I believe you know very well. There are some very unsavory people out there. We hear all sorts of horror stories, so before you let a man hang out with your four-year-old daughter, I would think you should know him a lot better."

Linnea gripped the back of her chair. The assumption her family had been dancing around formed itself into ugly words that Linnea spoke aloud. "You don't really think he's a child predator. That's not what this is about. You think I'm not good enough for him. I'm so bad that there must be something fishy about a guy who's interested in me."

Signy, Mamma, and Pappa looked at her in silence. None of them disagreed.

CHAPTER SIX

"Linnea, I hate to have to be blunt like this. We're not trying to hurt you."

Linnea held up both hands to ward off her mother's words. "No. Stop. Please just stop. You've said enough."

Hot tears burned her eyes as she grabbed the stack of dirty dinner plates and took them to the kitchen.

She knew they were staring at her as they sat there, weighing her in their scales and finding her wanting.

The only thing worse than the pain of their silent judgment was her fear that they were right.

She had come a long way since her life was an alcohol-soaked garbage heap of partying and sordid hookups. But even though she'd cleaned up and straightened out, there was nothing special about her to warrant the attention of a wonderful man like Andreas. She now came with the sorts of scars and baggage from which most men ran a mile.

Mamma, Pappa, and Signy drifted back to their seats in the living room as Linnea ferried the dishes from the table to the kitchen.

None of them offered to lend a hand, and she didn't want their help.

Today was supposed to be her chance to show her family how much she'd changed. But they just saw her as the sum of her many mistakes.

She stood in front of the sink, her back to her family as a few stubborn tears broke loose and rolled down her cheeks. They could think whatever they wanted about her, but how dare they insinuate such disgusting things about Andreas?

The doorbell rang. She needed to get a grip. It was Christmas, and Hanna deserved to have a good day. It didn't matter that her insides were cut into ribbons. She'd wear a smile and make sure her little girl enjoyed today.

Linnea dried her eyes and went to the front door.

"Mamma, we saw the Northern Lights!" Hanna gushed as she ran into the apartment.

"Wow, did you? That's wonderful."

Andreas followed the little girl inside. "They're stunning. What colors could you see, Hanna?"

"Green and pink and purple."

"Did you really see purple ones?" Linnea asked, looking at Andreas. "That's very rare."

"We did indeed. I've not seen a display like that in years. It's a special Christmas." He kissed Linnea's forehead, and she fought to hold the dam around her wounded heart in place so her tears didn't burst out in an unstoppable flood.

God was still painting the heavens. He was the creator and sustainer of all, and the loving Father who welcomed his prodigal sons and daughters home, laying out a feast before them and forgiving all. She stood still for a moment, her eyes closed. God loved her. She was good enough for him.

She opened her eyes and turned to her daughter. "Shall we look at our presents now?" The dinner things weren't completely cleared away, but so what? She wouldn't make Hanna wait a second longer to get her gifts.

The little girl hopped from foot to foot. "Really? Already?"

"Yes, really. As soon as you get your things off."

"Andreas, could you please help me with my boots?"

Linnea went into the living room where her parents and sister sat. "We're going to exchange our gifts now."

Mamma looked at the half-cleared dining table. "Now?"

"Yes. Now." She knelt on the floor in front of the tree and picked up a wrapped package as Hanna skipped toward her. "You're just in time, darling. This present has your name on it."

Hanna grabbed the gift with a pure delight that soothed Linnea's hurting heart. Despite all her mistakes, she had this lovely child. Another undeserved blessing from the God who unstintingly showered her with grace.

As the minutes went by, the pile under the tree dwindled. Most of the presents were Hanna's, ranging from stuffed toys to Legos, clothes, and jigsaw puzzles. She got a winter jacket from her grandparents and coloring books from Signy.

While everyone watched Hanna opening a Lego set, Linnea managed to slip into her pocket the gift that was supposed to go to Signy's fiancé.

Mamma and Pappa politely received their personalized "Grandma" and "Grandpa" mugs, and Signy looked happy with her scented hand lotion and bath products.

They'd all chipped in and gotten Linnea a gift card for the day spa at Solsiden.

Andreas gave Linnea a handmade snow globe, and he gave Signy, Mamma, and Pappa matching woolen scarves.

"I'm so sorry—we didn't get you anything," Mamma said as she took her package from Andreas. "We didn't know you were coming."

He waved his hands. "Don't even think about it. I wasn't expecting a gift. Linnea, this is from my parents."

He handed her an oblong box. She slid it open and gasped. Inside it was an exquisite gold-plated nurse's pendant watch. Tears blurred her eyes as she read the handwritten note.

Dearest Linnea, you've worked so hard this year and we know you'll do everyone who loves you proud when you graduate. You never cease to amaze us with how well you handle your work, studies, and being a wonderful mom to our precious little friend Hanna. Don't forget to take time to rest and play. Much love from Unni and Bjørn Nygaard.

Her heart ached with an exquisite pain.

"What does the paper say?" Hanna asked.

Linnea shook her head. She didn't trust her voice. She passed the note on to Andreas, and he read it out loud.

She caught the look Mamma and Pappa exchanged as Andreas read. Signy kept her head bowed as she fiddled with her new scarf.

Mamma cleared her throat. "That's a very pretty note. You must have made quite an impression on those people, Linnea."

The space under the tree was empty, and Andreas turned to Linnea. "I've got something else for you."

"You already gave me a gift. Wait. What are you doing?"

He lowered himself onto one knee and pulled a small velvet box from his jacket pocket. "I didn't wrap this one."

Linnea's heart galloped like a troop of wild horses.

"I've been wanting to ask you this for some time, but when you told me your family were coming, I decided to wait until today." He stared into her eyes. "Do you remember what you said to me the first day I asked you for a date?"

Linnea nodded, pressing her hand against her chest. "'If you really knew who you're talking to, you wouldn't be asking me out.'"

"And what did I say?"

Her answer came in a choked whisper. "You said, 'Try me.'"

"Mamma, why are you crying?" Hanna's soft hand patted Linnea's cheek.

"I think she's crying because I want her to marry me," Andreas said. "And if she says yes, I'm going to cry, too."

A frown creased Hanna's forehead. "Why? Does it hurt?"

"Sometimes nice things can make you cry because you're really happy. Can I ask her, *lille venn?*"

"Okay."

Linnea laughed through her tears as Hanna plopped herself down cross-legged between her and Andreas.

Andreas opened the box, revealing a three-stone diamond ring that reflected the twinkling Christmas lights into a thousand multicolored sparkles. "Linnea Birgitta Moen, will you marry me?"

There could only be one answer. "Yes. Yes, yes, yes!"

Andreas slid the ring onto her finger and pressed her hand to his lips. She brushed away the tears from the corners of his eyes.

"Yay!" Hanna clapped her little hands.

Andreas scooped the child up with one arm while he wrapped the other around Linnea.

He held them in a tight embrace. "I'll do my utmost to make you both safe and happy."

After a moment, Hanna squirmed and pulled out of the three-way hug. "Can I see the ring?"

Linnea held out her hand, and her daughter inspected the ring.

Pappa stood slowly and walked over to Andreas. He held out his hand. "Congratulations. Good luck to both of you."

Andreas wrung Pappa's hand, grinning from ear to ear.

Mamma inclined her head. "Congratulations. What a day of surprises. I'm happy for both of you."

Linnea's gaze slid to Signy. A pang of sympathy sliced

through her delirious joy. Her sister's engagement ended today. Was this adding to her pain?

Signy lifted her head, her features arranged into a smile. Only a slight tremble in her lips betrayed what might be going on inside. "Congratulations."

"Thank you," Andreas said, circling Linnea's shoulders with his arm. "And thank you for saying yes."

Linnea leaned against his chest, turning as Signy and Mamma stood.

"We'll be leaving now. We have a long drive back home."

"Won't you stay for dessert and coffee?" Linnea asked.

Mamma shook her head. "No, thank you. It's been a long day for Signy, as you know, and we'd better see her safely home."

Linnea understood. Once again, Signy needed her parents' support. She was okay with that.

Mamma, Pappa, and Signy said goodbye to Hanna and got into their coats and scarves.

Linnea followed them to the front door.

As they stepped outside, she glimpsed undulating waves of green in the black sky. The Northern Lights!

Mamma leaned forward and pecked Linnea on the cheek. "About what I said earlier . . . I really hope I'm wrong. Good luck."

Sensing a warm presence behind her, Linnea turned her body slightly. Andreas stood there. He rested his hands on her shoulders. Mamma *was* wrong. Linnea may not deserve anything good, but God was a gracious father to his prodigal children. Luck had nothing to do with it. She leaned against Andreas and waved at her family as they walked away under the colored sky.

A NOTE FROM THE AUTHOR

I love Jesus' parable about the Prodigal Son.

Above all, I'm floored by the abundant grace the Father pours on the wayward son. The boy who deserved everything bad that happened to him instead received forgiveness and restoration from his father.

But I also wonder about the "good" child who remained behind. He thought it was unfair that his wastrel brother seemingly got away with so much and even apparently got rewarded for his sins.

My story, *The Prodigal's Feast*, explores that dynamic.

I also wanted to consider the question of what happens when the prodigal straightens up his (or in this case her) life, but her family can't see past her mistakes.

I set the story in Norway at Christmastime, where the main celebration meal and gift exchange happens on Christmas Eve and not on December 25th.

Blessings and love in Christ, who welcomes all prodigals who repent.

ABOUT MILLA HOLT

In the distant past, **MILLA HOLT** was a journalist, a public information officer, and a copywriter. Now, she has her dream job: writing stories while being a homeschooling mom, so any day can be a pajama day. She lives with her husband and four children in the east of England, where they enjoy country walks, visiting stately homes, playing video games, and making up silly lyrics to their favorite songs.

Please visit Milla's website to explore more of her books and to subscribe to her newsletter:
www.millaholt.com

TITLES BY MILLA HOLT

THE MOSAIC COLLECTION: NOVELS
Seasons of Faith series
Into the Flood
Through the Blaze
Within the Storm
Amid the Ashes

THE MOSAIC COLLECTION: ANTHOLOGY STORIES

"Lost and Found"
(*All Things New: Stories to Refresh the Soul*)
"The Prodigal's Feast"
(*A Thrill in the Air: A Mosaic Christmas Anthology V*)

UPCOMING
Seasons of Faith series
After the Frost

A MERRYTIME CRUISE

Lorna Seilstad

* * *

Christmas is not the time to announce their marriage is over, so Rick and Merrideth Stevens agree to join forces one last time and give their children a magical family holiday that they'll treasure. After the family embarks on the jolliest vacation ever, a Christmas cruise to the Bahamas, Rick and Meredith find there's more to Christmas—and to their marriage—than carol-oke and cookies.

To my friend Dawn
Your friendship is a gift I treasure.
We've had a whale of a time cruising life and the writing world
together.

When they had gone, an angel of the Lord appeared to Joseph in a dream. "Get up," he said, "take the child and his mother and escape to Egypt. Stay there until I tell you, for Herod is going to search for the child to kill him." So he got up, took the child and his mother during the night and left for Egypt.

Matthew 2:13-14

CHAPTER ONE

Merrideth twisted the white gold wedding band on her left hand. She pulled it off and, weighing it in her hand, she looked down at her barren finger. Fifteen years of marriage had left the flesh indented where the ring had been. How long would it take for that mark to go away?

"Merri, are you listening to me?" Rick's tone bristled with irritation.

She blinked and slipped the ring back on her finger. "Sorry, what did you say?"

"I said I'll be home late. Something has come up here at the track. Don't wait up."

"But we were going to decide when to tell the kids about"—she paused and lowered her voice to a whisper —"about us."

He heaved an audible sigh. "It's almost Christmas. We can't do that to them. We'll tell them after. What's a few more weeks going to matter?" He paused. When he spoke again, his voice held a note of softness. "Merri, let's do something special for Christmas. One last hurrah."

"Such as?"

"I don't know. Go to the North Pole?"

She rolled her eyes. Inconsiderate fool. "Rick, you know I don't like the cold."

"Then, let's go somewhere warm: The Caribbean. The Bahamas. Mexico. A cruise somewhere."

"A cruise?"

"Sure." He sounded like a child begging for a new toy. "You've always wanted to go on one. We have the money. Let's give the kids a family Christmas to remember."

A whiff of cinnamon from her wax warmer tickled her nose, and she fought the urge to sneeze.

"Let me look into it. I'll see if it will fit into everyone's plans."

"Merri, for once just do it." The enthusiasm slipped from his tone. "Sign us up without scheduling everything down to the bathroom breaks."

"This might work. Let me think." She sneezed into a tissue then jotted down a few notes on everything she'd need to consider. Could a cruise line handle Simon's peanut allergy on a ship? What about bringing Christmas gifts for the boys? And if she remembered right, they'd both outgrown their swimsuits. Could she even find new ones this time of year?

She tapped the pad with her pen. She'd have to hand it to Rick. This time, he'd had a good idea, but was it practical?

Creating a memory the kids could hold onto was appealing, especially since the next year would be a difficult one for them. "Rick, do you think we could pull this off? I mean, can we get along well enough to fool the boys for seven days?"

"We've been fooling them for six months. What's seven more days? Besides, if you recall, I was a thespian."

"Oh, I'm all too aware of your acting abilities." She bit her lower lip and looked at the family photo hanging over the mantle of their last family vacation. What a day that had been!

Like herding feral cats. How would she corral her two active boys, eight-year-old Simon and ten-year-old Thaddeus, for seven days? She should put this crazy idea to bed right now.

He cleared his throat. "Okay, I found a Christmas cruise and booked all six of us.'

"Six?"

"The four of us and your parents. We normally spend Christmas with them, so why not? It'll be our Christmas gift to them."

She could think of a thousand "why nots," including one gigantic one. They might be able to fool the boys for seven days, but never her parents.

"It's done," he declared as if he were a judge with a gavel in hand. "Operation Christmas Cruise is underway. Six nights in the Western Caribbean including the Bahamas, Puerto Costa Maya, and Cozumel onboard the *Sensation of the Seas*. I'll send you a link so you can start planning everyone's bowel movements."

"Wait!" But it was too late. Rick had hung up and, once again, left her with a mess of things to clean up.

CHAPTER TWO

"Hey boys, look." Rick stopped and pointed up to the towering water slides on the top deck of the cruise ship. Standing at the rail was the right jolly old elf wearing a Hawaiian shirt, red shorts, and flip flops. He waved as the passengers filed on board.

Both boys shielded their eyes.

"It's Santa!" Simon bounced on his feet. He wacked his brother's arm. "I told you Santa would find us here, Thad. Daddy, can we go explore?"

Meredith nudged Simon forward. "Not now, sweetheart, and don't hit your brother. We have the tree lighting to attend to at four, but we can go swim after we check in at our muster station. According to Cruise Gurus, the most important thing for us to do on embarkation day is to get our swimsuits on because most people were not smart enough to put their suits in their carry-ons. That way, we'll miss the crowds."

Thaddeus adjusted his heavy backpack. "But I'm hungry, and I don't want a hotdog."

"Hotdog?" Grandma Bev asked, glancing at her husband to see if she heard right.

Grandpa Jessie chuckled. "Muster station. Not mustard, sport. It's where we'll go if there's a nautical emergency."

Simon's brow scrunched. "A naughty emergency? They have a special place for timeouts?"

She placed her hand on Simon's shoulder and gave the laughing men a side-eyed look of warning. "Nautical is a word for the sea."

"So we go to the mustard station if there's an emergency like sinking?" Thad's eyes lit up. "We studied about a big ship in school that sank when it hit an iceberg. Will we see any icebergs?"

"No, sport, there are no icebergs around here," Rick said. "And we won't be sinking, either. It's like a fire drill at school. It's practice in case there's ever a problem."

"Oh." Thad's stomach growled. "Will they have food there or even snacks?"

"No, but we'll grab something on the way." He ruffled his son's dark curls.

"Remember, darling, we have a schedule, and you promised to stick to it." She forced a smile. "For the children."

"I did, but sweetheart, we have to feed our growing boys, or we may end up with a whole different kind of nautical emergency to deal with called mutiny." He planted a kiss on her cheek.

Did she just blush? More likely she was flushed with anger. Merri did not like her schedules to be altered even for hungry ten-year-olds.

Despite the fact that her scheduling was over the top, he had to admit that their check-in had gone smoothly. Merri had filled out the health checks and everything else that she could in advance. She'd arranged the paperwork in a file, insisted they arrive on time, and made sure no one was carrying any open chip bags. Their excursions were booked and their bags checked. In truth, they had sailed through the line. He chuckled. Now, all they needed was a miracle to keep this charade afloat.

The group came to a stop as they entered the atrium. Christmas had exploded in the open space with an enormous Christmas tree taking center stage, flanked by a sprawling gingerbread village. The tree, however, was not lit. Oh yeah, the tree lighting was at four. That was good. The kids would enjoy seeing the fake spruce come to life.

"I'm so hungry I think I'll die." Thaddeus doubled over, hugging his stomach.

Grandpa Jessie draped his arm around his daughter's shoulders. "Merri, my girl, I could do with some lunch, too. What do you say we make an unexpected stop? I read that the best burgers on this ship are on Deck 10."

Merri sighed. " Really, Dad? You can't wait?"

Grandma Bev giggled and patted his stomach. "He's a growing boy, too."

She shrugged. "I submit to the needs of the masses. Dad, lead us to lunch."

After burgers, shakes, and mac-and-cheese bites had been consumed, the group made their way to Deck 6 and located their assigned muster station. The muster officer checked their name off the list and reminded them to report back during the cruise's official safety briefing.

"Now, can we go swimming?" Simon pleaded.

Rick grabbed his youngest son by the waist and flipped him upside down. Simon squealed with delight, and Rick tickled his belly. He set the giggling boy back down. "Hey, what are you doing laughing like that?" he teased. "I thought you wanted to go swimming. Let's go find a bathroom to change into our bathing suits."

Merri huffed. "If you two are done, according to the ship's map, there's a restroom around the corner." She pointed to her left. "Once you're ready, your dad can take you up to the water slides."

Rick frowned. "Where will you be?"

Merri checked off a box on her list. "I have to check in with the maître d' and confirm that Simon's peanut allergy is listed. Then, I want to check on our show reservations, purchase an internet package, and check in at the kid's club to sign the boys up for some Christmas fun." She paused and took off her backpack. Digging inside she pulled out blue lanyards with snowflakes dotting them and the key cards to their rooms. "I almost forgot these." She began to pass the items out. "Wait. They've got the boys listed in the wrong room. "

His in-laws exchanged knowing grins before Grandma Bev spoke up.

"No, it's not." Bev's southern accent thickened. "I called the cruise reservations and made sure the boys would be in a room with Grandpa and me."

Merri gaped at them. "How did you do that?"

Grandma Bev plucked the keys from her daughter's hand. "Where do you think you got your organization skills, Merrideth? And you know your dad's mischievous side. It was his idea. I simply called and pretended I was you. I know all your personal identifying information." She ticked them off on her fingers. "Reservation number, social security number, mother's maiden name, name of your first pet. So, no arguing. We want our grandsons with us, and y'all deserve some quality grown-up time—alone." She winked at her daughter.

Merri shot a look of helplessness at Rick, and his gut clinched. He and Merri hadn't shared a bedroom in over three months, and they could barely be in the same house without declaring war. How would they manage to remain civil in a tiny cruise ship cabin for a week?

CHAPTER THREE

Merri checked her watch for the umpteenth time. Where was Rick? If he didn't bring her parents and the boys down to their cabin soon, they would miss the tree-lighting ceremony. Her nerves zinged. He'd promised to get them there on time. Why had she believed him? Once Rick started to have fun, he forgot everything.

At least she'd had time to unpack her things, hang up the empty over-the-door shoe organizer she'd brought to hang on the bathroom door, and slip her toiletries in. Since she thought the boys would be with them, she figured the extra room the shoe organizer offered would be important. Now, Rick would probably accuse her of being ridiculous. But the one thing Rick never seemed to grasp is that she had to be the responsible one so that he could be the kid.

Laughter in the hallway made her swivel toward the door, and a second later Rick and the boys poured into the room, stories of waterslide triumph pouring from their lips.

"Whoa!" She held up her hand then pointed to her wrist. "I can't wait to hear all about it after the tree lighting. If we don't rush now, we'll miss it." The boys stared at her. "Go change in

Grandpa and Grandma's room. That's where your suitcases are. Thaddeus, help your brother."

The boys scooted out of the room, and she whirled on Rick. "How could you?"

He shook his head and held out his hands. "How could I what?"

"You promised to have everyone here by three fifteen. Now, we might miss the tree lighting."

He shook his head, flung a towel over his shoulder, and tossed his suitcase onto the bed.

"We're on vacation, Merri. Lighten up."

She pressed her lips together. Words she had best leave unsaid threatened to erupt. "I'm going to go see if the boys need help."

"I wouldn't if I were you. Not unless you want to see your father changing." He chuckled as he pulled out a coral polo and slipped it on. "I'm not sure what kind of therapy the boys will need after this week in their grandparents' cabin."

"I'm more worried about what kind of therapy they'll need because of us."

"They'll be fine." He pulled on a pair of shorts and ran a comb through his hair. "Ready?"

She rolled her eyes and tried to step around him. He caught her around the waist. "Merri, I'm sorry. I lost track of time. Let's not start this week off like this. Remember, one last perfect holiday for the kids?"

A knock on the door made her jump out of his arms. She swung the door open and took in her waiting sons. "You two look great." Her parents stepped into the hallway, too. "Everyone got their lanyards? Alrighty, then, let's get a move on."

All of the best viewing spots had been taken by the time they arrived, but Rick managed to find them a spot on by the railing on the second floor where they could see most of the tree if they leaned around a large potted palm.

The Christmas tree had been roped off to keep guests from getting too close. As guests continued to pour into the atrium, carols played, but that did little to dampen the wails of young children who'd most likely missed their naps.

An elf-hat-bedecked cruise director stepped forward with a microphone in his hand. "Are you ready to light the tree?" He held a hand to his ear for the crowd's enthusiastic reply. "Then I need your help." He had a pleasant Irish lilt to his voice. "Count down with me. Ten, nine, eight." The crowd chanted with him, and when he reached one, "O Christmas Tree" blared as the tree exploded with thousands of tiny white lights. Then, a light show began that added to the event.

"Mommy, look!" Simon pointed to a swirl of light that looked like it was wrapping around the tree.

Merri smiled. Her sweet boy had no idea this fantastic illusion would evaporate as soon as the projector was turned off. He'd be sad once it was gone, but at least he had this magic for the moment.

She pressed her hand to her stomach as the comparison to what she and Rick were doing with this cruise punched her. Was this experience going to make it easier or more difficult for Simon and Thaddeus?

Ooohs and aaahs drew her out of her reverie when the lights changed, making it appear as if it were snowing in the atrium.

"Wow," she breathed.

"It's stunning." Rick took her hand and squeezed it. He motioned with his head toward Thaddeus who stood with his mouth gaping and eyes wide. "We did the right thing with this trip. They're going to have great memories to hold on to. I promise."

She released his hand and pulled hers away. Rick's

promises were as fickle as the swirl of light around the tree—there one minute and gone the next. Oh, sure, he'd kept his promise of faithfulness, but the rest of the wedding vows? Love, honor, and cherish? The only thing Rick cherished was fast cars, and she was far from a Lamborghini.

No, this isn't about him. It's about the boys. Focus on them.

She forced a smile and let herself be swept up in the joy of the moment. The tree. Her boys. And Christmas.

She could do this. Couldn't she?

At least Merri didn't make him wear a tie to the Captain's Welcome Dinner in the dining room on their first night. Instead, she'd produced dark green polos for the boys, her father, and him to wear.

She and her mother had coordinated with dark green dresses that sported elegant Christmas trees and poinsettias. As they were shown to their table, he had to admit the dress hugged Merri in all the right places.

After the six of them were seated, another couple joined their table. Gabriel and Angelica Vargas, a vivacious retired couple from Florida, had booked this trip since they planned to celebrate Christmas with their adult children at the end of the month. They'd barely had time to exchange introductions when the waiter appeared and introduced himself. He presented everyone with their menus and said Thad and Simon's orders would come out before everyone else's. Merri had arranged for them to go to the kids' club for some special evening activities rather than have to remain at the table with the adults.

Thad had no trouble deciding on pizza from the children's menu, and Simon selected mac and cheese. To her credit, Merri didn't say anything about them having had mac-and-cheese bites for lunch. She did, however, insist they get vegetables with their entrees, and she double-checked that there would be no cross contamination with peanuts.

"What do you do for a living, Rick?" Gabriel asked after they'd all placed their orders.

Thad blurted out, "My dad is a race car driver."

Gabriel raised his eyebrows. "Are you?"

"I was." Rick placed his napkin in his lap. "I run Fast Track Racing School now. We teach racing, provide racing experiences, and even do a little stunt work for the movie industry."

"He worked on the movie *Talladega Nights*," his father-in-law said with pride in his voice. "And was in an episode of *Blue Bloods* last year."

"Really?" Angelica leaned forward. "Did you meet Tom Selleck or Donnie Wahlberg?"

"I wish." Merri's smile didn't reach her eyes. "But he did get to meet the show's stunt coordinator. What was his name?"

"Roy Farfel. Their normal stunt driver was out with Covid and needed someone to fill in, so I got the call since I look a little like Will Estes."

"Which one is Will?" Angelica asked.

"The youngest Reagan. Jamie." Rick didn't want to talk about racing anymore. The track was a sore subject between Merri and him. She had pinned most of their problems on it, so he needed to change the subject and fast. "So, Gabriel, what did you do before you retired?"

Conversation came easily to the group while Thad and Simon devoured their pizza and mac and cheese. Even the vegetables were gone before the kids were picked up for kids' club. Gabriel and Jessie had a lot in common as they'd both been building contractors. Angelica was fascinated to learn

Merri was an interior decorator and had her own home staging and design business.

Inevitably, conversation returned to the racetrack, and Gabriel asked Rick about the racing experiences he'd mentioned. "I always wanted to drive a race car. What kind of cars do you have?"

Merri tensed beside him. What choice did he have but to talk about what he did? He didn't want to be rude. Besides, it was more interesting than pillows and throw rugs.

He speared the last bite of his prime rib. "Most people come to take a spin in a full-sized, Indy-style race car. If they don't want to race, they can do a ride along."

Angelica's eyebrows rose. "You just let them get in a car and drive?"

He chewed and swallowed the meat then smiled. "No, ma'am. They have a period of classroom training and instruction first. Depending on the package they selected and their skill level, they either have a driver in the car with them or they have an instructor or spotter who communicates through an earpiece."

Gabriel looked at his wife and arched his brows. "Can they go as fast as they want?"

She swatted his arm. "You don't need to drive as fast you want."

"The RPMs have stops set based on the amount of time you're signed up for. The longer you drive, the more experience you'll have and the faster you can go."

Angelica turned to Merri. "Do you ride with him?"

"On the track?" She shook her head. "No."

"She used to." Rick slipped his arm around the back of her chair. After all, he had to keep up the appearance that they were experiencing marital bliss. "But not anymore. Too hard for her to give up control."

Bev looked up from the dessert menu. "Oh, she can trust you. You'd never let anything happen to her."

The words struck hard. His heart rate kicked up a notch, and the fine meal he'd eaten felt like a stone in his stomach. Why couldn't Merri be like her mother? It was true that trust was their biggest issue, but he had no idea why. He'd never done anything to deliberately break Merri's trust, and no one could live up to her standards. Every time he turned around in the last few months, he'd disappointed her in some way. He'd been praying about it for months, but there'd been no angel coming to tell him to "be of good cheer" or to tell him what to do.

Gabriel glanced at Merri and grinned. "Your wife seems like a capable woman. Maybe you should let her drive. Let her be the one in control."

He gave a wry chuckle. "I'm sure she'd like that more than you know."

CHAPTER FOUR

Since her parents wanted to take a walk under the starlit sky on the deck, Merri found herself alone with Rick. They had to pick up the boys in thirty minutes. She knew they were watching *Rudolph the Red-Nosed Reindeer* outdoors on the Lido deck on the giant screen. Thad and Simon would be furious if they picked them up earlier and ruined the ending of the show, even if they had seen it a dozen times.

"Let's walk." Rick held out his hand.

Out of habit, she slipped hers into place. His grasp was firm and warm—and comfortable. They could at least be friends, couldn't they?

They sauntered in silence along the deck, a cool wind gently blowing off the sea. She listened to the sounds of the water churning beneath them and paused at the railing to watch the moonlight ripple across the inky night ocean as the ship cruised along.

Rick joined her at the railing, standing so close Merri could smell his cologne. She loved that scent. Fresh, suave, and woodsy, it had top notes of bergamot, pepper, grapefruit, and rosemary over a base of musk, amber, and cedarwood—or so the sales lady had told her last Christmas.

He clasped his hands in front of him with his elbows resting on the top rail. "Merri, I'm sorry there was so much talk about the racetrack tonight."

"Ssh." She drew in another deep breath and closed her eyes. "I'm counting my three things."

He straightened and turned to her. "What three things?"

"I was listening to a podcast that said to find three things about your spouse every day to thank God for. I figured it won't save our marriage, but it might keep me from killing you this week." She laughed softly.

"And?"

"And what?"

He crossed his arms over his chest. "What are the three things?"

She shot him a glare. "I'm not going to tell you."

"You tell me yours and I'll tell you mine."

"You just heard about this. You don't have three things."

"I have more than three, Merri." His voice held a serious note. "Deal?"

He had more than three? Even though she doubted it was true, he had certainly piqued her interest. "Three. Every day?"

He nodded. "Agreed."

She stepped away from the railing and began walking. This was a dangerous game, but she had to follow through now. "Number one. The boys adore you." The words clogged her throat and she swallowed. "You are their hero."

He fell in step beside her. "Okay. Two?"

"You're a good provider. We've never wanted for anything."

"Are you forgetting the Ramen noodle days when we first got married?" He chuckled.

"I could never forget Noodle au Gratin by candlelight. But

even then, you took an extra job so we could have meat once a week."

Her traitorous feelings sparked at the memories. What were they doing playing this dance?

He tripped over a deck chair and caught himself. "And three?"

"You know, this is probably really silly. In case you forgot, we're getting a divorce."

"Not yet." He grabbed her by the waist and spun her towards him. She placed her hands on his chest to keep from toppling, but he held her firm. "My turn. Number one is I'm thankful for how hard you've worked to make this trip memorable—including these ridiculous Christmas outfits."

She quirked a smile. "There's more to come."

"I imagine there is." He pulled her a bit closer. "My number two is that you supported my dream and were with me every step of the way, even when it was clear I wasn't going to be the driver on the podium." His gaze dropped to her lips, but he drew in a breath and cleared his throat. "So, what's your number three for today?"

"You first."

"Uh uh. This was your idea."

She sighed. "Oh, all right. You smell really, really good."

"I'm glad I took that shower." He pressed a kiss to her forehead.

"And your third item?"

"Ready? My number three for today is that you've got a great dad."

"My dad? That's your third reason?" She pulled away and marched toward the elevator. His words had stung. What had she expected? Rick singing her praises to the high heavens?

"I was going to say you smelled good, too, but I thought you would say that was cheating." The elevator chimed and they stepped inside.

She jammed her fists onto her hips. "Because it would have been."

"Hey, I only heard about this three things challenge a few minutes ago. I was doing this on the fly. You've had all day to think about it." The elevator came to a stop and they exited. "Merri, wait."

She turned and hiked her eyebrows. "You said you had more than three."

"I do." He held his hands out in a pleading motion. "Can I have a redo? A number four?"

Tilting her head to the side, she tapped her foot impatiently. "We should get the boys."

"Number four." He stepped close, his hot breath tickling her ear. "I love that you only ate half your dessert and let me have the other half. That raspberry tarte was phenomenal."

She elbowed him. "You're incorrigible. You can't be serious for five minutes."

"And you love it."

He flashed her a devilish smile that made her frozen heart melt a little more. She did love Rick's playful side. Sometimes. At other times, she felt like she had another eight-year-old on her hands.

Merri quickened her pace as they drew near to the kids' club. All this emotion had her stomach flip-flopping. She was worried about their boys being shy and not enjoying themselves since they both got grumpy when they were tired. Rick agreed. Thad, especially, was slow to warm to people. All they received from the boys, however, were hugs and smiles upon their arrival. Merri signed them out with their kids' club counselor, Susie, who gushed about what great boys they were.

Merri thanked her and ushered the boys toward the elevator. Simon thrust the picture he'd made in her direction, but she ignored him and glanced at her watch.

"Boys, we'd better get a move on. It's way passed your bedtime."

"Mom, it's vacation," Thad whined.

She gave him a little nudge. "And that is why you need your sleep."

On the elevator, she closed her eyes and rested her cheek on the elevator's cool wall. Rick asked the boys about what they did and listened while they took turns unloading the stories of their adventures. Before the movie, they'd made snow paint and created a picture.

The elevator dinged, and as soon as they were out, Simon held his picture up. "Look, Daddy, it's a snowman. We made him with shaving cream and glue and glitter. Smell him. But be careful because he's not totally dry yet."

He took the picture and inhaled. "Peppermint?"

"You smell it too, Mommy," Simon ordered.

Not sure she could handle the smell, she pretended to take a quick whiff. "Oh yes, it does smell like peppermint. I'm glad you had fun. Come on boys. Let's pick up our pace. Your grandma and grandpa will be waiting."

"I got to add the peppermint oil to the paint 'cause I was the oldest in our group." Thad puffed out his chest as they walked. He then produced his own artwork for inspection.

Merri didn't think the green blob looked like any snowman he'd ever seen. And was that a mask or a bandana? She stopped in the middle of the hall and cocked her head to the side. "Why is your snowman green and yellow?"

"Miss Susie let me put green in my paint."

"Because?"

"Mom, how else could I make a ninja turtle snowman?" He pointed to the center. "All my new friends liked it. This is the best Christmas ever."

Merri certainly hoped so. What would Christmas be like for the boys in the future? She didn't need to worry about that now, and God had taken care of at least one of her concerns. Her boys had certainly come out of their shells.

Merri hugged the left edge of the bed and willed her breathing to steady. What if she accidentally touched Rick in the night or snuggled up to him if she got cold? Maybe she should put a pillow between them. That would be a good barrier. *A barrier? What is wrong with you? You've slept with this man for nearly fifteen years. He's the father of your children, not an ax murderer.*

She closed her eyes and felt the sway of the ship. At least the Dramamine was kicking in. She'd not told Rick, but she was a little seasick tonight. That's why she was rushing the boys back so fast. He probably thought she was being over the top about the boys' bedtime. Maybe she should have explained, but what was the use?

He'd been sweet tonight and fun. Maybe they could be friends after all. As long as she kept her distance, both in life and in this bed.

She bunched the pillow under her head and listened to his soft snores. He must have fallen asleep while she was still in the bathroom doing her night routine after he'd tucked the boys in next door. There it was again. One of the three things about him to be grateful for today. She'd have to find three new ones tomorrow, or had the podcaster said you could do repeats if you couldn't think of anything new?

Lord, help me make it through this week and have a grateful heart. I want to cherish every minute. This is the last time our family can be whole.

CHAPTER FIVE

Merri couldn't breathe. Where had they come from? Four men. Black masks. Sledge hammers. Glass shattering. Shouting. Screaming. It burns!

Please, don't take it.

"No!" Merri jolted awake, gasping for air.

Rick turned on the light. "Merri, is it another nightmare? About the robbery?"

She nodded, pressing her hand to her hammering heart. "I'm okay now. I'm sorry. You can go back to sleep."

He placed his hand on her arm. "You're trembling. Come here. Let me hold you."

"Rick . . ."

"Just this once." He pulled her gently down beside him and turned the light off.

She should resist, but the whole event had left her disoriented and panicky. She leaned against his chest as his strong arms enveloped her. "Just this once."

He pulled her close and stroked her hair. "You're safe. Go back to sleep. I won't let anything happen to you."

But something bad had happened, and even Rick couldn't have prevented it.

When Rick awoke, Merri wasn't in his arms. He reached out. She wasn't even in his bed. He cracked open one eye and found her dressed for the day—with a pink Christmas tree?

Maybe he was the one dreaming this time.

"Good morning, sleepy head, and happy Christmas Eve day." Merri fluffed out the little branches of a feathery, twelve-inch pink tree and set it on the desk. She topped a red tennis skirt with a black t-shirt that said "Momma Elf" on it. Beneath the words on the tee, the striped elf-legs with pointy red boots made him smile. To top it all off, she'd also donned a matching elf hat. Perfect.

Rick pushed up in bed and caught sight of himself in a mirror. Wow, it looked like he was the one who'd had the nightmare. "How are you going to keep that tree from falling if the ocean gets choppy?"

She tipped the base up so he could see. "I put a magnetic strip on it. Nearly every solid surface here is metal. I have some magnetic things for the boys to decorate the cabin doors with, too."

"You think of everything." But that was his Merri. He swung his feet to the floor. "Want to talk about your nightmare last night?"

"No, it was only a dream. I'm going to take these decorations over to the boys." She motioned to the end of the bed. "There's your 'daddy elf' t-shirt. And don't forget your hat. We'll meet you at the Santa meet and greet."

"No breakfast?"

"After the meet and greet." She put her hand on the door knob.

"Yes, ma'am." He saluted and she pinned him with a glare as she left their cabin.

By the time he arrived at the meet and greet, he had to navigate a queue that stretched around the atrium to reach his family. Grandpa Elf, Grandma Elf, Big Brother Elf, and Little Brother Elf were easy to spot beside their Momma Elf. They'd have a great photo when they were done.

Only a few minutes after he arrived, Merri took the boys up to see Santa. Previously, Thad had said he was too old for Santa, but at the last minute he relented.

He turned to his in-laws. "How did you sleep last night? Did the boys keep you up?"

Jessie chuckled. "They were out within minutes. They'd had quite a day. And you?"

He rubbed the back of his neck. "I slept great but Merri had a nightmare."

"Another one?" Bev asked. "That poor thing. I know I'm not telling you anything new, but she's been having those all the time lately. I'm worried about her, Rick. And I know she's been in control overload ever since the robbery."

All the time? He'd had no idea. He glanced at Merri standing by Simon, who was waiting his turn. "Control overload?"

"Hyper-fixated on schedules, to-do lists—anything she can control." Bev adjusted her elf hat. "Jessie, remember when she was in the car when you got rear-ended? Her room was spotless for months."

Jessie rubbed his hand over his jaw. "I sure do. She organized all her books by color, and she was only in second grade."

"I didn't know that." Rick shoved his hands into his pockets. Sure, he'd seen Merri's organization binges, but how had he missed all this with the burglary? "But she got over this overload?"

Jessie shrugged. "In time. At least she stopped making to-do lists for tea parties." He leaned forward. "I know she can be a lot. Thank you for keeping your vows and loving her even when she's unlovable."

Bev playfully hit his arm. "Our girl is never unlovable. Maybe a little hard to like, but not hard to love. Oh, she's ready for all of us."

The perky cruise elf made quick work of arranging them around Santa, taking extra care to make sure their t-shirts could be read.

"Say 'Sugarplums!'" The elf clicked the photo and told them they could pick it up at the photo station.

As they stepped away, Rick squatted and told Simon to hop on for a piggyback ride. "Boys, it's time to eat our weight in bacon!"

"Don't encourage that," Merri chided.

He galloped along with Simon giggling. "Hey, we're on vacation. We must indulge."

Once they had all settled at the table with heaping plates of food, Merri withdrew the day's schedule and laid it on the table.

Bev stilled Merri's hand. "Honey, we have something we need to talk to you about." She looked at her husband. "Jessie, do you want to tell them or should I?"

CHAPTER SIX

Merri looked from her mother to her father, and her palms began to sweat. What did they have up their sleeves now? Or were they going to give her bad news? Was one of them sick? Dying?

Jessie motioned with his hand. "You go ahead, sweetheart."

Bev plucked the schedule from the table. "I'll take that, Merri. You aren't going to need it because your dad and I bought you and Rick a day pass to the spa, including a couple's massage. It's our Christmas present to you, so you can't refuse."

Relief washed over Merri. No one was dying. Then, her pulse quickened. She pressed her hand to her chest. A whole day together in the spa? No kids. No parents. Nothing to do but relax together. With as much fighting as she and Rick did lately, how could they not turn a spa day into a sparring day?

Merri's gaze locked on Rick's. He gave her an almost imperceptible nod. She knew what it meant. If they were going to continue this ruse, somehow, she had to look excited and accept this gift. Otherwise, her parents would know something was wrong with their marriage.

Squaring her shoulders, Merri pasted on the biggest smile she could muster. Her parents seemed to buy her effusive thanks. Then, with a wave of the list, they gathered the boys and sent Momma Elf and Daddy Elf off to the adults-only spa to play.

Rick had never been to a spa. Sure, he'd had a massage once or twice, but he'd never envisioned a place like this. With its seafoam-blue colors, fancy artwork, and variety of textures, it screamed elegance and indulgence. Even the music playing had a new age flair. Merri looked around and beamed back at him.

They were welcomed by Dasha, a spa therapist with a low, melodious voice and a thick accent. Rick couldn't place the accent. Had Dasha been chosen to work in the spa because she sounded so exotic and calming? She pointed out that the spa specialized in alternating hot and cold therapies. They could go back and forth between saunas, jacuzzies, vitality pools, and rain showers.

"And here's our treasure." She pointed to a steamy glass door. "It's our snow room. You'll love it. It's so refreshing. It awakens all of your senses, and it's chilled to a steady fourteen degrees."

"So, where do you keep parkas and mittens?" Merri asked.

Dasha smiled. "Your swimsuit and robe will be fine. You can stay as long or as little as you like. Did you know that cold therapy can make your hair shinier?"

"I guess the shiny hair will detract from my frostbitten nose." Rick grinned at Merri, but Dasha didn't seem amused.

Dasha took them to another area. "This is our thermal suite, and these are our heated loungers. There are over thirty, so you should have no trouble finding a spot. Feel free to enjoy the view of the ocean and drink some of the fruit-infused water found at that station."

Back at the welcome desk, Dasha passed them each a clipboard. "Fill this out before your massage. We'll come and get you when your therapist is ready. The dressing rooms are this way. Men on the left. Women on the right. Robes and slippers are provided, and here are the keys to your lockers."

By the time they'd filled out the forms and tucked their belongings away in their respective lockers, the therapists were ready for them. After introductions, they were shown to the couple's suite, where two pristine beds awaited them. Since they each had their own massage therapists, the two women took turns giving them directions on how to prepare and asking them if they had any questions. The therapists left while they got into position for their massages.

Once the massage began, Rick was shocked at how quickly he relaxed under the combination of lavender-scented oils, the movement of the therapist's hands, and the hot stones. He turned his head so he could see Merri. Her eyes were closed, and there was not a line of tension on her face. He couldn't recall the last time he'd seen her so relaxed. When had he stopped noticing things like her stress levels and her nightmares?

He tensed, and the therapist asked if the stone was too warm. After he assured her it was not, he tried to push marriage thoughts aside. But like the hot stones, the thoughts burned.

"Empty your mind," his therapist instructed as she rolled the stones along his neck. "Let your body and soul be restored."

He liked the sound of that. He'd do anything for a little restoration, but having the desire wasn't going to make his marriage whole again. Is that what he wanted? Or did he simply want to be free from constantly failing in Merri's eyes?

The therapist placed hot stones along the length of his spine, and he moaned softly as muscles released even further. He forced Merri from his thoughts. He'd think about all that after the massage. Right now, he was determined to enjoy every minute of his Christmas gift.

Now clad in her swimsuit, Merri eased into the vitality pool beside Rick. He'd said almost nothing since the massage. What was on his mind? Was that how Rick was going to handle this day together? Give her the silent treatment?

She'd been able to set her concerns aside during the massage, but now that they were alone, her worries returned with the force of a tsunami. How was she going to survive? Would Rick want shared custody of the boys? How were they going to break the news to them? And what about telling her parents?

Rick sat beside her, his head resting on a rolled-up towel on the edge of the pool. If he were in one of those heated loungers, he'd probably be sound asleep. He appeared to not have a care in the world, and that irritated her even more. Didn't he realize that tomorrow was Christmas? Their last Christmas together as a family?

Her massage therapist had recommended the vitality pool for detoxification. She glanced at her husband. He was the only toxin she needed to get rid of. Unable to remain in one spot, she moved under the waterfall at the other end of the pool and imagined it washing him out of her life.

Tears flowed down her face, mixing with the warm water

sheeting down. She pressed her fists to her eyes, anger coursing through her. How had it come to this? She didn't want to rid her life of Rick, but she also needed more. She needed him to be there. This whole situation was such a mess, and there was nothing she hated more than a mess.

CHAPTER SEVEN

"What do you want to do next? The mud room?" Rick passed Merri a towel after they'd climbed out of the vitality pool. If he didn't know she'd been under a waterfall, he'd swear she'd been crying. He helped her into her fluffy white robe before donning his own and sliding his feet into the slippers provided by the spa.

She tied the belt on her robe. "I guess we should go to the snow room since you've been giving me the cold shoulder all day."

"What?"

"You've barely said a—"

The sound of glass shattering on the tile floor stopped her sentence.

Rick whirled. No big deal. Someone had dropped their frou-frou fruit water. He turned back to Merri, who was pale and breathing fast.

Tilting her face up, he looked into her wild eyes. "Merri, what's wrong?"

"The glass," she whispered.

Why did a broken glass make her turn into a ghost?

Realization hit him hard. During the robbery, the perpetrators had smashed the jewelry cases before grabbing everything they could carry.

He led her to a secluded seating area and held both of her hands in his. "You'll be okay. Breathe. I'm here any time you need me."

"That's a lie," she breathed.

He sucked in his breath. "Excuse me?"

She pushed away and stood. "I needed you, and you weren't there."

Suddenly, his blood boiled in his veins, and he wanted to explode. When had she needed him? They were going to get this out once and for all, but not out here in the open.

"Come on." He didn't give her a chance to protest. Instead, he took hold of her elbow and directed her toward the snow room. He motioned his protesting wife inside before entering himself. Good. They were alone. Snow clung to the artistically designed, stacked stone walls, but he was in no mood to appreciate its beauty. He needed to hurl something.

"Now, let's clear the air." His words created puffs of vapor between them. He picked up enough snow to form a snowball. "When was I not there for you? I came to the hospital as soon as you called. I was beyond relieved when the doctor said the mace wouldn't leave any permanent damage." He heaved the snowball at the wall, watched it burst, then scooped up another handful. "I held you every night for a month, asking nothing of you." He let another snowball go, and this one burst on the wall behind her. "I put up with your schedules and the fact that you try to micromanage every single facet of my life, but still I've failed you? What have I done, Merri? When wasn't I there for you?"

She brushed the snow from her hair and packed a snowball of her own. When she threw it, it caught Rick's shoulder, but he didn't flinch.

He stood there, his toes growing numb with cold, while she threw snowball after snowball at him. He dodged a few and let others hit their mark. Tears fell down her cheeks, and she dashed them away with her hand.

"Wait a minute." He stepped forward and caught her wrist, then he studied her wet, icy hand. "Merri, where's your engagement ring? Why are you only wearing your wedding band?"

She pulled her hand free and wrapped her arms around her shivering body. "They took it."

"Who?"

"The jewelry store robbers."

"But you never said anything."

"I . . . I . . . I couldn't." Her lower lip trembled. "You were supposed to come with me that day to have it resized, but something came up at the track. If you'd been there—"

He sank down onto the wooden bench as the truth dawned on him. "Then you wouldn't have been alone." He rubbed the back of his neck, all the tension coming back at once, and sucked in a frigid breath. A crushing sense of powerlessness bore down on him. How many times had something at the track come before her? How often had his need to succeed stolen her sense of being cherished by him? And now, it had even stolen her sense of safety.

Dear God, how can I fix this?

Merri put on her clothes as fast as she could. She had to get out of this spa. She needed to escape this chaos with Rick and get back to their cabin. It was Christmas Eve. She had things to do. Presents to set out. Stockings to fill. Maybe order cookies for Santa from room service.

Thankfully, Rick was nowhere to be seen. Perhaps he'd had the same idea and had gone off by himself. More likely, he'd do something where he could experience some kind of thrill. Wasn't there a zipline on deck 15? That was right up Rick's alley.

"Merri, wait!"

Even with Christmas calypso music over the speakers, she heard Rick's voice, followed by his heavy footfalls as he jogged towards her. Slightly winded, he took a deep breath before speaking. "We need to talk about this."

"We did and nothing has changed. Can't you let it go? It's Christmas Eve." She glanced at her watch. "The Christmas Eve dinner is formal, and then we have the Christmas show in the theater. I need time to get ready."

He moved in front of her, forcing her to stop. "This is more important than you primping for dinner. I want you to know that I'm sorry I hurt you. I'm sorry I wasn't there that day. I've let you down."

She clutched her bag to her chest. "Saying you're sorry isn't enough anymore, Rick. I can't live with the unpredictability of it all."

"Of my schedule? I can work on that."

"No, the unpredictability of us." She pressed her lips together. "I'm going to our cabin now. Please, I beg you, let me have enough time to gather myself, so we can continue this charade for a few more days."

Unshed tears filled his brown eyes, but he stepped to the side and let her pass.

CHAPTER EIGHT

Rick stood at the top of the platform, waiting his turn, sensing excitement in the air. The near vertical drop of the waterslide would be the adrenaline kick he needed. It was no race car, but the sign said it reached speeds up to thirty miles an hour. The clear tube sections over the side of the ship would amp things up as well. Since he couldn't go back to their cabin in the state he was in and Merri wanted time alone, he'd had to do something, and this waterslide would at least make him forget his wife for a few minutes.

After the operator motioned him forward, he stepped onto the launch chamber's trap door and crossed his arms over his chest. His heart hammered, and the mind-blowing uncertainty of when he was going to drop made his nerves zing. Suddenly, the door opened, and he fell straight down the shaft. He let out a whoop. Knowing enough about aerodynamics to maintain top speeds, he kept his core muscles rock solid as his body careened through the twists of the tube and out over the ocean.

The tube launched him into a brightly striped giant bowl, where water spun him around as if it were a sink drain until he fell into a hole. He landed with a splash in the pool and sank deep. With strong kicks, he propelled himself to the surface. After exiting the pool, he grabbed a towel from the cart, dried his face, and vigorously rubbed his hair.

"Rick!"

Rick turned to see his mother-in-law frantically waving at him, her eyes wide.

He bolted toward her. Something was wrong. He could feel it. Had something happened to Merri? The boys?

"Bev, what's going on?" he demanded. "Is it Merri?"

"No, isn't she with you? Never mind, I'm just glad I found you." She hugged him and stepped back. "It's Thad. He checked himself out of kids' club, and we don't know where he is. When we went to pick the boys up for the Cookie Decorating Extravaganza, he wasn't there."

Anger flared in Rick's chest. "They let him leave?"

"Apparently, any children aged ten and over can come and go as they please." The ridiculous elf hat Bev wore jingled when she spoke. "Jessie and I have been looking all over for him. I came up here hoping he might want to go down the waterslides. That's when I spotted you, thank the Lord."

"We need a plan." Rick glanced around the Lido deck. "You go back to the cabin in case he comes there. Merri should be back there soon. Have you tried calling or texting her?"

"I know she tried to teach me how to connect the wi-fi so we didn't get roaming charges, but I couldn't figure it out."

Rick released an exasperated sigh. His phone was in his room. "Here." He removed his ever-present lanyard and passed it to Bev. "Use this to get in our room, and you can use my phone."

"But I don't know your phone's password."

"Merri's birthday. 10-14-85." He scanned the deck and spotted a large clock. "Have Jessie stay at the Christmas tree like we all agreed to do if we got separated. I'll be meet up with y'all at five." He squeezed Bev's arm. "And Bev, tell Merri I'll find him."

Every step away from Rick had been harder than the first, but still Merri made her way along the deck. She wanted to stay and leave and scream and curl in a ball all at the same time. Her heart raced, and she could barely breathe. What was wrong with her? Was she having a nervous breakdown?

Merri sank into a deck chair, riffled through her bag, and found her earbuds. She stuck them in and pulled up a Christian podcast she'd downloaded. Thank goodness, she'd arranged to have internet. She trusted the smooth, bass voice of the podcaster to settle her spirit and calm her frazzled nerves. He welcomed the listeners and wished them all a Merry Christmas before introducing the podcast's topic—two lessons from Joseph, the earthly father of Jesus.

That sounded appropriate since it was Christmas Eve.

"The first lesson we can learn is to hear God in chaos," the podcaster said.

Really, God? This is how you tell me what you think I should hear?

The last thing she needed right now was more anxiety, so she paused the podcast and changed to some easy listening music she had on her phone. Then, she leaned back and let the sunshine drench her face.

Merri knew the story of Jesus' birth well but hadn't thought about how Mary's pregnancy had upturned Joseph's life. He had plans in place, and the next thing he knows, an angel is telling him to go ahead and take Mary as his wife and raise this child who was to save his people from their sins.

The longer she remained in the deck chair, the more she

wanted to hear the rest of the podcast. Maybe she could handle listening to a little bit more.

She pulled out her phone and made the switch.

"Even when his world felt out of control," the podcaster said, "Joseph chose to obey God."

During the commercial break, she pressed her eyes closed and considered the podcaster's statement. Was she choosing to obey God in all this?

The podcaster returned. "Our second lesson from the life of Joseph is to embrace the mess and press on."

Really God, this isn't even funny now.

The man pointed out the situation Joseph faced seemed to intensify after the birth of Jesus. After the wise men visit them in their home, an angel again appears to Joseph and warns him that Herod is going to search for Jesus because he wants to kill him. Joseph immediately gets up, packs up Mary and Jesus in the middle of the night, and leaves for Egypt.

"People are messy." The man's rich voice spoke to her heart. "Relationships are messy, and situations are messy. As Christians, we have to learn to embrace the mess like Joseph did, knowing God is in control."

Tears again filled Merri's eyes. *God, is this what you want me to do? Embrace the mess? Please don't ask this of me. I'm not sure I can do that. Maintaining control is all I have left.*

Merri woke with a start. Amid her pleading prayers, she must have dozed off at some point. How long had she slept? She checked her phone for the time. Nearly four. At least she wasn't running too far behind. If she didn't go overboard on her preparations, she'd be fine.

Her eyes felt puffy from crying, but she'd made a decision. As she walked toward the bay of elevators, she reminded herself that Merri Stevens was embracing the messy parts of her life. It wasn't going to be easy, but she was determined to give up control. She chuckled softly. Was she trying to control giving up control? This was going to be harder than she thought.

She pressed the deck 6 floor where their cabins were, but instead the elevator went up and opened to the Lido deck. Deck 15. Wasn't that where the zipline was?

Go!

She felt the word more than she heard it, but did God send a person ziplining? It didn't seem to be a God thing to her. Joseph at least got angels telling him what do in his dreams. She shrugged. Admittedly, there was nothing that would lead to her giving up control more than ziplining, but she doubted she'd have the courage to even step on the platform. At least she was obeying.

She made her way past the waterslide area and the cabana club toward the zipline. Due to the size of the cruise ship, it was quite a trek to the back of the ship. When she reached her destination, she stood at the base of the tower and stared up at the zipline. The queue held about a dozen people waiting for their turn, so she drew in a deep breath and joined the back of the line.

A posted sign gave the requirements for guests to participate. They had to be forty-two inches tall and at least seventy-five pounds in weight but not more than 275 pounds. At five feet six inches, she had the height covered, and her weight did indeed fall within those parameters. Participants also needed to have shoes with ties. She looked down at her sandals. Relief and disappointment mingled inside her. She started to step out of line when she heard someone call her name.

She glanced around and spotted Rick running towards her. Did he want to zipline, too?

"Merri, have you seen Thad? He's missing."

Her stomach twisted. Few things rattled Rick and he seemed alarmed. She pushed her way out of the cue. "What do you mean he's missing?"

"He checked himself out of the kids' club."

"But I told him he wasn't allowed to do that."

"You knew that he could? Why didn't you say something to me? I would have made sure he knew he had to stay there." He huffed and glanced around the area. "Listen, we need to focus on finding him. I've looked at the waterslides and here. Where else do you think he might have gone?"

"I don't know. If he wasn't so much like you, he—"

"Merri, stop." Rick's chest heaved and his eyes held an icy note. "Everything bad that happens in your life cannot be my fault. It's not fair. I feel like you resent the air I breathe."

She blinked several times. Did she resent Rick? Is that what had eroded their marriage?

Rick pressed on. "Now, think. Has he mentioned wanting to do any particular activity?"

She rubbed her temple, trying to remember anything that would help. "Yesterday, I remember he said he wanted to do something. He was upset because I said Simon was too little to do it, but I can't remember what it was."

"The arcade? Putt-putt? IMAX?"

She shook her head and wrapped her arms around her torso. "What if he's not there? What if he's lost or someone took him?"

"Merri, we'll find him."

She studied his face and the strong, determined set of his jaw. "Even when everything is going wrong, you're a rock."

He grabbed her by the shoulders and kissed her. "That's it! It has to be the rock-climbing wall."

CHAPTER NINE

With Merri in tow, Rick zigzagged through thinning crowds and towards the ship's forward area. He'd seen the rock wall earlier and thought the boys would love to give it a go.

They stopped at the base of the forty-foot wall and looked up.

Merri squealed and grabbed Rick's arm. "Look! There's Thad in his Big Brother Elf shirt."

"Ssh. Don't distract him." Rick watched as his son navigated the final fifteen feet of the wall. Thad grappled for his right foot's purchase and finally found one. Then, he grasped the next rock-peg and hoisted himself up a little further. "See, he's doing great."

"But he's up so high."

"He's fine." Rick took her hand. "And we're here if he falls. Truthfully, the harness, helmet, and safety lines will do more good than our presence to protect him, but if he falls, we'll need to pick up the emotional pieces. We'll have to tell him we're proud of him."

She shot Rick a sidelong glance. "Do we praise him before or after we ground him for life?"

Rick chuckled. "After. Definitely after."

Thad scrambled up a few more rocks and reached the bell. He gave it a resounding clang.

"Good job, buddy! Come on down," the operator shouted.

Thad didn't budge.

"Why isn't he moving?" Merri shielded her eyes. "Something's wrong."

Rick moved toward the queue, not taking his gaze off Thad. He heard the operator telling Thad to just let go and the pulley would lower him down. Still, Thad remained frozen in place.

"Excuse me. That's my son." Rick barreled through the line toward the front.

One of the staffers held up his hand. "Sir, you'll have to wait your turn."

Rick pointed to the wall. "That boy up there. He's my son. He's only ten. I think he is too scared to move. Please, let me go up. I can talk him down."

The staffer continued to block the way. "We can't do that, sir. We'll take care of it."

"Please. I know how to climb, and he needs me."

"Wait here." The staffer left to consult with the operator. A minute later he returned, handed Rick the harness, and found him a pair of climbing shoes. Finally, he gave him a helmet. "Good luck, sir."

The operator clipped the safety line to Rick's belt. "Take it slow, sir. All you have to do is get him to let go."

Palms damp and heart racing, Merri watched Rick traverse the rock wall at breakneck speed. He only slowed when he drew near Thad.

She wished she could hear what he said. She imagined him telling Thad to trust him. It would be okay if he would just let go.

Wasn't that the same message God was trying to get across to her?

Her cell phone dinged, indicating she had a message. That could wait. Everything could wait until Thad was on the ground.

Then, Rick pushed away from the wall without Thad. What was he doing? How could he leave him?

Once he was on the ground, he took the safety line from the operator. "Okay, sport! I've got the safety line. I won't let you fall." He braced himself. "On three. One, two, . . ."

Thad launched off the wall and began his descent. The few seconds it took for her son to end up in his father's arms lasted an eternity.

The crowd cheered, and the operator patted Rick on the back. "If you need a job, we can find a place for you."

"Thanks, but I'll stick to race cars." He draped his arm around Thad's shoulders. "Thank you for letting me go up there."

"No problem. Merry Christmas, sir."

As soon as they'd returned their climbing gear, Thad ran to Merri's outstretched arms. She pulled him into a hug and pressed her nose into his sweaty, boy-smelling hair. She lifted her face and mouthed the words "thank you" to Rick.

Wriggling, Thad tried to break free. "Mom, let me go. This is getting embarrassing."

Her phone dinged again, so she released him and dug it out of her bag. "Rick, it's a text from you."

He laughed. "I think your mom finally figured out how to text you that Thad had gone AWOL."

"What's AWOL?" Thad asked.

Merri placed her hand under her son's chin. "It's a fancy way of saying leaving without permission."

He drew circles on the ground with his tennis shoe. "Oh."

"Yeah, sport. We have some things to discuss." Rick lifted his gaze to Merri. "And we do, too."

She nodded. Her heart was too filled with thanksgiving to deny Rick anything.

CHAPTER TEN

Rick knocked on his in-law's cabin door. The boys had stuck a collection of magnet-backed foil bows on it. There was also a stocking in the center filled with candy canes to share with other passengers.

Jessie opened the door. "Come on in. We're almost ready."

"No, I only stopped by to ask y'all to go ahead with the boys to the dining room. Merri and I will be there shortly."

"My girl taking her sweet time? I understand. We'll meet y'all there."

When he returned to his own cabin, Merri was putting on dangling earrings. Her hair twist made them stand out, and they brought the perfect amount of sparkle to complement the shimmery, crimson, floor-length dress .

He cleared his throat. "You look amazing."

"Thank you." She walked over to him and straightened his tie. "You look pretty good, yourself. Ready to go?"

He captured both of her hands in his. "Not yet. Your parents are taking the boys to the dining room, but I want to make another stop on the way."

After tucking their lanyards in the pocket of his suit coat,

Rick followed her out the door. They walked in silence along the corridor toward the elevators. He rehearsed what he wanted to say in his mind, but nothing seemed right.

It didn't take them long to reach the observation lounge. He paused at the entry, drawing in a steadying breath and taking in the ocean and night sky through the wall of windows. "I thought this would be a good place for us to have that talk." They settled into comfy chairs, across from one another. "You probably know where this is going, but I don't know where to start."

Merri bit her lip. "I do."

"Okay, go ahead."

"I need to ask for your forgiveness." She averted her gaze. "I realized today that I have let little things pile up, and it's made me bitter and resentful. I've been a nightmare to deal with. Because I was hurting, I thought it was justified, but I was wrong." She swallowed and turned back to face him. "I made you feel like you couldn't make me happy, when nothing is further from the truth. You're confident and honest and genuine and all the things I want our boys to grow up to be."

"Even if they're risk-takers."

"Yes, even then."

"Good, because it's probably too late to avoid that one." He shook his head. Wait. This wasn't right. Merri was apologizing to him?

"Please, don't say no." She leaned forward and took his hand in hers. "Joseph, God, and a podcaster with a velvety voice made me see that I need to embrace the mess and let God be in control."

"You're going to embrace the mess?" He emphasized the last words and chuckled softly. "This I've got to see."

She traced his knuckles with her thumbs. "Will you? Will you be there to see it?"

"That's up to you." He pushed to his feet and strode over to the window. Stars flickered in the night sky, reminding him of Merri's earrings. "Today, when I was climbing that rock wall, I realized that only one thing mattered to me—my family. You. The boys." He shifted so he could see her face. "Then, I remembered your dad thanking me for keeping my vows to you. At the time, I thought I had. I have always loved you, but I haven't honored and cherished you, and that was so wrong. Merri, I don't need to find three things to love about you every day. I love a thousand things even when you're at your worst. I want us to commit to this marriage like we should have been doing all along and let God be in control."

She joined him at the window, snaking her arms around his waist. "It won't be easy for me to learn to embrace the mess, especially when I am the mess."

"We'll embrace it together." He lowered his lips to hers, and for the first time in months, kissed her like the gift from God that she was.

CHAPTER ELEVEN

Even Merri's taste buds seemed elated tonight. The dinner was sublime and so was the man at her side. Near the end of the meal, their waiter appeared with a tray of traditional Christmas cookies. Gabriel and Angelica shared their Christmas traditions as the group consumed the cookies. Rick then excused himself to go pick up the boys from the kids' club, since they'd be attending the Christmas show at the theater as a family.

As soon as he was gone, her mother turned to her. "So, that must have been some spa day. Y'all look more in love than ever."

Merri grinned. Her mother didn't need to know all the details. "I think we've learned some things about each other."

"And remembered what's important?" Her father took her mother's hand. "We all need a wake-up call now and then."

Merri set her napkin aside. "And on that note, we should get going. Rick said he'd meet us."

Inside the theater, Merri fought the urge to turn around every few minutes. Rick was capable of getting himself and their sons there, and if they were a few minutes late, they'd most likely still get in. Just as the lights were being dimmed, he slipped in beside her with the boys in tow. They had discarded their ties but still wore their sharp, white dress shirts.

The Christmas show was everything she could want. Lights and songs. Laughter, dancing, and good cheer. When the show concluded, the audience gave the performers a standing ovation, and the boys clapped so hard she imagined their palms stung.

Outside the theater, her parents offered to take the boys back and set out the two cookies her mother had taken from the dining room for Santa. Rick thanked them and said he had plans for the two of them tonight.

Merri slipped her hand into the crook of his arm. "And exactly where are we going?"

"You'll see."

The sign in front of the lounge read "Carol-oke."

She came to a stop. "Are you kidding me?"

"Not at all. Let's go sing."

"You can't sing."

He laughed. "And you can't drive, but I let you do it anyway."

Merri was delighted to discover that the "carol-oke" was more of a community sing along. Although some of the participants had clearly had a little too much Christmas cheer already, she and Rick found their virgin eggnog a perfect treat. She let her voice soar on "Silent Night" and nearly spit out her eggnog hearing Rick's version of "You're a Mean One, Mr. Grinch."

But her favorite came after they left and Rick treated her to the "Twelve Days of Christmas: Nascar Version," which included five checkered flags, four pit stops, three short tracks, and a Sprint Cup silver trophy. What he lacked in pitch, he made up for in performance.

"Tomorrow is the Ugly Sweater contest." Merri squeezed his hand.

"What do I have to wear? Something with flashing lights?"

She shrugged. "I have no idea. My mom insisted on being the Sweater Chair."

He groaned. "She's going to put me in something atrocious."

"Maybe." She giggled. "Probably."

Rick led them into the atrium. It was less crowded than at any other time, and the immense Christmas tree, sporting thousands of twinkling lights, beckoned them. But first, they walked around the gingerbread village, marveling at how the artists had been able to create such intricate designs with frosting and candy. Even the evergreens next the houses had been crafted from green-tinted cereal and dusted with "snow."

Merri's heart was full. All was well and her future felt bright. She wanted to dance up the garland-clad staircase of the atrium and sing as if she were in a Broadway musical, but she refrained. Embracing a mess didn't mean creating one.

Finally, they stood in front of the Atrium's Christmas tree, taking in the magic of the moment. Rick dropped her hand, and when she turned to see why, he held out a black box wrapped with a red ribbon. "Open it."

"Now?"

He grinned. "Or next week. It's up to you."

She tugged the ends of ribbon and opened the box. "Rick—"

He took the ring from the box and lifted her left hand. "It seems you're missing a diamond." He slipped the engagement ring in place. "Merri Stevens, will you continue to be my wife?"

"I will."

He cupped her cheek and kissed her, reverently at first, and then building with a passion that made her heart explode. As they broke away, she heard the words of a Christmas carol playing, "There's a thrill in the air—"

Yes, indeed there was.

A NOTE FROM THE AUTHOR

Thank you, dear reader, for taking the time to travel with me. Although there are many Christmas cruises and cruise lines, the one in this story is fictitious, so don't go trying to book a passage on Sensation of the Seas for next December.

I also know Christmas doesn't feel magical to everyone. If you are one of those who is struggling at this time of the year, please reach out. I care and so do many others.

"God bless us, everyone!"

ABOUT LORNA SEILSTAD

LORNA SEILSTAD brings history back to life using a generous dash of humor. She is a Carol Award finalist and the author of the **Lake Manawa Summers** series and the **Gregory Sisters** series. Her stories are also part of several novella collections. When she isn't eating chocolate, she teaches women's Bible classes, volunteers with 4-H, and is a wedding planner. She and her husband have three adult children and live in Iowa.

Learn more about Lorna at www.lornaseilstad.com.

TITLES BY LORNA SEILSTAD

THE MOSAIC COLLECTION: NOVELS
Watercolors
More Than Enough

THE MOSAIC COLLECTION: ANTHOLOGY STORIES
"Claus-trophobic"
(*The Heart of Christmas: A Mosaic Christmas Anthology III*)
"The Magic of Christmas"
(*A Whisper of Peace: A Mosaic Christmas Anthology IV*)
"A Merrytime Cruise"
(*A Thrill in the Air: A Mosaic Christmas Anthology V*)

THE GREGORY SISTERS SERIES
When Love Calls
While Love Stirs
As Love Blooms

THE LAKE MANAWA SUMMERS SERIES
Making Waves
A Great Catch
The Ride of Her Life

NOVELLA COLLECTIONS
Seven Brides for Seven Texans

MEG AND THE E-MONSTER

Eleanor Bertin

* * *

Meg is a young mom with Pottery Barn taste on a thrift store budget. For the sake of the husband she loves, she's determined to keep wearing her "contented mom" mask, but a monster named Envy is eating her from the inside out.

And with every new day bringing more costly bad news, Envy creeps through Meg's smiling persona to spill his poison onto hapless victims close to her. When Meg most needs someone in her corner, she ends up at odds with her new best friend, Hayley. Can she find a way to defeat the E-monster for good and salvage what's left of a great friendship?

To Marena

"Now godliness with contentment is great gain.
But those who desire to be rich fall into temptation and a snare,
and into many foolish and harmful lusts . . .
For the love of money is a root of all kinds of evil."

I Timothy 6:6, 8, 9

MEG AND THE E-MONSTER

That notification ping meant something. Something bad, no question. These days, it always did, usually to the tune of a whole lot of money Meg and Scot didn't have. A thousand dollars seemed to be the magic number of late. Everything cost a thousand dollars.

Meg's fingers itched to reach for the phone, but the rosy, damp face of her one-year-old son weighed down her left arm. With her right, the cell was out of reach. Did she really want to know the auto shop's diagnosis? Not badly, no. At the moment, there was a lull in her usually hectic day, and she wanted to savour the calm. For once, four-year-old Bentley and two-year-old Dex played peacefully in the living room. From where she sat in her bedroom rocking chair, she could just glimpse the tops of their heads and hear their occasional, high-pitched giggles. What blocked the full view was the plastic bin she had decked with a thrift-store tablecloth folded three times to cover it and serve as an end table.

No, the phone message could wait until Scot got home after classes today. Or better still, after he got home from his on-campus cleaning job. Last Saturday, they'd been on their way home from picking up a free Christmas tree—the smallest, scraggliest tree ever, but gift horses and all that— when a noise started. The ominous, intermittent rumbling coming from under the hood of their aging rust bucket of a minivan had prompted worried looks between Meg and Scot.

Scot had guessed $1500 might fix it. Might as well have been ten thousand. Where were they going to get that kind of money? Already this month, they'd shelled out an enormous sum for vehicle insurance, and their utility bills were higher now due to the cold. In January, there would be a big hit for Scot's tuition, and his next round of expensive seminary textbooks would be coming up in the new year, too.

Or maybe the phone notification wasn't the auto shop. Her gut spasmed again. What if it was a message from Mom? More bad news about Grandma? At the beginning of December when Meg's mom had called, her voice had gone squeaky with uncharacteristic fear, sending a shot of matching dread through Meg. Grandma had been taken to hospital with pneumonia. Never a good thing, Mom said, when a person was eighty-four and as frail as Grandma was since her stroke two years ago. But Mom's most recent message had said oxygen and antibiotics had perked Grandma right up. *Please, God, don't let it be about Grandma.*

Meg escaped her fears by focusing on the makeshift end table. She'd been so proud of the way it turned out. She'd topped it with Grandma's antique lamp that her mom had passed on to Meg before they moved state-side. Though Meg had never been much into antiques, the ironstone lamp with the graceful silhouette and vintage floral paper shade had been a wedding gift to her grandparents back in 1950. She had imagined an elaborate plan for decorating her whole place around it. It was one of the few truly lovely things she owned. For a second, she wondered what it would bring if she were to sell it to help pay some of their bills, then firmly rejected the idea. How could she part with such a special gift? Was it too much to ask to have just one nice thing?

But even her one tiny vignette of pretty in this swamp of toys and ratty furniture had been spoiled when the new friend she'd met in her first week here in Michigan had come over. Hayley, fellow boy-mom, whose middle was thicker and hair thinner than Meg's, had a joyful smile and infectious laugh. Since the day last summer when they had met at the park, Hayley had shared everything from juice boxes and snacks to name-brand kids' clothes that her boys, seven and nine years old, had outgrown. But the day she visited, she had looked around Meg's shabby apartment, spotted the cloth-covered plastic bin, and laughed. Yes, actually laughed.

"Oh, how cute!" Hayley had giggled. "I remember the years of decorating Early Student style, pinching pennies, and having to buy second hand."

To Meg the words were a kick in the stomach. What she heard was, "Look at the poor student's wife and her pitiful makeshift décor." She seethed under the condescension, barely noticing Hayley's wistful pause when she added, "Those were such good days."

And then Meg was invited to Hayley's house. The contrast couldn't be greater. Her mouth had watered as she took in her friend's beautiful Craftsman home in a fine neighbourhood, shaded by huge elm trees. Inside was even better, with its pristine woodwork and designer kitchen. Luxuriating in the plush wool rugs in every room as Hayley gave her a tour, Meg couldn't help thinking of the green, chipping, vinyl flooring at home. Was that the first time Envy sank his fangs into her insides? If so, it wasn't the last.

When they went to the Children's Museum together, Meg felt it nibble as she compared the ease of Hayley's van's automatic door-close to the wrestling she had to do to shut her own stubborn van doors. And again, it nipped inside her when Hayley offered to pay for all of them to see the latest Pixar movie with popcorn and treats, too. Feeding on her comparisons, the evil creature fattened and grew.

That evening after supper, Scot had launched into a point of theology he'd been wrestling with that morning. He must have finally noticed her absent responses because he'd asked, "Babe, what's eating you?"

Meg was ashamed to say. How could she load Scot down with her petty jealousies when he had slaved so hard for three years, paying down their debt and saving just to get them here at the school he'd been dreaming of? Once, in her frustration, she had griped about having no money for a snowsuit for Bentley. The tears that filled Scot's eyes had broken Meg's heart.

"I can't even afford to keep my little boy warm," he'd murmured, his hands hanging helpless at his side. She vowed she'd never do that to him again. And she knew, too, his unwillingness to mention any whiff of financial struggle to their parents, who they both knew would be all too quick to help. A man had his self-respect, after all.

But the evening after the free movie, Scot kept coaxing and, finally, Meg hinted at her embarrassment when she hadn't had enough cash to cover the movie admission for her and the boys. He'd taken her in his arms. "I'm sorry you were put in such an awkward spot," he whispered into her ear. "I don't blame you for feeling lousy." Which only made her feel lousier. None of it was Scot's fault.

The high-pitched beep of the stove timer sounded from the kitchen, bringing her back to reality and signalling that the bread was ready. One bright spot in the day. At least Meg's baking skills were something Hayley didn't have. Grandma had taught her the art of yeast baking when Meg was a young teen. From there she'd branched out into raisin bread, cheese bread, sourdough, and other artisanal types. She'd already planned what she would be baking for a glorious Christmas morning breakfast, too. But for today, it was just regular sandwich bread. She anticipated the golden loaves, fragrant with yeast. Wait! Why didn't she smell them?

Her sudden jerk woke little Toby, who protested with a creaky cry. She set him on the floor to rub his eyes with chubby fists while she dashed to the stove. Opening the oven door, she expected a blast of heat, but none came. Inside, the four loaves that had risen so promisingly earlier now sat sunken and lumpy in their pans. They had started to bake, but somehow the oven must have quit, hardening them into pale, leaden bricks. She groaned in dismay, checking the control knob. Yes, she'd turned on the heat.

A bitter cry escaped her. If she were a swearing woman, it would have been more than a cry. "Of all the—!" she muttered, switching off the useless oven and thinking of what she had paid only three days ago for a small jar of yeast. With all the expenses piling up these days, there was no margin for wasting money on cooking calamities. She swallowed the hot lump in her throat, fighting tears of frustration. What next?

Bentley had trailed her into the kitchen and stood looking up at her with large, dark eyes. "Are you sad, Mommy? Do you need a hug?"

Meg ignored the question, not trusting herself to give him a kind response. Instead, she gripped the oven door handle as though she would rip it from its hinges. Poor little guy was only trying to help. But what she most needed now was to run away. Better still, to win a lottery and then run away.

She sighed, releasing the handle. What a dumb notion. Where would she go? She always said she was living her dream. A husband who loved her, three precious little boys. A loving family, though now long distance, and a supportive church. What more could she want?

An extra five or ten grand would about do it, that's what. Lately, that thought showed up all too quickly.

Crouching to take her sweet boy into her arms, she eyed the dough bricks. What to do with them? Doorstops? Bookshelf supports? Disgust at the disaster overwhelmed her again. She tipped her head back, screwed her eyes shut, and wailed. "What next? What else could possibly go wrong?" A rent hike? An emergency trip to the dentist? A surprise tax bill?

True to Murphy's Law, something else did go wrong. A squeal of protest sounded from the living room. She opened her eyes in time to see Dex pushing Toby's chubby hands away from the boys' giant block tower. Toby howled, sitting down hard. He twisted and stood to head toward her, his mouth wide open with the grief of rejection. But as Meg watched, helpless, the tablecloth from the end table unfurled behind him, snagged by the rubber grip on his sock. The antique lamp teetered.

"Toby! Stop!"

The toddler bawled louder at her sharp tone, a big pout forming on his face. But he kept coming. Meg dived toward him. Too late, she reached for the lamp. It smacked the uncarpeted floor, cracking into a dozen jagged pieces.

"Oh no!" Fresh tears of frustration flooded Meg's eyes. "Oh no, oh no, oh no!" She knelt in front of the carnage, hugging her arms and sobbing. It shouldn't matter so much, but it did. Dex and Bentley stared at her, cringing at her distress. Toby, still crying, toddled toward her.

"No!" she shouted, pivoting to prevent him from stepping on the sharp fragments. As she gathered him in a tight embrace, he sobbed harder, and she joined him.

Meg's steps slowed as she and the boys returned from their impromptu walk around the block. The fresh air had calmed her now, yet she felt a little guilty, too. The boys had been unusually timid with her as she hurried them into jackets and boots to go outside. Around the neighbourhood, they did not ask, as they often did, to stop at the school play center nearby. No snow angels or shaking snowy bushes on each other, either. Even Toby sat quietly in his stroller, sucking his thumb.

She'd fled the apartment in all its horrendous disarray with only escape on her mind. Now she had to face it. She folded the stroller and, with one arm, lugged it up the stairs while carrying Toby in the other. As usual, halfway up the second flight, she cursed the dump they lived in for its lack of an elevator. It had meant a hundred-dollar difference in rent each month, but how could she have known what a toll it would take on her arms and shoulders? She gritted her teeth for the rest of the miserable, upward slog. Envy invited his odious little friend, Self-Pity, to join him.

Once the boys were unbundled and winter togs hung up, she set about making them some lunch. There was no bread for sandwiches, so she arranged cheese and crackers and apple slices in happy faces on the boys' plates. She glared at the wicked appliance that had so cruelly let her down. At least it wasn't their responsibility to repair. Hopefully, the landlord would get on it right away.

"So boys, what face do your little cracker men want to make at the big bad oven that wrecked our bread?"

Grinning, Bentley turned his apple slice upside down into a frown. Dex copied him, giggling, and Toby, clueless but happy, looked bright eyed from one to the other and chortled his adorable belly laugh. Their sweet faces mellowed Meg, at least for a while. After lunch, she herded them all to the couch, where she read them as many stories as they asked for, then put the two youngest down for naps and sent Bentley to her bed for a quiet time.

She scurried around, clearing away lunch, then the toys, and finally the shards of porcelain that had once been her beloved lamp. Even her best glue job would never salvage it. She sorrowfully lowered the pieces into the trash. Then she called the landlord to report the stove malfunction.

At last, she settled on the least bony end of the couch to relax. On their trip down here from Canada last summer, Scot had indulged her with a browse through an outlet mall. Of course, they couldn't afford to buy anything at any of the beautiful shops, not even at discount outlet prices, but a girl could dream, right? Pottery Barn and Anthropologie, Lulus and Francesca's, Gap Kids and Bebe Organic. Her long-suffering husband only smiled as she gushed over all the gorgeous goods. Since then, she allowed herself a few moments of escape each day to scan the websites of those stores as well as other fashion and décor sites. She worked hard being a mom and saving their limited funds. A little indulgence was only fair.

Scot let her have their only phone during the day in case of emergency, but she knew it was a sacrifice, limiting his research and note-taking ability. Meg used to set a timer to limit the time she spent dreaming online, but lately she hadn't bothered. E-monster eagerly opened his hungry maw to catch the flesh she willingly tossed him.

A small burst of anticipation shot through her as she opened her Pinterest app. E-monster licked his chops. Scrolling through the images, Meg drank in the beauty, the symmetry, the textures, soft neutrals, and perfect lighting of the featured rooms. Oh, for a trestle table like that! And that fabulous, tufted leather couch with all those pillows. How she would love to breathe new life into her space with some of these "decorating must-haves." A gnawing inside made her stomach ache with longing as she studied the tasteful designs. Finally, she lifted her eyes from the screen to scan the reality of the room she had to call home. The stark contrast was depressing.

Without the inspiring antique lamp, all her ideas to make the cramped living room something special turned to dust. Why bother anyway? No matter what she did, it would always be a boring, charmless space lacking character. Even Hayley's fantastic carpets couldn't have redeemed these dingy floors, nor could her beautiful artwork ever hide all the dings and chips on the dismal walls. There was no point dreaming. It would be years before she and Scot would ever have a home of their own. Hopelessness tasted sour in her mouth. Munch, munch. Big E devoured and digested more of her.

A message appeared at the top of her phone screen. She opened it to find Hayley inviting Meg and the boys to the Birthday Party for Jesus she was planning for moms and kids next week. No doubt there would be an enormous array of perfectly coordinated party décor and a great big, custom-designed bakery cake. Bah. Why would Meg want to subject herself to more of that? Something chewed at her insides. She was about to type her refusal when another text showed up.

Mom this time. Meg sat up straight. It was just what she'd feared. Grandma had taken a turn for the worse. In fact, they weren't even re-admitting her to the hospital but would be keeping her comfortable in the personal care home, expecting the worst. Then Mom asked the impossible: *Is there any way you can come?*

Meg sprang to her feet, pacing the short distance from couch to chair, then repeating the loop. No, there was no way. How could they possibly manage a flight back home now? She and Scot had already agreed they would stay here in Grand Rapids for Christmas. So dire was their financial picture that they were counting on whatever the grandparents sent to provide the only Christmas presents the boys would have. Meg hated missing the fun of shopping for stocking stuffers and all that, but it was the only way. So, airline tickets were absolutely out of the question.

And yet, Mom needed her. She wouldn't have asked if she didn't. And Meg longed to see Grandma again, too. Her throat constricted. Why, oh why, did this have to happen now?

Meg stared vacantly at the simmering vegetable soup she was stirring. With the oven kaput, she couldn't even make biscuits to go with the soup. Maybe dumplings? She'd never tried those. And frankly, she didn't feel up to an experiment that might waste more precious ingredients. This whole tight budget thing was making her a stingy and unadventurous cook.

But the worst thing on her mind was her grandma's health. Tears threatened again as she remembered Grandma's lessons in soup-making, lessons that had turned out to be a lifesaver in surviving a tight budget. She racked her brain trying to work out a way they could make the trip home so she could be with Grandma one last time. And if she died, wouldn't they at least want to go to the funeral?

Meg debated keeping this new crisis from Scot. The last thing she wanted to do was put pressure on him in his last week of the semester while he was finishing up a major paper and studying for exams. But her grandma . . . Near to bursting from worry and stress, Meg picked up her phone and started a message to Hayley. *Are you available for a phone call?* She was about to hit send but paused, biting her lip.

For the past several weeks, she'd been distant with Hayley, answering texts in monosyllables, avoiding her at Mom's

Morning Out, and declining a recent Sunday dinner invitation to their place using Scot's studies as an excuse. Not that Meg would have breathed a word of it, but Scot hadn't exactly hit it off with Hayley's husband, Chris. Scholar versus salesman. So, there was that. But the real reason for the cooling was that Meg could only take so much exposure to the wide gap between their lifestyles. Directly after the Jesus Birthday Party, for instance, Hayley and Chris and the boys were off to Cancun for Christmas with her side of the family. No doubt there would be a pile of pricey gifts for Hayley's boys. Maybe some flashy new jewelry for Hayley, too. The E-monster tore a piece out of her flesh that almost physically hurt.

No, she'd wait to share her worries about Grandma with Scot alone. "Boys, come and eat!" Scooping Toby into his highchair, she set a couple of crackers on his tray before draining some of the soup vegetables for him, blowing on them to cool them. Bentley and Dex clambered up to their seats as well.

When they were finished eating, and she finally had a chance to eat her own serving of lukewarm soup, Meg's heart was still making desperate attempts to come up with a way home.

Cleaning up the aftermath of the meal, she tried to field the questions that shot rapid-fire into her brain. Where could they scrape up money for airfare? There was no time for her to earn any money now. She would want to leave tomorrow. Didn't the airlines have some sort of discount in cases of bereavement? She checked online for the price of tickets. But cheaper wasn't cheap enough. And besides, there hadn't been a bereavement yet.

What about using their credit card? Couldn't Scot make an exception for this? Meg's Grandma was dying, after all. But it was useless to ask. She knew he would never agree. After the bind they'd found themselves in during the first couple of years of marriage, they had cut up their credit cards together and vowed never to go into debt again.

Then perhaps they could ask the church for help? Once a month the church took up a collection for the benevolent fund. Maybe? Her heart sank lower. If Scot refused to ask his parents for financial help, he certainly wouldn't let her mention it to their new church. Bother his convictions. Why did everything have to be so hard for them when it was so easy for people like Hayley? Invisible sharp teeth tore at her vitals.

Meg stomped to the tiny bathroom and started the evening bath ritual. With her three-men-in-a-tub routine and all the requisite splashing going on, she didn't hear footsteps or the door open. The boys' giant grins alerted her to Scot stepping inside the steamy room.

"Daddy! Dada!" they shouted.

Scot bent to give her a quick kiss. "I'll take over for you. There's not room in here for both of us."

Grateful, Meg edged out of the bathroom and changed into dry clothes, then dressed each of the little ones as Scot sent them out, damp and shivering. She tried to curb her frustration about their finances, but several times throughout the bedtime story and prayer, Scot raised his eyebrows at her. Meg only mouthed *Later*.

Finally, all was quiet in the boys' room. She followed Scot into the darkened living room.

"Hey, what happened to the lamp?" He flipped on the glaring overhead light instead, took a seat on the couch, and patted the spot beside him.

"That's such a harsh light. Let me get a couple of candles." Meg struck a match to a pair of tapers and finally snuggled in next to him.

"Did you finish your last paper?" she asked.

"Pretty much. I'll go over it one last time tomorrow morning before turning it in." He shifted to look her in the face. "But what's up with you? You've been skittish ever since I got home. And what about the lamp?"

Meg hung her head. As much as she tried to put him first, he could always see through her. And though she'd been determined to stay rational, now her throat was swelling and her eyes filling with tears. "Toby's foot caught on the cloth and pulled the lamp off. Smashed to bits."

"Ah, I see." He pulled her to him again. "I'm sorry about that. I know it meant a lot to you."

"Also, the oven quit on me in the middle of baking this afternoon. So now there's no fresh bread. And then these." She handed him the phone to show him the messages, one from the auto shop, the other her mother's plea to come home.

"Hm." Scot read them, stroking his jaw. "So I was right about the van repair bill." But he said nothing more.

She waited, knowing it was impossible yet still hoping somehow that he could dream up a way for them to travel north.

Finally, he took her hand. "Why don't you go up on your own? Toby can still fly for free, so it would only be the cost of one ticket, not four, and I won't have classes, so I can manage the boys."

Meg stared at him, mentally calculating. "But the money?" she asked weakly, excitement rising inside her against all reason.

"We'll juggle a few things. I'll work more hours. Whatever. We'll find a way."

"But what about Christmas? I don't want us to be apart for that."

"The boys are young enough they won't really notice if we celebrate it another day, will they? It'll be fine."

Meg threw her arms around him, hope spreading through her like yeast in a batch of dough.

Calling Hayley to ask for a ride to the airport was the last thing Meg wanted to do. She was ashamed to ask a favour of someone she had practically been ghosting the past few days. But she had no other option, what with their van still in the shop.

"Sure, no problem. Chris will be home, so he'll be able to watch the kids."

Meg felt a twinge of discomfort at Hayley's cheerful willingness to help, but not for long. They planned for Hayley to come for Meg and Toby the next evening right after supper.

Despite the somber reason for her trip, Meg couldn't squelch her excitement. She woke early the next day to wash and pack clothes, cook a couple of meals ahead, and write out the boys' routines for Scot. She couldn't bring herself to ask but felt sure that Scot had purchased her ticket with the money set aside for his tuition. What would they do come January? Payment was due by the end of the first week of classes. His sacrifice filled her heart with gratitude but also a smidgeon of guilt. She determined to spend as little cash as possible on the trip, packing everything in a carry-on bag, bringing their own snacks, and even using cloth diapers. The first flight was only half an hour, but hopefully the baby would sleep through the second leg of the evening flight.

After an early supper, and emotional goodbyes with her family, Meg and Hayley left for the airport through the now-darkened streets.

"I can't believe this actually worked out!" Meg gushed.

"Yesterday, when Mom texted, I had no hope that we could ever afford this. But here we are."

"Of course. It's your grandma." Was there less than usual enthusiasm in Hayley's voice?

Meg smiled at her friend, thankful she understood. "I should probably be sad, but I'm so excited to see everyone at home. My sister and her family will be there, too. Scot convinced me the boys are too young to know the difference, so we'll have our Christmas when I get back."

"Mm-hm."

Meg let the conversation lag, mentally double-checking the instructions she had left for Scot and planning her check-in procedure. He had let her have their phone, saying she would need it to contact her parents on arrival.

At the airport, Hayley quietly helped her with her belongings while Meg seated Toby in the baggage cart. His feet both went into the same slot on the first try, making him cry at the tight fit. She got him settled on the second try. With a final hug, Meg left her friend and headed for the ticket counter.

She sighed in relief once she was seated on the plane with Toby on her lap. While she had been navigating boarding, he had taken in all the bustle calmly. Now she pulled out a small pouch of Cheerios and a book to read to him. The seat beside her remained empty, allowing Toby space to play for the duration of the short flight.

Meg hoped for the same arrangement on the second part of the trip, but no such luck.

"Excuse me." A forty-something woman in an expensive-looking suit slipped past Meg into the window seat. Something about her carefully put-together outfit, classic jewelry, and professional manicure made Meg see an older version of Hayley. The old familiar twinge inside her made

Meg sit up straighter. Why couldn't she get free of that monster?

The woman settled in her seat and smiled at Toby. "How old is he?"

"Just past a year."

"Such amazing long eyelashes!" The woman met Meg's gaze. "I'm Tricia, by the way."

"Oh, right. I'm Meg, and this is Toby." He stuck his thumb into his mouth, twirling the hair behind his ear.

Tricia checked her smart watch. "They said there could be a delay. I hope we won't get in too much later than planned." Soon, however, the engines revved, and the plane began taxiing. "Ah, here we go."

Meg pulled out Toby's favourite blanket, and he leaned against her, growing more relaxed.

"You're heading home for Christmas?" Tricia asked.

Meg grinned. "Yes! I'm really looking forward to seeing my family again. I haven't been there since last summer."

"So that'll be fun then."

"Mostly. It would have been better if my husband and our other two boys could have come, too. But we hadn't planned to come up at all, except my grandmother's health suddenly got worse. She doesn't have much time left."

Genuine concern showed in Tricia's eyes. "Oh, I'm so sorry."

Glancing at the drooping baby, the older woman patted her own lap. "You can let him stretch his legs out if you want."

Meg shifted the little guy down so he could lie across the two of them. His eyelids barely fluttered. She tucked his blanket around him and whispered to her seatmate, "Thank you."

Tricia smothered a yawn with one hand. "Looking at him makes me sleepy. I think I'll try to catch some z's as well." She shut off the overhead light and leaned against the closed window.

When the seatbelt light came on again and the captain announced landing preparations, Toby fussed a bit and Meg worried he would disturb the other passengers. But she found a drinking box for him, which seemed to settle him. The flight attendant passed out customs statements and Meg filled hers out, then dug in the inside pocket of her tote for their passports. As she did, a thick wad of paper came out with them, one piece drifting under the seat in front of her.

Meg stared at it dumbly. Money. She gasped, retrieved the stray twenty, and lifted the cash toward her for a closer look. A thrill shot through her, raising her hopes sky high as the meaning of it sank in. More than enough to replace what had been spent on her plane fare. And some left over for Christmas gifts! For a few moments, she was floating on a cloud of ecstasy. The E-monster danced a jig inside her chest, slashing at her with his happy claws.

Then she paused, glancing around at the passengers nearby. No one paid any attention to her as the plane taxied in for the landing. Puzzled and thoughtful now, she riffled through the bills, then checked the tote to be sure it belonged to her. It was hers alright, the same one she'd schlepped around since college. And the money had been inside her passport. She fingered the bills, awe struck but bewildered. They were twenties. Her heart sped up the more she counted. A thousand dollars! Maybe Scot had found the money someplace other than his tuition savings. Maybe they could finally afford a couch that didn't throw your back out after fifteen minutes of sitting on it. Maybe— No, the money would have to go to something sensible. She thought of the van repair expenses and tuition. Deflated, she came back to reality with a thud. What made her think she could keep the money? Maybe it was a mistake.

Sensing she was being watched, she glanced at Tricia. "I don't understand. I mean, I don't know where this money came from. It isn't mine. I have to give it back to whoever it belongs to."

"How do you know it wasn't meant for you?"

Meg studied Tricia's face. "Did you put this in here?"

"Me?" Tricia's eyes widened. She shook her head with a smile. "No, why?"

"You must have." Meg held out the money. "You'd better take it back. I can't accept this. It's too much."

Tricia laughed softly. "Listen, honey. I don't carry that kind of cash around with me. It's too dangerous. But I love a good mystery. Do you think that husband of yours is sneaky enough to surprise you with this?"

Meg shook her head, frowning. "Absolutely not. We're barely squeaking by. We just paid a super big heat bill, our oven quit working yesterday, and paying our vehicle insurance drained our bank account." Her voice went hoarse. "I even had to beg a friend for a ride to the airport because our van is in the shop. We can't really afford this trip at all. I think my husband paid for my ticket with savings that were supposed to go toward his schooling."

Tricia tilted her head. "I remember the days of being poor students, living on noodles and love. It was hard, but they were such good days." For a moment, an undertone of sadness and longing crept into her voice.

It was the second time Meg had heard that sentiment. Seemed like only rich people thought back fondly of their misery when they were poor.

Then Tricia brightened. "Not every husband would do something like that for his wife. Sounds like he's a keeper."

Meg nodded. "I know." She caught sight of the older woman's bare ring finger and quickly averted her eyes. "But this," she said, holding up the bills again, "I can't think where it came from."

Tricia raised a finger. "Maybe that friend who gave you a ride to the airport was the one who gave you the money."

"Oh, I don't think so. She's well off and generous. But a thousand dollars?" Yet could it have been Hayley? Meg tried to remember how the dropping off had happened. Hayley had been awfully quiet on the drive. Scheming how to hand off the money? Come to think of it, Hayley had managed the luggage while Meg was getting Toby seated in the cart. But it had all happened so fast, there didn't seem to have been time.

"See? I bet that's it!" Tricia tapped Meg's arm. "Your friend knew your situation and came to the rescue. She knew you needed some cash."

"But how will I ever pay it back?" Because of course they would have to. The thought of another debt weighed heavily on Meg's shoulders. Scot would not be pleased at the prospect.

Other passengers were making their way up the aisle to disembark.

"Believe me, girl," Tricia told her as she rose from her seat, "someone sneaking money into your purse anonymously is not looking to be paid back. Just accept it and enjoy it. You've got one awfully sweet friend there."

Toby was getting active with the commotion surrounding them, but Meg's head still reeled from the impact of the gift. She gathered Toby's blanket and books, then put the money back with the passports into the pocket it came from and closed the zipper.

"It's been nice chatting, Meg," Tricia said as she reached for her belongings in the overhead bin. "I hope you have a very merry Christmas." She winked at Meg, then leaned down. "And just so you know, you won't always be poor."

"Merry Christmas to you, too." Still dazed, Meg pulled her

suitcase out of storage, slung her tote over her shoulder, and carried Toby down the aisle and into the airport. After what Tricia had said about the danger of carrying large amounts of cash, she felt jumpy and watchful. The customs lineup was long, and Toby grew fretful. A couple of kind souls let her move ahead of them in the line. She fed the baby goldfish crackers and, while he munched, she reactivated her phone.

Several messages pinged at once, mainly from her mom, but one was from Hayley. Curious, Meg opened that one first.

Hey Meg, I hope you got there safely. Sorry I was so silent on the drive to the airport earlier. Something happened this morning. I'd rather you heard it from me before you hear it on the news.

"I can help you over here, ma'am," one of the uniformed customs agents called, waving her hand. Meg stuffed her cell into her pocket and strode toward the desk, fumbling with the zipper on her bag for the passports and customs declaration. The sight of the money again gave her a fresh jolt. She mashed the bag between herself and the customs counter to keep it safe while answering the agent's questions.

"Welcome back to the motherland," the agent said, handing back Meg's passports. Meg followed the signs to the arrivals gate. As eager as she was to meet her mom and dad, she searched first for a place to sit down. Hayley's text had spooked her. Had something happened to Scot or the boys? She found a near-deserted waiting area and sat on a backless bench, allowing Toby to toddle freely in the open space.

Hayley's text continued: *I'm shaking as I type this. Can hardly believe it.*

What? That was it? Spit it out already, girl! There was a second text farther down, which had come an hour later.

Early this morning cops came and arrested Chris. It all happened so fast. Fraud, they said. Embezzlement. I don't really understand what it's all about and I'm sick to my stomach over it. The kids were awake when the police came so they answered the door. They had to see the whole thing, their dad being taken away in handcuffs. They're shaken up pretty bad and so am I. Please pray.

Meg looked up from her screen, stunned. Poor Hayley! It seemed like she had no clue anything illegal was going on. Would Chris go to prison? What would happen to Hayley and the kids then?

But maybe they got the wrong guy. Sure. Yeah. It must be mistaken identity. Chris would be released, and everything would be fine for Christmas. For all Meg's envy of her friend's life, she never wanted something bad to happen to her. Suddenly, Meg desperately, fervently wanted nothing more than for Hayley and her family to be back to normal, enjoying their Christmas, and able to go on their luxury vacation. The monster choked and staggered, gasping for air.

Meg checked for further messages. None from her friend. Should she ask Hayley if she was the one who stuffed the money in Meg's tote? Now didn't seem to be the time. And yet, she wanted to thank her. Wanted to hug her and apologize to her and comfort her and be there for her. Oh Hayley! What must you be going through? And maybe now with everything in Hayley's life going so badly, maybe now she would really need this money. Meg would be glad to give it back. Starving for fodder, E-monster shrank three sizes.

Then it dawned on Meg that Hayley had given the money just hours after experiencing the worst shock of her life. With all the fear and threat of loss she must be going through, Hayley had given this generous gift.

Meg was ashamed of herself. She had resented Hayley, wanting all that Hayley had. She'd coveted the house and the furniture, the new vehicles and vacations, all of the easy and free-wheeling spending. She'd even envied Hayley's ability to be generous. Never had she dreamed what was going on behind the façade. How horrible to be living amid all that loveliness, not knowing what catastrophe was just around the bend. "Things are not always what they seem," Grandma often used to say. And still, Hayley had freely given.

Meg was too overwhelmed by her friend's kindness and too taken up with Hayley's worrisome situation to notice that Envy had shriveled to gnat size, his fangs disabled and his impotent claws flailing uselessly. In his place, pity and sorrow grew. She fingered the wad of cash again. What a gift she'd been given!

"Toby," Meg called. She stuffed the money back into her bag and hurried to catch up to her toddler, who had made it too far down the hallway for a lone one-year-old. Scooping him up, she rushed the rest of the way to the arrivals area, where she spotted her parents scanning the emerging passengers hopefully.

A smile lit Mom's face. "Megan! And Tobykins!" She enfolded Meg and Toby in a joyful squeeze, covering the wee one in kisses. He giggled. "You're such a big boy now!" Then it was Dad's turn. He hugged Meg and the baby as one, then took over pulling her suitcase.

Mom swung Meg's bag onto her shoulder. "Did you get my texts?"

"I saw them but hadn't read them yet. I figured I'd see you in a couple of minutes."

They moved in the direction of the carpark. "The first was to tell you that Grandma has stabilized," Mom explained. "I sent the second after Scot called. He was calling from the neighbour's, he said, but he wanted you to know they were all fine. Then he said something about someone from your church being on the news? Asked you to call tomorrow." She scanned Meg's face for a clue. "I hope everything's alright?"

Meg paused, closing her eyes for a moment as they stepped outside into the frosty air. She would call tomorrow. Not only Scot but Hayley, too. For now, though, Meg looked up past the concrete layers of the parking garage beyond the bright terminal lights to the velvet sky above. Letting a taxi pass by, she took an expansive breath, feeling a lightness inside that she hadn't realized she had missed. There was a vacancy in there now as if a nasty tenant she'd been helpless to evict had finally moved out. A vacancy that made room for something new to fill the space. Something like peace and love, yet more than that. Ah, contentment. That was it!

"Yes, Mom. Finally, everything is alright. It's so good to be home for Christmas."

A NOTE FROM THE AUTHOR

Dear Reader:

Do you know that old stinker, the E-monster? I certainly do. Many of us know him all too well. He especially likes to make himself comfortable in our lives at Christmastime, when our expectations and longings are heightened and opportunities for comparison abound.

We get a whiff of him whenever we compare what we have or are to what we wish we had or wish we were. The points of comparison can be material, like they were for Meg, or less tangible. But Envy is a sure and certain friendship killer. We can envy someone's upbringing, talents, health, personality, accomplishments, relationships, or opportunities. But scripture tells us that covetousness is idolatry (Ephesians 5:5). When we practice it, we're putting something or someone else in first place instead of God.

Meg found, almost by accident, that the less she fed the monster that had grown fat on the fodder she had provided, he shrank to insignificance.

My prayer for myself and for you is that the things of earth will grow strangely dim in the light of His glory and grace. And may you all have a most contented Christmas!

Yours,

Eleanor

ACKNOWLEDGMENTS

I owe a debt of gratitude to my mother, who passed into the arms of Jesus last Christmas Eve. She so beautifully and consistently modelled contentment throughout her life that I have longed to follow in her path.

I am particularly thankful for Janice L. Dick's insightful comments on an early draft of this story, and Sara Davison's whimsical, adorable cover art. Thank you to the sisters of the Mosaic, as well, for their consistent encouragement and for allowing my work to take its place alongside their own inspiring writing.

Most of all, I thank my Saviour, Jesus, who has gently at times and severely at other times worked to wean me of covetousness through the years.

ABOUT ELEANOR BERTIN

Before raising and home-educating a family of seven children for thirty years, **ELEANOR BERTIN** worked in agriculture journalism. She returned to writing with her first novel, *Lifelines,* followed by *Unbound, Tethered,* and *Flame of Mercy.* The memoir, *Pall of Silence,* is about her late son, Paul.

Eleanor lives with her husband and youngest son in the Before of what will someday be a beautiful century home in central Alberta where she reads, writes, and sweeps up construction rubble.

Visit her website, www.eleanorbertinauthor.com, to learn more about her books and subscribe to her newsletter, or join her Facebook page, **Read with E's.**

TITLES BY ELEANOR BERTIN

THE MOSAIC COLLECTION: NOVELS
Ties That Bind series
Lifelines
Unbound
Tethered

A Flame of Mercy

THE MOSAIC COLLECTION: ANTHOLOGY STORIES
"Like Wool"
(*Hope is Born: A Mosaic Christmas Anthology*)
"Grounded"
(*Before Summer's End: Stories to Touch the Soul*)
"Love and Unexpected Stress Responses"
(*A Star Will Rise: A Mosaic Christmas Anthology II*)
"A Portion of Grace"
(*Song of Grace: Stories to Amaze the Soul*)
"No Night There"
(*The Heart of Christmas: A Mosaic Christmas Anthology III*)
"How Life Begins"
(*All Things New: Stories to Refresh the Soul*)
"Christmas at the Crossroads"
(*A Whisper of Peace: A Mosaic Christmas Anthology IV*)
"Who Sends the Rain?"
(*Dancing in the Rain: Stories to Shelter the Soul*)

"Meg and the E-Monster"
(*A Thrill in the Air: A Mosaic Christmas Anthology V*)

NONFICTION
Pall of Silence
(a memoir)

THE OTHER WAY

Sara Davison

* * *

Lawyer Cassandra White has always wanted to spend the holidays in New York City, and this is the year.

Except God is clearly calling her to go see her sister, Daria, instead, a call Cassie seriously objects to. After all, given what Daria did to her, Cassie owes her nothing.

So, even if reconciling with her family is the only way to experience peace this Christmas, Cassie is heading the other way.

And no one, not even God, is going to stop her.

Where can I go from your Spirit?
Where can I flee from your presence?
If I go up to the heavens, you are there;
if I make my bed in the depths, you are there.
If I rise on the wings of the dawn,
if I settle on the far side of the sea,
even there your hand will guide me,
your right hand will hold me fast.

Psalm 139:7-10 (NIV)

CHAPTER ONE

Cassie shifted in her window seat. Could they just take off already? The faint hint of jet engine fuel drifted in the air of the cabin, tempered by the aromas of stale coffee and the baby shampoo emanating from the toddler in the row of seats ahead of hers. The female flight attendant's voice rose above the buzz of conversation and shuffling of feet and carry-on luggage. The young Black woman in a navy blazer and pants gestured to the exits and issued instructions about what to do in case of an emergency. Cassie knew the drill. As a lawyer in the small town of Elliot Lake, Ontario, she flew to the States a few times a year for conferences or to meet up with friends. The flight to Minneapolis three days ago had been uneventful. No doubt this direct, two-and-a-half-hour flight to JFK would be the same.

As instructed, she switched her phone to airplane mode and fastened her seatbelt. The intercom crackled before the pilot came on. She listened to his reassuring message—a blizzard was pummeling the American Northeast, but they would be flying well over it and should land in New York at the scheduled time—as she tugged a novel from the bag on her lap. It was a relatively small jet plane, with only two seats to either side of the aisle. If no one took the one next to her, she might be able to finish the book before they reached their destination.

Everyone she knew, and a few strangers at work or in stores, had raved about *The Happiness of Bluebirds* and insisted she read it. For some reason, that tended to make Cassie dig in her heels and avoid a book. When she saw it in the lost and found at work last week, though, she figured that, with the extra time she'd have to read over the holidays—a rarity for her—maybe she would give it a few pages. Last night, a slight anxiety over her trip prodding her awake every time she started to drift off, she'd reached for it. Two hours later, she had forced herself to close the novel, knowing that, if she didn't, she'd sleep through her alarm and miss her flight.

The book was so engrossing, and the emotions the characters wrestling with after going through unimaginably painful experiences so close to her own struggles, Cassie felt as though the story had been written for her alone. After setting the novel on her bedside table, she'd touched her fingers to her cheek, surprised to find it damp with tears.

A man who'd been fighting with his bag, trying to shove it into the overhead compartment above the seats three rows ahead of her, finally managed to hold it in place with one hand long enough to slam the door closed with his other. The male flight attendant had been shooting him heated looks that didn't appear to faze the man. He only turned and started in her direction.

Don't sit next to me. Don't sit next to me.

He dropped onto the empty seat beside her, knocking the book from her hand and onto the floor.

A look of chagrin crossed his face. "Hey. Sorry about that."

They both reached for it at the same time, knocking their heads lightly as he grabbed it. Cassie straightened, rubbing her temple. So much for an uneventful flight. And they hadn't even started down the runway yet. Since she was stuck with the guy for the next couple hours, she bit back the words threatening to spill from her mouth and simply held out her hand.

He grimaced as he set the book on her palm. "Again, I apologize. Are you okay?"

"I'm fine." She spoke the words through gritted teeth, which likely undermined them somewhat. Was it her job to make him feel better for showing up late and stampeding into her presence like one of the bulls those crazy people ran with?

"Good." He did up his seatbelt with a loud click and then circled his finger through the air. "I didn't hear what the attendant said. Did I miss anything important?"

Cassie repressed a sigh. "Exits front and back, storm over the Northeast that shouldn't affect us other than maybe a little turbulence, oxygen masks go over the nose and mouth, life jackets are under the seats on the off chance that if we crash into Lake Erie we'll actually have need of one. The usual."

The man flashed her a grin. "Helpful information about the oxygen masks. I might not have figured that out on my own."

"You're welcome." Now that he wasn't encroaching on her personal space, she could take him in a little better. Her age or maybe a few years older. Dark hair and eyes, skin tone that hinted at an interesting ethnic background like Columbian or possibly Ecuadoran. The faint hint of an accent, like a second-generation English speaker who'd spoken a different language before starting school. No ring on his finger.

Irrelevant, your honor.

Cassie rubbed her own bare ring finger absentmindedly, phantom pain carving an ache in her chest. The engines roared to life, vibrating beneath her heeled boots. She clutched her book tighter and glanced out the window. The seat she'd requested was toward the front of the plane, ahead of the wings. Although she was reasonably comfortable flying, she didn't love taking off or landing, and the idea of looking out the window to see flames leaping from the engines after a bird strike, like videos she'd viewed online, did keep her tossing and turning the few nights before she caught a flight anywhere. Once they were in the air, she would bury her nose in her book and be fine. Before she knew it, she would be sitting in a theater watching the sugarplum fairy and the nutcracker prince dance on stage or wandering past Rockefeller Center filled with skaters or admiring the decorations in the window of Macy's Department Store.

Daria.

Seriously? Her gaze darted to the rows of fluorescent lights on the ceiling of the plane. *We have been over this. I am not going to see my sister.* The plane taxied to the runway. *Even if I wanted to, which I don't, it's too late now.* They were on their way. By the time they landed at JFK, she'd have no way to get back to Pennsylvania, given the weather. *Which, incidentally, is your fault and not mine. If you really wanted me to go to Clearview, you wouldn't have sent this big snowstorm, would you?*

Ha. In her business, that was what was known as an irrefutable argument. Case closed.

Reveling in her victory, it took Cassie a moment to realize her seatmate was watching her. Warmth crept into her cheeks. Had she said any of that out loud? Rehearsing her speeches to juries in front of the mirror or in the shower was a quirk of hers, so maybe. Before she could ask, the plane lunged forward down the runway, pressing her against the back of the seat. Dropping the book on top of her bag, she clutched both arm rests and focused on taking deep, calming breaths for several minutes.

"You okay?" The guy next to her nodded at her white knuckles.

They'd leveled out and, when she shot a look through the glass, Minneapolis had disappeared from view. Cassie unclenched her fingers. "Of course." She picked up her book, opened it. Would he take the hint?

"Heading home for Christmas?"

Apparently not. "No. Just going to NYC for the holidays." She ignored the expectation hanging heavy in the pause that followed as long as she could before exhaling and sticking her finger between the pages. "You?"

A shadow flashed across his face. If he hadn't wanted her to ask, why had he—

"I'm going there to see family."

Okay. Not as mysterious as that look warranted. Traveling to see family four days before Christmas wasn't unusual. A cliché, really. Before those thoughts could drag her along a path she didn't want to follow, she shifted to look out the window again. Dark clouds swirled below them. That storm the pilot had mentioned? When she'd checked the weather for New York that morning, forecasters had promised a crisp, clear Christmas week, so they should fly out of this in an hour or so.

"What do you do?"

Resigned, Cassie faced him. "I'm a lawyer."

"Impressive."

She shrugged. Not a lot of crime in their small Canadian town, so most days it wasn't exactly scintillating work. She contemplated him, attempting to guess what he did before she indulged him by asking. Expensive-looking dress shirt, pants, and shoes but no jacket or tie. "Stockbroker?"

He laughed. "Nope."

The man did have a nice laugh, she had to admit. Low and soft enough it felt as though the two of them were sharing a private joke. Had she ever felt that with Cole—the guy who'd told her after a couple dinners that he didn't see them being more than friends and who later ended up marrying Tala, who'd become Cassie's best friend—or any of the other men she'd dated? Not that she could remember. Also irrelevant, though, as this was most certainly not a man she was interested in dating. Cassie straightened in her seat. "Brain surgeon?"

"Ha. If my mother'd had her way."

Past tense? "Is she . . ."

"Gone? Oh no. Very much alive and running constant interference in my life."

Cassie propped her elbow on the armrest and rested her chin on her hand, fascinated despite herself. On a page, those words could be read many ways, in many tones of voices. This man's voice was filled with affection, and a small smile played around his mouth as he spoke of his mother. So why the shadow earlier, when he'd mentioned family?

Of course, Cassie had been close to her mother too. And her father. That didn't mean the word *family* wasn't fraught with pain now. She closed her eyes.

Her seatmate was watching her again. Even though she couldn't see him, she could feel it. She opened her eyes and sat up.

As she'd sensed, his dark eyes were fixed on hers. "And your mother . . . ?"

"Is no longer running interference in my life." The words didn't come out lightly, although she'd meant for them to. Even after three years, *lightly* was not a way she could talk about the loss of her parents.

"I'm sorry." The stranger didn't speak the words lightly either. He held out a hand. "I'm Jared."

She hesitated briefly before sliding her fingers into his. "Cassie."

Although he let go of her almost immediately, the warmth of his fingers lingered on hers. Cassie lowered her hand to the armrest, tracing a groove etched in the burgundy plastic with the tip of her finger. How had someone done that? Since 9/11, no one had been allowed anything sharp on board a plane. Maybe not before then either; she couldn't remember.

A rattling sound drew her from her musing. A man with reddish hair, also dressed in navy, gold buttons gleaming on his blazer, pushed a wheeled cart along the center aisle, stopping next to Jared. "Anything to drink?"

Jared looked at her. Cassie surveyed the few options. "Ginger ale, please."

The flight attendant reached in front of Jared to hand her the can, a plastic cup, and a small packet of pretzels. She smiled at him. "Thanks."

Jared chose water to go with his pretzels before the attendant pushed the cart past them to the people in the seats ahead.

She tugged the tray from the seat back in front of her and laid it flat. Tipping her cup, she slowly poured the soda into it. Ginger ale. Daria's favorite. She set the can abruptly on the tray. *Stop thinking about her.* Cassie was taking this trip to get her mind *off* memories of her family. Instead, they were coming to her more and more often, like the flakes of snow pelting people and buildings and cars thirty thousand feet below them.

Staring out the window, she sipped the cold, fizzy drink. What else should she do in New York? Dinner cruise around the harbor, maybe? Carriage ride in Central Park? A number of companies offered Christmas light tours, which could be fun. Her mother had loved Christmas lights. She'd conscripted Cassie and Daria into service every year to help her . . .

Releasing a soft hiss of frustration, Cassie swung her attention to the toddler bouncing on her father's lap in front of her. The child, soft baby hair pulled into a ponytail that sprayed out like a fountain on top of her head, pressed her forearms to the tops of the seats and peered over at Cassie and Jared. Jared laughed and tapped the chubby arm with his fingers, making the little girl giggle. When her mother pulled her around a couple minutes later, Cassie glanced over at him. "You still haven't told me what you do."

He grinned again. "I'm enjoying your guesses too much." After popping the last pretzel into his mouth, he crumpled the package and tossed it onto the tray. "Go ahead. Give it another try."

She touched a finger to her chin. "Hmm." A dinging sound accompanied the *fasten seatbelt* message lighting up the consul above her and flashing around the cabin. Cassie frowned. What did that mean? She hadn't noticed the plane bumping around. Still, the attendant who'd been serving drinks and snacks wheeled the cart past the last few rows without stopping, steering it directly behind the curtain. The female who'd been issuing instructions at the start of the flight grabbed the handset from the wall and spoke into it. "Ladies and gentlemen, the pilot has asked that you return to your seats and fasten your seatbelts immediately."

Without any further words reassuring them it was only a bit of turbulence or some other minor issue, she hung up the set and immediately sat down next to her colleague. They both did up their seatbelts. Cassie shot a look at Jared, who met her gaze and shrugged. Neither of them had unbuckled their seatbelts, so they waited as others returned to their places. The man in front of them took the toddler from her mother and settled her on his lap.

Cassie's stomach tightened as she glanced at the attendants and noted the concern on both their faces. Was something wrong? What did they know that they weren't—

The plane dipped a little and she gripped the armrests again. Suddenly, the oxygen masks dropped from above their heads, something that had never happened to Cassie on a flight. Several people gasped. Almost everyone reached for the masks and began slipping them over their faces.

This is my fault.

The thought slammed into her. Where had that come from? Why would something happening to the plane be her fault? She pressed her palm to the soft armrest between her and Jared and rubbed back and forth, attempting to hold the panic at bay.

She should have listened to God. For days now, her sister's name and face had repeatedly intruded into her thoughts. As much as she'd tried to ignore it, to resist the force compelling her, Cassie knew God had been telling her to go see Daria.

"Cassie."

The muffled, urgent voice of her seatmate called her back and she blinked, trying to focus on him. He'd already slid the mask over his face, and he reached over and tapped hers now, lifting the mask slightly away from his mouth. "Put it on. I'm sure it's nothing, but just in case . . ."

For a few more seconds, she clung to the armrests, until he grasped the mask and brought it closer. "Here."

Cassie forced herself to let go of the arms and take the mask from him. After sliding it over her nose and mouth, she risked a glance outside. Were the engines on fire? Through a break in the dark clouds, she caught a glimpse of icy blue. Lake Erie. The weak joke she'd made earlier, about the unlikelihood of needing a life jacket if the plane went down in the water, drifted through her mind, haunting her. That wouldn't happen, would—

Without warning, the nose of the plane dipped a little and then the plane dropped. Less a dive and more a plunge, like the elevator in that *Speed* movie. Cassie barely registered the screams of other passengers or the glasses and soda cans flying through the air. The whole world narrowed to the thudding in her chest and the thought beating out the same rhythm in her brain.

This is my fault. This is my fault. This is my fault.

If they crashed, if all the people on board the plane perished, she would have to answer to God for that, wouldn't she? Was she ready to die and face him? It appeared as though that might be a moot point.

Cassie squeezed her eyes shut and gripped the armrests until her fingers ached. Her whole life did not pass before her eyes—only one scene. Two young girls, auburn hair streaming halfway down their backs, holding hands as they skipped through a field of flowers, singing loudly. And laughing.

After what felt like an eternity, the fact that they were no longer dropping sank in. Someone still clutched her hand. Had that vision been real? Had the pilots gotten control of the plane? Was she dead?

"Cassie? Are you all right?"

She opened her eyes. Was she? They hadn't crashed, so she probably shouldn't complain about the pounding in her ears or that some kind of liquid—likely the ginger ale—dripped from the tips of her short, auburn hair. Jared's fingers—colder now than when he'd shaken her hand—had found hers at some point and were tightly wrapped around them. "I think so. You?" Her voice rasped and she cleared her throat.

He nodded as the intercom crackled again and the pilot's voice boomed through the aircraft. "Attention, please, passengers. We apologize for that sudden descent, but we discovered a cabin depressurization that means we need to land. Air traffic control is diverting us to Erie International Airport in Pennsylvania, just on the other side of the lake, so we can attend to the technical issues. You are not in any danger, and it is now safe to remove your oxygen masks. Please keep seated and wait for any further information."

The toddler in front of them was wailing so loudly Cassie

struggled to catch the words. The pilot's assertion that they were *not in any danger* was hard to believe but, if true, excellent news. Other than those words, the only one breaking through the haze in her mind the way the plane was slicing through the thick, dark clouds pressing against the glass was *Pennsylvania.*

Seriously? Is this some kind of great, cosmic joke? Whatever happened to free will?

Cassie straightened and her fingers slid from Jared's. They both tugged the masks from their faces and left them dangling. The man in front of them wrapped an arm around the woman's shoulders and pulled her and the child close until the toddler's wailing eased to a whimper. Like the soundtrack accompanying Cassie's furious prayers heavenward.

Jared picked up the bag that had tumbled off her lap and handed it to her with a weak smile. "Well. That was interesting."

She clutched the bag to her chest as she drew in a slightly shuddering breath. "That's one way to put it."

"Pretty sure you had nothing to do with it, though."

Her forehead wrinkled. "What do you mean?"

"You mentioned a couple of times that this was your fault." He tilted his head. "Why would you say that?"

Her cheeks warmed. She'd said that out loud? "I have no idea. We were plummeting to our deaths at the time, so I'm not surprised I wasn't making a lot of sense."

"Huh."

Clearly, he didn't buy it. Just because he'd helped with her mask and held her hand when she thought they were about to die didn't mean she owed this stranger any more than she owed her sister, right? Because she had no intention of revealing that she was pretty sure God had called her to go somewhere, and their near-death experience might very well have been his response to her stubborn refusal to listen.

Not that they were in the clear yet. Cassie glanced out the window. Now that they had descended below the cloud cover, thick flakes of snow pelted the glass. Would they even be able to land, or would they be stuck where they were, unable to go higher or lower until the plane ran out of fuel and they . . .

The thrumming had started up again in her chest, and Cassie drew in a few slow, deep breaths. It didn't help. *What do you want, for the flight attendants to open the hatch and throw me out? Would that appease you?*

"Hey." Jared touched the side of her hand before pulling back. "They can land in this."

So, he could read her mind now? Seriously, who *was* this guy? Cassie pried her fingers from around the ends of the armrests and bent and straightened them to get the blood flowing. "Psychiatrist."

His lips twitched. "Are you calling for one or is that another guess?"

"A guess." Although she could likely use one too, since it appeared she might be losing her mind. The plane veered to the left, clearly circling around to take a run at the Erie International airport. Maybe a game would take her mind off the agonizingly slow descent into thickening snow and ice.

"Nope." He held up a finger. "I'll give you a minute to think about it and then you can take another shot."

Twisting away from her, he leaned a little into the aisle, closer to the elderly couple in the row of seats opposite theirs who were clutching each other's hands and looking ashen. "You folks okay?"

The woman, white hair cut in a chic bob around her jawline, offered him a shaky smile. "We're worried we won't get to our daughter's for Christmas now. We so wanted to see the grandchildren opening their presents Christmas morning."

Worrying about seeing family instead of the fact they'd nearly hurtled to their deaths? Cassie bit her lip. Would her parents have been the same if they had lived and she and Mack had been able to give them grandchildren? The deep ache that had settled in her abdomen three years ago and never been dislodged intensified, and she pressed a palm to it. Of course they would have.

Everything would have been different then.

CHAPTER TWO

Jared was right. Thick snow had stolen Cassie's breath every time she'd foolishly glanced out the window. Even so, after nearly thirty harrowing minutes of circling and slowly descending, the pilot managed to land the aircraft without skidding off the tarmac. Flashing red lights outside the window indicated that emergency teams had set up at the scene in case of disaster, but the plane rolled slowly by them and stopped at a gate. Everyone unbuckled their seatbelts and staggered toward the front of the plane, gripping the tops of the seats as they passed by.

No one seemed to be injured. Many of the passengers had been splashed by the drinks flying around the cabin during the descent, but none were complaining about that, as far as Cassie could tell. Everyone was strangely quiet as they made their way to the exit, as though trying to process what had happened—or nearly happened—to them.

She managed a tremulous smile in response to the flight attendants' murmured apologies as they disembarked. Jared followed her through the tunnel, but neither of them spoke. What was there to say? As soon as she emerged into the arrivals area, Cassie nodded at him and then headed for the nearest women's room.

What should she do now? No way she was getting back on a plane. Besides, from the signs she'd caught as she made her way to the restroom, most if not all the flights in or out had been canceled. Theirs was likely the last one to land, barely ahead of the worst of the storm.

For twenty minutes, she splashed water on her face, attempted to clean the soda out of her hair and off the front of her pale green blouse, and paced the small room, ignoring the questioning looks of other women coming in and out of the cubicles. Her heart continued to skitter around in her chest, clearly not getting the message the danger had passed. How long would the storm last? Could she find a nearby hotel to sleep in? Likely not, since she'd waited so long to get on that. Still, she tugged out her phone and tried three of the closest ones. As suspected, no room at the inns.

For a few seconds, she gripped the sides of a porcelain sink. Then she straightened and squared her shoulders. If that guy in the movie *The Terminal* had lived in an airport for weeks or months, she could manage a night or two.

Hitching the strap of her carry-on bag more securely on her shoulder, she strode for the door and flung it open. Jared stood directly across from the women's room, one shoulder propped against a white pillar. When their eyes met, he straightened and held up his hand, a set of keys dangling from one finger.

The sight of a familiar face, even a man she'd met only a few hours earlier, sent an irrational thrill of . . . something coursing through her. Hope, maybe? A little less alone-in-the-worldness, for sure. Cassie walked over and stopped in front of him. "Planning a road trip?"

He grinned. "Seems like a lovely day for it."

She glanced toward a wall of windows. The snow had

165

tapered off a little but still fell in thick white flakes from an iron sky. "Oh yes, lovely."

"Care to join me?"

Jumping into a car with a strange man and heading out into a blizzard. Was that better or worse than setting up camp on the airport floor for days? Cassie scanned the arrivals area. Everywhere she looked, people were sprawled across chairs or the cold, hard tiles. Without exception, they looked frustrated and miserable. Even setting out in a storm had to be better than that. And hopefully they would drive out of it well before they reached their destination. Still, it definitely wasn't smart, accepting a ride from a man she didn't know. Especially since, if she did run into trouble, she had no one to call to come help her. Her stomach tightened. At least she knew he wasn't armed, since he'd just gotten off a plane.

Before she could talk herself into anything either way, Jared pointed to an elderly couple standing near the exit. The man and woman who'd been sitting across the aisle from them on the plane. "So you know, I invited the McClintocks to join us."

"You did?" If he had less-than-honorable intentions toward her, he wouldn't have offered to take other people with them, would he?

"Yes. But they called their daughter, and she didn't want them to drive in this weather. She got them a hotel room a few minutes from the airport. The storm is supposed to last a couple days, but their daughter said if they can't get a flight by the twenty-fourth, they would delay opening gifts and having a big dinner until they arrived, since she said it wouldn't be Christmas without the whole family there."

"Ah. That's really nice." Although Cassie tried to keep her voice neutral, she couldn't keep the wistfulness out of it. It had been three years since she'd had Christmas with her whole family. The memories of those holidays were good, even if thoughts of everything that had happened since made her stomach drop like the plane had during those terrible moments when she'd thought they might die.

He shot her a look, but before he could press her on it, Cassie pulled her brown leather gloves from her coat pocket and tugged them on. "Let's do it."

"Great." He held a hand toward the exit.

Cassie fell into step next to him. "How did you get a car?"

"I knew they'd go fast, so I went straight to the rental counter after getting off the plane."

"Smart. How did you find me?"

"I figured you'd still be in the arrivals area, since there weren't a lot of other options. When I ran into the McClintocks, Mrs. McClintock said she'd seen you pacing in the restroom." He waved at the couple as they passed by, and they both smiled and wished him a Merry Christmas.

Despite the blast of cold air that struck her when she pushed through the exit, warmth crawled up Cassie's neck. "Oh, right. I was trying to figure out where to go from here."

"And what had you decided?"

"To stay in the airport until the weather cleared. I figured if Tom Hanks could do it, so could I." She gripped her wool coat at her throat to block the bitter wind.

Jared chuckled as he pointed the remote at a car in the rental parking lot. Lights flashed and the two of them headed toward the dark blue Ford Escape. "You do know the guy that movie is based on spent eighteen years in a Paris airport, right?"

Cassie blinked. "Seriously?"

"Yep." They reached the car, and Jared hit another button to release the trunk lid. He lifted it and reached for her bag. After loading their luggage into the trunk, the two of them jumped into the vehicle, out of the snow. Jared touched the brakes and pressed the button to start the engine, and within a minute or two, warm air blasted from the vents.

Cassie pulled off her gloves. "Do you think the roads will be okay?"

Jared shrugged. "We'll take our time. And it should get better as we go along since we're heading south. If we have to stop somewhere and wait it out, we will, but I'm pretty sure we can plow through."

"Hopefully not literally."

He smiled and turned out of the parking lot. The roads appeared to have been recently cleared, and despite the large flakes splattering against the windshield, only a thin layer of pressed-down snow covered the surface. Even so, as promised, Jared stayed a little below the speed limit. After a minute or two of driving, Cassie caught a glimpse of a green sign on a corner and realized they were traveling on Grace Street. Grace. Is that what God had shown her by allowing the pilot to safely land the plane? By providing her a ride with this man she'd been hoping wouldn't take the empty seat next to her on the flight? Maybe.

Cassie dragged a fingernail through the condensation on her side window. Of course, she hadn't made it to New York City yet. Lots could happen along their journey. The thought made her tired, and she leaned against the headrest. Jared appeared to be concentrating on the road which, given the conditions, was likely best. After a while, though, he glanced over. "Is anyone expecting you in New York?"

She exhaled. "No."

A silence settled over them as thick as the snow drifting from gray clouds, as though Jared was prepared to wait for her to offer more. When she didn't, he looked over again. "We're alone in this car, and no one in the world knows where we are."

When she raised her eyebrows, he grimaced. "Sorry. That

came out more ominous than I intended. I only meant we'll be stuck together for hours, and it might help take our minds off everything that's happened if we get to know each other, open up about ourselves a little."

"You mean like free therapy."

"Exactly." He offered her a crooked smile before returning his attention to the few feet of road they could see ahead of them.

Staring out the front window at the storm blowing around them was not helping the ongoing skittering in Cassie's chest, the tightness that had yet to release from every nerve and muscle. The sight offered the strange, simultaneous feelings that the whole world had narrowed down to only a few feet in front of them before ending in a wall of snow and the sense that they were driving into some vast, infinite tunnel of white. She tore her gaze from the mesmerizing flakes and turned a little on her seat so she could observe him. "Priest?"

He laughed. "Nope."

"I'm assuming you're not a lawyer, since you likely would have mentioned that when I shared that I was."

"I am not a lawyer, you're right."

She chewed the inside of her lower lip. "So, not a priest, lawyer, or psychiatrist."

Jared's forehead wrinkled as though he was trying to draw the lines between the three to come up with the connection. After a moment, his face cleared. "You're wondering if I would be legally or ethically bound to keep anything you shared with me confidential."

"I guess I am."

When he spoke, his voice was gentle but firm. "Not legally, but I promise you I would consider myself ethically bound not to tell another soul what you share with me, regardless of what I do for a living."

"What if I confess to murder?"

He sent her a look that was half amusement, half apprehension. "If you're a murderer, then, given our current situation, I'm thinking the least of my worries is whether or not I'll be sharing what you tell me with anyone else."

Cassie grinned. "I could be a murderer, but I'm not."

"Kind of a weird brag, but okay."

The nervous tension in her muscles eased a little when she laughed. "I meant I've studied the criminal mind and researched so many cases that I know how it can be done, even how to increase my chances of getting away with it, but I don't have the inclination or desire to carry it out."

"Good to know."

Her throat tightened. The trauma they'd undergone earlier had clearly stirred up long-repressed emotions she had no desire to deal with at the moment. Cassie pressed the tips of her fingers to the cool glass of the side window. "In my line of work, I have met a few people who have killed someone. I will say, in some of those cases I did understand the motivation."

She felt his eyes on her as she had on the plane but kept her gaze on the swirling snow, the brief glimpses of ditch or buildings passing by.

"There's a story there." Jared's voice held compassion.

"Maybe."

When she didn't speak again, he said, "Would you like to request a continuance, counselor?"

Her lips twitched. "You're offering me time to prepare?"

"If you want it."

"But you're not a lawyer."

"That is correct."

"Some kind of criminal? You do seem alarmingly familiar with the language of court."

He chuckled. "Trust me, everything I know about the legal system I learned from Atticus Finch."

She pressed her fingers harder against the glass, fighting

the increasing draw she felt for him. *He's a stranger. And a man. Do not lower your defences so easily.* Something about the cocoon they were wrapped in offered a false sense of security it would likely be detrimental to fully trust. Still, she couldn't fault his literary taste. "I love *To Kill a Mockingbird.*"

"Me too. One of my favorites."

Huh.

"All I'm saying is I could go first, if that would help."

She nodded, still staring out at the Narnian world on the other side of the glass. "I believe it would."

"All right then." He took a deep breath. "I have a daughter."

Although Cassie waited, Jared didn't expound on the pronouncement. On paper, the words, much like his earlier assertion that he was going to New York to meet family, would have waved softly, like long grasses in the prairies as the wind blew across the endless fields. Nothing of particular note. Something in his voice, though, hinted at layers of strata built up beneath the prairie dirt that would take a great deal of time and effort to mine through.

She shifted around to contemplate him.

Jared let go of the steering wheel with one hand and held it in the air, palm up. "Sorry. Not trying to be melodramatic. It's just . . . that's only the second time I've said that out loud. I mean, I've repeated it in my head a thousand times, but telling someone else, hearing it with my own ears, makes it incredibly real."

Her forehead wrinkled. "Was she just born, then?"

"No. She's five. Only I had no idea she existed until a few days ago."

"Ah. So your . . . girlfriend didn't tell you she was pregnant?"

"She was never my girlfriend." Jared drove his fingers through his short dark hair before returning his hand to the wheel. "As we established earlier, I'm not a priest, but I do have a faith in God that usually informs how I live my life, and that includes not sleeping around. Six years ago, though, I was going through a rough time. A woman I thought I was going to marry had just dumped me and I had lost my job and was pretty much feeling like the biggest loser on the planet. I went out with a few friends for drinks—something else I rarely did—and met a woman at the bar. She was beautiful, and she offered me comfort, flirted with me, generally made me feel a whole lot better about myself.

"I ended up going home with her, which was the stupidest mistake I've ever made. I deeply regretted it the next morning —repented of it, to be more accurate. I told her I couldn't see her again, which she did not take well. She threw me out of her place, and I didn't hear from her again until she called me out of the blue a couple weeks ago."

"Why did she decide to tell you now?"

"Apparently, she's had enough of taking care of our daughter on her own. She's an actress trying to make it in New York City, and she said if I didn't come get Mira right away, she planned to put her into the system."

"Wow." Actually, Jared had drilled down through that rock pretty quickly. The intensity behind the innocuous-sounding statements suddenly made sense. And he had a faith in God? The man was becoming more and more interesting.

Which terrified her.

Cassie cleared her throat. "Who did you say those words to first?"

"My parents. A few days ago." He winced. "That was a difficult conversation. They were really good about it, though. Mira is their first grandchild, so they're excited about that."

"Mira. That's pretty."

His features softened. "Yeah." He slid a hand beneath the zippered opening of his royal-blue Columbian jacket to tug a cell phone out of an inside pocket. "Here." Keeping his eyes on the road, he tapped a couple buttons before handing Cassie the device.

The little girl whose face filled the screen was adorable, with a mischievous smile, beautiful brown skin, and soft, dark hair that brushed her shoulders. Cassie bit her lip, fighting the wave of emotion. "She's really cute. She looks just like you." Her cheeks heated. "Those two statements are, of course, completely unrelated."

Jared laughed. "Obviously. But she is cute, isn't she?" He took the phone Cassie handed back to him, glanced at the screen with a small smile, and then returned it to his pocket. "When I got the call about her, my first thought was that this was God's punishment for my recklessness. The more I look into those big brown eyes, though, the more I've started to think the opposite—that, despite the circumstances around the start of her life, she's a precious gift from God I don't deserve but that I'm incredibly grateful for."

"Yes. A child is always a gift, no matter what."

He shot her one of those shrewd looks that saw far too much of her, as brief as they were. Before he could push her on it, the SUV skidded slightly on the road. Jared calmly steered into the skid and brought the vehicle under control, but Cassie's heart had taken up the thudding it had begun when the *fasten seatbelt* sign had flashed across the front of the plane.

She rested the side of her head against the glass. They traveled in comfortable silence for a while, until Cassie glanced at her watch. They'd been driving two hours but weren't able to go very fast. Had they made much progress? "You doing okay?"

"Yeah, I'm good, although I wouldn't mind stopping for a break, maybe grab a coffee if we see a place."

"A break would be good." A break from driving. From being reminded every second of the precariousness of life.

From sharing deep, intimate stories with this man. Cassie peered through the flakes continuing to twirl thickly through the air. Weren't they supposed to drive out of this at some point?

"There." Jared signaled and then eased onto a ramp leading off the interstate. "Should be a coffee shop or restaurant here. Once we've had something to eat, we can get back to it. I still haven't heard your story."

Was she ready to share it? Cassie peered out her window, trying not only to spot a place for them to stop but to avoid Jared's gaze—those brown eyes, so like his daughter's, that conveyed much more than his words did.

Whether she was ready or not, Cassie guessed the continuance he'd offered her so she could prepare herself was about to come to an end.

CHAPTER THREE

They had coffee and sandwiches at a small diner just off the interstate. By the time they finished, it was late afternoon and the storm had abated slightly. Cassie scrutinized her travel companion as they trudged through the snow to the SUV. His eyes were a little bloodshot and rimmed with shadows. Not surprising, since it had been a long day and he'd had to stare into the pelting snow for two hours already, trying to see enough of the road ahead to keep them on it. "Are you all right to keep going?" If he wasn't, maybe they could ask someone at the diner if there was a hotel nearby. As anxious as Cassie was to get out of Pennsylvania, she couldn't ask this stranger to push himself beyond his ability, to risk his life, even, simply to ease her tension. Or her guilty conscience.

Jared ran a hand over his face before stopping at the passenger side door and pulling it open. "I'm game to go on a while longer if you are."

Cassie paused on the other side of the door and rested her gloved hand on the top of it. "When are you supposed to pick up Mira?"

"The twenty-fourth at four in the afternoon. I'd planned to

arrive in the city a few days early, buy gifts for her, maybe put up some decorations at the Airbnb I rented to make it feel a little like Christmas, since we don't fly out until the twenty-seventh."

Christmas Eve. That gave them three days to get to the city, although arriving at least a day or two early so Jared could prepare—mentally and emotionally as much as any other way—would be a good idea. That would also allow Cassie to enjoy some of the festive activities New York had to offer before she flew home on the twenty-sixth. "All right then." She tapped the top of the door. "Let's go a bit farther. If you need to stop for the night, though, just say so. We can get a room at a hotel. Rooms," she added quickly, her cheeks heating despite the frigid temperatures and flakes of snow landing on her neck and sliding between her shoulder blades.

Jared gave her another crooked smile but didn't say anything, only waited until she had climbed in before closing the door and then rounding the front of the vehicle. Her adjournment lasted another ten or fifteen minutes as he navigated through ruts in the snow and got back onto the interstate, eventually settling in behind a snowplow. Slow going, but it meant the road was fairly clear and they had steady lights to follow, helpful in the gathering dusk.

Still, Jared didn't speak, didn't remind her it was her turn to share. His easy silence felt less like pressure and far more like an open invitation. Which was creating in her a deep, driving need to spill to him everything she'd held clenched inside for so long. Shrouded in a heavy white silence, it did feel as though the two of them were the only occupants of the planet. Jared didn't know or care about any of the people she might talk about, and as soon as they reached New York City, they would part ways forever. What better opportunity might she have to unload everything she'd gone through the last few years, something she had yet to do with anyone other than a therapist she paid to listen?

Still, it took her another minute or two to summon the words. And the courage. Propping her feet on the dash, she wrapped her arms around her knees. "Eight years ago, I married a man named Mack."

Jared nodded but didn't say anything.

Cassie took a deep breath. "A couple years in, we decided we were ready to have a child. I got pregnant right away but lost the baby a few weeks later."

Jared winced but didn't offer any of the well-intentioned but meaningless platitudes others had over the years. "A few months later, I got pregnant again and the same thing happened. With that baby and then three more."

He exhaled. "I'm sorry, Cassie. I can't imagine how painful that was."

No, he couldn't. No one could unless they had experienced it for themselves. Which she wouldn't wish on anyone. "It was." Remarkably, his voice held genuine sorrow, which meant the words sounded anything but meaningless. Of course, he'd recently found out he had missed out on the first five years of his own child's life, which had to hold a deep sorrow of its own.

"Anyway, we tried in vitro—twice—which pretty much bankrupted us. Then, three years ago, my parents died suddenly."

"Both of them?"

"Yes." Cassie rubbed a palm along the arm rest, over and over, the cool plastic grounding her, keeping hysteria at bay. "They had a woodstove in their home, and something went wrong one night. There was a carbon monoxide leak. The two of them went to bed and never woke up." She rubbed harder, a strategy her therapist had given her to keep herself from being sucked into that black hole she'd been so often lost in the days and weeks and months after they got that terrible phone call.

"Cassie." Jared breathed her name out more than spoke it.

"Yeah. It was terrible. But it did remind me how fragile life was, how precious time with the people you loved was. The fertility stuff we'd been going through was all-consuming, and I had missed out on so much time with my mom and dad. I realized I couldn't keep doing it. So, one day, six months after we buried my parents, I brought up the idea of adoption to Mack."

Although she'd worked to keep it level, something in her voice must have tipped him off. Still staring out the front window at the taillights partially obscured by snow, the flashing blue on top of the snowplow reflecting off every icy surface, Jared frowned. "And he didn't want that?"

Her throat had tightened, and she pressed her fingers to it, waiting until the ache eased enough for her to answer. "No. He didn't want that. Apparently, he didn't want any of it, not anymore. Including me."

His head jerked a little. In the near darkness inside the vehicle, his eyes sought out hers, held them a moment before he returned his gaze to the road. "Idiot."

Cassie let out a shocked laugh. Definitely not the response she'd expected. Exactly what she needed to hear, though.

"He left you?"

"Yes. He packed a suitcase that night, walked out the door, and headed straight to the woman he'd fallen in love with while I was doing everything I could to give him the child, the home and family, I thought we both wanted."

CHAPTER FOUR

The memories she'd dredged up drained the last of the adrenaline that had been flickering through her like sparks of electricity since the plane plummeted through the sky. Cassie sagged against the back of the seat.

Jared's knuckles gleamed white in the darkness. Had what she told him about Mack upset him, or was he struggling to keep the car on the road? He didn't say, only inclined his head in her direction. "It's been a crazy day. Get some rest; I'll wake you if I decide to stop at some point."

Although she doubted her body—or her mind—was ready to settle after the trauma they'd gone through or the story she'd shared, Cassie nodded and closed her eyes. When someone quietly speaking her name roused her what felt like seconds later, she bolted upright, shocked to realize she had somehow fallen asleep.

Jared held up a hand. "Sorry to startle you. Unfortunately, the weather's getting worse, not better, so I got off the interstate a few minutes ago when I spotted a sign for an inn up ahead. Are you okay if we stop for the night?"

Cassie gazed out the front windshield at the mesmerizing

flakes driving straight into the glass, a relentless onslaught of white. How could he even see a sign? Or the road? "Yes, I definitely think we should stop." What was one or two fewer days in New York City? As she'd told Jared, no one was waiting for her there. They'd still be able to make it in time for Christmas, right? She ran a hand over her eyes. "Where are we?"

"I'm not sure. The GPS doesn't seem to be working, possibly because of the weather. We've been driving on I-80 for almost four hours, but pretty much crawling, so we're maybe a third of the way to NYC?"

She blinked. "Four hours?" That meant she'd been sleeping for two. Several sleepless nights and a brush with death had clearly taken more out of her than she'd realized.

"Yeah." Jared signaled to make a turn. "I kept hoping visibility would improve, but, as you can see, it didn't."

Cassie held her breath, unable to see the road coming up on their right until the last second, just before he turned onto it. Two minutes later, he signaled again and pulled into a small parking lot. She caught a glimpse of the sign in front of the two-story wooden structure, half buried in snow on the front lawn, as he pulled close to the building and stopped the car. The Orange Grove Inn. Ha. Somehow, she doubted there were a lot of orange groves in this area. Whoever had named it was clearly a wishful thinker. Or maybe they'd moved here from Florida and wanted a reminder of home.

Cassie tore her gaze from the sign and reached for her seatbelt. Jared grabbed both their bags from the trunk and followed her as she waded through eighteen-inch snow drifts and up the three stairs to the wide front veranda. A snow-covered swing hung at one end of the porch, beneath the large overhang. In nice weather, this would be a great place to sit and chat or read a book.

A frigid gust of wind carried icy bits of snow that pelted

her cheeks and throat, reminding her that this was not nice weather. The sooner they got inside, the better. Cassie pulled open a red wooden screen door, knocked on the oak one with an arched, stained-glass window set into it, and then pushed inside without waiting for a response. She held the screen for Jared as he brushed by and stepped onto a multi-colored carpet with the words *Welcome to the Family* woven into it.

Although any warm, dry place would have been welcoming tonight, entering the Orange Grove Inn felt like walking into the arms of a friend. No one sat behind the counter tucked under the spiraling wooden staircase ahead of them, so they stood on the carpet a moment, stamping the snow off their boots. A dining room to the left housed a massive oak table, ten or twelve chairs arranged around it. Cassie's gaze was drawn to the right, past a set of double French doors that opened into a cavernous living area.

Stockings hung from the mantel set into a floor-to-ceiling stone fireplace. Crackling flames cast a warm glow over the whole room, infusing the air with a hint of smoke. A ten-foot-tall pine tree loaded with lights twinkled brightly in one corner, vintage stars and balls hanging from every branch. Couches and chairs sat in clusters perfect for conversations, and every wall was covered in shelves filled with books and games. It was quite possibly the most inviting room Cassie had ever seen. And somehow they had stumbled across this magical place where they could seek shelter in the midst of a raging blizzard.

If she and God weren't on the outs at the moment, Cassie might have considered it a miracle. Or a divine gift.

A door behind the counter swung open, and a woman in soft-worn jeans and a knitted sweater—Santa riding a reindeer on the front of it—bustled into the foyer. "Welcome, welcome." She was a bit too young and slender to play Mrs. Claus, and her short, curly hair was dark, but her bright eyes and rosy cheeks did call the mythical North Pole queen to mind. She rounded the counter and headed straight for Cassie. "You poor thing. You look done in. You must be if you've come very far in this storm."

Cassie was just exhausted enough in body and soul that, if the woman had opened her arms, she might have fallen right into them. Except that would have likely snapped the fragile strands woven of sheer willpower holding her together, and she could very well have burst into tears and thoroughly embarrassed herself in front of this stranger. Strangers, really, although Jared didn't feel like one anymore.

What she needed more than anything was to be directed to a room with a nice soft bed, lots of thick blankets, and a table with a lamp she could curl up next to and finally get back to *The Happiness of Bluebirds*.

As if sensing she was close to losing it, Jared touched the back of her cream-colored wool coat lightly with his fingers. "Do you happen to have two free rooms?"

"You're in luck." The woman hooked her arm through Cassie's and guided her to the counter. "We only have four rooms and were fully booked earlier today, but then three people canceled because of the weather. Mr. Thompson in room four is a long-term guest, but otherwise you'll have the place to yourselves."

Which sounded heavenly. As though as enamored by the living room as Cassie was, Jared lingered in the opening between the French doors while she paid for her booking. When the woman tore the receipt from the debit machine, she said, "You're in room one, darlin'. No rush to come down in the morning. Buffet will be laid out in the dining room until eleven."

"Oh, we'll likely be on our way before that."

The woman blinked as she held out a key. "Honey, I don't think you'll be going anywhere tomorrow. They'll close the roads tonight, I'm sure, since the forecast is for this storm to settle in for a day or two. Even getting into town will be tricky until this snow tapers off and the plows get out, so you might want to plan on simply relaxing until things settle."

Cassie looked over at Jared, who lifted his shoulders. "If we're going to be snowed in, this is a pretty great place to be. We'll still have time if we leave on the twenty-third."

She couldn't argue with either of those statements, so she only closed her fingers around the key. "Okay, thank you." Being stuck in this lovely place, resting, reading or playing games in front of the fire, and—judging by the incredible aromas of cinnamon and other spices drifting from the kitchen—eating fabulous food was certainly not the worst way to spend a little time.

"You're very welcome. My name's Fiona. Don't hesitate to ring the front desk if you need anything at all, you hear?"

Cassie smiled. "All right. Thank you."

Jared slid her bag off his shoulder and held it out as she walked over to him. "Sleep well, Cassie."

"Thanks. I'm sure I will." Something the woman said had twigged a question in her mind, and she stopped at the bottom of the stairs, her hand gripping the round wooden knob. "You mentioned driving into the nearest town. What town would that be?"

Clutching Jared's credit card, Fiona looked over at her. Before she even opened her mouth, it struck Cassie what the innkeeper was about to say, and she gripped the knob tighter to keep from bolting up the stairs before she heard the answer.

"It's Clearview, Pennsylvania, darlin'."

CHAPTER FIVE

Clearview. Of course it was. The small town Cassie's sister Daria had moved to after their parents had died and she and Cassie had fallen out completely. The town Cassie had sworn to never set foot in. The one she'd felt God calling her to for weeks. That Clearview.

No doubt she'd gone as white as the snow pelting against the windowpanes when Fiona had confirmed Cassie's sudden suspicions that the storm had driven them to Daria's doorstep. Somehow, she'd managed to nod and stumble up the stairs, once again feeling Jared's intense gaze on her as she went.

In her room—as warm and inviting as the rest of the inn with a handmade quilt on the four-poster bed, plush blue area rug on the wooden floor, and white rocking chair in the corner by the window—Cassie locked the door behind her, lowered the bag to the floor, and dropped to her knees next to the bed. *Why are you doing this to me? I can't do it. You know I can't. And you know why.*

Although she waited for it, no answer came from God. Had he abandoned her? Cast her away? Her heart ached at the thought. As much as she might not like what he was asking her to do now, Cassie knew she would not have made it through the last three years without him.

With a low groan, she pushed to her feet, got ready for bed in the small bathroom off her room, and tugged the book from her bag before switching on the lamp and crawling under the warm quilt.

She hadn't expected to get through much of her novel before dropping off to sleep, but once again she found herself caught up in the story. What was it that moved her so deeply? It certainly wasn't preachy, but the flawed, broken heroine was on a faith journey that spoke to Cassie's heart. Beckoned her like the soft lights and hint of woodsmoke drifting from the Orange Grove Inn as she and Jared made their way through the snow and ice toward it. The warm glow didn't ebb when she finished the last page hours later, closed the book, and set it reverently on the bedside table. It only seemed to burn brighter, filling the parts of her that had been cold and dark for so long.

Cassie pressed a hand to her chest, to the flames flickering there. Maybe it wasn't the story itself. Perhaps it was the way the words made her feel, as though the long, terrible journey she had been on would, in the end, lead her somewhere beautiful. *Is that what you're trying to tell me? That you are still with me, guiding me to a place of refuge the way you guided us to this wonderful inn?*

If God hadn't abandoned her, then maybe she actually could . . .

The thought threatened to drive out the warmth like a cold north wind. *Look, I'm grateful you're with me. I really am. But you're asking too much.* She closed her eyes and draped an arm across her forehead, wrestling with letting go the way she had for years. *All right. Here is the best I can do.* Cassie leaned over, switched off the light, and plumped up her pillow before burrowing deep under the mound of blankets. *I'll think about it.*

Cassie slept late the next morning, barely making it down to the dining room before eleven. When she ambled into the room in jeans and a sweatshirt, her short hair tousled, Jared sat at the table reading, an empty plate and half-empty cup of coffee in front of him. When he looked up and smiled, the same sensation she'd felt when she had come in out of the storm the night before wrapped itself around her. Cassie lifted a hand. "Good morning."

"Morning." He nodded towards a credenza at the far end of the room. "Coffee's hot and there's fruit and yogurt and fresh carrot muffins."

Which explained the hints of cinnamon and nutmeg that still lingered in the air, mingling with the rich aroma of coffee. "Perfect. Thanks."

She glanced out one of the eight-foot-tall windows as she passed by. Snow and ice covered the glass halfway up. Through the cleared part, she glimpsed swirling flakes and gray sky. The storm wasn't over yet. Cassie couldn't bring herself to be sad about that as she loaded a plate with fruit and a muffin and carried it and a cup of coffee to a seat at the table across from Jared.

"What are you reading?" She took a sip of coffee and nearly moaned with pleasure. Hazelnut. Her favorite.

Jared held up the book. "*Moby Dick.* I found it on one of the shelves in the other room."

Hmm. Cassie pursed her lips. "English professor?"

He grinned as he set the book down. "Nope."

She contemplated him. In jeans and a plaid shirt, he looked

less like a stockbroker today. Since they had more time together now, she'd figure it out. "Where's Fiona?"

"Working on lunch already, I believe. She said her husband, Clark, went to an outlet store up north for supplies. He had hoped to get back before the storm, but it moved in too quickly, so she's on her own until he can get through. I told her to let us know if she needed help with anything. And Mr. Thomas was down earlier. Nice man. Retired."

"Not married?"

"He was, for fifty-seven years. His wife, Jean, died last year."

"Ah." A pang shot through her. What would that have been like, spending more than half a century with someone? Actually staying together until death parted the two of you? "I can't imagine how hard that would be, losing someone you'd been married to for so long."

"Me neither."

Cassie unwrapped her fingers from around the warm mug and reached for the muffin, casually peeling off the wrapper. "You've never been married?"

He shook his head. "No. I've had a couple serious relationships, but in the end, neither woman felt like the one I was meant to spend my life with. Or maybe . . ." He toyed with the linen napkin crumpled next to his plate.

"Maybe what?"

Jared looked up and met her gaze. "Maybe, on some level, I wouldn't let myself think that way. To accept that kind of love or happiness. A penance, of sorts."

Cassie winced. "That's a lot of penance for one mistake."

"Kind of a big mistake."

"You said you had a faith, right? Did you ask God to forgive you for it?"

"Repeatedly." His dark eyes probed hers. "Do you think he has?"

"Yes." Her voice held more vitriol than she'd intended, and Jared's eyebrows rose.

"You have a problem with God forgiving people?"

"Not you, no."

"Someone else."

"Yes."

His features softened. "Your husband."

Cassie broke off a piece of muffin but didn't put it in her mouth. "For one. I don't know this for a fact, since I haven't spoken directly to him since the night he walked out on me, but he grew up in church and claimed to be a Christian. It's possible he asked God to forgive him and, knowing God, he did. Which would make things nice and easy for Mack, wouldn't it?"

"I can't speak for Mack, but I can tell you that knowing in your head God has forgiven you doesn't automatically make things nice and easy. It can be a pretty long journey from the head to the heart."

The sadness in his voice banished the bitterness drifting through her. Cassie set the muffin on her plate and reached for the mug again. "That's a lot more than I was planning to get into before coffee."

Jared flashed her that crooked smile that warmed her more than the hot drink. "You're right. After everything we went through yesterday, we should likely be a bit easier on ourselves today. Why don't you finish your breakfast, and then we can sit by the fire. Do you have a book to read?"

"I don't, actually. I brought one with me I thought would last my whole trip, but I ended up finishing it sometime in the early hours this morning." She popped a green grape into her mouth.

"That good?"

"Amazing, actually. I'm not sure I'll be able to get into

another one today, as I have a bit of a book hangover. Lots to process."

"The best kind of book."

"I agree."

After she'd eaten and finished a second cup of coffee, Cassie trailed after him to the living room. There had to be hundreds of books on the shelves in this room. As she'd suspected, none caught her interest even after perusing dozens of covers and titles. In the end, she grabbed a puzzle off a large stack and settled at a card table near a window to put it together while Jared relaxed in an armchair in front of the fire.

They chatted off and on, keeping the topics of conversation much lighter than they had at breakfast, but the lengthy silences between them when she was concentrating on finding the right piece to fit into the puzzle and Jared was deep into *Moby Dick* were as comfortable as the crackling fire and the soft, twinkling lights on the tree and threaded through the pine garland on the mantel.

After a couple hours, she rose, back muscles cramped and her neck sore. "I'm going to get a cup of tea. Do you want anything?"

Jared stuck a finger in his book and looked up. "Tea would be great, thanks."

She nodded and made her way out of the room and past the counter to the kitchen door. When she rapped lightly, Fiona called out a cheery "Come in," and Cassie pushed into the room. The kitchen was large and bright, despite the sullen skies outside. Fiona's smile was even brighter and drew Cassie in as much as the aromas of baking bread and roasting meat. "I just came to get a cup of tea, but is there anything I can help you with while I'm here?"

Fiona grabbed the kettle off the burner. "Oh no, darlin'.

Thank you. With only the four of us here, I'm keeping things simple."

"Good. Jared and I don't need much."

Fiona filled the kettle at the sink before returning it to the burner. After wiping her hands on a towel hanging over the handle of the stove, she came over and reached for Cassie's hands. "Are you doing okay?"

Cassie blinked. "Of course. Why do you ask?"

Fiona squeezed her fingers. "It's just that a lot of people come and go from this inn, and I listen to many of their stories. I know sadness when I see it."

Shock tingled across Cassie's skin. "I'm not . . ." She trailed off when her eyes met Fiona's warm hazel ones. Although the woman was only a few years older than Cassie, those eyes held wisdom and understanding.

"You don't have to talk about it if you're not ready. I only wanted you to know that I'm here if you are. Although that man of yours might be better medicine for you than I would be."

"Oh." The shock rippling across her flesh morphed into prickles of heat. "He's not my man. We just, I mean, we're . . ." She trailed off again. If they weren't strangers, what *were* she and Jared? Friends?

A knowing smile carved dimples into Fiona's rosy cheeks. "Whatever the two of you are, I'm pretty sure he sees the same thing I do when he looks at you. Which he does, often. And given the concern in his eyes every time, I'd wager he would do pretty much anything to ease that burden you carry."

Mercifully, the kettle whistled, sparing Cassie from having to reply. Fiona let her go and bustled around the room, making a pot of tea that she set on a tray with two cups and a plate of cookies. When she finished, she handed Cassie the tray, flashed her another warm smile, and then returned to her work.

Her head spinning, Cassie returned to the library, diving back into her puzzle to avoid dealing with all the new thoughts Fiona had put into her head. By late afternoon the room was growing dark, and Jared closed his book and went around switching on lamps and tossing a few more pieces of wood onto the fire. He paused a moment in front of one of the large windows. "Looks like it might be clearing up out there."

"Really?" Cassie looked up, the thrill of finding the exact piece to finish the cat lying on the rug in front of the fire still shivering through her. Only a dozen or so more pieces and she'd be done. When was the last time she'd sat long enough to complete an entire thousand-piece puzzle. Had she ever? Somehow, the pleasant task, the quiet, steady presence of Jared, and the warm comfort of the room had kept her from thinking about much else for hours. The slight buzzing in the back of her mind, the reminder that there was something she was meant to be doing, something she had, so far, refused to do, was all that marred this perfect day. She rose and walked over to join Jared at the window, not wanting to think about that.

"Yeah. We might even be able to—"

Before he could finish the thought, Fiona bustled into the room. "Storm appears to be about over." She wiped her hands on the red-and-white-striped apron tied around her waist. "The roads have been plowed, apparently, so I think I might slip into town, pick up a couple things for dinner."

Jared turned from the window. "I could go."

The buzzing grew louder in Cassie's head. Before she could change her mind, she said, "I'll go with you."

He half turned to scrutinize her, that concern Fiona had mentioned flickering in his eyes again. Likely because she'd ground out the words with exactly the amount of enthusiasm with which someone might announce they were about to head off to the gallows. "Are you sure?"

No. I've never been less sure about anything. Cassie drew in a slow, deep breath. "Yes. I have to go to Clearview. There's something I need to do there. Someone I need to see."

CHAPTER SIX

Jared eased the SUV to the curb and shifted the transmission into park. Cassie stared at the house she'd seen only in a picture. A photo tucked inside a curt missive Cassie hadn't responded to. She hadn't received another one. Jared hadn't asked her what it was she had to do in town, who she needed to see, but she sensed it was taking everything he had not to. Maybe it would ease his mind for her to tell him that much.

She ran the tip of her finger along the side window, following the post at the top of the porch stairs. "This is my sister Daria's place."

"Ah." Somehow he managed to convey relief, curiosity, and compassion in that one small word. How did he do that?

"We . . . haven't spoken for a few years." Would he ask why? Cassie had no desire to get into that. Not now. Certainly not here.

"Do you want me to go in with you?"

Everything in Cassie wanted to say yes. She swallowed the lump in her throat so she could answer him. "Thank you for offering. But this is something I have to do alone."

"I could wait here."

She tore her gaze from the house and, even knowing it wouldn't fool him, forced a smile. "I'll be okay. Go get the things on Fiona's list."

He nodded. "All right. But I'll be back in a few minutes. Take as long as you need, but when you're done, I'll be here."

That helped. "Thanks." Drawing in a deep breath, she pushed open the door and stepped out into the snow.

"Cassie?"

She gripped the top of the door with one hand and, pressing her other to the roof of the car, leaned in. "Yes?"

"I'll be praying."

Her smile came easier this time. "I appreciate it." She closed the door, turned, and took a deep breath before starting along the front walkway someone had recently shoveled. She nearly changed her mind when she reached the bottom of the stairs. Jared hadn't pulled away yet. Was he waiting to see if she would flee to the vehicle without even going to the door? One foot on the bottom step, she paused, gathered every bit of courage she had, and started up.

At the door, she pressed the bell and waited, not turning around. If she did, if she saw Jared sitting there, ready to take her anywhere she wanted to go—which was pretty much anywhere but here—she might go to him. But she'd tried running the other way, and it hadn't gone very well. *Okay look. I'm here, like you asked. But I can't do this alone. So I really hope you're—*

The wooden door swung open. Daria stood on the other side of the screen. She let out a small cry and pressed a hand to her mouth. When she lowered it, every bit of color had drained from her cheeks, and she pressed her fingers to the doorframe. "Cassie."

"Hi, Daria."

"What are you . . . I mean . . . I wasn't expecting . . ." Daria swiped her auburn hair off her forehead. Although Cassie had cut her hair short, her sister still wore hers long, halfway down the back of her black sweater.

"I know you weren't. Can I come in?"

Daria didn't answer, only staggered backwards, out of her way. Cassie pulled open the screen door and stepped into the warm kitchen. Not until she turned and pulled the screen closed, lifting a hand in Jared's direction, did he pull away from the curb.

When she faced her sister, a tsunami of emotions roiled in Daria's eyes—fear, anger, longing, hope. Then, just as quickly, a shutter came down and her features hardened. "What are you doing here?"

"I needed to see you. Could we—"

"Dar? Is everything okay? I heard . . ." A man strode into the kitchen and skidded to a stop, his face paling the way his wife's had. "Cassie."

Cassie swallowed back the sudden lump in her throat. "Hi, Mack."

Mack wrapped an arm around Daria's waist and pulled her to his side. Protective, like he'd been with Cassie every time she'd gotten . . . Pain spiraled through her, and she pressed a hand to her abdomen as she shifted her gaze to meet her sister's. "You're pregnant."

Daria reached up to touch a knuckle to Mack's chest. "Could you give us a few minutes to talk?"

He hesitated before letting her go. "All right. I need to finish shoveling the driveway anyway."

Cassie didn't move as he brushed by her, grabbed his winter coat from a hook next to the door, and slung it on. Her sister's gaze was still shuttered, almost cold, and Cassie crossed her arms over her chest. "Look, this won't take long. I just came to give you a message, and then I'll go."

"What message?" Daria's voice was as cold as her eyes.

This was your idea. Give me the words to say. Cassie pressed her arms harder against her ribs. Here goes . . . "What you and Mack did to me was very, very wrong. You hurt and betrayed me in the most egregious way, and you sinned greatly against God."

When she stopped, Daria lifted her chin slightly. "Is that all?"

There was lots more Cassie could say, many more accusations she could spew against her sister and her ex-husband, but that would degenerate quickly. No doubt they would both say things the other would never be able to forgive or forget. And it would deviate from the path she'd been compelled to follow, something she'd already done more than enough. "Yes."

When Daria didn't respond, Cassie nodded and started to turn away.

"Wait."

Cassie faced her sister, bracing herself for a hostile response, but the cold had melted from Daria's face. She jerked a hand toward the table. "Could we sit?"

Cassie's knees were weak, and sitting suddenly seemed like a really good idea. She stumbled across the linoleum floor and sank onto a wooden kitchen chair. The room was cozy, with white lace curtains on the windows, a chandelier over the table, and a pot of something that smelled like vegetable soup bubbling on the stove.

Pressing both palms against the tabletop, Daria lowered herself onto the chair across from Cassie. She propped her elbows on the table and lowered her face to her hands. After a moment, she murmured, her voice ragged, "You're not wrong, Cass. What we did . . . what I did . . . is unforgiveable."

Yes, it is. At the hot-needle jab to her conscience, Cassie exhaled. "No, it isn't. Not to God, anyway."

Daria lifted her head. The raw pain in her eyes stole Cassie's breath. "Do you really believe that?"

"I do." Unable to look at her sister, to witness her agony, Cassie followed the shape of a knot in the wooden table with the tip of her finger. "I didn't want to come here, Daria. For weeks I've felt God calling me to come see you, but I resisted. I bought a plane ticket to New York City and planned to fly straight there to spend the holidays. Then the plane had to make an emergency landing at Erie Airport, and while a friend and I were attempting to drive to New York, the storm forced us to stop at an inn near here. Finally, I gave up and came. And I think that's what God wanted me to tell you. That you hurt me terribly, you grieved him terribly, but if you repent he is still willing to forgive you."

When Daria didn't respond, Cassie pushed back her chair. "Well, I've said what I came to say, so I'll go."

She stood and took a step toward the door, but Daria pushed to her feet. "Not yet." She rounded the end of the table and stopped in front of Cassie. "Please, Sass."

A pang shot through Cassie's chest at the childhood nickname, short for Sassy Cassie, their father's pet name for her.

Her sister reached out with both hands but stopped before they touched Cassie's and lowered them to her sides again. "I can't imagine how much courage it took for you to come here."

Cassie almost laughed. "Actually, there was a great deal of cowardice involved."

"Even so, you did come. I've wanted to reach out to you for so long. I've started a hundred letters to you, entered your number into my phone countless times, but in the end I couldn't do it. I didn't know how, after betraying you so

197

horribly." Daria rubbed trembling fingers across her forehead. "I've tried to justify what I did in my head, but I always knew, deep down, that what you said is true, that it was a terrible sin against you and against God. I've struggled with that as Mack and I have tried to build a life together. I mean, we're happy, but in some ways it has felt like trying to build a home on the blackened ruins of the one that burned down before it. Some days it feels like we'll never get rid of the stench of smoke that permeates everything. I haven't even been able to experience joy over this child." She touched a hand to her slightly rounded belly. "But now, for the first time, I feel like there might be hope." When she met Cassie's gaze, Daria's eyes brimmed with tears. "So, thank you."

Cassie nodded.

When she took a step toward the door, Daria touched her arm to stop her. "For what it's worth, I'm terribly, terribly sorry." Her voice broke. "Do you think you could ever forgive me?"

Cassie's stomach clenched. "I don't know, Daria."

Her sister pulled back her arm, pain flitting across her face again. "I get it. And I don't blame you."

Those terrible moments on the plane, when they were plummeting toward earth, it was Daria who filled Cassie's thoughts. The love and friendship they had always shared. Was it possible their roots went deep enough to survive everything that had happened? Even fire sweeping through a forest left roots that allowed for new growth. She reached for her sister's hand, Daria's fingers cold in hers. "I can't promise you anything except that I'll try. Carrying around all this anger and bitterness toward you and Mack has been an unbearable burden. I'd love to be able to let go of it."

Daria managed a watery smile. "That's more than I deserve. I'll understand if you never do, but I really hope you can find a way someday. For your sake and for mine. I . . . miss my sister."

"So do I." Cassie let go of her sister's hand and brushed her fingers lightly across the front of Daria's sweater, over the tiny bump there. "Take care of yourself. And this little one. And let me know if I have a niece or nephew."

"I will."

With nothing left to say, Cassie made her way to the door and stepped out into the cold. The blue SUV waited at the curb across the street, and relief poured through her. Jared must have hustled around the store to get back here this quickly.

Her eyes on the car, she heard Mack's boots crunching across the frozen ground before she saw him walking toward her, shovel in hand. Cassie paused at the bottom of the stairs, and he stopped and shoved the metal tip into the snow. "Can we talk?"

She shot a glance at the car. Jared was watching the two of them. Was that why he'd parked facing that direction, so he could see her? The warmth of the thought uncoiled the muscles that had tightened at the sight of Mack. "You can have one minute."

He nodded at the SUV. "Who's your friend?"

Cassie sighed. "That's not really your business anymore, Mack."

"Fair enough." He gripped the handle of the shovel as though he needed the support. "Look, Cassie. I've never had the chance to apologize to you for everything that happened. I know there's nothing I can say, no way for me to make up for what I did, but I want you to know that I am genuinely sorry. I don't expect you to forgive me, but I hope you and Daria can work things out. She—" he scuffed the toe of his boot through a small mound of snow, "—she cries at night. A lot. I don't think she's aware that I hear her, but I do, and I know it's because she still struggles with how badly she hurt you. We both do."

Cassie shot another look across the street. Jared had cracked the door open, as though prepared to come over if he thought she needed him. The sight of that gave her the strength to push her shoulders back and face her ex-husband. "I appreciate you saying that. I told Daria I would try to forgive her, and I will. I'm going to try to forgive both of you."

"That's all I ask. Thank you."

"Tell Daria I'll call her sometime."

Some of the tension left his shoulders. "That would mean a lot to her."

"Goodbye, Mack."

He paused, as though as aware of the magnitude of those words as she was. "Goodbye, Cassie." Things had ended so badly between them, so abruptly, they'd never really had the chance to say those words to each other.

Cassie made her way the end of the walk and started across the street. Before reaching Jared, who had climbed out of the car, she shot a look at the sky. *Well, it's done. I hope you're happy.*

Jared pulled open the passenger door for her as she approached, and Cassie slid onto the front seat. She didn't glance back, only stared out the windshield as they pulled away from the curb.

After a minute of silence, Jared touched the back of his hand to hers and quietly asked, "Are you okay?"

Excellent question. *Was* she okay? Her emotions were as tangled as the strings of Christmas lights her dad had pulled out of the box of decorations every year, and she struggled to separate one from the others. "I think so."

"Was that your sister's husband you were talking to outside?"

"Yes." She bit her lip. "It was also Mack."

Jared shot her a look, his dark eyes wide. "Mack? I thought. . ." He exhaled a long breath, his fingers tightening around the steering wheel again. "He left you for your sister."

It wasn't a question, so Cassie didn't answer, only rubbed her palm over the cool plastic of the door handle. After a moment, she fisted her hand and pressed the side of it to the condensation on the window. Then she added five little dots over the top of the impression with the tip of her finger, like she and Daria had so often done when riding in the car. She contemplated the finished image. A tiny, perfect little foot. "They're having a baby," she whispered.

Jared didn't speak. What could anyone possibly say to that? He did reach over and take her hand, the warmth of his fingers curling around hers comforting her far more than any words would have. He let her go quickly, but, as it seemed to do each time, the heat of his touch lingered on her skin.

Cassie relaxed into the sensation as she leaned her head against the seat and they wended their way back to The Orange Grove Inn.

CHAPTER SEVEN

If she'd thought carrying out her mission to deliver a message to Daria would unburden her enough to let her fall into a deep sleep, Cassie was mistaken. She tossed and turned until after midnight before finally giving up and heading down to the kitchen for a cup of chamomile tea. A few minutes later, steaming mug in hand, she started for the stairs but paused at the bottom and glanced into the softly lit living room. Maybe she'd drink her tea in front of the dying fire before heading up and trying again to get some rest.

The room was empty but as cozy as ever with warm coals in the fireplace, soft lamps glowing in the corners, and the lights twinkling on the tree. Cassie set her tea on a small table and wandered over to admire the vintage decorations. Branches had been cleared from about a foot and a half of trunk at the bottom of the tree, the way her father had liked to do it when they were growing up. The sight of it sparked a memory—of her and Daria crawling under the tree to lie beneath it and stare up at the lights sparkling off red and gold decorations and mounds of tinsel.

Cassie glanced around the room. The house was silent.

She pressed her lips together. Did she dare? Without giving it any more thought, she stretched out on the floor in front of the tree and then shimmied under until she lay on her back beneath the spreading branches. The world down there was as magical as she remembered. For the first time in a long time, memories of the past, with Daria, didn't send electrical shocks of pain shooting through her. Instead, a warmth spread through her chest, and she smiled, hearing again the laughter of those two little girls. They'd been inseparable, she and her little sister. As she never would have imagined she and Mack wouldn't make it, she never could have dreamt that such a chasm of hurt and betrayal would have opened between her and Daria.

You've forgiven them, haven't you? Cassie stared up through the heavily laden branches. Both her sister and her ex-husband had seemed sincerely remorseful and repentant today. No doubt they had already asked God to forgive them and, knowing him, he had. Exactly why Cassie hadn't wanted to go and confront them in the first place. They didn't deserve to be forgiven. Did they?

That hot needle—everything she'd read in the Bible and knew to be true about God—pricked her chest again. *I know, I know, it's not my place to decide that. And yes, I'm aware I wasn't blameless in the situation, since I was not easy to live with when we were going through all that. Still . . .*

Soft footsteps padding across the floor interrupted her thoughts. Cassie didn't move when Jared stopped in front of the tree, only kept staring up at the glowing lights. When he spoke, his voice held a mixture of concern and amusement. "Mind if I join you?"

"Be my guest." Cassie waved a hand toward the other side of the tree. "How did you know I was here?"

"Heard your door open and close, so I came down to see if you were all right." Jared lowered himself to the floor and wriggled under the lowest branches on the other side of the trunk. For a moment, he didn't speak, only lay there quietly, then he said, "Well. I don't believe I've ever seen a Christmas tree from this angle."

"Really? I'm sorry you had such a deprived childhood. My sister and I used to lie under ours every night when we were kids."

Jared chuckled. Then, after a moment of quiet, he said, "Speaking of your sister, do you want to talk about how it went with her today?"

Did she? Maybe it would help to share, enough for her to finally be able to fall asleep when she returned to her room. "You've already figured out most of it."

Still gazing up at the branches, Cassie filled in the rest for him—what it had been like losing the babies and going through the fertility treatments, how she had, admittedly, become obsessed with having a child and hadn't noticed she and Mack were drifting apart, that he was turning more and more often to Daria for comfort and a shoulder to cry on.

"When he finally left, I was so hurt and angry. I moved to a new town in northern Ontario where I didn't know anyone, where I could start over. I fooled myself into thinking I was okay. Then one day, I drove out to see a guy I'd gone out with a couple times but who had made it clear that nothing was going to happen with us. Even though it had ended months earlier, I was struggling to let it go. When he introduced me to the woman he was now with, I was awful to her. It wasn't like me, and I felt horrible about it afterwards. Thankfully, they both forgave me, and Tala is now one of my closest friends, but it showed me I wasn't doing as okay as I'd thought. That I was still filled with anger and bitterness. Which was why, even though I felt God calling me to, going to their place today, seeing Daria and Mack for the first time since he'd left me, was the last thing in the world I wanted to do."

"Did it help?"

Cassie contemplated that a moment before answering. "I think so. I mean, as you know, I was really struggling with the idea of God forgiving them. But it did make it a bit easier, seeing how sorry they are, hearing them say the words."

"Can you forgive them?"

"Honestly? I don't know. But I told them both I would try. I'm not as angry as I was, anyway, so that's a start. I still have a lot to work through."

"Of course you do. Anger and bitterness are the ice that forms over the river of sorrow beneath. They save us from drowning in that sadness and allow us to keep moving forward, but they can also trap that sorrow inside. Sounds like that ice cracked a little today, which is a very hopeful sign."

Her chest tightened. Sadness. Fiona had seen that in her too. But if that ice was truly cracking, what if she crashed through? Could she flounder through those waves of sorrow alone? Words from a verse she'd once memorized for the sheer beauty of it drifted through her mind. *When you pass through the waters, I will be with you.* Was that true? Could she trust that God would stay by her side as she waded through all that pain?

She drew in a slow breath, heavy with the scent of pine needles and sap. He'd sent her to confront Daria and Mack about what they had done so they would know he hadn't forgotten them, that they could be forgiven. So why did she think he would abandon her when she needed him? The sweetness of that thought drove out the fear of what lay ahead. Jared was right. The ice needed to crack so she could pass through the waters beneath to get to the other side of her grief. The loss of those five precious babies and the life she had thought she would have. The betrayal of those closest to her.

How had he found the exact words to paint the picture that would help her see . . .

Cassie turned her head a little, just enough to see him in her periphery. "You're a writer."

He'd been quiet, giving her time to process. Now he looked over, the corners of his eyes crinkling when he smiled. "Yep."

Cassie frowned. Was he one of those authors who used strangers they encountered as characters in their stories and everything people shared with them as fodder for their plotlines? Chills tingled across her skin, and she rubbed her arms, bare beneath the sleeves of her navy T-shirt.

Jared's smile faded. "That's an unusual reaction."

"Is it? How do most people react?"

"Interested, usually. A bit awed, sometimes, as though being an author is some glamorous profession. What we typically try to hide is the fact that, for the most part, being a writer is about as unglamorous as it gets. I spend a lot of time banging my head against the wall because I can't think of a thing to write."

"What does that feel like?"

"Banging my head against the wall? It hurts."

She rolled her eyes. "I meant writer's block."

"Oh." He grinned. "That hurts too, in a different way. When you were a kid, did you ever fall off the monkey bars or a swing and land on your back, get the air knocked completely out of you?"

"Sure."

"Remember lying there, gasping for air, getting nothing, and thinking there was a very good chance you might never breathe again? Well, it's exactly like that. Only with words instead of breaths. And when the words do come, most of the time I read them over later and think they're absolute drivel no one in the world would want to read, let alone pay money for."

"And if the writing is going well and the story is coming together?"

"Then I get so lost in it that everything else falls by the wayside—including family and friends. Not to mention personal hygiene. It's a horrible profession really. No idea why anyone would choose to do it."

Cassie managed a smile at that. "How many books have you written?"

"Written or had published?"

"Written."

"Eight."

"And published?"

A sheepish look crossed his face as he glanced away. "One."

"Ah." He couldn't be that great a writer then, if he had seven books no one wanted to touch. "Why only one?"

He shrugged. "I haven't submitted any of the others to a publisher yet, much to my agent's frustration."

"Because?"

He exhaled. "Fear, I guess."

That she could relate to. "Fear of what?"

"That my next book won't live up to the first one."

Cassie turned onto her side, propped her elbow on the hardwood floor, and rested the side of her head on her hand so she could see him better. "So, your first book did well?"

Another shrug. "*Well* is relative. It was no Harry Potter. I did make enough to live off while I try to screw up my courage to put another one out into the world, so I guess I'd have to say yes, since that was far more than I expected." His self-deprecating smile was endearing, and Cassie found herself hoping against hope that he truly was a good writer. Jared touched a shiny silver star with the tip of his finger. "But what if that was a fluke? Like when you're lying in the grass at night staring up at a bazillion stars and suddenly one goes shooting across the sky and you watch for hours, waiting and hoping for another one that never comes."

"Still, the alternative, never gazing up at the stars again, has to be worse, doesn't it?"

"Huh." Jared nudged a sparkling red ball hanging from a low branch with a knuckle, sending it rocking back and forth, spilling drops of ruby across the wooden floor. "I never thought of it that way."

"Would I have heard of your book?"

He tapped a gold angel, still not looking at her. "I believe you have, yes."

She blinked. "How do you know?"

"Because you were attempting to read it on the plane when I boorishly knocked it from your hand."

Years of disciplining herself not to react, no matter what she heard in court, flew out the window as her mouth dropped open. "*You* wrote *The Happiness of Bluebirds*?"

"Guilty as charged, counselor." He turned to gaze at her again, his lips twitching. "Have to admit, the incredulity hurts a little."

"But . . . but the author's name is J. E. Huntwell."

"I guess we never have told each other our full names." He reached around the trunk of the tree for her hand. "Jared Eduardo Huntwell."

Stunned, Cassie let him wrap his strong fingers around hers. Since he was stretched out on his right side, he'd taken her hand in his left, which felt more like holding it. "Cassandra Lydia White." Unlike the first time they'd introduced themselves to each other or when he had wrapped his fingers around hers to comfort her, he didn't let go of her quickly. Their eyes met beneath the glittering boughs of the tree.

"Was Lydia . . .?"

"My mother, yes."

"Ah." He held her hand a moment longer before squeezing it gently and letting her go. "Eduardo was my grandfather. Venezuelan, like my mother."

Which explained his looks. And his daughter's. Cassie rolled onto her back and rested her bent arm on her forehead. "Reese Witherspoon raved about your book." The words came out in a raspy whisper.

"Reese, yes. She's lovely. She called me shortly after it came out to tell me how much she liked it."

Cassie was beginning to grasp why Jared had seven manuscripts languishing on his computer—he'd set the bar pretty high with his debut novel. How could he hope to top the success of that one? But what if his other stories were as powerful as *Bluebirds*, only they were never able to reach anyone, make them feel—when they were going through the worst, darkest times of their lives—seen, heard, understood? She sat up and crossed her legs, leaning against the floral wallpaper. "You have to put out another book."

Jared sat up too and faced her, his back to the wall. "Why?"

"Because people need your stories, your words. You have no idea . . ."

He waited a moment, then asked, softly, "I have no idea what?"

"How much this one means to me. It . . . it spoke to me. Or rather, God used it to speak to me. It changed me."

"Cassie." Jared scrubbed his face with both hands before resting his forearms on his knees. "That's it right there."

She tilted her head. "That's what?"

"The reason anyone chooses this profession. What you just said? It's everything. Far more meaningful than a phone call from Reese Witherspoon."

"I mean it."

His eyes locked on hers again. "I know you do. Which is

actually making me believe, for the first time, that maybe I *can* send one of my other manuscripts off to my agent." In the twinkling lights, they gazed at each other a moment, until Jared cleared his throat. "We've got a few hours to drive tomorrow. I think I'll try to get some sleep."

"Me too." Her back brushing the soft felt wallpaper, Cassie edged past a branch.

"Here." Jared stood and held out a hand. When she placed her fingers in his, he tugged her to her feet. As soon as she was standing, he let her go and touched a strand of twinkling lights. "Thanks for introducing me to the wonders of lying beneath the branches of a Christmas tree. I think I'll see if Mira wants to try it sometime."

Cassie liked the idea of Jared and his daughter enjoying the magical view of the world from beneath the tree together, like she and Daria had always done. "I hope you do."

Jared studied her a moment before pressing a palm to the wall next to her head and leaning closer. "You know I would never use anything you've told me in a book, right? Your story is sacred. To God and to me. And so is your trust. I would cut off my arm before I would violate either."

His warm breath on her cheek sent shivers skittering across Cassie's skin. His words carried heat too, flowing deep inside and sending more cracks snaking across the surface of the ice that had formed there. "I believe you."

"Good." His smile was as warm as his fingers.

Where had this man come from? He'd almost literally materialized in thin air, thin enough he'd had to encourage her to put on an oxygen mask. "How are you still single?"

She'd meant to break the intensity between them, make him smile. Instead, he grew more serious. "I'm starting to think I just hadn't met the woman I was meant to spend my life with."

Cassie's breath caught as his dark eyes probed hers. Then

he pushed away from the wall and ran a hand over his head. "So, I'm going to try and let go of my need to do penance. If I've learned anything the last couple weeks, it's that God is a God of grace and second chances. He can take anything that's broken or sordid or ugly and turn it into something breathtakingly beautiful. Like that precious little girl I'm going to meet on Christmas Eve."

That resonated as deeply as the words he'd written in his book, and Cassie pressed a hand to her chest. "I think you might be right."

CHAPTER EIGHT

"Are you okay?"

Jared was shifting his weight from one booted foot to the other, despite the relatively mild temperatures in New York.

They'd arrived in the city late yesterday afternoon, and Cassie had offered to help him shop for gifts and decorate his rental place for Christmas. Jared had been unusually quiet as they'd worked and eaten pizza, no doubt because the enormity of what was about to happen—his life changing forever—had struck him as they decorated a small tree and hung strings of lights around the living room and the bedroom where Mira would sleep.

After Jared had held Cassie's wool coat for her to slip on, he grasped the sleeve and asked, "Would you come with me tomorrow?"

When she had hesitated, wanting to go but not wishing to intrude on Jared's initial meeting with his daughter, he'd added, "It might help Mira to have you there."

Which it might. Having to leave her mother and go somewhere with a strange man, even if she'd been told the man was her daddy and safe, would have to be terrifying for the little one. If Cassie could help ease the transition even a little, she was more than willing. "Of course I'll come."

So here they were, waiting at the base of the giant Christmas tree in Rockefeller Center. Every muscle in his body appeared drawn taut. Of course he was uptight. He was a single guy about to start solo parenting a five-year-old whom he'd never met. His entire world had been turned upside down and shaken the last few weeks as though he were living in some kind of massive snow globe.

Cassie nudged him in the arm. "You're going to be a great dad."

For the first time since they'd arrived at the tree, Jared stopped scanning the area and turned to her. "How do you know?"

"For starters, you were so good with that little girl in front of us on the plane. And when everything started going crazy, you took care of me, made sure I put on my oxygen mask. After we realized we weren't going to crash, you checked on the McCormicks to make sure they were okay. You treated the strangers around you like family you truly cared about. I think you might be the most empathetic, selfless person I know. Mira is extremely blessed to have you for a father."

Jared's eyes glistened a little in the twinkling lights of the tree. He reached for both her gloved hands and held them tightly. "Thank you for that. It might be the nicest thing anyone has ever said to me."

"It's true."

"I hope so." His eyes searched hers. "Cassie, I—"

"Jared?"

He let go of her and whirled around. A beautiful woman with long, blonde hair stood a few feet from them, clutching the red-mittened hand of a little girl. Jared took a faltering step toward them and stopped. As he had done for her the night they arrived at the Orange Grove Inn, Cassie touched the tips of her fingers to his back to steady him. He drew in a deep breath. "Shannon."

The woman nodded and looked down at the girl. "This is Mira."

Jared closed the space between them and squatted in front of his daughter. "Hi, Mira."

The little girl craned her neck to peer up at her mother. When Shannon nodded, Mira lowered her head and gazed at Jared. "Hi."

"Do you want me to take your backpack for you?" He straightened and held out a hand.

She hesitated, until her mother said, "It's okay, Mira," and helped her take it off before handing it to Jared. Shannon bent forward and took the little girl's face in her hands. "Goodbye, Mira. You be a good girl for your daddy, okay?"

She was less emotional than Cassie would have expected, but maybe she'd said her goodbyes already or was waiting until she returned to her empty apartment to let go.

When Mira nodded, Shannon pressed a kiss to her daughter's forehead and then turned to Jared. "Could we talk for a minute?"

"Sure." He glanced over his shoulder at Cassie, and she stepped forward. "I'll stay with Mira."

"Thanks." He followed Shannon a few feet, until she stopped and faced him.

Cassie crouched down so she was eye level with Jared's daughter. "Hi, Mira. My name is Cassie."

Mira shot a look at her mother. Poor thing. Did she have any idea what was happening here? That her mother was giving her up for good? Cassie's heart squeezed. "I'm a friend of your daddy's."

The little girl shifted her attention back to Cassie. "I'm going to live with my daddy."

"I know you are. And can I tell you a secret?"

Mira's dark eyes widened. "What?"

Cassie cupped her mouth with one hand and leaned closer to whisper, "Your daddy is super nice. One of the nicest people I know, in fact. You are going to love living with him."

For the first time, the girl offered her a shy smile. "That's good."

"It is good."

They both turned at the sound of clopping hooves. A white horse and carriage were passing by them on the street, and Cassie gazed at the majestic animal in admiration.

"A horse."

At the awe in Mira's voice, Cassie, still in a crouch, shifted back around. The little girl had clasped her mittened hands together in front of her. Cassie smiled. "Do you like horses?"

"Yes. I love them."

"Have you ever gone for a carriage ride?"

Mira shook her head, the long tassel on her red wool hat swinging. "No. I always ask Mommy if we can, but she says no. She doesn't like horses."

"Well, I love them too. And do you know what? My best friend lives on a ranch with horses."

If possible, the little girl's eyes widened even more. "She's so lucky."

Cassie laughed. After everything Tala had gone through, Cassie wasn't sure she'd call her friend *lucky*, but she was certainly happy now on the ranch with Cole.

Before she could respond, Mira touched her shoulder. "Can you take me to see them sometime?"

That thought sent such a rush of longing through Cassie that for a moment she couldn't draw in a breath. As much as she wanted to, she couldn't make promises to Mira she might not be able to keep. "I'm not sure, sweetie. You'll have to ask your daddy about that, okay?"

"Ask her daddy about what?"

At Jared's quiet voice next to them, Mira pulled her hand away and Cassie stood up. "Your daughter was telling me how much she loves horses."

"Is that right?" Jared, clutching a brown, legal-sized envelope in one hand, smiled down at the girl.

"Yes. And Cassie said her friend lives on a ranch with horses, and maybe she'll take me there someday."

Cassie held up both hands. "Whoa. I didn't say that." She met Jared's gaze. "She asked, but I didn't want to make any promises. I said she'd have to talk to you about that."

"Ah." His lips twitched. "Definitely something to think about." He flicked the red tassel on Mira's wool hat. "For today, how about we take a ride in one of the carriages?"

His daughter's mouth dropped open. "Really?"

He chuckled. "We don't have to if you don't want to."

"No." She pressed her red mittens together in front of her. "I do. Please."

"All right then. Let's do it."

The three of them strolled past the rink filled with skaters and along the sidewalk bustling with people clutching bags of last-minute gifts until they reached a row of carriages lined up at the curb. Jared spoke to the driver of the one at the front of the line before helping Cassie and then Mira up onto the seat and climbing into the carriage himself. The little girl couldn't sit still but bounced from Jared's bench, which faced backwards, to Cassie's across from him, and from side to side so she could see everything they were passing by.

Jared must have paid for extra time because the horse ambled around Rockefeller Center before making its way through the traffic to Central Park. Skyscrapers taller than any Cassie had ever seen towered above the trees, and she gaped at them for a few minutes before focusing on the beautiful sights around them. By the time they'd gone halfway around the park, Mira's energy had fizzled. Maybe it had helped to have Cassie there when her mother first left her with Jared, but, if anything, Mira had inched closer to her daddy now, as though she inherently knew she could trust him. Finally, she curled up on the seat next to him, her heavy eyelids drooping.

Cassie gazed at the trees and parkland they were slowly passing by. As they'd clopped through the park over the last hour, she'd recognized a few of the landmarks she had read about when preparing for her trip—Strawberry Fields, the memorial to John Lennon, where a man with a guitar sat strumming and singing "Let it be." All the statues of writers along the Literary Walk. The Chess and Checkers House. The beautiful stone arches of Bethesda Terrace Arcade and the nearby Bethesda Fountain, one of the tallest in New York City. The bronze angel hovering over the waters and the four cherubim below it took Cassie's breath away.

And they'd passed by the gorgeous, ornate carousel, catching glimpses of horses and tigers through the openings in the brick building surrounding it. Mira had wanted to ride it, but Jared told her they would finish the carriage ride today and come back the day after Christmas to go on the carousel, which seemed to satisfy her.

Now, darkness was falling over the city, and the skyscrapers and other buildings surrounding the park had lit up and were twinkling like jewels in a massive crown.

Jared had settled the backpack on the floor at his feet and tucked the brown envelope behind it. Hopefully those were papers making the transfer of custody between Shannon and Jared official. And permanent. It wasn't really her business, but Cassie had seen too many ugly, painful custody battles playing out in court, and that was the last thing she wanted for Jared. Or sweet Mira, who was so far bearing up remarkably well, given the circumstances. Likely she would have a lot to deal with in the weeks and months to come, though. They both would. Jared would have to find a good family therapist who could help the two of them as they adapted to the radical changes in both their lives.

Jared gently nudged Cassie's boot with his, and she looked over. Mira's eyes were still closed, but she had crept closer to Jared, until her head rested just above his knee. Jared's gaze locked on Cassie's, and he whispered, "My daughter is sleeping on my leg."

The wonder in his eyes brought a smile to her lips. "I see that," she whispered back.

"This," he circled his hand around the carriage, encompassing the three of them, "might be the best day of my life." He'd been careful not to touch Mira, Cassie had noticed, but now he rested a hand tentatively on his daughter's arm. She didn't stir.

"I'm praying you and Mira will have many more best days to come."

He contemplated her in the light of the lampposts lining the road through the park. "Maybe one of them could be us coming up to visit you and see your friend's horses."

"I'd really like that."

"Me too." Jared glanced down at Mira, whose breathing had grown slow and deep, before meeting Cassie's eyes again. "Look, Cassie, I know we've just met, but I've never felt this strongly about anyone before, certainly not this quickly. I think there could be something really special between us."

Ever since losing her babies and then her parents in such a sudden, shocking way, followed by the gut-wrenching betrayal of the two people closest to her, Cassie had guarded her heart fiercely. Except that she'd forgotten to do that with Jared. From the moment he'd knocked that crazy, wonderful book out of her hand, she had been drawn to him in a way she never had been with Mack or Cole or anyone else. "I think so too."

Jared held out his free hand, and she placed her fingers in his. His eyes held that concern Fiona had pointed out to Cassie. "After what happened with Mack, that has to be terrifying for you."

Tears pricked her eyes—more of that river of sorrow seeping through the ice—but she blinked them back. "It is, but the thought of never opening my heart up again is as sad as the idea of never gazing at the stars. I don't want to live that way."

"Neither do I." Jared tugged on her hand, pulling her across the carriage to the spot next to him. When she settled in, he let go of her and wrapped an arm around her shoulders.

For several minutes, they gazed in silence at the sky, glowing in the light of a half moon and a bazillion twinkling lights. Then something caught her eye and she straightened. "Jared, look." A star was blazing across the field of lights, trailing a stream of yellow behind it.

"A shooting star." The wonder was back in his voice. "That's so"—before he could finish, another star streaked across the sky, leaving shimmering gold in its wake —"perfect." Jared's breath was warm on the top of her head. "I can't believe it. Two of them."

Cassie tipped her head to grin up at him. "Now you have to send in your next book."

He touched his lips to her forehead. "Since you've found the courage to open your heart to the possibility of getting involved with someone again, then I promise you I will send it in as soon as I get home."

"Good. Because I'm already waiting for the next book by my new favorite author."

Jared pulled her close. Cassie rested her head on his shoulder and contemplated the kaleidoscope of twinkling lights overhead, each one placed there by the very hand of God. The God who had sent someone, even someone who would rather run the other way, to those who had wandered from him to show them it wasn't too late to come back home. And the God who sent stars streaking across the sky to remind two of his children they weren't alone, that he was with them. Not because any of them deserved it, but because he was a God of grace and second chances.

And tonight, possibly the best one of *her* life, Cassie was more than happy to accept both.

A NOTE FROM THE AUTHOR

Dear Reader,

We were created to be in community, to be part of a family. But the ones who are supposed to protect and shelter us from harm often end up being the ones who cause us the most pain. Sometimes the level of betrayal is so deep that forgiveness is unimaginable. And yet every one of us who has confessed our sins to God has received forgiveness. In turn, we are to extend that grace and forgiveness to others. It may not always be safe or possible to remain in that relationship, but to save us from carrying the burdens of unforgiveness and bitterness around with us—burdens we were never meant to carry—we must, with God's help, find a way to forgive.

Between the writing of this story and the book being published, I lost a family member in a sudden, shocking way. One of the many things grief does is remind us that life is fragile and fleeting. That every day we have on this earth, every moment we are given with the people we love, is precious and worth far more than gold.

So, dear ones, I pray that if you are harboring unforgiveness toward anyone in your life, that you are able to lay it at the feet of Jesus. And I pray that you will take every opportunity to tell those closest to you that you love them and you are grateful they are part of your life.

This Christmas and every day of the year, may you experience the unfathomable peace that comes from knowing that, wherever we go, whether we flee from God or run toward Him, he is always there, waiting for us, loving us, forgiving us, and welcoming us back home.

Blessings,
     Sara

ABOUT SARA DAVISON

SARA DAVISON has a passion for writing stories that keep readers on the edge of their seats—and maybe swooning a little. Beyond that, she longs for readers to discover, as her characters do, that whatever they are going through, they are never alone. God is always with them. A finalist for more than a dozen national writing awards, Davison is a Cascade, Word, and two-time Carol Award winner for romantic suspense. She lives in Ontario with her husband, Michael. Like every good Canadian, she loves coffee, hockey, poutine, and apologizing for no particular reason.

Get to know Sara better and subscribe to her short, monthly newsletter at www.saradavison.org.

TITLES BY SARA DAVISON

THE MOSAIC COLLECTION: NOVELS
Rose Tattoo Trilogy
Lost Down Deep
Written in Ink

two sparrows for a penny series
Every Star in the Sky
Every Flower of the Field

THE MOSAIC COLLECTION: ANTHOLOGY STORIES
"Taste of Heaven"
(*Hope is Born: A Mosaic Christmas Anthology*)
"Ten Bottles of Sand"
(*Before Summer's End: Stories to Touch the Soul*)
"Sixty Feet to Home"
(*A Star Will Rise: A Mosaic Christmas Anthology II*)
"I'd Like to Thank the Academy"
(*Song of Grace: Stories to Amaze the Soul*)
"Scarlet"
(*All Things New: Stories to Refresh the Soul*)
"A Single Spark of Light"
(*A Whisper of Peace: A Mosaic Christmas Anthology IV*)
"The Poppy"
(*Dancing in the Rain: Stories to Shelter the Soul*)

"The Other Way"
(*A Thrill in the Air: A Mosaic Christmas Anthology V*)

THE NIGHT GUARDIANS SERIES
Vigilant
Guarded
Driven
Forged

THE SEVEN TRILOGY
The End Begins
The Darkness Deepens
The Morning Star Rises

UPCOMING
The Color of Sky and Stone
Every Bird That Falls
Sharp Like Glass

THE HOME FOR CHRISTMAS CHALLENGE

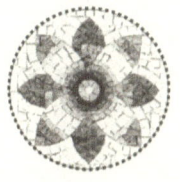

Brenda S. Anderson

* * *

A Coming Home Series short story

Christmas isn't Christmas without drama, and this season might be the worst of all.

Dating hasn't been on Lee Aldrich's mind since Amelia's mother abandoned the two of them over thirteen years ago. Since it's the last year before his daughter heads off to college, he wants to make the upcoming holiday season memorable. Unfortunately, Amelia has other plans, beginning with a blind date for Lee. A date that stirs up memories of the past that he has no desire to revisit.

But if Lee wants to have Christmas with his daughter, he and his date need to accept Amelia's Home for Christmas Challenge. As the months pass, Christmas nears, and the challenges continue, forcing Lee to face hard truths. If he doesn't meet the truth head on, he risks losing what he cherishes the most.

Therefore, confess your sins to one another and pray for one another, that you may be healed. The prayer of a righteous person has great power as it is working.

James 5:16

CHAPTER ONE

The father-daughter roles had been flipped on their head.

Lee Aldrich chuckled as he examined the clothes arranged neatly on his bed. A decade ago he'd done the same for Amelia for her first years of school. Now she was caring for him, although he wasn't terribly happy with the reason.

What kind of daughter sets her dad up on a blind date?

Apparently, his.

He dressed in the outfit Amelia had picked out for him during their excruciating afternoon of shopping. He would rather stick his finger in a live socket than go through that torture again.

The date tonight was going to be a different kind of torture. He didn't need a woman to fulfill him, hadn't since Elise had walked out on him thirteen years ago. But he'd do anything to please his daughter, even go on a lousy blind date.

A knock sounded on his bedroom door.

"Come in," he said, knowing it would be Amelia.

She breezed inside the room, and her gaze traveled from his black captain shoes to his new jeans, a blue button-down shirt, and then his hair she'd styled like Chris Evans's. Or so she claimed. Hey, if it was good enough for Captain America . . .

"You approve?" He crossed his arms, uncomfortable with the scrutiny.

She scrunched her lips and waved a finger, indicating she wanted him to turn around.

With a loud sigh, he obeyed, then turned back and splayed his arms. "If this isn't good enough, we can always call off the evening."

"Don't you wish." Finally, she grinned. "You look passable."

"Gee thanks."

"No, seriously, you look amazing. Who knew an electrician could clean up so nice?"

"Why do I feel like I'm being insulted?" With a grunt, he grabbed his wallet and phone off of his dresser and stuffed them in his back pockets.

"Sorry, that's not what I meant. You look fabulous. No qualifiers." She wrapped an arm in his and led him out to the living room, where she straightened his collar. "Promise you won't be home before ten."

"Ten oh one it is, then." That would be nearly two hours with a stranger. Wasn't that long enough?

At least Amelia had chosen Lee's favorite steak restaurant in Brainerd, one that wouldn't be too loud to hear each other. Hopefully, this woman could hold up her end in a conversation.

"Fine." She gestured toward the door leading to the garage. "Time to go, or you'll be late and set a bad first impression."

"I'm going." He raised his hands in surrender and aimed for the garage. "What's her name again?" He grinned as he listened for her response.

"Nuh-uh. I know you. I give you her name, and you're doing a google search to learn all about her and ruin the surprise. All you need to know is that you're perfect for each other. Her daughter agrees."

Lee had no response to that as he escaped the house and climbed into his pickup. He backed out of the garage and onto a quiet Granite Creek street that had changed little since his once-intact family moved there over thirteen years ago.

After all these years, why did Amelia need him to date now? At the beginning of his single parenthood, he'd longed for a helpmeet, a woman who would be a mom to Amelia, yet they'd survived the pre-teen and now most of the teen years with barely a hiccup.

All he knew was that he had no desire to date. Over the next year, he had one goal, and that was to make it a memorable year for him and Amelia before she left him for college. How could his daughter be old enough for college already? Wasn't she born just a year or two ago?

Work had gotten in the way too often, but raising a daughter while running your own electric business wasn't easy, even if Amelia spent half her weekends and holidays with her mother. This year, though . . . this year was for Amelia. Not for his customers, and certainly not for some stranger Amelia wanted him to meet.

He pulled onto the Minnesota state highway that was less crowded, since Labor Day had just passed and all the cabin owners had closed up for the season. He headed toward Brainerd and his date. If Amelia wanted him to meet someone, he'd appease her. He'd even try to be on his best behavior. Chances were, this woman was as thrilled to meet him as he was to meet her. He'd behave like a gentleman and treat a woman as she deserved, even if it was just one evening.

In his rearview mirror, he watched the sun edge toward the horizon, a beautiful way to cap off this early September day and a reminder that God was still in charge. Something he'd come to believe after his family fell apart.

He drummed his fingers on the steering wheel. What attitude would God want him to have tonight, beyond treating this woman as a precious child of God?

"You're going to have to help me with that." With a smirk, he briefly looked up.

The miles passed, the town drew near, and butterflies took flight in his gut. He was nervous? Didn't that mean he wanted to make a good impression, that maybe getting to know someone was a good idea? Life had to be more than working, and when Amelia left for college in a year, he'd be alone.

Alone. He gulped at the idea. Yeah, Amelia was right about this. A slow smile crept to his face. If tonight didn't work out, maybe he'd start putting himself out there, sign up for one of those online dating services. He laughed at that. Nah, technological dating wasn't for him. All that mattered was that he enjoyed the evening.

At last, the restaurant came into view, nestled among woods that surrounded one of the many lakes in the area. His stomach growled in anticipation of the steak.

He parked his pickup and glanced in the rearview mirror to check his hair. Dang, he was nervous. He climbed out, smoothed wrinkles on his shirt, then made his way inside.

The host, dressed mostly in black, greeted him with a smile. "Good evening. Do you have reservations?"

"I do." He gave his name. "I'm meeting someone and requested the corner booth with the lake view." That was what Amelia had told him anyway.

"Of course." She made a mark on the tablet in front of her and grabbed a menu. "Right this way."

Lee followed her through the dimly lit room filled with patrons speaking in hushed tones. A perfect setting for a date. They'd be able to talk and be heard. The scent of steak wafted toward him, and his stomach growled. Regardless of how the date went, he'd be happy to have a good piece of meat.

Someone already sat in the booth the host directed him to, with her back to him. Wavy blond locks that fell to narrow shoulders and slender arms, hands that already held a menu. This was a good start.

But what he'd give for some water right now, to calm nerves jumping as bad as a school kid's. "I will have a good night tonight," he whispered to himself to calm the jitters. If something came of the evening, he'd thank his daughter. And if it turned out to be a dud, maybe he'd let Amelia set him up again. Or maybe not.

Elise Kraemer tapped her manicured fingers on the table while staring out the window at Gull Lake brimming with boats, pontoons, and jet skis. Why she'd bothered with a manicure for a stranger, she didn't know. It wasn't as if she'd ever had difficulty attracting men, and not a one had cared about her fingernails.

They'd been more allured by her medical degree and her bank account, which had taught her to give up on the dating life.

But she'd do anything for Amelia.

"Hello, I'm supposed to—"

Her eyes widened as she turned toward the too-familiar voice, and her mouth hung open.

Oh, Amelia was in big trouble.

"Well." She cleared her throat and regained her voice. "If it isn't Leopold Aldrich?" Her ex. And her daughter's father.

Smirking, she gestured to the seat across from her. Their little sneak of a daughter was going to be grounded for life.

He crossed his arms and glowered down at her. "This was a mistake."

"Oh, no it wasn't." Amelia's voice came from behind Lee. Elise had been so focused on the man hovering above her, she hadn't noticed Amelia sneak up behind him.

Lee spun toward their daughter, his jaw tight. That informed Elise he was holding back a good tongue lashing.

"Uh-uh." Amelia wagged her finger and nodded toward the booth. "This is where you put on your big boy pants and sit down."

Elise chuckled. Their daughter had inherited Elise's temperament, that was for certain. She covered her mouth to hide her grin, even though she actually agreed with Lee that this—whatever *this* was—was a mistake.

He sat, that glower taking over his still-handsome face. No doubt, he was cooking up some punishment for when the two arrived home. Good thing for Amelia that tonight was Lee's night with her because the punishment Elise would dole out wouldn't be as charitable as his.

Elise scooted over for Amelia to sit, but she pulled up a chair and sat at the table's end instead.

"I won't be long." Amelia opened her massive purse, removed two notebooks, and handed one to her and the other to Lee. On the front of each, someone had scribbled "Home for Christmas Challenge." Perhaps written by one of the children Amelia babysat. "Since I plan to become a teacher, I figured now is a good time to start practicing giving out homework."

Uh-oh. Elise opened the book—a journal, actually—to the first page. Amelia had written "Find Your Center" at the top in all caps.

"What do you mean by this?" Lee practically took the words out of Elise's mouth.

"What do you think it means?" Amelia rested her elbows on the table and her chin on her folded hands.

The impertinent child. Oh, she was too much like her mother.

Elise paged through the rest of the journal. All blank.

"Sounds like some new age gobbledygook, if you ask me." Lee closed the notebook.

"You know me better than that." She took Lee's journal and wrote *Matthew 6:33* below the title. "There. That's the only hint the two of you are getting."

Oh, their child looked awfully smug sitting there, her arms crossed.

"When and where do we turn in this homework?" Lee grumbled like he'd done back in high school over any assignment. He liked problems with numbers and hard facts that to him were easily solved, not something vague.

"You have until this Thursday."

Elise opened the calendar on her phone, and Lee did the same.

"Oh, you're both free. I already added it to your schedules."

"What?" Lee jabbed at his phone. "You hacked my phone?"

"Well, it does sync with that co-parenting app you guys are signed up for."

"Oh," Lee mumbled.

Elise just stared at the entry on her phone. *Homework assignment #1 due* was highlighted in bright blue. Under *Location*, the calendar read *Paul Bunyan State Trail, Picnic Shelter*.

"And if we don't do the homework?" Lee beat her to the question.

Amelia pulled out her phone and tapped at it. "As you know, my eighteenth birthday is coming soon."

Elise knew that all too well. Her spirited daughter was about to leave her an empty nester, which was why she'd agreed to this so-called date in the first place. Even though

Amelia spent much more time at Lee's, her too-large house was going to feel awfully empty.

"What does your birthday have to do with this?" Elise waved her hand over the notebook and gestured to Lee. "With us?"

Amelia sat back in her chair, her sassy demeanor suddenly replaced with a flatlined mouth and dark eyes. "Katie is spending Christmas vacation with her aunt and uncle in New York, and she's invited me to go with her."

Elise glanced at her calendar again. Winter break began a day before Amelia turned eighteen, which was nine days before Christmas, and ended January second. Her daughter couldn't mean the entire vacation, could she? She studied her daughter's face, then dared look across at Lee. Clearly, he'd drawn the same conclusion, that their daughter was blackmailing them.

Lee laid down his phone and ran a hand down his face that held a perpetual frown, then stared at their daughter. "What about Christmas at Aunt Lydia's? We've been planning that week at the ranch for over a year?"

"I guess that depends upon you," Amelia said, her face expressionless.

"Okay, then. What's your goal?" Such a Lee question. "Because if it's that you want the two of us back together . . ."

"Would that be so bad?" A tear hovered beneath Amelia's eye, and she blinked it away.

Oh, yes it would. "Sweetheart." Elise slid from her seat and wrapped Amelia in a hug. "No matter what you bribe us with, your father and I aren't getting back together."

Amelia shrugged out of Elise's hug. She raised her chin and stood. "That's your choice. But also know, on my next birthday I'll be an adult, so I can make my own choices as well."

Their daughter spun and stalked from the restaurant, drawing stares from other diners.

Well, this was a mess. Elise slunk onto the bench and bowed her head. The air seemed to close in around her, stealing her breath. They couldn't miss Amelia's birthday or her last Christmas at home before going off to college, but her demands were too high. No way could Elise or Lee afford paying them.

Which meant she'd spend the rest of the evening on her knees, beseeching God for a solution. She grabbed her clutch and began to slide from the bench.

Lee's phone pinged, and his frown deepened.

"Is there another problem?" Elise hovered on the edge, wanting to leave, but her gut—or was it her conscience?—told her to stay.

Lee chuckled. Shook his head. "I'd promised her I wouldn't be home before ten, which means I have an hour and a half to kill."

"Sorry about that." Just because Lee had to stay late didn't mean she had to. She needed to get outside where she could breathe again. "Enjoy your steak."

"Yeah, there is that. The night won't be a total waste."

"I guess not." Elise serpentined around the tables and out of the restaurant, where she finally filled her lungs with fresh air. She'd meant it when she said they couldn't get back together, not when it was her fault that they'd broken up in the first place.

CHAPTER TWO

What a mess.

Lee picked up the menu and reminded himself of the words he'd thought when entering tonight. If the date was a dud, at least he'd have steak.

Tonight hadn't been a dud, though. It had been an implosion.

How could Amelia begin to think that he and Elise would get back together? His heart hadn't recovered from what she'd done to him thirteen years ago. Probably never would.

He glanced at the menu, his gaze scrolling down until he found what his watering mouth wanted: the filet mignon with buttery mashed potatoes and the chef's choice of veggie. Yeah, it was pricy, but after what Amelia had just put him through, it was worth the cost. He might even have an adult beverage to go with it. He'd planned on ordering wine with his date, but he'd settle for a beer.

He studied the beverage menu. Elise would have liked the cabernet sauvignon from Geyser Peak in California. Berry, chocolate, and smooth.

"Am I driving you to drink?"

Startled by Elise's voice, he dropped the menu and was struck mute as she slid in across from him.

"Let me see what they have." She took the menu from him and scanned it as if everything was natural rather than upside down and inside out.

"What are you—"

"That cabernet sauvignon from Geyser Peak sounds divine." She set down the drink menu and reached for the one with food. "What do you recommend? I'm assuming it's still a favorite place."

"Time-out here." He gave the time-out signal with his hands. "I thought you were leaving. I was going to enjoy a steak in silence."

She just shrugged. "I felt sorry for you. What can I say?"

"That you'll leave?" *Please?*

"Sorry. I think that promise you made to Amelia was for both of us." She set the menu down and smiled at him in a way that made his gut churn. "I can't be the reason you didn't keep it."

"Like you've kept your commitments in the past?"

She blinked and nodded. "Touché."

He sighed. That was a low blow that the Lee from thirteen years ago would have delivered, not the new, redeemed Lee. "Sorry."

"It's the truth." She shrugged as if he hadn't hurt her, but her silence and her intense focus on the menu indicated he'd hit her right where he'd been aiming.

"I hear their salmon is amazing," Lee said. Talking food worked as an apology, didn't it?

She flipped the menu closed. "Then salmon it is." She raised her gaze to his. "It's true that I came back because Amelia would have wanted it."

"Yes, but—"

"But we didn't listen closely."

"Are you ready to order?" Somehow the waitress had snuck up to the table without his noticing. They both ordered, and Lee informed the server to put it all on one bill, in spite of Elise's protests. Call him old fashioned, but he still believed a guy should pay for his date. Once upon a time, Elise had appreciated that, until her profession had changed her.

After the server left, Elise leaned toward him, resuming where they'd left off. "Our assignment isn't to get back together, even if that's what she ultimately wants, but it's simply to do the assignments."

"That sounds deceptive." And he wouldn't lie to Amelia.

"Not if we're up front with our intentions."

He considered that. If they told Amelia up front, which they already had, that there would be no reconciliation, that wouldn't be deceptive. Elise's plan could work.

"Okay, then." Lee flipped open the notebook and read out loud. "Find your center, Matthew 6:33." For the life of him, he couldn't memorize scripture. He opened his Bible app to look it up.

"That one's easy." Elise raised her brows in that way of hers that told others she was superior. "'But seek first the kingdom of God and his righteousness, and all these things will be added to you.'"

Startled, he gaped at Elise. She didn't have her phone out to search for the verse. "You know that one?"

"You'd be surprised at what I know."

"I'm surprised you even read the Bible."

She patted her heart. "Another well-aimed shot."

Oh, man, he was being an idiot, but seriously, when they had been together, her focus was all about science and God's being a crutch or proof of people's low intelligence. Still, he felt like sinking into the floor. If only they still had the menu so he could distract himself.

"You really didn't know?"

He forced his gaze to Elise and shook his head.

"Two years ago." Her face lit up with a genuine smile, with eyes that shone. "I realized that God and science weren't mutually exclusive but rather the opposite. Your daughter had something to do with that. She's quite the evangelist."

"Tell me about it." Although his conversion had taken place shortly after Elise left him and Amelia, thanks to Katie, Amelia's best friend then and now. His faith in Christ was the only thing that got him through those first years of being a single dad.

To a child that both he and Elise loved. They could put aside their differences for a few months, couldn't they? After all, they'd once been best friends. It wouldn't hurt either of them to get along for Amelia's sake.

He tapped the notebook. "You game?"

Elise showed a half smile. "Anything to keep our daughter home for Christmas." Her smile grew to a grin. "Even if it means spending time with you."

"Then Thursday is a date."

"No." She shook her head, a bit too vehemently, in his opinion. "Not a date. But I'll see you at the park."

Lee peddled hard for the last mile of the Paul Bunyan Trail, the reds, oranges, and yellows of fall exploding around him. Reminded him of when he'd first met Elise back in grade school. He was biking with his family, and his little sister lost her balance and fell. Elise happened to be biking toward them and saw the mishap. She was only eight years old at the time, yet she'd braked and hurried to help Lydia. She'd pulled a small first-aid kit from her fanny pack and taken care of the scrape.

Even as a nine-year-old, Lee had been impressed. Had his first crush. After that, Lee and Elise had been inseparable.

Until she'd cleaved them apart with the precision of a surgeon.

Affairs will do that to a couple.

He shook off that thought and banished the anger that frequently made its appearance at the thought of Elise.

Which was why this Home for Christmas Challenge made him more nervous than the blind date had. That evening had ended okay. They'd managed to play nice, enjoy their meals, and talk mostly about their daughter. He'd even held his tongue when Elise had left herself wide open for criticism. That meant he was growing, right?

Or did it mean he had a whole bunch of room to grow yet?

Probably a little of both.

Regardless, spending any time with someone he'd learned to despise wasn't something he looked forward to, but he'd made the sacrifice for Amelia.

He arrived at the shelter ten minutes prior to their scheduled time and was pleased to see that it was empty. That would give him time to prepare spiritually. After all, considering Amelia's assignment, that was what this evening was about.

He dismounted his bike, tugged off his helmet, and steered into the shelter that overlooked the Mississippi. He parked his bike beside a picnic table and removed Amelia's notebook from his backpack.

Beneath the words *Find Your Center* and the Bible verse from Matthew 6:33, he'd drawn a circle and placed a cross in the middle. After that, he'd poured out tough truths. Too often he was his own center, or Amelia, or his work. They all took the place where God belonged. The fact that his daughter made this part of his assignment meant that she could easily see his focus was off.

He'd already initiated making the changes in his life. Praying and reading the Bible the first thing every morning. Holding conversations with God throughout the day. Bringing everything—his praises and his problems—to God and laying them at His feet. For someone who liked to be in control, that was difficult but necessary.

No doubt, Elise was struggling with the same issues.

On his phone, he opened his Bible app to Luke 10. He now began his day with Proverbs and ended with the Psalms. This year, he was working his way through the rest of the Bible chronologically. Sandwiching the daily reading with Psalms and Proverbs had given him a new perspective.

Reading about Martha and her need for control gave him a different perspective of himself.

"Hey there."

Lee pulled his attention from his phone and looked back at Amelia. He patted the bench beside himself. "How was school?"

She shrugged. "Just school. When I'm a teacher, I'm going to make it interesting."

"I'm sure you will." Lee gave his daughter a hug, then glanced at the clock on his phone. Ten minutes after six already. For the ultra-precise Elise, that was unconscionably late. "Any sign of your mom yet?"

"No." Amelia checked her phone, and worry drew her brows together. "And no message either. She told me she wasn't on call, so that shouldn't be a problem, and even when she is called in, she always lets me know."

"I'm sure it's nothing." He held up the notebook. "But this sure wasn't." Then he attempted to distract Amelia by talking about what he'd learned this week, but couldn't help noticing her frequent looks back and peeking at her phone.

To be honest, when his phone showed six thirty, concern

nagged at him as well. "You don't suppose she stood us up, do you?"

"I thought of that." Amelia worried her lower lip. "But she messaged me this morning. Said she'd be here."

"Do you have a tracker on your phone?" Amelia was able to track his whereabouts and he hers.

"Ha! When I told Mom you'd let me follow you, she laughed."

"Has she ever done this before? Just not shown up for something?"

"Never. Not without letting me know."

"Maybe she went to the wrong picnic shelter. This isn't the only one."

"I sent her the map earlier, just like I did you. She said she knows right where it is."

He took his daughter's hand. "I'm sure it's nothing, but let's pray."

Amelia nodded.

Lee looked out over the mighty river as he brought Elise to God. "You know where she is, Lord. Protect her and strengthen our faith to trust in You." They continued praying for several more minutes as the sun crept down the horizon. Time ticked past, and full-blown worry now ate at his gut.

He couldn't sit and wait any longer. "Let's head over to her place." He didn't know what he expected to find, but he couldn't sit here and do nothing.

"I don't want to drive." Her voice trembled.

"That's okay. We'll take my pickup and get your car later."

With one arm around Amelia's shoulder and one hand balancing his bike, he hurried to the parking lot. He secured his bike in the truck bed, then hopped in the cab and hit the ignition button just as Amelia's phone sang.

"It's Mom!" She stabbed at the phone and answered. "Where are you?"

Lee heard mumbling on the other end of the phone, but couldn't make it out. "Can you put her on speaker?"

Amelia hit the speaker button. "Dad's listening now. Could you repeat?"

"Sorry I'm not there." Her voice was still shrouded by what sounded like heavy traffic. Had she been in an accident? That was what had continuously crossed Lee's mind.

"A bear ran out in—"

"You were hit by a bear?" Lee turned off the pickup so he could hear better.

She sighed dramatically, a trait he remembered too well. "If you'd listen, you'd hear the story."

"Fine. Zipping my lips."

"The car in front of me hit a bear. I had to stop and make sure everyone was okay."

Oh. Of course she had to. He wouldn't expect anything else.

"And calling you wasn't on my mind."

Amelie sniffled. "We were so worried."

"We?" Elise said with a happy lilt. "You do care, Lee."

He snorted, but couldn't come up with a clever retort, so instead he said, "So, you're okay? What about the people in the car?"

"What about the bear?" Naturally, Amelia worried about the animal.

"The family is okay. Just superficial injuries. Nothing that requires hospitalization or surgery, but I did recommend they get checked out at the hospital."

"What about the bear?" Amelie's voice grew insistent.

"I'm sorry, hon. He ran off and the authorities are searching for him. But I'm afraid his injuries will be too severe."

Lee wasn't surprised to see the trail of tears roll down

Amelia's cheeks. If he'd been telling the story, he'd have left that last part off.

"Do you mind if I beg off for the night, though, sweetheart? I'm used to dealing with injuries but not witnessing what brought them about, and I'm exhausted."

Amelia wiped at her eyes. "That's okay, if you can just tell us what you learned. Dad learned he has to stop putting himself at the center. That he needs to put God there instead."

Elise laughed. "Your father and I are too much alike in that respect."

Wasn't that the truth?

"I'm working on seeking God first. Was even praying as I was driving, and that's when I saw the accident. I know He put me here at this specific time."

"Then you both get A's on your first assignment."

Lee flexed his arm. "Of course, I did."

"Yeah, don't go getting a big head, Leopold."

He chuckled at the name that always humbled him, especially when Elise used it.

"This next assignment should be an easy one, but it's super important." Amelia pressed and swiped at her phone. "The next class is scheduled for three weeks from now, Friday. It's on both of your calendars. You'll find the details there."

"Very good." An engine roared on Elise's end. Showing off the power of her BMW, no doubt. "I'll be there." Elise's phone went silent.

Abrupt. Typical.

"You good driving home, kiddo?"

"Sure." She opened the door and slid out. "See you at home."

He watched her go to her shiny red Mazda coupe that Elise had spoiled her with when Amelia passed her driver's test. At least, Lee didn't have to pay the insurance. Amelia drove off, then Lee opened the family app schedule and looked up the next assignment. A Friday night football game at the high school. That wouldn't be too awful. The crowd would be too loud for them to have any conversation. He could just enjoy the game.

Then he read the assignment. "You've found your center. Yay! Now it's time to add to your team (think football). Bring their names and positions to the game and be prepared to tell me why you chose them. Also, bring your phone records to prove you've been in contact with them. Go Team Lee!"

Lee placed his phone in the center console and stared straight ahead into a night sky that had grown dark, save for the first twinkles of stars. A light shot through the sky. A shooting star? Was that a sign of some kind?

Who knew? What he did know was that Amelia was wrong. This next assignment wasn't an easy one. Over the years he'd become a loner, with all his efforts going to Amelia and his career. He didn't have a team, and clearly his very wise daughter knew that.

CHAPTER THREE

Elise strode toward the ticket booth, trying to recall the last time she'd attended a high school football game. Probably twenty-seven years ago during her senior year of high school. She and Lee had attended every game from that first one of their sophomore year when their relationship took a turn.

She almost blushed thinking about those young-and-in-love days. Part of her would love to recapture that feeling again. Just not with Lee.

"Mom." Amelia jogged toward her, with Katie and her younger sister lagging behind.

Interesting to see those two here. They attended the same small-town school that Amelia did. Choosing a school had resulted in many an argument between Elise and Lee. She wanted Amelia to attend the private school in Brainerd. Lee wanted her in the Granite Creek school system where his friend, and Katie's dad, was the principal.

Lee had eventually won that argument, mostly because he was the one who would have to drive Amelia to school. For years, Elise had held a grudge, but only recently had she admitted Lee's choice was best.

Oh, she'd hated Lee winning at anything. How very selfish she'd been. About so much more than school.

"Mom!" Amelia waved a piece of paper in Elise's face. "You daydreaming or something?"

Elise shook her head. "Or something." She smiled at Katie and Lilly who'd finally caught up. "I'm surprised to see you two here tonight."

"Katie has a boyfriend," Lilly said in a singsong tone, her entire face lighting up with her grin.

Katie looked down but not before Elise caught her blush. "He's playing tonight."

"How fun. I hope you girls enjoy your evening. Tell your parents hello."

"I will!" Lilly bounded away, and Katie sighed. "I'm going to be spending more time watching her than the game."

Oh, the challenges a child with Down syndrome brought. Elise had seen it often in her work with pediatrics, but Katie handled it well, and Lilly was a big part of Amelia's decision to become a special ed teacher. Which made Elise and Lee proud.

Speaking of Lee . . . she sighed. It was time to get her ticket and find him. She aimed for the ticket booth again.

"Mo-om." Agitation rang in Amelia's voice as she waved the paper in Elise's face again. "I have your ticket already."

"Oh, that's what that is. How nice of you to buy a ticket for me."

"Not from me, silly. Dad bought it. He said it was tradition."

Elise stilled, nodded. Other things were tradition, too. "I believe I know where he's sitting."

She hurried away from her daughter, toward the entrance. They'd always sat in the same spot in the bleachers. He'd treated her to whatever food she wanted. He'd been old fashioned in that way. Once upon a time, she'd appreciated that in his character, until her ego had gotten in the way.

She shoved that thought away as she entered the stadium and hung a right. Too often, she beat herself up, but her team —the one she'd organized, thanks to Amelia—was helping her to get over that, to see that she was redeemed and beloved, even with all her baggage.

She kept her gaze forward as she walked past three sets of steps, then took the last set up to the top to the far end of the bleachers.

Their spot.

Lee was there, of course, with the homework notebook on his lap. Hers was in her tote bag that she set at her feet. He handed her a bag of popcorn. "Can't break with tradition."

No, no they couldn't. Without saying anything, she sat, keeping an Amelia-sized space between them. This was too familiar, and it made her heart pump to a wacky beat that no patient monitor could follow.

"Are you okay?" Lee asked with his mouth full, a habit he still hadn't broken. It still irritated her.

"I'm fine," she said in a clipped manner.

"I can tell."

With that tone, she could almost see him roll his eyes.

"I'm sorry," they both said at the same time.

And she glanced his way. "That was uncalled for. I'm just trying to work through this homework Amelia has us doing."

"And the locations."

"Yes, that. The supper club you took me to on our first date."

"That didn't even cross my mind that night, but I did think about meeting you on that bike path where you stopped to help my sister."

"How is Lydia doing, by the way?"

He grinned. "Happy as can be with her five kids and cowboy husband in Wyoming."

"I never pictured her to be a rancher."

"Me neither, but God had other plans."

Yes, He did. "And now there's here." Elise looked out over the stadium filling up with blue and white. She'd intentionally chosen a blue sweatshirt for the night to match. As had Lee. As they always had since that very first game, sitting in this very spot where they'd shared their first kiss and their relationship had crossed over from best friends as naturally as night giving way to day.

"What happened to us, Elise?"

She felt his intense gaze on her but refused to turn his way, refused to reply when he full well knew the answer.

"Things were off long before . . ." He shrugged. "Well, you know."

The affair. He never could name it, as if saying it aloud made her deceit more painful. Now, that once-gorgeous cardiac surgeon she'd thrown her marriage away for had a keg-sized belly and not a lick of hair, while Lee . . .

She stole a quick glance at the man beside her. Strands of gray colored the hair by his temple, and his hairline might be receding a bit, but that didn't detract from his look. Actually, it made him very attractive. He'd never had a six-pack but had always kept himself in shape. Still did. It was a wonder no woman had snatched him up since their breakup.

But Lee was right about the affair. That had been the tip of their melting iceberg. "Do you think, if we'd gotten married, things would have turned out differently? I know I wouldn't have found it as easy to leave."

He shrugged. "I've thought about that but doubt it would have saved us."

"I've learned only Jesus can do that."

His eyes connected with hers, and that familiar feeling of

butterflies taking flight awakened in her belly. As much as she wanted to turn away, she couldn't, and for the life of her, she couldn't shake the desire of wanting him to kiss her like he had the first night here and then every Friday football game thereafter.

"Hey, Lee and Elise. Still in your ol' make-out spot, I see."

Elise tore her gaze from Lee and looked back. Squinted. "Benji?"

The rotund man laughed. "I go by Ben now, but yeah. How you two doing? Haven't seen you for forever."

Lee stood and shook the man's beefy hand. "We're well. And you?"

She appreciated that Lee didn't go into their sordid history. A stranger didn't need to know the details.

"Well, Hannah and I got married, had a couple kids. First grandkid is on the way. Life's treated us well."

"That's good to hear." Lee looked beyond the man's shoulder. "And here comes our daughter, Amelia."

The man turned and nodded. "Nice to meet you, young lady. Your folks used to steam up the bleachers here, back in the day."

Oh brother.

Amelia's face turned a bright red. Time to say goodbye to Benji before he embarrassed them further.

She forced a smile and held out her hand. "It was good seeing you again. You'll have to greet Hannah for us."

"I'll do that. Too bad she's not here. She'd love to see you both. Enjoy the game. Go Warriors!"

"Go Warriors," Lee repeated with half the enthusiasm, as the man bounded down the bleacher steps, shaking the seats as he went.

Then Amelia glanced between them. "Seriously? What if I came here with my boyfriend and made out?"

"Boyfriend?" Elise's eyes went wide and she plopped down on the bench.

"Fictitious boyfriend, okay, but geez, you two were that couple? You just said you shared your first kiss here."

Elise felt her own face grow red. "Well, that and a few other . . ." Elise cleared her throat. ". . . kisses." Her daughter didn't need to know all the details.

"Oh brother." Amelia rolled her eyes as only a teenaged girl can do, then she pointed to the now-narrow gap between Lee and Elise. "Mind if I squeeze in here? Nice to see you two getting along."

Elise scooted over. If only Amelia knew how very well she and Lee had been getting along before Benji came along and ruined their moment, she might have stayed away. Elise didn't know whether she should be angry at the man or thankful.

Music blasted through the loudspeakers, and a voice boomed over that, announcing the home team as the players ran onto the field flanked by the cheer team. Cheers erupted from the crowd, and the bleachers began filling in. The announcer welcomed the visiting team, who were greeted with boos.

From there on in, talking would be futile. Guess that was why she and Lee had spent the game making out. She smiled at the memory, but if they ever caught Amelia behaving that way? She'd be grounded until the end of the school year.

Oh, the two of them had done so many things wrong. It was a wonder they'd lasted at all. Nothing that broken could be fixed, could it?

Amelia pointed to Elise's tote bag and practically yelled, "Got your homework?"

Elise nodded and pulled out her notebook, then handed it to her daughter. She'd established a team, though it hadn't been easy, not when so many of her relationships with men and women were superficial.

Elise had spoken with Luella—a woman at church, whom she'd long admired—about being Elise's mentor. Luella had eagerly said yes and had taken her role to heart by connecting with Elise every few days. Then there was Gloria, the new nurse in the NICU section of the hospital, who was always praying for the babies. She had gladly agreed to be a prayer warrior. The last one had been tough. She wanted a mom who would be willing to speak difficult truths to Elise and finally asked Katie's mom—who happened to be a marriage and family counselor. Debbie said she'd be honored to be the truth teller on Elise's team.

Amelia studied both notebooks as the game got underway. After a few minutes, she placed the open books side by side and pointed to two names: Debbie and Jerry. Katie's parents. Then her finger underlined the name, Marcus, the man who'd given Lee a job after Elise left him. He also happened to be Katie's uncle.

That young woman and her family sure had made an impact on Elise's broken family's life.

Amelia found a marker in her own bag and drew a big A+ on each page as the crowd cheered during a long run play.

Lee grinned, and Elise felt pretty proud herself. Before they knew it, this challenge would be done, and life would go back to the way it was before, without the Lee distraction.

That shouldn't make her sad, but it did.

Her phone pinged, and apparently Lee's did as well, and they each awoke their phones. A text from Amelia. Well, that was one way to communicate in the middle of a crowd.

It read:

Your next class session is scheduled for November first. Check the date for your assignment.

Elise quickly opened the calendar and scrolled to November. She read the assignment, and her heart dropped. It fell even further when she read the location: Cameron Park in

Bemidji. The place where Lee had gotten down on one knee and asked her to move in with him. She'd found it romantic and believed that living together made much more sense than wasting money on a wedding.

Of all the mistakes the two of them had made, that was probably the worst and was the beginning of their downfall.

Now she'd have to face that dreadful moment once again.

Even as cheers filled the stadium following a touchdown by the home team, Lee felt sick as he read the instructions for their next assignment. It was bad enough that Amelia wanted them to meet at the place where he'd made such a stupid decision. They easily could have gone to a justice of the peace to get married, but no, they were modern and didn't need that license.

And they'd had no faith to ground or inform them.

What was worse, though, was the homework. It was titled "What I Did Wrong" with specific instructions to be honest about his part in the breakup. He'd never faced that truth before and wasn't sure he could bear it now. But he'd do whatever he had to in order to keep his daughter home for Christmas, even if it meant he learned that he was just as responsible for tearing up their family as Elise was.

CHAPTER FOUR

It was his fault.

Lee gazed out the window of his pickup at Cameron Park. Typical for November first, temps in the thirties with light snowflakes. Elise and Amelia had stayed the previous night at a hotel because she had a feeling she wouldn't want to drive home.

Snowflakes gathered on his front window, beginning to block his view of the park. With temperatures playing yo-yo with the freezing mark, he'd stay in the warm truck until Elise and Amelia arrived.

How was he going to tell her what he'd realized? That had been his prayer these past weeks. His team members' prayer as well. God sure had a way of shining the light on truth. Why did it have to be so painful?

He prayed still as he waited for Elise to arrive with Amelia. Hopefully, those two were enjoying their weekend in Bemidji. Their relationship had changed over the last months. They'd both matured, it seemed, and part of him envied their closeness, but mostly he was glad for Amelia to have the mother-daughter relationship she'd long desired. He prayed over them and this afternoon, that God would use all of them in a mighty way.

Elise laughed at Amelia's joke as they turned into the parking lot at Cameron Park. The levity sure helped prepare her for this coming "class" with Lee. She wasn't sure what Amelia expected, but she'd find out soon. What she did know was that her daughter would make a great counselor. These exercises the past couple of months had helped clear so much baggage from her mind and heart. She hadn't felt this light or free since high school.

And now witnessing the maturity of her daughter, there'd been a shift in their relationship. Still mother-daughter, but more now. In Amelia, she now had a confidant, not in all things but in those that mattered, and Elise thanked God for this gift.

Lee's truck was the only one in the parking lot, not a surprise with the frigid weather Bemidji anticipated today. His head was bowed. Praying, likely. Funny how a few years ago she'd regarded that as a weakness, and now she admired the strength it gave him.

Speaking of shifting relationships, something had changed between her and Lee. The animosity was gone and, to be honest, that old attraction was there. She didn't know what to make of it. But that was okay, her team had assured her. Just let God keep leading, and things would work out His way.

But, oh, giving over control was difficult.

She parked beside the pickup, and Lee's head bobbed up. He gave a small smile. A wave. Then he stepped out of his truck, pulled on a stocking cap and gloves. She and Amelia followed suit. At the end of winter, thirty degrees was practically swimming weather, but this side of summer, it took a while for her blood to thicken.

Lee came around the front of his pickup, a blanket around his arm and a steaming cup in each hand. He handed one to Elise. "Still like an oak milk latte?"

"Oh, bless your heart." She gratefully accepted the coffee drink and sipped, letting it warm her insides and her heart. That he had remembered her favorite drink was endearing. Lee was still the gentleman, something she'd scorned in her early days as a feminist and physician. That was one of the many items she'd recorded on her "What I Did Wrong" list.

Amelia ran ahead, leaving her to walk with Lee, which was okay. Another change that had occurred over the past couple of months.

"Do you know what to expect?" Lee asked, his gaze straight ahead. "Did she give any hints of what we're supposed to do? Are we to read our sins aloud?"

Our sins. Boy, that was a truthful way to put it.

"I don't know. Our daughter is good at keeping secrets. You seem concerned."

He blew out a breath, and a frozen cloud drifted from his mouth. "You could say I've had a revelation."

"You and me both." Elise stopped and turned to Lee. "How did two messed-up people raise such an amazing daughter?"

"Probably that team we've enlisted. My players have been with me all along." He placed a hand on her back, and Elise let out a little gasp as he guided her forward. The slight touch was a surprise but quite welcome, and it felt very natural.

They reached a bench Amelia was wiping off. It looked over the lake that would soon freeze if today's weather kept up. Lee stopped Elise from sitting and spread the blanket over the cold cast iron. When sitting, they did not leave an Amelia-sized hole between them but just enough to be discreet while allowing her to feel some warmth from his body.

Amelia stood in front of them, her arms crossed and her hands rubbing up and down her arms. "I know from both of you that it's been a tough few weeks."

Lee grunted and Elise chuckled at his response.

"What you do with what you've learned is up to you, but I'm giving you one direction for today, and that's to listen. I read this quote from Steven Covey recently. 'Seek first to understand, then to be understood.' What that looks like will be different for both of you." She pulled her phone from her pocket. "I'm heading to Latte Fun to work on some schoolwork. You can meet me there."

Elise sipped at her coffee and stared out at the lake, waiting for Lee to speak yet debating if she should set the tone for today.

"What do you want to do?" Lee finally said, pulling a crumpled piece of paper from his pocket. "Feel free to go first."

Was he being a gentleman or avoiding? Didn't matter, as she was glad to take the lead.

She turned to him, her knee barely grazing his, ignoring the desire to take his hand as well. "I won't rehash the affair. That's the easy *sin*, as you put it, to lay out."

Lee glanced down at his lap.

What to make of that, Elise wasn't sure, but she kept on. "I think what I've learned over the past three weeks is that the affair was the culmination of my other mistakes I made. Letting my career become my god and having an ego to match. Letting my gaze wander to greener pastures only to discover it was just dry grass painted green. That doctor had nothing on you except social status, which, I've learned, really has no value at all. I put my career above you and Amelia. Yes, I was helping sick children but was blind to the sickness creeping into our little family."

Lee raised a hand to his eyes. He was crying?

Still, she had more to say, the most important statement of all. She blinked back tears to get through it. "Basically, what it comes down to is that I messed up badly. I hurt you and Amelia and tossed away years together for my selfishness, and I can't tell you how sorry I am." Tears trailed over her cheeks. "I know I'm thirteen years late for this, but is there any way you can forgive me?"

She held her breath, waiting for a response, but Lee kept his head bowed. His hands were splayed open. His way of praying? Didn't really matter. Now was her time to sit quiet and listen, if not to Lee then to God's whispers. She closed her eyes, folded her gloved hands around her coffee, and listened to wind cutting through bare trees, to lake water fighting the freeze by lapping onto the shore, to cars motoring past on the highway behind them. To God's voice telling her that He delighted in her, that she was beloved, even with all her mistakes.

"I have a question for you." Lee's soft baritone slipped into her prayer.

She looked up. Nodded.

"That day here, when I proposed"—he made finger quotes —"did you anticipate, were you hoping for, a real proposal?"

She reviewed that moment in her thoughts. It had been spring, and she'd just completed all her pre-med courses. Lee had treated her to a picnic not far from this very spot, then he got up on a knee, and joy and dread shared equal places in her heart. No doubt she'd say yes, but was she ready to make that commitment, one her parents hadn't been able to keep?

Then he'd opened his hand. A key, not a ring, sat in his palm, and disappointment coursed through her. Elise didn't recall his exact words, but they did include an "I love you." They were also very practical. They'd save money by living together, especially since they often spent the night at his place. He was earning money as a journeyman electrician, and she was still accumulating debt. Then he'd promised to follow her wherever her job took her.

How could she say no to that? So they'd hugged, kissed, and then gone back to his apartment for that night and every night thereafter. A real proposal never came, and she was okay with that.

Or so she'd thought.

"The answer's complicated," she finally said. "But in truth, yes, I'd hoped for a proposal, a ring, that special day where I got to be a princess and you were my prince. Silly, I know."

"No, it's not. I'm sorry I took that from you. I know we weren't believers then, but deep inside, I still knew something was wrong, like I was saying na-na-na-na-na to nature or something, even though that's what everyone did. Now I can see that was the beginning of our end."

He sniffled and wiped at his nose. "I did so much wrong, Elise." He shook his head. "I took you for granted. I think I knew you wanted to get married, but as long as you didn't complain, I didn't pursue it. I didn't listen to you. I made the decision for both of us without getting your input. When I inherited Grandpa's house and insisted we move in, I ignored your complaint that it was too far away from the hospital. I didn't hear your opinions about small-town life. And then I made the decision to be a stay-at-home dad without consulting you. With every misstep, I pushed you further away. Maybe you had the affair to get my attention—I forgive you a hundred times for that and for everything else—but by then it was too late. We were too broken and had no faith in God to restore us."

He sat up and wiped a hand over his eyes.

She longed to give him a hug but kept her arms pressed to her sides. Her own mind swirled with his confession. For so long, she'd blamed solely herself, and, honestly, her actions did the final and permanent severing, but Lee wasn't an innocent in this.

"It wasn't until these last months that I've considered my part in our breakup, that it's really my fault. When I pushed you away, what did I think would happen?"

"Oh, Lee." This time she did wrap her arms around him. Sobs wracked his body, and her tears wet his whiskered cheek.

"I'm sorry, Elise, for everything," he said into her shoulder. "I've confessed to God, to my team. That was easy. I know they'll forgive. But you and Amelia, that's the hard part because my selfishness tore us apart."

He pulled away, looked her square in the eye. His eyes still shone with moisture. "I know I don't deserve it, but can you forgive me?"

Elise took his hands, cupped them between her own, and resisted the urge to kiss away his hurt like she used to do. "I do forgive you."

He sighed and his shoulders lifted as if they no longer carried a heavy burden.

"But I have a question now." She kept his hands between hers, very uncertain of his answer, though she knew what she wanted him to say.

His gaze scanned hers and landed on her lips, then reverted back up to her eyes. "I know what my feelings are telling me, but the last time I let them speak for me, I broke us. That can't happen again." He pulled his hands from hers, then wrapped hers in his. "I think the important thing is to ask God what our next step is and really listen for His answer."

CHAPTER FIVE

To say she was giddy was an understatement, even among this day-after-Thanksgiving crowd at the Mall of America. These past few weeks, Elise had almost felt like a schoolgirl in love for the first time.

She and Lee hadn't kissed. Nope. They hadn't even seen each other since the cold day at the Bemidji park, but they'd shared plenty of phone calls. No I-love-yous either. It was too early for that, but still she believed that was where they were heading.

Today was their final assignment from Amelia, though Amelia had already told them they'd passed the course and didn't really need this final step. Today was more about enjoying their time together.

With Christmas music playing over the loudspeakers, Elise squeezed among the shopping throngs, taking in the Christmas decor as she went. She loved it, but Lee probably couldn't wait to get home.

She passed Nordstrom on the way to their meeting place, Macy's. In past assignments, nostalgia had played a role in the location chosen, but she and Lee had no past with Macy's, so she was curious.

Tantalizing scents of fresh-baked cookies and hot coffee drifted past, tempting her, but she'd wait until she was with the family.

The family. Huh. When was the last time she'd thought that phrase with a smile and hope? It gave her a little lift as she walked. She checked her watch and quickened her steps. She wouldn't be late, but being early never hurt, especially since Lee tended to be an early bird.

She took a right at the corner leading to Macy's and spotted Lee and Amelia on a bench. He waved her over and handed her a cup.

She sniffed at the opening. "Mint mocha?"

"Yep." Lee grinned. "You still like it, I hope."

"Oh, absolutely." She took a long sip and sighed. Just what she needed for a winter day pick-me-up. "And let me guess, yours is just a regular coffee."

"Real coffee, you mean, without all the junk ruining it."

"Dad." Amelia groaned. "You don't know what good coffee is." She held up her cup. "I got a gingerbread latte. It's divine."

"That's my girl." Elise nodded to her daughter.

"Well." Lee rubbed his hands together. "I know you two love the mall, and you can stay all day if you want, but the sooner I get out of here the better. What's our assignment today, Miss Aldrich?"

Amelia set down her coffee and took both their hands. "Just this. Family."

Elise shared a glance with Lee, and his mouth lifted to the right, waking those butterflies in her stomach. His smile grew, which meant her expression gave away too much information.

"Lead the way." Lee gestured to Amelia then held out his hand for Elise. She looked at it for a second and another before grasping it, as if holding his hand was making a commitment.

Maybe it was.

Amelia led them to an escalator that took them to the first floor, then wound among shoppers until they reached an opening that led into the amusement park. "Remember when I was almost four and you guys took me here?"

Elise snapped her fingers. That was the connection. She'd forgotten all about that day-after-Thanksgiving event, probably because she'd wanted to put it out of her mind. She and Lee had argued that morning after a torturous Thanksgiving with her family, and they wanted to make it up to Amelia. Then they'd argued again after the trip. That day marked the beginning of their end. Thankfully, Amelia remembered the happy part of that day.

With Lee's hand in hers, Elise promised herself that she wouldn't make the same mistakes again. Today wasn't going to be another beginning of an end but the prelude to a beginning.

Lee might despise shopping, but he was always game for amusement park rides. Well, maybe not fourteen years ago. Oh, he was a jerk that day, letting Elise know at every opportunity how much he didn't want to be there.

Thankfully, Amelia didn't remember the tension that had sizzled between him and Elise that day. He had no desire to go shopping, much less at the overcrowded megamall. Add that to the torturous Thanksgiving meal the day before—who serves tofu instead of turkey for Thanksgiving?—and that entire forty-eight hours ended with an argument that relegated him to the couch for a week.

Now, with Elise's hand locked in his, they waited in long lines, screamed on the coasters—well, Elise and Amelia did the screaming—and rested shoulder to shoulder on the Ferris wheel, all with contented smiles on their faces. This was how family should be.

"Ready for some food?" Lee asked after getting off a spinny ride.

Elise shook her head. "It'll probably all come back up. I used to be able to ride these, no problem."

"The joys of getting old."

"Watch it, buster." She elbowed Lee in his side. "You'll always be ten months older than I am, and I plan to age with grace."

"Babe, you're already succeeding."

Her cheeks blushed as red as a rose, which looked adorable on her. He squeezed her hand and whispered in her ear, "You're looking amazing."

Somehow her cheeks grew more red.

She squeezed his hand as they walked past the toy brick store. "Why don't the two of you play for a bit? I need to find a restroom."

"Sure thing."

She tried to release her hand from his, but he held on to do something that had been on his mind since he saw her walking toward them this morning. It was a risk for sure, but he needed to know her feelings, so he kissed her on the cheek.

Her gaze rose to his, her mouth open in an O. Yeah, it had been worth the risk. He grinned as he released her hand.

Silently, she left for the restroom, and he watched the gentle sway of her hips as she gracefully cut through the crowds until he could no longer see her.

Yeah, it was just a cheek kiss, but, still, it was a signal to her that he cared without promising a future. Yet. But he'd been praying, along with his team, for discernment, and he wasn't getting any stop signs. Later, he might make a riskier move, but that depended on how the day went.

"You still love Mom, don't you?" Amelia tore him back to the moment.

He shrugged and gestured to a table with loose bricks for people to build with. Did he love Elise? Boy, that was difficult to tell. Was it love or infatuation or him just wanting to have someone around when Amelia left for college? Or all of the above?

"I don't know," he said honestly as he stacked bricks into a house shape. "I'm enjoying our time together, our talks. I'm enjoying not being angry with her. I feel lighter without carrying around a grudge. So, do I love her? Absolutely. But in love? We'll have to see."

"That's all I need." Amelia wrapped her arm around his back and leaned into him.

"So, does this mean your challenge was successful? That you're staying home for Christmas?" He picked up the house he'd created and offered it to her.

She shrugged with a sly grin. "I don't know. The day isn't over yet."

"So you're saying that, when the clock strikes midnight, you're staying home?"

"If you and Mom keep playing nice, there's a good chance." She set three brick people figures next to the house Lee had created.

That would be nice. Really nice, actually.

He glanced at his watch. "I think I can hold out another nine hours."

"I think you can, too."

They continued playing with the bricks, adding a Christmas tree outside, and a garage and truck.

"Are you two children having fun?" Elise knelt beside them.

"I am." Lee thought about stealing another cheek kiss but decided to wait until later, when he might take a risk and go for her lips instead. Yeah, he'd do that.

Elise's phone pinged, and her brows furrowed.

"Problem?" Lee gestured to a bench that another couple just vacated. Amelia continued to build while Lee sat alongside Elise.

"I guess that depends upon your answer."

Uh-oh. Why didn't he like the sound of that? "What is it?"

"Mom and Dad are going to be at my brother's place for Christmas. Actually, the entire family plans to be there."

"Sounds like fun," he said sarcastically, then added with a grin, "Christmas with the crazy Kraemers."

"That's my family we're talking about."

"Hey, I'm just repeating what I've heard you say. I remember that Thanksgiving fourteen years ago. Besides, what does this have to do with me? I'm not stopping you from spending time with them." He certainly wasn't invited, and even if he was, he'd give a flat-out "no way." They'd probably serve some kind of veggie ham.

"They want to see Amelia."

"Of course, they . . ." He cut his reply short then shook his head. "Christmas Day?"

"And Eve." She jutted out her chin, asserting her position.

"No." He shook his head. "I've had the trip to Wyoming planned since last Christmas. You had Amelia last year. You can see your family on your own."

"And we can't make an exception one time?"

He laughed. "If I was the one asking you to make an exception, can you imagine your response? You'd have laid into me for being selfish."

"Wow." She backed away from him. "You're right. Instead, I'll lay into you now for being selfish. Mom and Dad are in their eighties."

"Barely."

"And who knows when we'll all have an opportunity to get together again? Amelia should see her cousins."

"I agree, which is why we're going to Wyoming."

Elise laughed. "And here I thought you'd grown up." She draped her purse over her shoulder and opened her mouth, but a shadow hovered over them, quieting both her and Lee.

Amelia stood above them, with her phone to her ear, her jaw tight and eyes glassy.

"Hi Katie." Her tone smiled, but the look she seared down on Lee and Elise was anything but friendly. "Yeah, I have good news. I'm coming to New York with you for my birthday and Christmas."

Lee's mouth fell open, but he didn't dare say another word. His mouth had already done too much damage.

"Let's talk about this, Amelia." Elise patted the open spot beside her.

Amelia just held out her hand to Elise. "I'd like your keys. You two lovebirds can drive home together."

CHAPTER SIX

The temperature inside the truck had been more frigid than the below-freezing temps outside. Elise could become the ice queen faster than any woman he knew, and she'd turned the cold shoulder on full blast for the past two hours on the drive home.

Not that he didn't deserve it. He was a selfish, unthinking, foam-at-the-mouth idiot. All of his apologies landed on deaf ears.

Elise's had as well.

So, she'd surrendered her car keys to Amelia, who'd torn from the mall faster than an Olympic skier racing downhill.

Now they had nothing left to say to each other.

How could a budding romance reconciliation wither in mere seconds? Worse than that, they'd included Amelia in their demise.

He sighed for what had to be the fiftieth time as he drove up the driveway of her house that was far too large for just two people, and Amelia was only there on weekends and every other holiday.

Elise clutched the door handle, turned to him. "I'm sorry."

His gaze barely brushed hers. "Yeah, me too."

"Why do we keep making a mess of things?"

"My only answer is that we're human, but I feel like that's just an excuse. I need to get home, get on the line with my team, pray it over, see if there's any way to salvage this mess."

"Same here." Elise opened the door, letting in a blast of cold air, then looked back. "For the record, I do care about you. My apologies up in Bemidji were real. I guess I was hoping to relive our past and forget about all the hurt in between then and now."

"Maybe we took it too fast."

"Maybe." She looked away then stepped out of the truck. "And maybe *we* never should have been."

With that, she closed the door, lightly, but it felt like a slam to his heart. He put the truck in gear, backed down the driveway, and tore home.

Then he gathered his team on a conference call and prayed for wisdom to pull out a win.

"Hi, Debbie. I have a problem," Elise said over the phone.

When she'd arrived home, Elise had taken a hot, soaking bath to relieve her muscles, but that did nothing to ease the burden of her heart. So she got on the phone, first to Luella, then Gloria. They'd both prayed over her following her confession, but Debbie always seemed to have insight the others didn't.

"I gathered you did." How did Debbie always know what Elise was feeling or thinking? Even over the phone? "Amelia's here, by the way. Asked if she could stay the night. I told her it was up to you, at least for a couple more weeks."

When she would turn eighteen. Elise felt far too young to

be a mother to an adult, but that was the reality, and that scared Elise to death. She didn't want Amelia to make the same bad choices, to go through the same hurt, yet she knew that, this side of heaven, that wasn't a possibility.

"Yes, she has permission."

"You want to talk about it?"

"No." Always was the response to Debbie's question. "But I will." She inhaled a slow breath and let it out to the count of ten. "We went to the megamall for Amelia's last assignment, we were having a great day, and then I threw a monkey wrench into our perfect day." She explained the argument from her perspective and then told about Amelia's angry departure. "Was that just a teenager whim, did she overreact, or did we really blow it?"

"A question for you?" That was always Debbie's response, it seemed. "Did you or Lee let Amelia have any say in your Christmas plans?"

Elise closed her eyes, relived the argument, hoping for something that would show she and Lee hadn't both been selfish, but no. They'd fought over her as if she were a doll, not their precious daughter.

Finally, Elise responded. "No. We didn't."

"Hmm." Dead air meant Debbie was thinking, and Elise had learned to give her that space.

But an idea formed in the silence. "What if . . ."

Elise relayed her idea to Debbie, who affirmed it might work. Then she scheduled tomorrow afternoon on the family app for her, Lee, and Amelia, and called Lee to explain.

And they even prayed together.

Whatever happened tomorrow was in God's hands.

CHAPTER SEVEN

Lee sat alongside Elise in their booth at the supper club where they'd begun Amelia's assignment over three months ago. This time, the room was lit with Christmas lights on each window, and a large, undecorated pine filled an entire corner of the room. "Do you think she'll show?"

"I think so." Elise toyed with her napkin. "But she is a teenager."

"True." He took a sip of his coffee and wished he had something to munch on to bide the time. The easy banter he and Elise had shared just a day ago had hardened into silence. They'd apologized and forgiven each other but had nothing else but remorse to share between them.

"There she is." Elise sat up straighter, as did Lee.

Amelia slid into the booth opposite them. "Well, this is interesting." Her poker face gave away nothing.

"We have an in-class assignment for you." Elise slid a fresh notebook across the table. On the top she'd written, *Home for Christmas Challenge, part 2.*

That got Amelia to smile, anyway.

"Go ahead." Lee made a turn-the-page motion with his hand.

And she did. She stared at the page for a second then glanced from Elise to Lee. "Talk?"

"Yep," Lee said. "We learned that we've done all the talking and didn't give you an opportunity to voice your opinion."

Her eyes lit up. "Oh."

"And we'll sit here and listen." Elise folded her hands on the table. "And be honest. There will be no judgment from us."

"Are you sure?" She looked from Lee to Elise and back again.

"Hundred percent," Lee said. "I put on my big boy pants this morning, so I can take it."

That made both Amelia and Elise chuckle. A little levity didn't hurt, right?

"Okay, then." Amelia folded her hands over the notebook and bowed her head.

Silence was not what Lee expected or wanted, but he then realized Elise's head was bowed as well. Duh. He followed suit and lifted this afternoon up to God. He prayed that God would give Amelia the right words, and that they would do a work in his and Elise's hearts. He prayed that whatever the outcome of today's class would be God's will and nothing else.

"Yesterday was my goal." Amelia began.

Lee gripped Elise's hand, and thankfully, she didn't pull away.

"I have this vague memory of being at Camp Snoopy." Amelia's eyes lit up. "And riding the train and carousel and the two of you smiling together. We were a team. A family. Maybe that time sticks out because I saw so little of it growing up."

Wow. What a sad depiction of his parenting.

"And whenever I'd go to Katie's house, I saw an intact family. They weren't perfect—Katie'll tell you that—but even in their imperfections they stick together. Same goes for her uncles' families in Brainerd and New York. I thought going to New York with Katie, I'd get to experience the family Christmas I've missed out on, not the celebrate-at-Dad's-on-Christmas-Eve and then shuttle-to-Mom's-for-Christmas-day experience."

Elise's hand gripped his harder.

"I just wanted one Christmas." Amelia shrugged. "Just one Christmas at home. With the three of us. Even if it was pretend. And then I saw the way you two were getting along, and I hoped for something I hadn't planned. To think that maybe the two of you would get together again was really beyond my hopes."

She sighed. "And then yesterday was so much fun, until it wasn't. I wanted you to see me as a grown-up, not your little girl who you had to use an app to make sure you each got equal time with, because none of it was fair."

Lee felt sick to his stomach at how he'd treated their daughter.

"When you decided for me yesterday, I felt I didn't have any other choice. If you'd invited me into the discussion, I'd have told you that I wanted one Christmas at home, just the three of us. Not the Kraemers and not the ranch, but just one Christmas at home where we'd go to the candlelight service on Christmas Eve. We'd all stay the night, and then I'd wake up and hurry to the fireplace to see what Santa brought and then have you both there for breakfast before opening presents. A real family. Together. I know you've always told me that just because I want something doesn't mean I'll get it, but I hoped. And I prayed so hard."

Amelia sniffled and Elise handed her a tissue.

No surprise, Elise was wiping her own eyes.

"You're right. About everything." Lee clenched his jaw so his emotions wouldn't spill out.

"Is it too late for this year?" Elise gripped Lee's hand so tight he felt he'd lose circulation.

"So no Kraemers and no ranch? You can get along for two days?"

"We won't be perfect," Elise said.

"I don't expect perfection. Just one Christmas together. Just the three of us, and whatever happens from there happens."

Lee exchanged a look with Elise, and she nodded. "Then that's exactly what we'll give you."

EPILOGUE

1 Year Later

Amelia's alarm went off at six a.m. Way too early on a normal day for a college student, but this was Christmas Day, the celebration of Jesus's birth. And she was home, in her own bedroom, with Mom and Dad sleeping under the same roof, if not in the same bed.

For the second year in a row!

Last Christmas had been a bit awkward with her parents not quite knowing how to function under the same roof. She'd seen their shared glances, with them trying to figure out where they stood with each other, but they'd survived without one argument.

And this past year, they'd even grown to like each other again. That had been more than she dared hope for.

Amelia hurried downstairs and found her stocking hanging from the fireplace mantel right in between Mom's and Dad's. She flicked a switch, turning on the fireplace. Something soft nudged her ankle, and she bent down to pick up Data, the tabby cat Dad had adopted after she went off to college. He'd always told her he wasn't a cat person, but the truth lay in Data's purr. This kitty did love attention.

"You're up." Dad, wearing his pj's, came out of his office, where he'd spent the night on a blow-up mattress. He'd refused to let Mom lie on the floor, and Mom hadn't argued.

"Of course." Keeping Data in one arm, she hugged her dad with the other. "Any sound from Mom's room?"

"Other than her snoring?" He chuckled, thinking he was hilarious, but the truth was Mom did snore, though she'd deny it.

"You're so funny." She set down the cat and knelt by the Christmas tree to see what she'd find with her name on it. Seeing gifts for Lee and for Elise under the tree, something that hadn't happened for years until last year's challenge, made her do a kneeling dance.

She loved seeing that her parents still liked each other. Beyond that, she didn't know. Two days home with only Dad around, and then the candlelight service last night, didn't give her any clues. If romance didn't blossom between them, that was okay, too. As long as they could have family Christmases.

Behind her, a door opened and closed, then another door closed.

"Mom's up," Dad said. "Want some breakfast? Coffee?"

"I'll pour myself a coffee, but can we do the stockings before breakfast?"

"Before, huh." Dad looked to the bathroom. Smiled. Nodded. "Yeah. That would work."

Okay, that was strange. But whatever. Dads were naturally strange, right?

About twenty minutes and two cups of coffee later, Mom finally came out of the bathroom, looking awesome. That was a clue, for sure. Back at her house, Mom didn't care what she looked like around Amelia, but here? Very interesting, indeed.

Dad handed Mom a cup of coffee. "Sorry, it's just black."

"That's perfect." She squinted at Amelia. "Someone insisted on getting up at six a.m. on my day off."

"Can you blame me? It's Christmas!"

As Mom and Dad sat side by side on the couch—another clue?—Amelia leaped from the floor and hurried to the fireplace. She removed all the stockings and handed them out. Yes, she was acting like a five-year-old, but she had years to make up for.

"You go first," Dad said as Data jumped up on his lap.

"Yay!" Amelia sat cross-legged on the floor and dug into her stocking. A toothbrush. A pair of socks with *Star Wars* characters on them. A pair of panties. "Dad!"

He held up a hand and pointed to Mom. "I had nothing to do with that, believe me."

"I hope not." Amelia dug in again and hit pay dirt. Chocolate. She poured the rest of the stocking onto the floor and grabbed a Hershey's Kiss. "Breakfast."

"I don't think so." Mom held up her stocking. "Me next?"

"Nope." Dad pulled it away. "You got to go first last year. My turn."

Mom pretend pouted. "Fine. Go ahead."

Dad also got a toothbrush, a pair of socks, and chocolate. Instead of underwear, he got new winter driving gloves. "Would you look at that?" He tugged them on and winked at Mom—another clue. "Santa knew just what I needed."

"I wonder how." Mom smiled at him, and her toe nudged his.

Okay, they were no longer giving clues, but this was affirmation. Amelia could barely rein in her excitement.

"What's in yours?" Dad sat up taller and leaned over, trying to sneak a peek into Mom's stocking, but she pulled it close to her chest. "Patience, dear."

Dear? Amelia did a small jig where she sat.

Mom reached into her stocking and pulled out a toothbrush, socks, and chocolate, then dug back in. Something was stuck in the toe.

By the grin on Dad's face, Amelia knew it was something special.

Mom finally pulled out the item.

A ring box! Amelia squealed.

"Lee, you didn't." But the shine in her eyes told Amelia that she certainly hoped Dad did.

Dad winked and put a finger to his mouth as he got on one knee on the floor.

Mom's fingers shook as she lifted the lid, then she leveled the meanest stare Amelia had ever seen, at Dad. "I am not going to just live with you."

"What?" His eyes twinkling, he took the ring box from Mom and showed it to Amelia.

A key. No wonder Mom was livid.

Amelia took her dad's place on the couch, snuggled against her mom.

But then Dad, still kneeling, reached into his pajama pocket, kept whatever he dug out tight in his fist, so Mom couldn't see it, but let's face it, they both knew what he held.

He took Mom's hand. "You know I'm not one for speeches, so I'll make this short. This past year has been the best one of my life. It's amazing what happens when you let God take control of your life, thanks to our daughter, who is the most mature young woman I've ever met and who will be the best special ed teacher out there."

"I agree." Mom kissed Amelia's cheek.

"Thirty-some years ago when we moved in together, I was clueless about the amazing woman who'd agreed to share my life, but now, only due to the grace of God, she's back in my life in a fuller and more beautiful way than ever before."

He opened his hand, and Mom gasped.

Amelia did too.

The ring was understated, really. Three strands of rose gold woven like ivy.

"It's perfect," Mom said under her breath.

It really was.

"Would you be willing to give me another chance, Elise? Do it right this time." His voice shook, and he closed his eyes, but not before a tear fell. "Will you marry me?"

"Yes! Yes!" Amelia jumped up and clapped and then realized she hadn't listened to Mom's reply and slumped back on the couch. "Sorry. Go ahead, Mom. Give Dad your answer."

"Well, if you weren't screaming loud enough for the neighborhood to hear, you would have heard me say, absolutely yes."

And Mom and Dad kissed. Really kissed. Not that peck on the cheek she'd seen him give her, but a full, not very child-friendly kiss either, but that was okay. Amelia was an adult now, so she could watch them and be ecstatic for them without telling them to get a room, which would be a really bad idea.

And to think, this never would have happened if she hadn't challenged them to be home for Christmas. Well, that and a whole bunch of prayer.

If God could reconcile these two, which was about as easy as moving mountains, then He absolutely could do anything.

Put on then, as God's chosen ones, holy and beloved, compassionate hearts, kindness, humility, meekness, and patience, bearing with one another and, if one has a complaint against another, forgiving each other; as the Lord has forgiven you, so you also must forgive. And above all these put on love, which binds everything together in perfect harmony.
Colossians 3:12-14

A NOTE FROM THE AUTHOR

It's been over two years since I've sat to write a story, two years since I've typed the end as my husband's Alzheimer's has changed priorities in our lives. Still, God nudged me. Scratch that, He shoved me face first into telling this story of reconciliation that I didn't know needed writing.

I first met Lee, Amelia, and Elise in *Pieces of Granite*. They were side characters in another broken family story and insisted they be allowed to reconcile. Who was I to argue?

I loved the role that grown-up Amelia played in her parents' lives. I also recognize that their story is a unique one and not all marriages or relationships can be or should be reconciled, but this story gives hope for those that can. And that hope can only come from a God who forgives and moves mountains.

A God who was born miraculously over 2000 years ago to become the Savior of this world.

Praying you have a blessed Christmas!

ACKNOWLEDGMENTS

This story came together in one week, which is very quick for me, but it could not have been written without the prayers of my Mosaic sisters. My sister Gayle read my unedited draft and offered enthusiasm for the story and much needed encouragement. And Lesley Ann McDaniel managed to squeeze proofreading this story into her busy schedule to make this story pretty.

Special thanks goes to the cover designers for *A Thrill in the Air*. Sara Davison and Roseanna M. White worked together to create an eye-catching cover.

Also, thank you to Camry Crist for formatting this anthology, making the inside as beautiful as the outside.

ABOUT BRENDA S. ANDERSON

Brenda S. Anderson writes authentic, gritty, life-affirming fiction that shows God at work in people's messy lives. She enjoys live music and theater, walking the shores of Lake Superior, and sharing hot cocoa with friends and family. She lives near Minneapolis with her newly retired husband. Together, they plan to travel across the United States, checking items off their bucket list, beginning with a bus trip to Niagara Falls.

Please visit Brenda's website for more of her books and to subscribe to her newsletter:
www.brendaandersonbooks.com

TITLES BY BRENDA S. ANDERSON

THE MOSAIC COLLECTION: NOVELS
A Beautiful Mess
Pieces of Granite
Broken Together

THE MOSAIC COLLECTION: ANTHOLOGY STORIES
"A Beautiful Christ-mess"
(*Hope is Born: A Mosaic Christmas Anthology*)
"Hot Cocoa Summers"
(*Before Summer's End: Stories to Touch the Soul*)
"A Christmas Homecoming"
(*A Star Will Rise: A Mosaic Christmas Anthology II*)
"Broken Noel"
(*The Heart of Christmas: A Mosaic Christmas Anthology III*)
"Coming Home"
(*All Things New: Stories to Refresh the Soul*)
"The Home for Christmas Challenge"
(*A Thrill in the Air: A Mosaic Christmas Anthology V*)

THE POTTER'S HOUSE BOOKS | ONE
Long Way Home
Place Called Home
Home Another Way
The Potter's House Books box set, books 4, 11, and 18

THE POTTER'S HOUSE BOOKS | TWO
Hands of Grace
Song of Mercy
Season of Hope
The Potter's House Books (Two) box set, books 4, 12, and 20

WHERE THE HEART IS SERIES
Risking Love
Capturing Beauty
Planting Hope

COMING HOME SERIES
Pieces of Granite
Chain of Mercy
Memory Box Secrets
Hungry for Home
Coming Home – A Short Story
A Christmas Homecoming – A Short Story

SCRABBLING

Deb Elkink

* * *

It's time for their annual Yuletide tournament, anticipated by house-bound Kristen despite the apprehension of worldly-wise Taylor. After all, even disjointed game tiles might divulge hidden motives. The two young women, friends since university, hold differing perspectives regarding their student trip to Amsterdam a decade ago—and the incident that left them both profoundly maimed.

But rejoice and be glad with your banners unfurled,
For the Christ that is come is the hope of the world.

"Sing, Merrily Sing" by Lillian Gray

Kristen leaned forward in her wheelchair to raise the blinds. She settled back in front of the living room window, hands slack and palms cupped on top of her lap blanket. Cold radiated from the glass, ice crystals forming at the corners brilliant against the backdrop of the night. Soft blue light from the string of miniature bulbs winding around the banister illuminated only the front step, but she peered through the naked maple branches and beyond the gate for any movement in the outer darkness. Taylor was—as usual— running late.

So what? Kristen puffed a laugh through her nostrils. She had all the time in the world, in contrast to her expected guest, who was always on the run—quite literally.

Kristen rearranged the quilt. It was a long-ago patchwork hug from her mom, who'd never have guessed back then how her daughter would, in her thirties, warm useless knees beneath its riotous cotton print.

She smoothed a wrinkle. She'd had a productive day punctuated by a refreshing nap to ensure her energy for the evening ahead. Up very early this morning, she'd sent her housemates off with fresh baking to share with their families —shortbread stars, Nanaimo bars, and gingerbread men adorned with pink icing buttons. Maybe Taylor would take a few with her, too, depending on what diet she was following these days.

Kristen's hands were still useful enough despite the ever-present threat of atrophy, the intermittent tingling and numbness. Use it or lose it, she'd been told. So she baked and she embroidered and she typed messages like a madwoman while tutoring her online ESL students.

"Kristen?"

At her caregiver's ethnic lilt, Kristen swivelled towards the kitchen and, with mock sternness, chastised Mariel. "Your home is full and waiting for you." All the aide's income since emigrating had gone to bringing her relatives over from the Philippines; finally, they were together. "Leave already."

"*Salamat.*" Mariel bobbed her head in gratitude. "But I wanted to take your cake out of the oven for you first." After placing the pan on the cooling rack, she traversed the open corridor to Kristen's side. "And I don't like it when you're completely alone."

"I'm never completely alone." Kristen's fingers sought out the gold cross at the end of her neck chain, a gift from Mariel herself.

"I know what you mean." The squat woman, her hair in a neat bun, squeezed Kristen's shoulder. "But the guidelines say you need a companion close by at all times."

As if Kristen needed reminding. Now, if she'd had family herself—siblings or even cousins—the night stretching before her would look completely different. But having been born to older parents, no relatives rallied around her on special occasions. Her own dad couldn't be part of any celebrations these days. Or Brandon, of course; that cake had been baked long ago. She plucked at the quilt stitches, tears prickling, but shook her head free of encroaching distress.

And it could always be worse. Instead of dead legs, for example, Kristen could have a crippled soul. Like Taylor.

"When will your friend be here, *bata*?" Mariel checked her watch.

The smattering of Tagalog throughout her speech brought a flavour of multiculturalism into Kristen's day-to-day existence. "Any minute, I'm sure."

The dark window drew Kristen's attention again, but now she spied a sprinkling of stars twinkling afar, the vault of creation glimmering at her. She so missed her Christmas Eve stroll with her parents beneath the eternal sky—that revelation by the heavens, that declaration of incarnation shimmering out to the ends of the earth.

She shrugged off shreds of melancholy and sucked in a slow, steadying breath. How could she be downcast in the presence of the primordial? And what could be more festive than a games night on December 24th? That, too, had been a part of every Yuletide. As she'd progressed through her childhood, the after-walk sessions of Chutes and Ladders had given way to Checkers and Monopoly and then, eventually, Scrabble—Mom seated on a floor cushion, Kristen lying flat on her belly with her toes tickled by the pom-pom fringe on the red velvet tree skirt. Dad was usually snoring in his easy chair by then.

Not restricting themselves to Christmas, Mom had continued to play the word game with her at the table after supper during junior high, and then through high school around her volleyball calendar, and then when she was home for weekends from the city, where she studied education on an athletic scholarship—back when she was planning to be a Phys Ed teacher. And, of course, hours on end when Mom had been in hospice, ultimately leaving their last match unfinished, an implicit promise that they would meet again.

Kristen only wished she'd had Mom when it was her own turn in a hospital bed.

Taylor stalked the unlit block of nighttime sidewalk towards Plumberg's assisted-living group home. Frost stuck her lashes together, and her breath was brittle—coughed-out shards that ballooned into ethereal vapour. Small-town Canada in winter was not for the faint of heart. Why had she left her fleece-lined boots in her downtown Winnipeg condo and taken the ninety-minute drive straight from the gym in her trainers? Her ankles were getting frostbitten.

She picked up her pace, but what was the rush? Kristen was going nowhere fast.

As she trudged up the ramp of Bethesda House, a festooned tree—topped by an angel in star-spackled gown—sparkled at her through the front window. She poked at the doorbell, stamping her feet and shivering, her eyelids lowered against the black canopy of sky now dusting the air about her with glittering specks. Just great. It would likely start to blizzard before she left again for the city.

Kristen finally opened the front door, releasing a tantalizing swell of cinnamon-laced baking, but Taylor had to wait another moment until her friend backed her wheelchair up enough to allow for her entry.

"You've brought carollers along, have you?" Kristen peeped out past Taylor.

Indeed, at that moment a gaggle of flush-cheeked teens swathed in scarves rounded a corner, caught sight of them in the entrance, and burst into a cheery cloud of song: *Joy to the world* . . . Kristen waved and called out a few names before Taylor wormed her way into the warm interior and slammed the door shut tight against them.

"You're looking well," Taylor lied. Kristen's wizened complexion could sure use a dousing of hyaluronic hydrating cream. Maybe Taylor had some samples in her backpack. She kicked off her shoes and hung her jacket on a hallway hook before heading towards the dining table, where the game board was set up and waiting.

Instead, Kristen rolled in the direction of the sitting-room couch. "Let's eat some coffeecake first, while it's still warm. Mariel just cut it."

At the mention of her name, the Filipina caregiver turned from the kitchen sink, her almond eyes gleaming hospitality at Taylor—same as last year and the year before. Taylor steeled herself against the inevitable and offensive "Merry

Christmas" that came with the season, but Mariel only said something foreign as she wiped her hands on a tea towel.

"Carry the cocoa?" Mariel handed two steaming mugs to Taylor and took the plates herself, setting them on the coffee table. "There's juice in the fridge for later. I'm on my way, now, so I'll leave Kristen to you."

Taylor's belly clenched, and moisture beaded on her upper lip. "I thought you stayed overnight with her." She wouldn't know what to do in the case of choking or if Kristen needed oxygen for her breathing issue.

"Mariel will be back by twelve—before you leave." Kristen locked her wheels and manoeuvered her chair tray into place, her movements more laboured than ever. "The other residents are gone, and poor Mariel needs a break." She glinted a crooked smile towards the doorway and raised her hand goodbye as the aide zipped up her parka and left them alone.

Taylor hadn't met any of the other half-dozen tenants, coming here as she did only this one six-hour period of the year for a board game she played only, ever, with Kristen. But she'd heard of their various disabilities requiring long-term support—cerebral palsy, MS, epilepsy. Over the past decade, a few had cycled out to be replaced, and all but Kristen had somewhere to go over the holidays.

Taylor set the mugs down. She retrieved her backpack from the front hall and dug into it—no facial cream samples tucked away there, after all—then drew out and deposited her tissue-tufted bag beneath the tree beside a long tubular package wrapped in Kristen's signature butcher paper tied up with raffia. What had her old friend bought her this Christmas? Kristen's gifts were unique and even exotic, maybe a substitution for international souvenirs she'd never had a chance to buy—wistful purchases ordered through the 'Net in her cyber walk-about: a Waterford bud vase from

Ireland, a bit of French Alençon lace, tulip bulbs postmarked Amsterdam.

Amsterdam! Taylor shuddered. She'd planted those wretched bulbs in a ceramic pot but in the end had let them wither and die, their fresh green-and-pink growth reproaching her with every glimpse she caught of them blooming on her windowsill.

The cake was scrumptious and full of calories she'd jog off tomorrow—something Kristen would never again be able to do. How did her friend handle the immobility?

Kristen lifted a napkin from her tray and dabbed at her cocoa moustache. "Where are your parents cruising this vacation?"

"The Caribbean again." Taylor blamed them for her insatiable wanderlust, though she herself preferred air and ground transportation to avoid water. She checked her phone for their latest message. "They've just docked in Bahamas—with my sister and nieces, of course."

"How delightful." Kristen's reply held no hint of a grudge.

Fully employed and no longer counting on her parents' handouts, Taylor saved her own travel budget for independent adventures—this past fall, two luxurious weeks in an adults-only Cancun resort. She'd lounged and swum and joined in on Spanish instruction under blowing beach palms: *Chico guapo* and *Más cervesa, por favor.*

"The official family online Santa call comes in from Nassau tomorrow."

"Right." Kristen tilted her head to one side. "Last winter their ahoy was from South America—Rio, wasn't it? So glamorous."

Taylor nodded. All Kristen had to anticipate these days was being chauffeured to the town's nursing home for a one-sided chat with her elderly father, the missus having passed on already. But Kristen seemed chill about it all—contented.

Kristen's contentment slapped Taylor in the conscience.

Time to get out of this headspace. If Kristen wasn't upset about her situation, Taylor had no intention of dwelling on it or of fuming about her own life realities: folks who had invasive expectations of her private life, a bank account insufficient for her desires, and disappointing relationships that needed ending. In fact, she'd just this week burned the latest bridge to her parents' potential happiness by kicking out her live-in, putting an end to his pensive references about someday becoming a daddy. Too much fervour, as was usual on the part of the men in Taylor's life.

Of course, she would not be tricked into sharing that detail with Kristen. Such newsy bits of romance, or lack thereof, were best stored away for dumping at her next girls' night out, where throbbing music and booze effectively muffled unwelcome emotions.

"Let's get at it, then." Taylor stood, brushed sticky crumbs from her jeans, and sauntered towards the game board set up on the kitchen table.

Kristen extracted her replacement tiles from the drawstring pouch. Halfway through their first round, she and Taylor were running neck and neck, with several interesting words laid out already, such as *F-E-A-R* and *H-O-P-E* and *G-L-O-R-Y*. Taylor's *B-E-D* had become Kristen's *O-B-E-D-I-E-N-C-E*. Kristen's *Q-U-I-T* had grown into Taylor's *I-N-I-Q-U-I-T-Y*. The board tonight was murmuring more than the trite conversation at the surface.

Kristen cared less about score than creative vocabulary. She particularly enjoyed pulling the *X* and finding the perfect little word to please her—say, *P-A-X* or *C-R-U-X*. She'd refuse to play a poisonous term such as *H-E-X* or *E-X-P-L-O-I-T*, instead saving the high-scoring letter until the meaning held positive significance.

She surveyed her opponent through half-shuttered eyes. Taylor was biting her bottom lip in concentration, taken up with technique so that she'd momentarily ceased her restless shifting—so much movement! She'd certainly kept in shape; Tay was a career girl, after all, and in a top position, by the sounds of it. Yet she had been coming all the way out to Plumberg year upon year, ten times now, when she surely had many other activities on the go.

Why did Taylor keep returning?

Kristen fostered hunches about that but had never managed to break through Tay's protective demeanour to ferret out her friend's honest feelings and beliefs. She didn't seem to have changed one bit since uni days—same lack of restraint, same strong will and self-focus that diverted all conversations back to thin observations about her job and parties and globetrotting.

Same scratching and clambering for some sort of purpose, as though she could work herself into worthiness.

Kristen licked a cinnamon smudge off her lower lip. Oh, to really delve into discussion, to explore Taylor's essential values and describe her own inner musings, the personal changes Kristen had been undergoing for a long while. Ever since Amsterdam, actually—her crossroads in more ways than one. Didn't friends do that—expose inner growth? Discuss the past and face its truth? Dive into the chaos of life to somehow find cosmos there?

Kristen contracted and relaxed her shoulders, repositioning her backbone—what was left of it that moved or felt anything. Her paraplegia was complete, the result of injury high on the spinal cord that had caused her strange and vast rages for a while, she admitted, until the stillness had finally spread to her spirit.

Rages? Kristen checked her letters. She actually had an *R* to add to Taylor's *A-G-E-S*, though maybe she'd hold out for a *W*. Not that the image of wages was necessarily positive, especially when cast as a biblical concept.

An interesting board indeed.

Taylor tapped four wooden tiles into place, their edges worn smooth and the printed letters beginning to blur.

"That's not a word." Across the table from her, Kristen's cheeks dimpled.

Taylor stuck out her chin. "Are you formally challenging me?"

"Look at your spelling, Tay." Kristen tittered—a trilling, catchy bit of mirth that Taylor tried to ignore. Kristen's joyfulness was what she most loved and hated about her.

"Oops." Taylor rearranged the letters: not *E-V-N-Y* but *E-N-V-Y*. Short word, great score. "My dyslexia kicking in."

As if dyslexia were a real disability of hers like paralysis was for Kristen. Taylor had used the excuse of her self-diagnosed reading disorder all through university to qualify for an extra hour during exams. Kristen hadn't needed to beg such a handicap in the classroom back when she was still enrolled, preceding their interrupted summer trip before their final year of studies. And yet Taylor was the successful one with the undergrad marketing degree and a job as a rep for a high-end cosmetics start-up that took her pretty far afield—Vancouver, Calgary, Montreal. No trade show in Paris yet, true, but she'd eventually go to the Continent again as a tourist—without Kristen, of course.

Her old roomie seemed willing to let the spelling switcheroo pass without insisting Taylor lose her turn, though she'd lifted her fingers from the board already and jotted down the score. Good thing, too, as that penalty might have put a win right out of her reach.

She and Kristen were evenly matched—at least Kristen let her think so. Kristen, who had unlimited opportunity to read. With all that time on her hands, she had an unfair advantage that Taylor could hardly criticize aloud without appearing small minded.

Not that they followed strict game rules, of course—never using a timer, for instance, but allowing themselves to "ponder every delicious word choice," as Kristen put it. Impatient as Taylor might get when a best-two-out-of-three series ran past midnight, she owed it to Kristen, right?

Taylor jiggled her leg, bumping the table. The pen rolled from the score pad onto the floor, and she bent from her seated position to pick it up. Such a simple action she took so for granted. She squelched surging shame over her physical well-being—no need to dredge up such emotion—and drew in a yogic breath filling her nose, chest, belly. The last thing Kristen would want was her pity. She'd said so from the beginning.

Or maybe it wasn't compassion in Taylor but fear of exposure arising from that whole Amsterdam scenario.

"More OJ?" Kristen nudged the pitcher closer to Taylor.

"Sure." Too bad there wasn't any vodka to make a cocktail in holiday celebration, some liquid cheer. No use even asking. Taylor had learned that lesson when Kristen first moved into the group home. Mariel—still in her forties then and slightly slimmer—had confiscated her flask, forbidden by the church-sponsored facility. Good thing the matron hadn't patted Taylor down on that initial visit or she'd have found something a bit more incriminating than alcohol. Taylor didn't bother to carry a hidden joint around with her these days, now that weed was legal in Canada and so widely available.

Just as it had been in Amsterdam back then.

Taylor served herself juice from the sweating pitcher before topping off Kristen's glass. Pathetic thing didn't have enough core strength to lift much more than a game tile. Which she did quite handily, with lots of points adding up on the board.

Taylor's opponent shuffled her letters around on her rack, then sat back in her wheelchair and absently fiddled with one of her waist-length copper braids—the dominant point of beauty Kristen retained from her academic period. Along with her adorable freckles, of course. Thirty-one wasn't officially young anymore, though Taylor herself still received constant flattery from men, to the annoyance of her ex until she'd ushered him out . . .

She dismissed reminiscence of that recent scene and returned her scrutiny to Kristen's complete lack of make-up. Well, maybe the girl couldn't wield a lipstick tube any longer. And who was there to admire her anyway? No guy since the fiancé. Kristen had been wise, even generous, to let Brandon go so he could live a whole life, unfettered by her infirmity. So, no—it wasn't like Kristen had a social life.

Thanks to her, to Taylor herself.

The twinge of contrition almost compelled her to cross herself, a long-laid-aside religious habit. She gritted her teeth against the invasive self-censure. Her therapist had toiled for so long already to help her silence her inner critic's false guilt, based—they both agreed aloud—on her mother's coercing her to attend Mass as a girl. Taylor had developed effective behavioural techniques such as displacement when she felt triggered, but she'd hidden from the psychologist the actual source memories that assaulted her in unguarded moments.

She forced her gaze from Kristen to stare at her wooden rack of letters. Seven tiles. Her mind raced ahead, redirecting her thoughts: seven seas, seventh heaven, lucky seven, seven-year itch.

And seven deadlies, of course. Taylor cleared her throat to rid her of the mental sputum, but she couldn't unhear the long-ago recitation by the priest: "The seven virtues of chastity, temperance . . . The seven deadlies of pride, greed . . ." She covered her ears.

"You okay, Tay?"

"It's nothing." She winked in fake gaiety. "My turn, right?"

At that moment, she consciously identified the word that had likely fed into her obsessive liturgical fancy just now: *L-U-S-T*. She had a perfect place to play it, and the irony was rich given the juxtaposition of her deeply rooted sensuality with Kristen's ongoing celibacy. But the score for *L-U-S-T* wouldn't be that high. Anyway, she swore Kristen could read her thoughts through the board. She'd use something less indicting.

R-U-S-T. That would do for now. Kristen, in turn, transformed it into *T-R-U-S-T*, which Taylor negated by prefacing it with *D-I-S*.

And so the sparring continued until Taylor, messing around with her low-scoring tiles, spotted a fantastic possibility. She feigned indifference and crossed her fingers.

Kristen built *J-O-Y* vertically on an earlier move, to Taylor's relief.

"Good one." In reality, Taylor's compliment was due to Kristen's having left the *V* open for her use. With a flourish—and only the briefest pang—Taylor spelled out *V-I-R-G-I-N-A-L*, using all of her letters and placing the final *L* on a red square.

Kristen didn't gasp or hesitate. "Wow, that's a whopping"—she counted on her fingers—"eighty-six points." Her tone rang with honest congratulation, which somehow dampened Taylor's glee over her snide innuendo. "Your game." Kristen's saucy eyebrow rose. "But watch out—I'm coming for you."

They set up for the second of three rounds in their annual tournament.

Taylor's annual penance.

No matter the score, Kristen grew ever more expansive as the second round progressed. Almost careless. How could she live so freely when Taylor felt so bound? Kristen was confined, yet Taylor was the one with the impairment.

Kristen yawned, wide awake but filling her lungs in a satiation of breath—not always guaranteed, given her condition. Along with this came a profound sense of satisfaction in the moment. It was Christmas Eve, after all, that most magical and miraculous of times, when stardust and sugar delighted imagination and appetite, when carols and crèche brought to mind swaddling cloths and manger. Background music sang truths to her: *Peace on earth and mercy mild . . . All is calm, all is bright . . .*

She pivoted towards the countertop and reached for a packet of her favourite dark-chocolate caramels, a treat from Mariel. She rattled the cellophane to entice Tay to help herself to a piece. No response.

Taylor sat across from her, as usual by the midpoint of the evening bearing down in concentration. She furiously paged through the dictionary, ran her finger along the column of entries, shook her bleached and tousled tresses, then flipped halfway back to the front. Tay took winning very seriously.

So Kristen unwrapped a bonbon for herself and popped it whole into her mouth, its creaminess coating every single taste bud and bringing back thoughts of Brandon, who'd introduced the confectionary to her when they'd met in youth group as teens. It had been their signature candy. These days, each one she ate was a sort of homage to him, who'd given so much to her—not least of all his faith. She glanced down at her ringless left hand, still grateful for Brandon despite his shortcomings.

Taylor by now was complaining about the lack of vocab available. From the start of their tradition, in keeping with how Kristen had been taught to play, she and Tay accepted words found only in the tattered paperback original to the game inherited from Mom—no checking online, no using alternative sources or external shortcut lists of two- and three-letter cheat words.

And as usual by this point in the evening, Kristen's curiosity about Taylor's inward thoughts was whetted— tasted, but not sated. Ten years of unspoken remembering made Kristen question if Tay recalled anything of the incident at all.

Amsterdam had really been a phenomenal city—what she'd seen of it in those first two days, at least. Its ambience had seared itself into Kristen's mind, and she retained vivid memories of their disembarking at Schiphol, giddy with adventure, and riding the train to the city centre in search of their third-story lodgings. They'd trodden narrow alleyways between quaint buildings topped by gable façades. They'd ambled over arched bridges spanning one canal after another. Cathedral bells had chimed, pigeons fluttered, and bicycles swarmed—riders' skirts flying and satchels flapping. Some cyclists had doubled up on one-person bikes, with passengers teetering on the handlebars or riding side-saddle on a rack over the back tire.

Oh, she and Taylor had had plans! They would ride a canal boat to drink in Amsterdam's history, they promised one another, and view all the art of the Dutch masters, and tour Anne Frank's house, and find a functional windmill.

But first, Tay had insisted, they must check out the famous red-light district with brothel windows full of exposed flesh. And, of course, the coffee shops.

"Ta-da!" *Taylor* fairly crowed over her grand-slam of the high-counting *Z-I-P-P-E-R*, which she fittingly cuddled up next to *L-A-D*. "Beat that, if you can, you brainiac, you."

This seemed to bring Kristen back from her far-away daydreaming. "I accept that challenge." She flared her nostrils in mock fierceness, but that did nothing to stifle her general merriment.

Taylor recorded her points, not bothering to hide her smirk. Even as she exulted over her score, she had to remind herself about her larger motive in coming here—her self-made, inflexible vow to pay off her dues. All said and done, she wasn't really a bad person, was she? Surely the good she did outweighed the bad.

But Kristen won the second round anyway, with ridiculous words like *S-W-E-E-T* and *M-E-E-K* and *P-E-A-C-E*. What drivel had the girl been filling her mind with? Taylor let her vision wander to the wall of shelves holding multiple rows of books and movies thick and thin, classic and current —*Paradise Lost* and *It's a Wonderful Life*, *Little Women* and *Pilgrim's Progress*. And, of course, a big, fat Bible. She crossed her legs in the opposite direction. It was time to get on with the order of business.

"Want to pause to open our gifts?"

Kristen's whole face lit up. "Of course."

They typically broke away from the intensity after the

second match—even if a winner had been confirmed by then, which it had not tonight—to open the other's present. It helped calm the tension. Okay, to calm Taylor's tension. Every year she forgot, until this point in the tournament, how her jaw ached, whether or not she was winning.

Taylor collected the two gifts from beneath the tree while Kristen wheeled over to the television in the sitting room, where a two-dimensional fire burned on the screen. Kristen grabbed the remote and increased the volume so the sacred music couldn't be ignored any longer. Strains of "The First Noel" filled the air. Taylor was sure Kristen, swaying from the waist up, would have glided off her chair into a tippy-toe Nutcracker rendition if she'd been able.

"You go first." Taylor set her bag, with its distinctive Hudson Bay stripes, on Kristen's lap. The same-sized bag as ever.

"What could it be?" Kristen's gentle mocking got both of them chuckling. Every year Taylor brought Kristen slippers, the only footwear she owned—this year a pair of made-in-Canada, felted wool booties. Kristen must have a closet shelf full of the non-shoes by now—the pink silk mules with polka-dot bows, the cork-soled clogs, last year's rawhide moccasins —and not one pair with scuffed bottoms. Taylor would never surprise Kristen.

On the other hand, Taylor could never guess what was in store for her. She now lifted the brown-paper cylinder onto her lap and shook it but heard nothing. "A wizarding wand from the Harry Potter park in Japan? A bamboo flute from India?"

Kristen beamed. "Open and see."

Taylor loosened the raffia twine and tore off the paper to expose a mailing tube printed with the official logo of the Museum of Modern Art.

"Up to your old tricks of souvenir shopping?" Taylor had

not yet experienced NYC, but likely she wouldn't bother with the MoMA anyway—or any museum worldwide that Kristen might fantasize about.

As for the Big Apple's very lively club scene—now *that* held fascination for Taylor.

At least this present had nothing to do with the Netherlands and the fated trip. When all was said and done back then, Taylor hadn't needed to set foot in the Rijksmuseum that had been near the top of Kristen's must-see Amsterdam list. But what artwork had Kristen judged Taylor might value enough to get online from the MoMA?

Tedious as she found the ritual of celebrating, as it were, in Plumberg, Taylor had to admit that the giggles of gift opening with this most childlike of friends brought her a rush of anticipation. That moment of holding an unopened parcel, wondering at the contents beneath its paper veil, thrust her back to her own age of innocence and aroused the strangest hope in her breast, something Kristen called "holy expectancy." It was all nonsense, of course, Kristen's underlying presumption that a girl—a virgin—could carry the humanity of divinity within.

But she pried off the plastic cap from one end of the tube and gingerly tugged on the edge of the paper until it was free —a rolled scroll fastened with a gold foil seal, an unread missive holding a secret she hadn't yet comprehended. She drew out the moment of revelation, savouring the suspense as though she were a girl again. Since early adulthood, Taylor'd had very few gifts to open, as Mom and Dad generally handed her a cheque early in December before gallivanting off. Now she slowly peeled the seal away and unrolled Kristen's scroll to find a glossy poster of a famous painting. What was its title again? She raised her gaze to meet Kristen's.

"*The Starry Night*," Kristen volunteered without being

asked, eyes glistening. "Painted by Dutch artist Vincent van Gogh while in a lunatic asylum in the South of France."

Sudden fury ignited Taylor's gut, an inner detonation. She clamped her teeth against the sharp rebuke that threatened to slice through the gaiety of the background music. Kristen just couldn't help herself, could she? She had to bring up that cursed trip to Holland.

Kristen, apparently not noticing Taylor's reaction, continued babbling. "Of course, that original piece itself isn't kept in Amsterdam, but we might have seen so many of van Gogh's other works while there—*Sunflowers* and *The Potato Eaters* and *Almond Blossom*—if only . . ." Her voice faltered, and then, with a brightness that must have been manufactured, she said, "Let's get going on that last round. I'll trounce you this time."

Kristen shrank inwardly, as though her chest were caving in. She knew, as soon as she'd uttered the phrase "if only," that she'd made a real mistake. She could see it in Taylor's expression of—what was it?—loathing or ire. Poor Tay, hypersensitive and so very hardened all at once. Kristen busied herself with the final game, as Taylor was doing, until the silence got a bit too loud.

"So, where are you off to next?" Kristen made a point, whenever they talked, of asking about Taylor's future destinations, birdie of clipped wing that she herself was. For now, at least she could allow her imagination to soar.

"I have a trade fair in Vegas next month to pitch the new growth serum." Tay, seemingly recovered from Kristen's blunder, fluttered her eyelashes in a look-at-these demonstration.

"Not extensions? They really are long. Someone got the chemical formula right." Kristen chortled as a mental picture came rushing back. "Remember our overnight parties cramming for Chem 101? Our consumption of junk food and caffeine to stay awake?" Dorm life had been such a blast.

"To be honest, not really."

Huh. It had been a required first-year course taught by the coolest professor. Kristen could have sworn Tay had been part of her group project to design a sports massage balm, studying the interaction between the test-tube substances—scooping and measuring and weighing ingredients from the lab's muddle of bottles and jars full of acids and alcohols, waxes and solvents, minerals and thickeners and emollients. Making cosmetics out of chaotic clutter.

Like God had been creating order out of the turmoil of her life.

Taylor continued piecing words together, but at every chance Kristen redefined them: *L-I-E-S* morphed into *H-O-L-I-E-S* under her hand, *M-E-D-I-A* became *M-E-D-I-A-T-O-R*. Taylor placed *I-C-E* and fished for her next letters, snagging a *V* again, the second time in three games. If Kristen didn't take up the spaces, she might create *A-V-A-R-I-C-E* on her turn.

But instead Kristen again played off Taylor's move: *S-A-C-R-I-F-I-C-E.*

Taylor stiffened. Was she reading into the board, seeing something not there? So often she'd asked herself if she'd made a sacrificial lamb out of her friend—abandoning her on the banks of the canal, bent and bleeding and dripping wet from near drowning, to be taken alone to the Amsterdam emergency ward before any cops might show up. Yes, she'd made sure a random passerby—possibly one of the crowd that had spilled out of the coffee shop—called the ambulance before she bolted, and she did go to the hospital herself as soon as she was sober. Kristen hadn't come to before then anyway. But had she done enough?

Taylor banished the gruesome image and, to get on with it, settled for another quick choice: *V-O-I-D*. Anything to dislodge the recurrent, ten-year-old picture Kristen kept hammering into her head, rousing spasms of self-reproach.

The verb meant to empty the bladder. In the past, she'd puzzled over how petite Mariel managed to help Kristen onto the toilet, maybe using the lift-and-sling contraption to get her dead weight from chair to commode. Or, by *V-O-I-D*, maybe Taylor had another definition in mind. Was she subconsciously expressing unspoken horror at that great, empty sky above Plumberg just waiting to glare down at her in familiar accusation when it was time to return to the city?

Displacement wasn't working.

"Aha. Easy points for me." Kristen added a prefix, creating *A-V-O-I-D*.

Taylor snapped her face up towards the clean, clear visage across the table. Was Kristen sending her a deliberate message, suspecting her evasion?

Well, she could send her own mute curse: *R-A-S-H*. The red and itchy noun, not the impetuous adjective.

Kristen, uncharacteristically negative, laid out *C-R-A-S-H*.

Taylor sucked in her breath—she couldn't stop herself. Kristen's hazel eyes above her freckled cheeks were fixed on Taylor without evident malice and maybe even with compassion.

Kristen couldn't miss the mood emanating from across the game table, could almost smell Tay's apprehension. Poor stray sheep who'd lost her way, scrambling down a long, wrong path, tattered and muddy in the mire. Kristen had been there herself, once, floundering in the mundane rather than flourishing in the supernatural. Fighting against the unfairness of fate—fighting for life.

She reached out her hand to touch Taylor's bare forearm. "Do you want to talk about it?" Tay jerked back and didn't meet her eyes, focusing on the layout before them.

Kristen had never before broached that question aloud, only soundlessly pled a thousand times. A pictorial synopsis of the summer night in Amsterdam flashed through Kristen's mind: The coffee shop with the neon sign advertising cannabis, where Taylor had so boldly ordered a high-THC brownie and eaten the whole thing on an empty stomach. Tay's insistence that they go dinking like the locals, with Kristen perched on the handlebars and teetering with every jostle of the bike tires rattling over the street's brick surface. Taylor, peddling furiously, singing at the top of her lungs when the tires caught on the tram ruts that ran close to the canal. And then Kristen's weightless flight through the air and the watery impact and oblivion . . .

Taylor played a word and Kristen thought about re-voicing her query, asking again if Tay wanted to discuss the accident, but Tay seemed so intent on counting up her points, on dipping into the pouch for her next tiles, with her brows bunched into knots and her forehead vein popping. Would there be any benefit in pushing the issue now?

What an all-around catastrophe Amsterdam had ended up being, by anyone's standards—not only that prematurely shortened sightseeing tour but the continued fallout. Kristen had been in a coma for over a week. When she awoke, her dad was there—dear Dad who was still lost in his grief over

Mom's death and already displaying symptoms of the encroaching brain disease that would soon after swallow everything precious to him. But he'd had enough presence of mind ten years ago to bring along Brandon, his would-be son-in-law. The three of them—Dad, Taylor, Brandon—got Kristen to Canada and coached her back to mitigated health, sitting beside her in the hospital for the long months of recuperation, spelling each other off until Dad got too fuzzy to take his turn and Tay's study schedule grew too demanding and Brandon . . . Well, with a heavy but determined heart, Kristen had ultimately set him free. He'd protested, of course, but she wouldn't hear of tying him down to her invalidity once she'd learned her full diagnosis.

Yes, Kristen had lost so much in one fell swoop. But, on the upside, she'd been forced into a kind of independence through her total dependence on others—on God.

Taylor kept her vision glued to board and tile pouch and score pad. Did she want to talk about it? What had Kristen been thinking, asking a question like that? Hadn't they implicitly agreed long-ago to the rules of this relationship? They took another few turns at the game, and abruptly, just when Taylor had unclenched her jaw, Kristen spoke again.

"It hasn't been the end of my life."

Taylor gulped. "Well, no—you're here, after all." As though Kristen had any quality of life.

"I'm not really talking about my disability or the trappings of it." Kristen tapped her metal armrest with her fingernail. "I am not *one* with my wheelchair, you know."

"Of course not." But Taylor could never have lived through the whole ordeal—the medical part that Kristen had valiantly fought through and the relational part Kristen had no idea about. Maybe Taylor could salvage this conversation after all. She'd been dreading it for so long, and maybe it was time to bite the bullet or at least flatter her way out of it. She patted Kristen's arm.

"You are a real person with value and character. You have meaningful work"—didn't Kristen enthusiastically take on new tutorial students?—"and you keep yourself in relatively good condition." It wasn't bald lying; fudging the truth would encourage Kristen.

"I count my blessings, Tay. It's not the physical and emotional alone that need nourishing." Kristen's left hand crept up to touch her gold cross—the hand devoid of the diamond Taylor was *de facto* guilty of removing.

"Right." Taylor dragged out the single syllable. What was Kristen getting at? Maybe she meant her social life needed nourishing, too—which of course Taylor had been trying to feed, if only once a year at Christmas.

She closed her eyes against the insufficiency of her excuses, the incompetence of her pathetic attempts to worm her way into Kristen's good graces. Or was it to convince herself of her own character and worth? Weren't the physical and emotional—the paraplegia and the psychological effects— enough of a curse for Taylor? Counting blessings was all fine and good; positive attitude enabled healing. But Kristen's optimism was straight-out naïve.

Across from her, Kristen pushed the board aside and leaned forward on her forearms, brows arched. "The walk of life isn't limited to body and soul. There's the spiritual aspect of redemption, too." She paused. "I needed forgiveness."

"*You?*" What a bizarre thing to say, given the circumstances. "Kristen, if anyone has been a good person, it's you. You've gone through so much and yet you don't seem bitter at all."

But Kristen *would* if she ever discovered the whole story. Taylor trembled.

"Being good has nothing to do with it." Kristen picked up her empty glass and rotated it between her palms. "I've made my share of mistakes and struggled through a pile of resentment. Everyone sins, after all."

Taylor had nothing to say in defense. She braced herself. Maybe she should officially apologize for the whole Amsterdam thing? Well, at least the part about the weed and her vehicular recklessness . . . Maybe that would be enough to assuage Kristen's potential prying and divert the direction of the conversation away from her untimely moral gaffe that summer.

"Kristen," she began, "I'm so sorry for my stupid decisions back then, when—"

But Kristen's tinkling laughter bubbled up and drowned out the sentence. "Oh, I forgave you ages ago, Tay!"

Taylor sloped away, resting her shoulder blades on the chair's vertical spindles. She wished for a backbone half as strong as Kristen's. "Just like that?" Kristen would not offer such hasty absolution if she suspected the whole story. "It's that easy for you?"

"When you've been forgiven yourself, you can re-gift forgiveness to others."

Hm. That would be nice, but it wasn't that simple. Childhood catechism couldn't stand up to grown-woman indiscretions. "I don't even believe in God."

Kristen grinned at her. "I didn't bring Him up. You did."

Taylor stared over at the tree—at the sequined stars dangling from faux pine branches and the angel lording it over her. Now she'd get preached at.

But when had her friend ever done that? No, it was her own conscience condemning her. She'd realized it before she stepped into Bethesda House earlier—when, outside, she'd as usual ignored the real, non-sequined stars in that black sky probing her black heart.

"But you're right," Kristen continued. "The Nativity is all about God, about reconciliation between the divine and the human, about His forgiveness reaching down to us."

"Some things that can't be reconciled." Taylor should know.

Kristen's lips puckered to one side, then she drew the board close again, her hand hovering over her letters as though she were in deep thought, and then she formed another word—short, piggy-backed on her *V* so she didn't score much: *L-O-V-E.* Kristen studied her, and a searing knife of conviction pierced Taylor.

Then, from somewhere inside and beyond her control, Taylor belched out in a rush, "Okay, I did it."

She slapped her hand over her mouth.

But Kristen's eyes welled with moisture that trembled on the brink of spilling over. She nodded and kept mum, but she still couldn't have a clue about the cheating. Could she? Taylor's shoulders sagged. She might as well speak bluntly.

"I stole Brandon from you, Kristen. I saw how he looked at you when you were broken and suffering—with all that longing and tenderness. And I couldn't help myself." She glanced up into eyes that were not at all clouded or confused but, rather, full of mercy. Taylor broke the visual connection, dropping her gaze back down towards the battered old game board. "You thought you were the one to give him freedom, but I'd gotten to your loyal fiancé first."

How could Taylor be admitting this? She couldn't staunch the flow, as though the seal of her guilt were being peeled back after a decade of covering up. "It started innocently enough at your bedside." Was she really claiming innocence? "We touched hands and it was pure electricity"—which of course she'd intended it to be.

But Taylor, lowering her head and setting her jaw, wouldn't go into more detail, wouldn't allow herself to mention how Brandon had responded to her sly flirting, her suggestive bantering. It hadn't been that difficult, really, starved as he must have been by Kristen's demure abstinence. Taylor had only toyed a bit with him, and his flustered craving had done the rest of the job. And all this while Taylor had allowed Kristen to think letting her fiancé off the hook was her own doing.

That seduction had been as easy for Taylor as kicking her ex out of the apartment a couple of days ago.

In the hush, Taylor's inner judgment screeched at her until she came out of her stupor and raised her head.

Kristen's tears had breached the boundary and were flooding down over her freckles and dripping off her chin— tears of the sort Taylor had not shed since youth. But Kristen, with a soft smile, was nodding in rhythm to the lyrics being sung out from the television—*Fall on your knees, O hear the angel voices* . . . She clasped her hands to her chest.

"You've finally confessed."

Taylor bolted upright, her mouth falling open, her tongue suddenly dry. "You knew?" All these years Kristen had known about her betrayal? All the talk about forgiveness and reconciliation tonight wasn't about only the accident?

"Of course. I'm paralyzed, not blind."

"But . . ." Taylor had no more words.

The door opened and a freezing gust slammed into her ankles. "*Kamusta*. You two all good?" Mariel pulled her parka hood back to expose a face ruddy with the cold. She pointed to the wall clock. "Told you I'd make it back by midnight."

Kristen swept the last tears from her cheeks. "We're finished here."

"You still have letters left." Mariel pried off her boots and hung her jacket on a hallway hook beside Taylor's.

"Yeah." Kristen flicked her eyes over towards Taylor. "For the next game . . . Right, Tay?" Her brows rose. "Maybe in the spring? We've played long enough."

Ten minutes later, after Kristen pressed hugs and baked goodies on her, the door closed behind Taylor, the lock clicked, and the string of blue bulbs blinked off.

But alone in the blustery darkness, strange warmth and light glowed inside her.

Kristen watched Tay stride out of her view beneath maple branches that clutched a fistful of stars against the background flashes of aurora borealis.

"Help me to the bathroom, Mariel? I need a shower."

But more than that, she wanted to get settled in bed, which faced the large bay window that gave her an unobstructed panorama when the curtains were opened. She wanted to observe the sky's glorious display, to read its bedtime story from down here on earth tonight, to dream of the day she'd not only walk again but fly.

Taylor, having stepped from the residence onto the sidewalk, made footprints in the skiff of powder. At the icy corner where she turned towards her car, she stopped dead and forced her chin straight up—no trees or tall buildings to obstruct her view out on the prairie. But nothing, either, to hide behind. Nothing to protect her from the scrutiny of the heavens in its corresponding examination of her own soul—

that deep and boundless infinity with its countless stars looking right back down at her.

She could almost hear the snap and sizzle of the northern lights, their edges wavering like the parchment of an unrolling scroll, a banner unfurling to proclaim a transcendent message to all the world—to Taylor herself: *Let every heart prepare Him room . . .*

Just then, low on the horizon, a shooting star momentarily bridged heaven and earth, the celestial coming down to the terrestrial.

"Merry Christmas," she murmured, in case the sky had ears.

A NOTE FROM THE AUTHOR

Synonyms for the word *scrabble* include *scuffle, skirmish, battle, fight, row.* I confess that I have scrabbled with God.

Of course, so have some of the "greats" in the Bible, Jacob coming most readily to mind—that deceiving supplanter who wrestled with God on the banks of a river and earned a dislocated hip as a penalty before receiving amazing blessings from the same disciplining hand of the Lord (Genesis 32:22-32).

Scrabbling against the will of God, I've found, can lead to a limp in life. For example, I still carry sorrow over some past flailing in my earthly relationships when I didn't listen closely to the Word of the Lord. In this fictional story, Kristen and Taylor are both fighting against elements that handicap them in one way or another—scrabbling in the mud beneath the expanse of the sky that so loudly proclaims the presence of the Creator.

What about you? Do you have the battle scars of guilt from resisting the principles of the Bible, or maybe wounds inflicted upon you by others or circumstances? Be encouraged; our disciplining, forgiving, reconciling, and healing God of Christmas yet has blessings for you.

ACKNOWLEDGMENTS

I would not have written this story without somewhat recent family troubles that have been reaffirming to me the truth that God, who fairly shouts for our attention, redeems us from our sin and walks with us in our suffering, granting us the birthright we could never have earned—to be called heirs of God and fellow heirs with Christ, justified by His grace according to the hope of eternal life (see Psalm 19; Romans 1:19-20; 8:17; Galatians 3:29; Titus 3:7).

Thank You, Abba, for the undeserved gift of Jesus!

ABOUT DEB ELKINK

DEB ELKINK writes from her cottage on the banks of a lovely creek in the rolling hills of southern Alberta, Canada, a stone's throw from the Montana border and home base for international adventures with her husband of 45+ years. Her award-winning novels and short stories—literary fiction with a theological twist—incorporate travel and tastebuds and tumults of the heart.

Please visit Deb's website to learn more about her books and to subscribe to her newsletter: www.debelkink.com. Join her Facebook street team, Retelling Timeless Truths.

TITLES BY DEB ELKINK

THE MOSAIC COLLECTION: NOVELS
The Red Journal
The Third Grace

THE MOSAIC COLLECTION: ANTHOLOGY STORIES
"Ever Greening"
(Hope is Born: A Mosaic Christmas Anthology)
"Blue Genes"
(Before Summer's End: Stories to Touch the Soul)
"Reconstituted"
(Song of Grace: Stories to Amaze the Soul)
"Taste Budding"
(All Things New: Stories to Refresh the Soul)
"Clanging Symbols"
(Dancing in the Rain: Stories to Shelter the Soul)
"Scrabbling"
(A Thrill in the Air: A Mosaic Christmas Anthology V)

NONFICTION
Roots and Branches: The Symbol of the Tree in the
Imagination of G.K. Chesterton

UPCOMING
Vagabond Come Home: Collected Stories

THE ANGEL VOICES

Candace West

* * *

All will not be calm and bright for estranged sisters Natalie and Chloe Frost. A bed and breakfast is the last thing they want for Christmas, but their aunt signs it over anyway.

Cookie-cutter smiles for their holiday guests split open old wounds between them. If they could wrap up the past and stash it with the oodles of gifts under the tree, they would survive the season.

Hiding the ugly truth will prove much more difficult, however.

To the crushed in spirit who keenly feel their loss during this season.
Know you are abundantly loved.

And suddenly there was with the angel
a multitude of the heavenly host
praising God and saying,
Glory to God in the highest, and on earth peace,
good will toward men.

Luke 2:13-14

CHLOE

~ Long lay the world in sin and error pining ~

The slam of a car door jerked Chloe Frost from her story world and back to reality. A frown nipped the corners of her mouth as she slid a crocheted bookmark into the novel before laying it beside her on the porch swing.

The mid-December breeze swirled through Rosewood Inn's wraparound porch, hardly chilling Chloe through her light fleece sweater. Though winter was technically a few weeks away, it didn't bother showing up in south Mississippi until it was good and ready.

From the side yard, slow footsteps clipped over the brick driveway towards her. Scooting to the edge of her seat, Chloe curled her fingers around it and stiffened her shoulders. For three days, the sound of every vehicle and person venturing to the bed and breakfast had frozen the blood in her veins. The constant freezing and thawing wore thin.

If Natalie didn't show her face soon—

A dog barked and rounded the hedge, tugging on its leash.

The Scottish terrier paused and shook itself as though happy to be outside.

Chloe dragged her stare farther up the leash to the manicured hand that held it. Farther still over the designer tweed jacket framing a woman's slender lines. With a blink, she focused on the face of her older sister.

A tense grimace marred Natalie's pretty features as she hesitated. Blue eyes, identical to Chloe's, darted from one end of the house to the other as though searching for a way to escape.

Chloe pushed up from the swing and rubbed her arms. Wordlessly, the women stared at each other.

Five years stood between them and their rift. No one else knew the true reason they hadn't spoken during that time.

Natalie's success shone from the blond highlights in her chestnut hair to the red patent leather shoes peeking from her navy bootcut slacks. For goodness' sake, she was even sporting the dog of Chloe's dreams.

On the opposite end of the spectrum, she wore faded jeans, a sloppy sweater, and a pair of clodhoppers she'd dug out of a thrift store bin.

All of Natalie's trinkets could have been hers, but that wasn't the deepest wound nor the sharpest pain now throbbing against Chloe's ribs.

Natalie licked her ruby lips and took a breath. "Chloe."

Her resolve to remain cool and polite shattered under a wave of bitterness. "How's the bestsellers' list treating you these days?"

There. The long-awaited barb crossed the space between them and found its mark. Dipping her head, Natalie murmured to the dog and continued down the brick path to the porch steps. She climbed them without a glance in Chloe's direction then crossed to the antique oak door.

With a twist of the knob, Natalie let herself inside. Once

more, Chloe rubbed her arms. Rather than freeing her, the words burrowed the hard feelings deeper.

From inside, Aunt Lottie's ecstatic greeting reached Chloe's ears. The happy exclamations slid over her like cheese over a grater. Despite herself, a wry smile curved her lips. Of all the moments to think of food.

"Chloe, hon, come on in," Aunt Lottie called.

Let Christmastime begin. Pulling in a breath, Chloe entered the house, her stare fixed on a nondescript spot down the sprawling hallway. To her left, the staircase swept upward to the bedrooms of their five guests.

The fragrance of cinnamon, apples, lemons, and cloves thankfully drowned Natalie's stout, flowery perfume—the smell of fame and city living. Her older sister hovered out of her line of sight, clinging to the leash.

Natalie cleared her throat. "Aunt Lottie, is it all right if I get unpacked first? I need to get Skye settled and fed."

"Sure. When you're finished, come to the office."

Aunt Lottie smiled over her coffee mug at them, the nostalgia shimmering in her hazel gaze. "My, but you're both a sight for sore eyes. How long has it been? Five years?"

She'd always been the queen of small talk. Affection warred with anger under Chloe's ribcage. Her aunt had taken her and Natalie to raise when their parents died in a plane crash. She'd been five and her sister nine years old. Rosewood Inn became their haven, a place filled with love, stories, and a bit of magic.

Charlotte Frost had given up dreams. The moment the girls had arrived, she yanked the *For Sale* sign out of the yard and tossed it into the bin behind the family's Victorian farmhouse. She dropped out of the doctorate program at the university to focus solely on raising them and building a business.

With a lot of grit and hard work, Rosewood Inn, bed and breakfast, had become one of the leading vacation destinations in the state.

Far from being the stereotypical matronly, spinster aunt of novels, she embodied a modern-day Myrna Loy, sporting wavy bobbed hair straight out of a 1930s' fashion magazine. Eyeshadow and eyeliner didn't scare her none. Neither did any shade of lipstick. She wore them with style and flair whether she was greeting guests or weeding the garden.

If Chloe hadn't loved Aunt Lottie to bits, she would've bolted from the chair that instant.

When neither of them responded, a small sigh blew through Aunt Lottie's lips, a flicker of dread replacing the wistfulness in her stare. She set the mug aside and swept a hand over a thin stack of paper.

"Let's get to it, then. From a business standpoint, you know why I've called you both together. It's time I retire. You know I have a nest egg. I'd like to do a little traveling before settling down in a small, low-maintenance house. Adventures are waiting. Rosewood Inn is your home, and I'm signing it over to you."

The silence deepened.

"By all means, let's not shower me with adulation or congratulations." Aunt Lottie quirked an eyebrow.

Natalie shifted in her seat. "I don't understand why you don't sign all of it over to Chloe. I've been gone for years, while she stayed and worked hard here. She deserves it."

"I can speak for myself." Chloe shot a sideways glance at her sister.

Natalie busied herself by twiddling with her fingernails.

"Well, I'm waiting." Aunt Lottie crossed her arms.

"I honestly don't know what to make of it. It's your home to do with as you please." Chloe massaged her pounding temples.

"And it pleases me to turn it over to you. You'll have to decide together the future of this place. Whatever that may be is fine. You're free to choose. Rosewood Inn is your home, and you will decide its fate. And yours."

Chloe shook her head. "Forcing us together won't work. You promised not to interfere."

"I had my fingers crossed." Aunt Lottie shamelessly shrugged.

Natalie glanced up from her fingernail gazing. "Do you really think this is fair?"

Aunt Lottie stilled. Even though she hadn't been stirring, everything around her settled like the calm before a thunderstorm. She blinked and tucked her chin, her response quiet.

"Is it fair for me to have poured my life into y'all just to watch you become hostile strangers? Dan and Maggie's memory deserves better. *I* deserve better."

The mention of their parents struck Chloe like a slap, stinging to her core. Beside her, Natalie patted her fingers against her lips.

Rising from the chair, Aunt Lottie pulled a pen from an assortment tangled in a cup. "This is my last Christmas at Rosewood Inn, and we will make it count. One way or the other." She dropped the pen onto the pile of papers. "Sign these. The places are marked and highlighted."

Chin lifted, she rounded the desk and whisked past them. Done. The door clicked shut behind her.

Aunt Lottie was also the queen of sucker punches. Another of her endearing qualities.

NATALIE

~ Till He appeared and the soul felt its worth ~

Groaning, Natalie collapsed onto the canopy bed and stared up into its rosy tucks and gathers. What a nightmare.

After signing the papers, she and Chloe vacated the office, never speaking a word. How were they going to make it through the holidays? Though Aunt Lottie's actions were spurred by love, she would never bridge a gap she didn't understand. Neither sister had ever discussed the rift with her.

Puzzling, really, especially since Chloe had every right to spill it. But her prevailing silence had grown louder with each passing year along with Natalie's guilt.

A firm rap at the door startled her. If she lived a hundred years, she'd know that insistent knock anywhere.

"Come in, Aunt Lottie."

The door swished open then shut softly before Aunt Lottie approached the side of the bed. For a moment, she studied Natalie. "I see you and Chloe signed the papers."

A wry smile twitched Natalie's mouth. "Did we have a choice?"

"Nope." Aunt Lottie gently pushed Natalie's legs. "Skooch over a bit."

Natalie scooted over, feeling like a teenager in trouble. "Oh no, it must be serious."

"A bit." After sitting, she scratched Skye's chin, a faraway expression tensing Aunt Lottie's face. She drew in a long breath. "I think it's high time you told me what happened between you and Chloe."

A fresh wave of sorrow crashed over Natalie as her mind drifted back to her once-bubbly sister, trailing her everywhere, copying everything she did, almost worshiping her every step. In Chloe's eyes, Natalie could never do wrong.

Until . . .

"Where do I start? When we were kids?" Natalie pressed a hand against the queasiness swelling in her stomach.

"Go back as far as you need."

The quiet calm of her aunt's voice allayed a bit of the dread of confessing her wrongs. *Lord, give me strength. Help Aunt Lottie not to hate me.* Fixing her gaze on the canopy, she ignored the hammering of her heart.

"No one knew how lost I was inside. You did everything to mother us, and Chloe needed my attention constantly. And it drove me nuts. I realize now how awful I was to feel that way. The anger and grief over losing my parents overtook everything."

Aunt Lottie gave Skye a final pat before sitting straight. "Though I couldn't walk a mile in your shoes, I knew you were suffering. I didn't know what to do."

"I hated that Chloe's memories faded while mine remained. The more she clung to me, the more I resented it. I tried to be the mother-sister figure she needed. But I lost myself. Nothing was good enough—this home, your sacrifices, or my sister's love."

Natalie's thoughts veered unwillingly to her senior year of college. "I wanted out. Freedom. Away from home, away from family, and away from Chloe. To leave the past in the dust of Rosewood."

Instead of leaving a trail of dust, she incinerated a bridge.

"God, forgive me," she whispered as the rays of sunset filtered through the lace curtains, casting a mosaic silhouette on the wall. "I didn't want Chloe to be an author like me. Her dreams of filling people's bookshelves and hearts made me sick."

Aunt Lottie frowned. "Pretty harsh."

Natalie's chest heaved. "There's no excuse. Are you sure you want to know the rest? It gets worse."

"I'm a big girl." She nodded, her jaw set.

"The way Chloe strung words together amazed me. Her talent far exceeded mine. Even though I excelled academically, my restlessness grew worse. When one of my professors suggested I apply for a master of fine arts at a university on the west coast, I snapped up the opportunity. You remember the application required a sample of my short stories, poems, and novel excerpts—ten to twenty pages?"

"Yes. You were nervous."

"Because I wanted escape more than the degree. At any cost." Squeezing her eyes shut as the memories assaulted her, Natalie shuddered. "The selection process narrowed my chances. I choked. I didn't think I was good enough, so I formed a deliberate plan."

Even now, a cold sweat popped out all over Natalie's body.

"When the time came to mail the portfolio, Chloe and I rode to the post office together. She sang most of the way, chatting in between about how she knew I'd be chosen. After we arrived, I bought a mailing envelope." Her voice wobbled.

"I can still see Chloe blowing bubble gum, leaning against the counter. The door jingled as someone came inside, and she twisted to see who it was. Then, her purse bumped into the stack of papers and scattered them to the floor."

Natalie's stomach quivered, her emotions strangling her. "I can't . . ."

Immediately, Aunt Lottie's soft hand closed over one of hers. "You've come this far, hon. You must continue."

Like a child, Natalie swiped a sleeve under her nose and gulped air. "We both dove to retrieve the stack. Never in a million years will I forget the look on my sister's face when she scanned the scattered pages." For the first time, she turned her head to look at Aunt Lottie. "I stole Chloe's work instead of using mine."

The descending quiet smothered Natalie while she waited for her aunt's reaction.

Though Aunt Lottie's shoulders sagged, her grip never left Natalie's hand. Only tightened. "What did Chloe do?"

"In her eyes, I saw everything she ever felt for me die. She said nothing, just thrust the papers into my hands and walked out before I could say anything."

"And you sent them anyway?" Surprise edged her tone.

"I did. Against my screaming conscience." Natalie clenched her teeth. "I thought I could make Chloe see my reasons and promise to make it up to her bigtime. How stupid."

In the following years, Natalie came to understand just how special Chloe was to her. The tag-along, copycat sister withdrew from her life, leaving something void and painful lodged deeply where Chloe's love once dwelled with abandon.

The freedom hadn't been worth the price.

After being accepted, she worked twice as hard, but nothing allayed her guilt. Once, she sent a letter to Chloe apologizing, but it was returned unopened. Though she earned the degree on her own merits, she had cheated herself and her sister.

Only when Natalie made things right with the Lord did a measure of peace enter her life. Remaining unreconciled to Chloe stole most of her joy.

Natalie scanned the bookshelf across the room. At eye level, Aunt Lottie had displayed three of her novels in the center, their front covers in full view. Inspirational stories. "What a mockery. You ought to toss them into the garbage."

Following Natalie's stare, Aunt Lottie groaned. "I'll never do it. Child, nothing I can do or say will punish you more than the torture you've already suffered. What a burden you've both endured."

Stunned, Natalie pushed herself up on her elbow. "You're not angry?"

"I'm angry it took us this long to get here, but we're going to get through it with God's help. No matter what happened, we still love each other." Lifting a hand, Aunt Lottie stroked Natalie's cheek. "We're going to make it through this valley, one step at a time. In the meantime, we'd better keep this conversation to ourselves and pray."

After Aunt Lottie left the room, Natalie replayed the conversation, shocked over the grace extended to her. She didn't deserve her aunt's forgiveness. Like a balm, it soothed the anguish.

Two black paws padded the side of the bed. Sweet Skye. Propping herself on an elbow, Natalie scratched behind the dog's ears.

"I wish I'd never written in the first place," Natalie trailed her fingers under Skye's chin. "You know what, girl? I'd give up everything if I could just go back."

Skye's pink tongue bobbed out and swiped her palm. Her button-black eyes glittered as though she understood.

A thought struck Natalie. "What can I lose going forward? If I try my hardest, I might gain my sister."

She sat up, swinging her legs over the side of the bed. After scratching Skye's ears a final time, Natalie linked her fingers together and bowed her head.

One thing she had learned well. Never jump into something without God's guidance.

CHLOE

~ A thrill of hope- the weary world rejoices ~

Heat seared Chloe's face at breakfast the next morning. The fork between her fingers slipped and clattered onto the plate, but the guests thankfully ignored the sound. Instead, they beamed and chattered over Aunt Lottie's proposed Christmas plans.

"Poetry, cookies, and cocoa." Marlene Stevens sighed with delight and elbowed her husband. "Alex, here, loves oatmeal cookies best." She slid a wink at Natalie. "What a great idea. I've never been a judge before."

"Neither have I." Brent Harlowe sipped his milk and dabbed his gray mustache with a napkin before grinning at Chloe. "A little healthy competition between sisters, eh? I'm sure you're used to it."

Good thing Chloe respected her elders. Not a person around the table except her and Natalie was under fifty. Swallowing, she curved her lips upward and darted a glance across the table. The color leeched from Natalie's face.

"It's perfect for Christmas Eve." Louisa Mae Thompson jabbed at the pile of hash browns on her plate. "Good thing we won't know whose dish belongs to which girl. You're both so sweet."

"Yep. Plus we can't be prejudiced for or against a New York Times bestselling author." Kent Walker chuckled, basking in the laughter at his joke around the table.

Chloe nearly gagged. At the head of the table, Aunt Lottie lifted a blue and white teacup, but Chloe caught a flicker of a nervous grimace before the cup touched her lips. Why was she doing this? Her glance bounced only to the guests, avoiding her nieces' covert glares.

Rising, Chloe lifted her plate then summoned into her voice all the sweetness remaining in her soul. "If you'll all excuse me, it's time I tidy the kitchen."

In less than five minutes, Aunt Lottie pushed through the swinging door trailed by Natalie. Chloe looked up from the skillet she was scrubbing at the kitchen island.

"What were you thinking?" she hissed. "Pitting Natalie and me in a poetry contest for our guests to judge?"

"Don't forget the cookies and cocoa." Without remorse, Aunt Lottie donned an apron.

Natalie puffed out an indignant breath. "Have you lost your mind?"

"I am in full possession of my faculties, last time I checked." She plucked up a dish towel and joined Chloe at the sink.

"You didn't even bother asking us." Natalie shook her head, looking mystified. "Don't we deserve just a teeny bit of respect?"

"Respect is highly overrated."

"I won't do it, Aunt Lottie." Water splattered the floor, but Chloe didn't care.

"Neither will I."

Their aunt eyed the skillet. "You're rubbing the finish off."

"Better the skillet than other things." Chloe thrust it into Aunt Lottie's hands. Unhurried, she rinsed it while Chloe tackled a speckled casserole dish.

"Don't you have anything to say?" Natalie jammed her fists onto her hips.

"Yes." Aunt Lottie tilted her head toward the refrigerator. "There's a grocery list under that magnet. Would you be a dear and go to the store?"

Natalie's eyebrows arched as her jaw slacked. "You just can't—"

Aunt Lottie started humming *Grandma Got Run Over by a Reindeer*. She tugged the casserole dish from Chloe's fingers and passed it under the faucet, all the while inspecting it for any missed spots.

For a fleeting moment, a spark of kinship stirred Chloe's heart as Natalie's horrified stare locked with hers. Tearing away her gaze, she snatched up a mixing bowl and plunged it into the soapy water.

Car keys jangled as Natalie yanked the list from the refrigerator and clipped toward the back door. A few seconds later it opened then snapped shut.

Aunt Lottie didn't miss a note.

"Okay." Chloe paused the washing. "I get it, but your tough love act isn't going to work."

"Oh, it's not an act, honey." Her feather-light voice morphed back to humming as though nothing out of the ordinary had happened. However, the glint in her eyes jabbed Chloe somewhere in the pit of her stomach.

Chewing her lip, she veered her attention once more to the dish in her hands. She hadn't seen that look on Aunt Lottie's face since Sam Irby of the town's zoning committee had demanded she tear down Rosewood Inn's picket fence.

Glancing up, Chloe caught sight of a cardinal as it landed on the fence, no worse for the wear after fifteen years.

Aunt Lottie didn't tolerate folks tearing down what belonged to her. Apparently, her nieces were no exception.

NATALIE

~ *For yonder breaks a new and glorious morn* ~

"Spending Christmas with two broken arms would be easier. That way, no writing, no baking for me." Natalie crammed the plastic grocery bags in the already ballooning keeper sack before switching off the kitchen light. Above her, the sound of a box shuffled across the attic floor.

Natalie shook her head. Aunt Lottie was at it already, dragging out the decorations. She'd barely parked the car when her aunt had hallooed from the attic window with instructions. She was to join Chloe on the front porch after putting away the groceries.

Had she switched places with her fifteen-year-old self?

After letting Skye out of her room, Natalie headed to the front of the house. Old, sweet memories hovered in every corner, around every bend, the taste whetting her appetite for home. She'd stayed away too long.

As she passed the rooms, she waved at several guests. A few of the ladies occupied the library while the men hunched around a game of chess in the parlor. Every December, they booked the last few weeks of the month. They seemed more like family than guests, either having no kindred to share the holiday or none that would have them.

Same as her.

Every Christmas, Natalie found an excuse to avoid home, but Aunt Lottie refused to accept it this time.

Natalie swept open the front door, led by Skye who wriggled through a maze of boxes and danced a circle around Chloe.

Freezing mid-step, her sister eyed the wiggling Scottie before finally stroking Skye's silky head.

"She likes you." Natalie ventured. Though every part of her longed to spill an apology, she sensed the time wasn't right. Chloe wasn't ready.

A shadow clouded her expression. She withdrew her fingers from Skye. "I guess Aunt Lottie wrangled you into decorating."

"What can I do?"

"You know the drill—a week of decking the house inside and out with every bauble of the season." Chloe gestured a hand over the brimming boxes. Ornaments, greenery, and lights spilled over, a lifetime of merry making held in store.

"Does she still have tree-trimming night with the guests?"

"Always. She never changes the schedule." Chloe reached into a box of wreaths and started piling them onto the porch swing. "Until this year."

Natalie knew exactly what she meant. The poetry contest. "You know, Chloe, I hate it as much as you do."

Chloe jerked her head, squinting in Natalie's direction. "Don't go there. The garlands are in that box. You can work on the porch railing while I freshen up these wreaths."

Easing a step closer, Natalie ignored the instructions. "Have you written anything since . . ."

"Since what?" Chloe straightened, a challenge sparkling in her blue eyes.

"Have you?"

She worked her jaw. "No."

Natalie's mouth ran dry. Asking the reason was pointless. All she had to do was look in the mirror and find it.

"I . . . I wish you hadn't quit. You have so much talent to give."

Instantly realizing her mistake, Natalie watched her poor choice of words slam into Chloe, whose chest heaved.

"I've already given it."

A mist stung Natalie's eyes. "Why didn't you tell? You could've told Aunt Lottie or contacted the university."

Chloe's lips quivered. "I almost did, but then I thought *why not let her go. It's better that way.* I wasn't some dumb kid, you know." She thrust her palms upward. "You resented me at times. I grated on your nerves, demanded your attention. I loved you too much and tried too hard to be like you. Made you a surrogate mom. All those stories—I poured everything I had into those words to make you proud of me. What a joke."

"You have no idea how much I regret it."

Chloe shrugged. "Why? You got what you wanted."

"No, I didn't."

"Save it." Turning to the wreaths, she wrenched another one from the box and tossed it onto the pile.

Seeing the damage she'd done to Chloe was worse than knowing it. A lone tear streaked down Natalie's cheek. Had she waited too long to repair the breach? After dashing the moisture away, she rolled up her sleeves and sent an unspoken prayer upward.

Time hadn't even started to heal the wounds.

Somehow, she had to cross the divide one ornament and garland at a time.

CHLOE

~ Fall on your knees! O hear the angel voices ~

Unwelcome emotions assaulted Chloe from every corner of her memories. The evident pain on Natalie's face twisted her heart into a tight, throbbing ball. *No.* She wouldn't soften. Better to keep her distance than allow herself to trust.

The betrayal hurt worse than the stealing of her stories. After getting caught, Natalie had gone ahead and sent them anyhow. Had life at Rosewood with her and Aunt Lottie been so awful? All families had bad and good times. Aunt Lottie's love and faith had carried them through.

In the midnight hours, she'd soothed their tears with prayers and funny stories of their parents. Many times, Chloe had woken to find Aunt Lottie standing at the foot of their bed, her head bowed and lips murmuring a petition of grace over them. Her arms surrounded them often, gathering them close to her heart. Her guidance nurtured them.

Despite difficulties, Aunt Lottie had worked to make Rosewood Inn their haven, a magical place of imagination filled with love. Like a little chick, Chloe found her nest and huddled into its shelter.

For Natalie, it hadn't been enough. She always seemed to be running from something. Holding back.

Frowning, Chloe shook the dust from a wreath with a bit too much fervor. What had Natalie been afraid of? Love?

The sarcastic notion halted the pounding in Chloe's chest. Stealing a peek over her shoulder, she observed Natalie laying out the length of garland on the brick walkway. A cherry flush stained her cheeks while her brows knitted in concentration. Beside her, Skye nosed a stick before snatching it between her teeth and tossing it into the air.

Their parents' death had shattered them, but Natalie had suffered the brunt of it. Maybe the pain of loving and losing had hardened a protective shell around her heart.

Like me.

At that moment, Natalie flicked a glance upward and collided with her watchful stare.

Chloe's throat tightened. Clenching her jaw, she turned her back and reached blindly into the box to pull out the last of the wreaths.

Why did it still have to hurt so badly?

"Girls, you're doing a marvelous job." Aunt Lottie took several steps backward on the walkway to absorb the full view of the house. A pleased smile crinkled the corners of her eyes. "You haven't lost your touch, Natalie."

An embarrassed grimace passed over her face as she brushed a sleeve over her clammy forehead. "Thanks."

"And I don't know how you manage to make those wreaths look spanking new every year, Chloe."

She cleared her throat. "I just shake them a bit."

Aunt Lottie tilted her head up and laughed, her caramel-colored curls bouncing in rhythm. Sunlight danced over the bits of silver weaving through them, making Chloe's heart pinch.

Sliding an arm around their shoulders, Aunt Lottie pulled them closer as she'd often done throughout their life. Without words, the three women took in the details of the house.

The garlands graced the length of the wraparound porch's railing while others wound the posts. In the downstairs windows, a wreath adorned the center of each. Next would come the upstairs windows. Then the trimmings. Last of all, the lights.

And then they'd start inside.

Normally, Chloe loved decorating, but she dreaded working closely with her sister. In the past, they'd shared the tasks with zest and laughter.

A conspiratorial twinkle entered Aunt Lottie's stare. "I'd say we stand a chance winning the town's neighborhood contest."

"We win every few years." Chloe shook her head.

"A dismal record to be sure." She breathed a mock sigh.

"You beat all, you know that?" Pressing her lips together, Natalie rolled her eyes.

"Not quite, but I'm working on it." Dropping her arms from their shoulders, she spatted their backsides as though they were still children. "Now, come inside. I've made pimento cheese sandwiches—your favorites."

She whisked up the porch steps, kissing to Skye who bounded up them two at a time. Aunt Lottie turned to find the girls still rooted in place. "Well?" She arched an eyebrow.

Spurred forward, they followed her inside, knowing better than to keep her waiting.

Logs crackled in the firepit to the notes of *It Came Upon the Midnight Clear*. With a guitar cradled under an arm, Alex Stevens picked the melody while everyone sipped hot apple cider and chatted. Usually, Chloe relished these times, but for now, she wished to be alone.

Dusting off an ash flake from her knee, Chloe stood then cupped her cider between her hands. With a slight smile at everyone, she ambled farther into the backyard, past the dormant flower garden. Beside her, Skye skipped through the brown grass, nipping at a stray leaf here and there. Chloe marveled at the dog's brisk glide across the yard, almost as though she were on parade at a dog show.

After picking her steps over a few magnolia roots, Chloe leaned against the trunk of the massive tree. She lifted the cup to her lips and sipped the tangy, sweet liquid. Violet dusk kissed every house, tree, and bush in the neighborhood. Lights of every color sprinkled houses and bushes throughout the quiet streets. The evening breeze feathered over her cheeks, hinting at the changing season. How she wished it were already over.

"Chloe." Louisa Mae approached, sidestepping the roots.

A bit startled, Chloe restrained the frown threating to tug down her lips and kept her tone light. "Can I help you with anything?"

Louisa Mae shook her head. Silver wisps of hair, loosened from her chignon, brushed her crinkled face. A concerned expression muted her usual smile. "Not this time, dearie. I'd like to know what I can do to help you?"

"Me?" Chloe grimaced, her heart dropping. So much for hiding her feelings in front of the guests. She'd have to do better. "That's sweet, Miss Louisa Mae, but I'm fine."

"Piffle tosh." She waved away the answer. "You're not yourself. I'm pretty good at smelling these things out."

"I appreciate the concern, but I'm okay. Really."

Louisa Mae simply stared until Chloe dropped her gaze. Gently, she patted her shoulder. "Sometimes it helps to talk with someone who's not family."

"I'm just a little tired, that's all." Chloe forced a smile, but Louisa Mae apparently didn't buy it.

"I've been *tired* lots of times too. You know, I've been coming every Christmas for several years, and I've shared my reasons. You and Lottie never judged. Let me be that listener for you." Louisa Mae squeezed Chloe's arm.

Sweet Louisa Mae's family didn't welcome her for the holidays. Or any day, for that matter. A terrible misunderstanding had barred communication between them. Chloe's heart ached for her.

A shuddered breath escaped her lips. "It's hard seeing my sister and having to compete with her."

"Ah, the contest." Louisa Mae nodded. "Because she's a bestselling author?"

Chloe shrugged. "Partly. But I haven't written anything in years. Stories are difficult enough, but poetry requires an extra level of inspiration. The timing and the moment have to be right. I don't have it in me anymore."

"Writers may get rusty, but they never forget the craft."

Chloe raised her eyebrows. "You sound like a writer."

"I've composed a line or two in my time—nothing momentous. It's pointless to advise you to forget Natalie is your sister plus a successful author. You'll have to push through it. However, you can absorb all the good things around you—the sights, conversations, smells, and most of all, the love. What inspires you during Christmastime?"

"The songs, especially the ones about the birth of Jesus."

A pleased twinkle filled Louisa Mae's eyes. "Perfect. What's your favorite?"

"That's hard." Chloe scanned the lines of lyrics and their melodies in her mind. After a few moments, she settled on one. "*O Holy Night*. It never fails to stir my soul."

"Here's what you do." Louisa Mae leaned closer in a conspiratorial whisper. "Look up the lyrics, read them, let the words soak in. Research the backstory. Listen to the music. Over and over. Let it take you through your memories and emotions—the painful and good. Inspiration will come."

"And if I still can't dredge up a syllable?"

"Then, pray hard." Louisa Mae chuckled. "I think you'll find what you need, though. It's locked away in here." She tapped an arthritic finger over her own heart. "Just remember a little word with the Good Lord might unlock the door."

"I'll keep it in mind." With a rueful grin, Chloe lifted the mug in a mock toast. "Thank you."

Louisa Mae held up a hand. "Beware. My motives aren't pure. I'm all about the homemade cocoa and cookies."

Their mingled laughter drifted upward as they turned toward the silhouettes circling the firepit.

With all her being, Chloe hoped her friend was right.

NATALIE

~ Led by the light of faith serenely beaming ~

"Done at last." Dusting off her hands, Natalie rose from her knees and surveyed the space. After a week full of work, every room and hall was decked.

She'd tackled the library all by her lonesome. Honestly, she needed the time to herself. The whirlwind of activity from sunup to sunset left little time to think. And now Christmas week yawned before them.

She, Aunt Lottie, and Chloe had spent all last week decorating every nook and cranny of the place until it resembled a Norman Rockwell scene. Straining her ears, she halfway expected the sound of sleigh bells to magically drift through the hall.

Like it or not, she'd fallen into the routine as though she'd never left.

I'm not ashamed to admit I've missed it. More than that, through the hustle, Natalie discovered she needed home.

Was this her way back, a second chance to make things right? The yearning to belong stirred her soul. Would Chloe accept her?

While they decorated, Natalie tried to engage Chloe in conversation, but her sister kept it short and cordial. Not much of an improvement. Occasionally, their glances caught, and something passed between them. Always, Chloe would shut it down, snapping her attention elsewhere. So much for working together.

Crossing to the desk, Natalie then straightened the skirt of a ballerina poised on its surface. The scene from *The Dance of the Sugar Plum Fairy* adorned the room, the character almost coming alive in its colorful surroundings.

Lord, help me to set things right as perfectly as I've arranged this room. Arranging a room and changing a person's heart were two different things, however. One required a pair of hands, the other an act of God.

"I got myself into this mess, Lord, but I can't get myself and Chloe out."

"You're too young to be talking to yourself."

Natalie whirled around.

Aunt Lottie stood in the doorway. Stepping inside, she glanced around the room, taking in every detail before settling her perceptive gaze on Natalie. "You're not getting anywhere with Chloe, I suppose."

"No. And the contest isn't helping matters."

"Think of it as bread dough. Give it time."

Despite her worry, Natalie laughed. "Only you can turn a rift into a bread dough analogy."

Aunt Lottie spread her fingers, making a show of counting them. "When you've ruined as many loaves as I have . . ."

Sobering, Natalie sat on the edge of a settee. "You know I've ruined a lot worse."

A pained look pinched the corners of Aunt Lottie's eyes. "I do know what will pull you together."

"Poems and treats aren't going to fix it."

"Nope, but the things that lie underneath will."

Crossing her arms, Natalie leaned back. "I don't like it when you talk in riddles."

Unruffled, Aunt Lottie scrutinized a wooden toy soldier standing guard beside the fireplace's hearth. "'A time to rend, and a time to sew; a time to keep silence, and a time to speak; A time to love, and a time to hate; a time of war, and a time of peace.'" She swiped a hand over the soldier's hat as though checking for dust. "Do you know what these lines speak of?"

Keeping silent, Natalie waited.

"The process of forgiveness." Aunt Lottie turned a pointed stare at her. "You've both run the gamut of every single stage. Except the last one. Chloe is ready, whether she realizes it or not."

A flicker of hope lightened Natalie's heart. "Do you really believe it's possible?"

"As long as there's breath." A sudden wink dissolved Aunt Lottie's serious expression. "And if I have anything to do with it."

Springing up from the seat, Natalie rushed across the room and flung her arms around the older woman's shoulders. The faint smell of toffee curled under Natalie's nose, sweeping her back to childhood. How many of those toffee-scented hugs had she put up with? They hadn't been Mama's arms. Now, Aunt Lottie's embrace anchored her.

"Thank you. For everything. And I mean everything."

A quiver rippled across Aunt Lottie's shoulders. For a long moment, she was quiet, her arms gathering Natalie a little closer.

"I'd do it all again."

"Any luck with the poem?" Lowering herself onto the wicker chair, Natalie tugged her jacket closer around her torso. Every day, the wind sharpened, winding through the neighborhood as though whetting its cold blade.

Crimping her lips together, Chloe smoothed the fleece blanket wrapping her legs. She thumbed through a thin stack of papers on her lap. "Not hardly."

Okay. A one-sided conversation it is. "I've managed a few lines. So far, I'm mostly stuck."

"Sorry. I'm fresh out of words."

Natalie winced, the fiery dart withering her insides. She gathered her crumbling resolve. "That makes two of us."

For the first time since Natalie came onto the porch, Chloe peered at her. Squinting, she frowned. "What do you want?"

Way too much, apparently. She clenched her trembling fingers together. "I'm trying to find my way through. Is there any way forward for us?"

Tunneling a hand through her sandy blonde waves, Chloe slid her eyelids closed. "Just . . . don't."

The quiet warning clued Natalie in on a forgotten fact. When they were children, she loved heights, but Chloe hated it. While the freedom of standing on edge dizzied Natalie's senses, Chloe always scrambled for safer ground.

Like now.

She was wavering on the cusp of opening her heart.

"Please, Chloe."

Snatching up the papers in one hand, she whipped aside the blanket with the other. She swung her legs over the edge of the swing. "Don't you get it? I don't want any of this—no contest, no tree-trimming, no *togetherness*. No . . . you. None of it."

A mixture of anger and determination stiffened Natalie's spine. "Well, you've got all of it, regardless."

Gritting her teeth, Chloe stormed to the front door, her socked feet padding a dull thunder across the porch.

CHLOE

~ He knows our need— to our weakness is no stranger ~

"Sometimes I hate myself." Closing the attic door, Chloe shuffled down the stairs while wrangling a box of ornaments. The heat from below inched up her legs as she descended. The day before Christmas Eve had blustered in with a cold front.

Since their confrontation several days prior, Natalie had avoided her—not in an angry way. More like one would avoid a tornado.

In silence, they had run the bed and breakfast with precision, the tension so thick between them she could hardly breathe. At night, sleep fled while her conscience battered her. She'd never felt so mean.

As for the poem . . .

In those sleepless hours, Chloe poured over the lyrics, jotted thoughts on paper, yet nothing sparked an idea. Only the phrase *the angel voices* rolled through her mind again and again.

What were the angels saying? Sure, she knew the biblical

account. On that starry night, as they filled the sky with proclamations and worship, they must have said more. How earthshattering was that moment to the shepherds?

If nothing else, why not let Natalie win by default? Maybe it would ease the guilt. If inspiration didn't strike tonight, the contest was a bust.

When Chloe reached the bottom of the stairs, merry voices meandered from the parlor down the hallway. Any semblance of joy abandoned her. *How am I going to make it through the tree-trimming party this evening?*

As she edged through the parlor's doorway, laughter ambushed her, each one a volley of pain. Pasting a grin on her face, Chloe wound through the guests to deposit the box beside the evergreen tree standing in front of the picture window. The balsam fir's spicy scent infused the room. Any other time, she would've welcomed it.

From her periphery, Natalie dipped hot lemonade from a steaming kettle over the fireplace and poured the ladleful into Louisa Mae's cup.

Standing at the record player, Aunt Lottie set a Christmas album on the turntable. An instant later, the room filled with the first strains of a choir singing *O Holy Night*.

The haunting melody churned in Chloe's heart. Her heavy footsteps led her to the window seat where she sat and surveyed the sprawling front yard, the shadows yawning across the brittle grass.

"Care for a sip or two?" Natalie's voice seized Chloe's attention. She held out a blue, speckled enamel cup like the ones in old westerns.

Before Chloe realized it, her fingers were closing around its handle. "Thanks." Her voice crackled like last year's wrapping paper.

Natalie settled on the opposite side of the seat, studying her. "You look exhausted. You haven't been sleeping?"

"Not much." Holding the cup to her lips, Chloe breathed in the aroma of honey and lemon before sampling it. Aunt Lottie always dashed in a hint of cinnamon. Heaven in a cup.

"Neither have I."

The forlorn admission pricked Chloe. With a little squirm, she took another sip rather than reply.

Turning to the window, Natalie exhaled a soft groan. "It's not the snowy wonderland we used to dream of, is it?"

"That's Mississippi for you."

A long silence stretched while the song subdued the guests' conversation.

Fall on your knees, O hear the angel voices . . .

Natalie scooted closer, her voice lowering. "I've tried to wait for the right time, but it never comes. I need to tell you how sorry I am. I did a horrible thing by stealing from you. I betrayed my best friend, and I wish I could take it back. I destroyed our relationship with my selfishness. I hurt you, and there's no excuse." Tears shimmered in her earnest eyes.

Hesitantly, her hand ventured out and gripped Chloe's. "Is there any way you can forgive me?"

The hard shell around Chloe's resolve splintered, but she floundered in the anguish hovering between them. The sensation was too sharp to endure. Chloe wrung away her hand.

"I don't know," she gasped. "Maybe I can't."

"I understand."

No, not that. Chloe scrambled to her feet. Blindly, she stumbled to the doorway, pausing only to thrust her cup into Aunt Lottie's hands before disappearing into the backyard.

Footfalls crunched behind Chloe in the maze. Decades ago, her grandfather had designed and grown the hedges for his children to spend happy times within their cozy walls. Perfect hiding places with a bench in the center.

Gritting her teeth against the chill and a confrontation, she stiffened her knees.

"You need this." Aunt Lottie draped a jacket over Chloe's shoulders. "Care to sit?"

Wordlessly, she shrugged into the jacket and lowered herself onto the bench.

Aunt Lottie joined her. "You might as well know I finally persuaded Natalie to tell me the reason for the fallout."

"How long have you known?"

"A bit. Since the night she arrived." No apology brooked Aunt Lottie's tone. "Would you like to elaborate?"

Why not? Weariness pressed hard. Chloe dipped her head, chin quivering. No need to hold it inside any longer. "It gutted me. Not just her stealing my work but wanting to escape me. You. Our home. That she would stoop so low."

Faltering over her words, she related that fateful afternoon, her tight voice roughing like gravel. Aunt Lottie neither moved nor spoke.

The last of the story faded into the evening air. Chloe filled her lungs with it, hoping to steady the roiling inside.

"Now, I need to 'fess up." Aunt Lottie tilted up her head, gazing into the heavens, her voice steady and unhurried. "Something I've never told you girls about your parents."

Ice cold dread trickled down Chloe's spine. "What?"

"The reason the plane crashed."

"It was an accident."

"Yes, but there's a detail I never shared." Aunt Lottie rubbed her arms. "It was quite a bitter pill to swallow. Senseless. Your father chartered a plane. He was quite a pilot. At first, I couldn't believe someone with his experience would

—" For a moment, she clenched her teeth together until she regained control. "The investigation revealed that a flight mechanic falsified several maintenance documents."

Chloe pressed a hand to her chest. "You mean, they died because someone else didn't do his job? Lied about it?"

Aunt Lottie nodded. "I was devastated. Angry. All they did was fine him and revoke his license."

"I can't believe it."

"Once the shock wore off, I promised myself I would make him pay dearly. After a little research, I learned his name and found his address. Oh, the things I planned to say—how he'd shattered the lives of two young girls. Then, I'd threaten him with a civil suit, break him."

The weight of her words sent a shiver down Chloe's spine. "What happened?"

"I found him one afternoon in a bar, slumped over a table. When I told him who I was, he started crying uncontrollably." Aunt Lottie covered her mouth with her fingertips as though witnessing it afresh. "The man I despised. Already broken. A dead man walking."

Chloe's eyes burned. "Did you tell him the rest?"

"I opened my mouth, but then, I couldn't." Shrugging, Aunt Lottie scanned the sky. "Instead, I sat across from him, grabbed his hand, and told him I forgave him—that my brother and sister-in-law wouldn't want him to be this way." A tear trailed down her cheek, widening into a silver stream. "I can't describe the look on his face."

"Do you know what happened to him?"

Aunt Lottie dabbed her jawline with the collar of her shawl. "I sent Devin Miller to rehab. He's been sober ever since. He calls a couple of times a year."

How brave and utterly selfless. All her life, Chloe occupied a front-row seat to her aunt's big, loving heart, but this reached far beyond anything she ever imagined.

Overwhelmed, she rested her elbows on her knees and buried her face.

Aunt Lottie's warm hand stroked Chloe's back. "I'm sorry I haven't told you both sooner. Maybe it would've saved you this trouble."

"No, you're not to blame. We are. Trying to keep you out of the fray only made it worse for you." Chloe rubbed her forehead. "Natalie asked me to forgive her tonight."

"Is that why you came out here?"

She nodded. "What if I can't? I don't know if I can overcome it."

Aunt Lottie's caress stilled. "Forgiveness is stepping out in faith, sometimes on nothing else but knowing what's right. I learned this the night I found Devin. If I had turned away, I truly believe I would've destroyed him and myself. God does the mending, Chloe. We lay ourselves aside and put our sorrows in His hands. That's why He sent His Son. He reconciled humanity to Himself. Apart from Him, there is no forgiveness."

Suddenly, everything within Chloe shifted and aligned with perfect clarity. Scenes unfolded from the long-ago night when the angels proclaimed the birth of the Messiah. The singing angels proclaiming the Gospel of hope, the greatest reconciliation of the ages. Speechless shepherds, awed by the Divine reaching down to gather His wayward children into His bosom. The offering of a precious gift. Forgiveness.

As Chloe raised her head and looked heavenward, the crushing burden of her grudge slipped from her spirit. Gratitude welled up. Just then, a shooting star streaked across the sky.

"What a glorious sight." Aunt Lottie whispered.

Wrapping an arm around her aunt's shoulders, Chloe kissed her cheek. "I understand now."

"I had no doubt you would."

Chloe stood, a bubble of inspiration rising deep inside. "If you'll excuse me, I have a poem to write."

A soft, serene smile lit the older lady's face. "Merry Christmas, honey."

Most of all, Aunt Lottie was the queen of perfect timing. The best of her endearing qualities.

NATALIE

~ Truly He taught us to love one another;
His law is love and His gospel is peace. . . ~

Skye's sharp bark jolted Natalie awake. Sitting up, she glanced at the glowing bedside clock. 5:00 a.m. Christmas Eve morning. Way too early for Skye to tear into a beribboned box of treats. "What is it, girl?"

A soft tap rattled the door, and Skye scampered to it, her nub of a tail wagging. Her fuzzy paw scratched at the doorframe.

"Just a minute," Natalie called softly, swinging her legs over the edge of the bed and rising. The chilled wood floor shocked the warmth from her feet. After sliding them into a pair of slippers, she donned a housecoat and crossed the room.

Shock threaded through her to find Chloe standing there, wrapped also in a housecoat, gripping a sheet of paper in one hand. A strange glow shone in her eyes. "I finished it. My poem."

Blinking, Natalie kept her voice steady, showing no trace

of surprise. "You worked on it all night?"

Chloe nodded. "I just finished. Will you come with me?"

A split second passed before Natalie realized what Chloe meant as she followed her down the hallway. When they were growing up, they often crept out to the front porch in the middle of the night to talk.

Even now, though, she dared not hope, especially after Chloe's response last night. The anguish in her answer had crushed Natalie. For the rest of the evening, she laughed, chatted, and trimmed the tree with the guests while her heart crumbled into a thousand pieces.

Once outside with the door safely shut behind them, Skye bounced down the steps while they settled on the swing. A frigid, crisp gust of air whirled past them.

"Okay. What is it?" Natalie ventured.

Chloe's eyes faltered under her gaze as she held out the paper which wobbled in her grasp. "Will you read it, please?"

"Sure." Swallowing, Natalie took it, hardly knowing what to think.

To mortals lost, in despair separated
Through the ages from God their Father,
A song unfurled to shepherds, consecrated
Hope forever with abounding pardon
The angel voices sang.

Stanza after stanza expressed the message of the angel voices on that first Christmas night. The stanzas composed the wonder of God's offer of peace to lost humanity coupled with unparalleled forgiveness. In true Chloe-style, she expressed it with unbounded grace and beauty.

On the page, the words swam while tears brimmed Natalie's eyes. Blinking, she patted her damp cheeks with the back of a hand. Natalie's chest expanded with pride. She'd never top it. Neither did she wish to.

After absorbing the last line, she raised her head and closed her eyes, the depth washing over her like a cleansing rain.

"I've been asking myself what the angel voices were expressing." Chloe's soft voice broke the silence. "It finally dawned on me last night. Pardon born of His love. And I had no right to withhold mine from you."

Though Natalie opened her mouth to respond, no words came.

"I'm sorry for being hateful and refusing to forgive you. We can't go back and undo that day, and there's no need to try to fix it. It's gone. But Lord willing, we have a lot of days ahead of us, and I'd like to make them count."

Unsure, Natalie ventured a glance at her sister. In Chloe's eyes gleamed the love and adoration she'd sorely missed. "So would I." Without hesitation this time, she grasped Chloe's hand. "What inspired you to write this?"

"You need to ask Aunt Lottie." Chloe squeezed her hand. "There's something she needs to tell you."

Natalie snickered, the feeling liberating. "God bless Aunt Lottie."

"No wonder I woke up with my ears burning."

They scrambled to their feet as their aunt softly closed the door and padded toward them. "I thought I raised y'all better than to speak ill of your elders, especially behind their backs."

"It was all good, I promise." Chloe sputtered.

Aunt Lottie scrutinized them, her gaze bouncing from one to the other. Understanding dawned in her face. "My girls, you've given me the best gift of all. My prayers and efforts haven't been in vain."

Chloe and Natalie shared a smile. Taking a step closer,

Aunt Lottie opened her arms and gathered them close. Coming home for Christmas had never felt so wonderful.

Moments later, light and feathery flakes brushed against their faces. Gasping, they hurried to the edge of the porch and held out their hands as snow glided down.

"I can count on my fingers the number of times it snowed here on Christmas." Natalie grinned as Skye whirled around in confusion. "Can you believe it?"

"I can. I specifically ordered it." Winking, Aunt Lottie quirked her head to one side.

Their hushed laughter filled all the empty, aching spaces they'd endured, exchanging it with promises for the future.

EPILOGUE

~ Sweet hymns of joy in grateful chorus raise we;
Let all within us praise His holy name ~

"And we have a winner," Aunt Lottie announced, waving a piece of paper as a hush descended over the dining room.

The results were in. The guests had dined on the sisters' own special creations while Aunt Lottie read the poems before handing out copies. No one knew which treat or poem belonged to whom. Afterward came the votes.

Chloe and Natalie joined hands, the anticipation growing as the guests leaned a bit forward in their chairs.

"Chloe Frost, congratulations and well done making an extra delicious treat with your poem, *The Angel Voices*."

Shock descended over Chloe while applause and cheers reverberated around the room.

Natalie flung an arm around her. "I knew it. You know, I think it's time you wrote the next bestseller."

Chloe assumed her best shrewd expression. "Only if you consider returning home to help me run this place."

"I thought you'd never ask." Natalie smirked, evidently pleased with her joke.

"Oh," Chloe elbowed her. "It's not a request."

She rolled her eyes heavenward. "One Aunt Lottie in the family is enough, don't you think?"

ACKNOWLEDGMENTS

A hearty thanks goes to Shannon Taylor Vannatter for her edits on this story. Your suggestions were spot on. Sara Davison, thank you for designing my Kindle cover for this story as well as the overall cover design for *A Thrill in the Air*. Phenomenal job! It's my current favorite. Also, a big shout out goes to each of my Mosaic sisters for their encouragement and friendship. What an amazing group of ladies! Thank you for the roles you undertake in our group.

And to our faithful Mosaic readers, thank you for loving our stories and inspiring us to write more stories to fill your hearts.

A special thanks belongs to Brenda Anderson who has taken the mantle of leading our group, organizing, creating graphics, and taking care of a million other details for us. And to Angela Meyer, you do a fantastic job spurring discussions and setting timelines for our stories each season. Not least of all, big hugs and appreciation goes to Camry Crist for everything she has tirelessly done to make The Mosaic Collection the brand it is today. We love you and your sweet family.

BIBLIOGRAPHY

O *Holy Night*, original text by Placide Cappeau (1847) *Minuit, Chretiens* or *Cantique de Noël*
English translation by John S. Dwight

ABOUT CANDACE WEST

CANDACE WEST was born in the Mississippi delta but grew up in small-town Arkansas. She is a graduate of the University of Arkansas at Monticello. Ever since the age of twelve, she dreamed of writing inspirational fiction. Over the years, she has published short stories as well as poems in various magazines. By weaving entertaining, page-turning stories, she hopes to share the Gospel and encourage her readers.

Please visit Candace's website to explore more of her books
and to subscribe to her newsletter:
www.candaceweststoryteller.com

TITLES BY CANDACE WEST

THE MOSAIC COLLECTION: NOVELS
Windy Hollow series
Through the Lettered Veil

THE MOSAIC COLLECTION: ANTHOLOGY STORIES
"A Garland of Grace"
(*A Star Will Rise: A Mosaic Christmas Anthology II*)
"Forever Mine"
(*Song of Grace: Stories to Amaze the Soul*)
"The Key"
(*All Things New: Stories to Refresh the Soul*)
"McDonald's Farm"
(*Dancing in the Rain: Stories to Shelter the Soul*)
"The Angel Voices"
(*A Thrill in the Air: A Mosaic Christmas Anthology V*)

VALLEY CREEK REDEMPTION SERIES
Lane Steen
Valley of Shadows
Dogwood Winter

Chiseled on the Heart: A Christmas Legacy Novella Collection

CHRISTMAS COMES TO SPRINGLIGHT

Johnnie Alexander

* * *

Lemora Violet McElhaney-Smythe is bewilderingly befuddled when a notorious newcomer arrives at the When at a Loss Pawn Shop on a bleak afternoon to return a purloined present. Meanwhile, her identical twin, Elmira Rose, is troubled by a tragical tragedy.

Will the sisters celebrate Christmas with acrimonious animosity? Or will a shooting star kindle kindred kinship?

To Each of You, Our Dear Readers,
Merry Christmas!

When they saw the star, they were overjoyed.

Matthew 2:10

WHEREIN LEMORA REFUSES TO WELCOME CHRISTMAS

At ten minutes past two o'clock on a Tuesday, Lemora Violet McElhaney-Smythe sighed a solemn sigh and stared a sullen stare out the picturesque picture window of When at a Loss Pawn Shop. Snowflakes fluttered from a sapphire sky dotted with winter white clouds onto the outstretched branches of the Spreading Chestnut Tree and atop the snow-blanketed lawn of Courthouse Square.

If you or I, dear reader, were standing in Lemora's pink stilettos—for she'd exchanged fur-lined boots for heels more befitting a professional proprietress before opening for business that morning—our breaths may have been taken away by the breathtaking beauty of the winter wonderland outside the pawnshop's picturesque window.

The three-story courthouse squatted across the snow-covered square. Each mullioned window displayed a delightfully decorated wreath, the big blue spruce was hung with giant ornaments and strung with strings of brilliant lights, and gaily wrapped presents with huge red bows were piled high in Farmer Boggs's old-fashioned sleigh.

Each business, store, and establishment surrounding

Courthouse Square exuded the Christmas spirit with twinkling lights and carefully hung stockings, candy canes and gingerbread men, angelic beings and lowly shepherds, poinsettias and—do not be shocked, dear reader—sprigs of mistletoe.

And yet, despite the pristine snow and holiday hullabaloo, Lemora sighed and stared, stared and sighed, her heart heavy with the loss of what had been and what could never be regained.

The minutes passed on the multiple clocks that hung on the walls and nestled on the shelves until an horological hullabaloo occurred as the chiming clocks and the cuckoo clocks chimed and cuckooed, a few too soon and a few too late.

"It's two fifteen or thereabouts," Lemora announced to Mrs. Jones, the fluffy, furry feline with gray-tipped ears who had resided in the pawn shop since she'd first arrived there on a dark and stormy day preceded by a dark and stormy night.

"And nary a buyer or a seller in sight."

Though Lemora spoke truth, she did not know and could not know that a pawn shop visitor existed who was *not* in sight. A visitor who, wishing *not* to be seen, at that very moment of two fifteen or thereabouts, lingered, nay, languished in anguish in the rear alleyway.

He pondered and paced, paced and pondered.

He summoned strength, he called for courage, he begged for bravery.

He pounded on the pawn shop's back door.

WHEREIN ELMIRA RECALLS A TRAGIC TRAGEDY

Tragedies rarely came to Springlight—the charming town, the quaint town, the strolling-along-the-sidewalks-on-a-Saturday-morning kind of town, which lies to the east of the mysterious Ravendark Woods—but woe to the charm, the quaint, the Saturday stroll when they did.

An especially tragical tragedy had arrived less than two months before when the Courthouse Square and the Springlight shops were festooned with harvest golds, orange pumpkins, and autumn leaves that colored the trees and crackled underfoot.

On that fateful day, When at a Loss Pawn Shop wasn't among the businesses, stores, and establishments that surrounded Courthouse Square. Papa's papa had built the original shop off the beaten path as he didn't want customers beating a path to his door. He preferred solitude to sales, dilly-dallying to deal-making, and tinkering to talking.

For all their growing up years, Lemora and Elmira played princesses who were two peas in a pod. The lackluster pawn shop was their palatial palace where they pirouetted, preened, and pretended among the shelves of pawned electronics, knickknacks, and fragilities; the glass cases of watches, rings, brooches, bracelets, pendants, lockets, cameos, and beads; and the cabinets of porcelains, pottery, and precious keepsakes.

A place of wonder and a wonder of a place.

For all their growing old years, Lemora and Elmira played proprietors who weren't two peas in a pod. The lackluster pawn shop was their bitter battleground where they bought, sold, acquired and redeemed electronics, knickknacks, and fragilities; watches, rings, brooches, bracelets, pendants, lockets, cameos, and beads; and porcelains, pottery, and precious keepsakes.

But the twins never bought or sold, acquired or redeemed, together.

Oh, no, dear reader.

If you visit the WaaLPS on a Monday or a Tuesday, you will find Lemora dusting the shelves and eager to greet you. If you visit the PS on a Thursday or a Friday, you will find Elmira eager to greet you and dusting the shelves. If you have the misfortune of visiting on a Wednesday, Saturday, or Sunday, you will not find a pink-clad twin dusting the shelves or a purple-clad twin eager to greet you.

Oh, no, dear reader.

You will find the door locked with seven locks and a CLOSED sign, painted in the McElhaney-Smythe custom color of Meloira Blue, in the window.

And now, our purposeful postponement and procrastination must pause as we revisit the scene of the tragical tragedy.

Here we find Elmira Rose McElhaney-Smythe, bundled in purple, sitting among the ruinous ruins of the palatial playground and bitter battleground, elbows on her knees, chin in her hands, tears on her cheeks. Snowflakes fluttered from a sapphire sky, blanketing the cinders and ashes, the angled shards of burnt walls, and the piled debris from that fateful, fearful night when a fire blazed, raged, and dazed the sisters who clutched one another in anguished agony.

Lemora comforted Elmira and Elmira comforted Lemora.

'Twas a day or two later when Frankie Franklin, the only firefighter fighting fires in Springlight, disclosed to Elmira the calamitous cause of the ferocious flames.

You may be tempted to avert your eyes, dear reader, as I recount the tragically tragic tale. But you must not! For if you do, how will you read these sorrowful words? Be brave and of stout heart, though you may take a moment to tuck a tissue into your sleeve before proceeding.

'Twas the night of the annual Springlight Harvest Festival when Elmira and Lemora joined figurative hands to provide, as was their annual custom, the hot dogs for the festival feast. An anonymous newspaper carrier had pawned the two-wheeled hot dog cart back in Papa's day before leaving town in a hurry to elope with the Widow McLarsen—a secret not revealed until decades later when a stranger came to Springlight.

But I digress.

After the harvest feast, Elmira stored the yellow hot dog cart in the lackluster pawn shop's even more lackluster back room. She removed the pink-and-purple striped umbrella that covered the cart and cleaned all the surfaces, including the sign pawned back in Papa's day that read, "Uncle Newton's Falling Apple Orchard."

But what Elmira didn't do, forgot to do, neglected to do was to turn off the switch that lights the lights and heats the rotating rollers on the sparkling clean hot dog cart.

And tragedy struck the lackluster When at a Loss Pawn Shop.

WHEREIN LEMORA RECEIVES A PUZZLING PRESENT FROM THE PAST

"It's Elmira pounding on the back door," Lemora disclosed to Mrs. Jones, the fluffy, furry feline with the gray-tipped ears. "Only she would be so bold and so loud."

Mrs. Jones daintily licked her paw.

"Why should I let her in?" Lemora demanded of Mrs. Jones. "If not for her negligent negligence, we would not be here"—Lemora stamped her pink-stilettoed foot on the hardwood floor—"we'd be there!" She gestured in the direction of the burnt building with the air of an actress, the grace of a dancer, and the poise of a performer.

Mrs. Jones daintily flicked her tail.

"She will never be forgiven!" Lemora declared to Mrs. Jones. "Though we live seventy times seven more years here in Springlight."

Mrs. Jones daintily tilted her head and eyed Lemora with her amber eyes.

The pounder pounded. Lemora flung wide the door.

The pounder stepped back. Lemora stepped forth.

"You are not the odious offspring of my dearly departed parents," Lemora asserted.

"I am a repentant thief," the dusty, dark-cloaked drifter avowed. "Here to return what I stole from your dearly departed parents on a long-ago December night."

"How long ago?" Lemora asked, suspicion furrowing her brow.

"'Twas your first December and the week before Christmas. Your papa planned a special gift for your mama that I, with jealousy in my heart, spirited away. During all my long wanderings, I intended to sell it. Alas, I could not. I tried to toss it. Guilt forbade me. I tried to gift it. Shame decreed no."

"And now," Lemora whispered, her mind befuddled and her heart bewildered, "you bestow it on me?"

He drew a black velvet drawstring bag from beneath his dark and dusty cloak. "With the only blessing I can give. A Christmas wish for joy, harmony, and peace on earth."

Lemora took the bag, an unexpectedly heavy bag, in both her hands. The drawstring, a thick golden braid, was tied into a knotted bow. Awestruck and struck with awe, she held the bag close to her heart and closed her eyes, imagining Papa's disappointment when his gift disappeared and Mama singing sweetly his favorite tune.

You are my star, my shooting star.
Lighting my dark sky.
I'm always with you, near or far.
My love, my shooting star.

The melody faded and Lemora opened her eyes to offer the dusty, dark-cloaked drifter a comfy chair by the pot-bellied stove to warm his outside and a steaming cup of chamomile tea to warm his inside.

But her invitation went unspoken, for the repentant thief had disappeared.

WHEREIN ELMIRA REVEALS ONE SECRET AND KEEPS ANOTHER

Lost in her memories of the tragical tragedy, Elmira noticed not how the snowflakes fluttered onto her toes, her knees, her shoulders, and her head. How they dampened her damp cheeks, moistened her parched lips, and tickled her sniffling nose. A finger of icy wind slipped between her purple plaid scarf and the dark purple collar of her pale purple coat to chill the nape of her neck. She felt it not.

She sensed nothing until a shadow as familiar as her own hid the mid-afternoon sun.

Lemora.

No doubt come to chastise and criticize, to condemn and convict. Elmira braced for belittlement and beratement, prepared to button her tongue and barricade her temper, and vowed once again that Lemora would never guess, never suspect, never know the true cause of the tragical tragedy.

Till now, they'd shared everything—a mama's womb, a papa's love. The shabby Victorian where they lived with Mr. Smith, the canary who chirped and chanted and trilled in his massive blue cage that stood prominently in the hallway between the parlor and the dining room. Their lackluster business, burnt and beyond repair, and now the splendid store on Courthouse Square where lived Mrs. Jones.

Absolutely everything.

But Elmira refused to share the burden for the loss of When at a Loss Pawn Shop. Even though the burden was as much Lemora's as her own. Perhaps more.

For it was Lemora who'd neglected to properly pack and put away the Fourth of July leftover fiery fireworks. A short in the two-wheeled hot dog cart created a spark, but the fireworks sparked the fire.

As the snowflakes fluttered onto the sisters from a sapphire sky dotted with winter white clouds, Lemora sat beside Elmira on what remained of the windowless window seat. She held a black velvet drawstring bag on her lap tied with a thick golden braid.

"A mysterious man gave me this," she said, her eyes fixed on a faraway tree. "A present from the past."

"What is it?" Elmira asked, her eyes fixed on a nearby shrub.

"Papa's Christmas gift to Mama the year we were born. The mysterious man stole it long ago and today he gave it back." Lemora passed the black velvet bag to Elmira without even a glance.

Elmira unknotted and untied the thick golden braid, widened the opening of the black velvet bag, and slid the fabric along the sides of the gift.

A bronze shooting star sculpture.

"You are my star, my shooting star," Lemora sang softly. "Lighting my dark sky."

"I'm always with you, near or far," Elmira sang softly. "My love, my shooting star."

"We miss them."

"We do." Elmira studied the bronze sculpture, running her sensitive fingers across the oval base, along the chiseled arc, and around the edges of the five-pointed star. "This beautiful bronze holds a Christmas secret."

Her fingertips tingled as they lingered along the base, touching here and tapping there, until a hidden drawer popped open. Two silver charms, miniature replicas of the bronze sculpture, rested on black velvet.

"An etched violet engraved with an *L*," Elmira said.

"An etched rose engraved with an *E*," Lemora said.

"Papa's gift to Mama," Elmira said.

"To celebrate her gift to him," Lemora said.

The sisters, for the first time, turned to each other as snowflakes fluttered from a sapphire sky.

"Us."

A NOTE FROM THE AUTHOR

Dear Friends,

Did you enjoy your Christmas visit to the quaint and charming town of Springlight? While you were there, I hope you dropped in at Mr. McPurdy's Dandy Land of Candy for a candy cane and at Mrs. McPurdy's Delightful Teas and Tasteful Delicacies for a sampling of her Christmas cookies.

Your trip wouldn't be complete without a shopping spree at the When at a Loss Pawn Shop where I'm sure you'll find a treasure or two among the knickknacks, fragilities, and keepsakes.

Lemora and Elmira—such adorably eccentric sisters—provide me with such joy whenever I spend time with them. Though I admit, they surprised me in this story. It wasn't my intent for Elmira to keep such a tragically tragic secret from Lemora. But she insisted, and I respected her decision.

If you've not been to Springlight before, then grab a copy of the Mosaic Collection's *Before Summer's End* anthology to read what happens when "A Stranger Comes to Springlight." (Plus, you'll have six other great stories to read!)

On behalf of all the Mosaic authors, we pray that our stories touch your hearts, bless your spirits, and deepen your relationship with our Heavenly Father.

And we wish you a Very Merry Christmas and a delightful, joy-filled, memory-making New Year!

Johnnie

ACKNOWLEDGMENTS

To all the Mosaic Collection authors ~ I value your friendships so much. How grateful I am that God joined our paths together. You're often in my prayers.

My heartfelt thanks to Sara Davison who created the ebook cover, warmed my heart with her encouraging comments, and edited the story.

Thanks, too, to Camry Crist for all she does to organize, format, and design our anthologies. Her talents are so appreciated.

As always, all my love to Bethany and Justin, Jill and Jacob, Nate and Bre, plus my growing-up-too-fast grands ~ Jeremy, Jedidiah, Kaydi, Josiah, and Presley.

ABOUT JOHNNIE ALEXANDER

JOHNNIE ALEXANDER is a wannabe vagabond with a heart for making memories. Whether at home or on the road, she creates characters you want to meet and imagines stories you won't forget.

Her award-winning debut novel, *Where Treasure Hides*, is a CBA bestseller. The World War II novel has been translated into Dutch and Norwegian. Besides historicals, she also writes contemporary romances, cozy mysteries, and romantic suspense.

Johnnie is on the executive boards of Serious Writer, Inc. and Mid-South Christian Writers Conference, and she co-hosts an online show called Writers Chat.

A fan of classic movies, stacks of books, and road trips, Johnnie shares a life of quiet adventure with Griff, her happy-go-lucky collie, and Rugby, her raccoon-treeing papillon.

Please visit Johnnie's website, www.johnnie-alexander.com, to learn more about her books and to subscribe to her newsletter.

TITLES BY JOHNNIE ALEXANDER

THE MOSAIC COLLECTION: NOVELS
The Mischief Thief

THE MOSAIC COLLECTION: ANTHOLOGY STORIES
"The Caretaker's Christmas"
(*Hope is Born: A Mosaic Christmas Anthology*)
"A Stranger Comes to Springlight"
(*Before Summer's End: Stories to Touch the Soul*)
"Paper Trail"
(*Song of Grace: Stories to Amaze the Soul*)
"Souvenir in my Pocket"
(*All Things New: Stories to Refresh the Soul*)
"Christmas Comes to Springlight"
(*A Thrill in the Air: A Mosaic Christmas Anthology V*)

WORLD WAR II NOVELS
Where Treasure Hides
The Cryptographer's Dilemma

MISTY WILLOW SERIES
Where She Belongs
When Love Arrives
What Hope Remembers

NOVELLAS
"The Healing Promise"
(*Courageous Brides Collection*)
"Journey of the Heart"
(*Erie Canal Brides Collection*)
"Match You Like Crazy"
(*Resort to Romance Series*)
"Blue Moon"
(*Homefront Heroines*)
"The Thistle Rings"
(*Love's A Mystery in Gnaw Bone, Indiana*)
"The Potter's Design"
(*Love's a Mystery in Crooksville, Ohio*)

SHORT STORIES
"Beneath the Christmas Star"
(in *A Cup of Christmas Cheer—Tales of Joy and Wonder for the Holidays*)

ANNIE'S FICTION
Johnnie has written novels in the following series:

Victorian Mansion Flower Shop Mysteries
Hearts of Amish Country
Inn at Magnolia Harbor
Sweet Intrigue Mysteries
Love in Lancaster County
Mysteries of Aspen Falls

UPCOMING
Three Dog Knight (Mystery of Cobble Hill Farms Series)

THANK YOU FOR READING!

We hope you enjoyed reading *A Thrill in the Air,* Mosaic's 2023 Christmas anthology. If you did, please consider leaving a short review on Amazon, Goodreads, or BookBub. Positive reviews and word-of-mouth recommendations count as they honor an author and help other readers to find quality Christian fiction to read.

Thank you so much!